Don't miss these ot

Vickie McKeehan

The Pelican Pointe Series
PROMISE COVE
HIDDEN MOON BAY
DANCING TIDES
LIGHTHOUSE REEF
STARLIGHT DUNES
LAST CHANCE HARBOR
SEA GLASS COTTAGE
LAVENDER BEACH
SANDCASTLES UNDER THE CHRISTMAS MOON
BENEATH WINTER SAND
KEEPING CAPE SUMMER (2018)

The Evil Secrets Trilogy
JUST EVIL Book One
DEEPER EVIL Book Two
ENDING EVIL Book Three
EVIL SECRETS TRILOGY BOXED SET

The Skye Cree Novels
THE BONES OF OTHERS
THE BONES WILL TELL
THE BOX OF BONES
HIS GARDEN OF BONES
TRUTH IN THE BONES
SEA OF BONES (2018)

The Indigo Brothers Trilogy
INDIGO FIRE
INDIGO HEAT
INDIGO JUSTICE
INDIGO BROTHERS TRILOGY BOXED SET

Coyote Wells Mysteries
MYSTIC FALLS
SHADOW CANYON
SPIRIT LAKE (2018)

The Bones of Others

A Skye Cree Novel

VICKIE McKEEHAN

beachdevils
PRESS

The Bones of Others
A Skye Cree Novel
Copyright © 2013 Vickie McKeehan

Published by Beachdevils Press
ISBN-10: 0615751911
ISBN-13: 978-0615751917
Printed in the USA

Cover design by Vanessa Mendozzi
Wolf designed by Jess Johnson

You can visit the author at:
www.vickiemckeehan.com
www.facebook.com/VickieMcKeehan
http://vickiemckeehan.wordpress.com/
www.twitter.com/VickieMcKeehan

Author's Note to Readers:

First, I want to say a huge thank you to all Seattleites for such wonderful hospitality while visiting your city. Next, I'd like to say for this novel, literary license was taken with the Seattle streets. Let's face it, I made up stuff, especially a lot of fictional streets and places, especially anywhere near or around a port area, that includes both Seattle and Tacoma. If the streets exist at all, it is in a purely fictional way and only in my mind. And to all those that say it rains too much in your fair city, I say posh. I lived in Houston for several years and it rains more there than it ever did on us in Seattle.

For the victims, the survivors,

someone's daughter or son.

The children.

If a man hasn't discovered something that
he will die for, he isn't fit to live.
Martin Luther King, Jr.
1929 – 1968

Excerpt from
A Man Young and Old: I. First Love
by
William Butler Yeats

The Bones of Others

A Skye Cree Novel

VICKIE McKEEHAN

PROLOGUE

Thirteen years earlier
Seattle, Washington

The fragrant grass and clover had been freshly cut, and the smell of it filtered to his nose, making him sneeze once, then twice more in rapid succession. He took out a handkerchief from his pants pocket to swipe at his runny nose. Today's pollen count had been seventy-five, the highest all summer long. It was obviously responsible for triggering his chronic hay fever. It reminded him how much he hated spending time outdoors. He'd much rather stay tucked into his apartment, sitting in front of his computer screen.

But little girls loved to play outside.

The warmth of the July day, along with the beautiful blue sky, invariably drew them out of the house to play, often unaccompanied by adults. And today, because of the balmy weather, the public park, his domain, the realm where he ruled, was a noisy place. Several families were hosting birthday parties while others picnicked to the sounds of rock music drifting from their stereos, which meant the playground was packed. What with the swings, the monkey bars, two slides, the spider rider, and the sandbox, there were almost too many children to keep track of.

But since he was good at what he did, he didn't mind today's outing if it got him the results he wanted. He'd been watching the kids at play for almost an hour now, studying his choices. The range of girls ran the gamut—chubby, slim, blonde, brunette—no doubt an assortment to pick from.

But one stood out. It hadn't taken long before he'd zeroed in on her. But there was a drawback. At the moment, the one he wanted threw a Frisbee back and forth to her father. He knew because he'd overheard the little girl call the man daddy. With the parents in attendance that meant he'd have to be extra vigilant. It didn't mean it couldn't be done, only that he'd have to take more precautions.

The one who'd caught his eye had long, black hair tied back in a ponytail held in place by a pretty red ribbon—bundled up like a gift—especially for him. Her running and bouncing had caused her cinnamon skin to all but glow under the summer sun.

He had only to bide his time to wait for that perfect opportunity, that seamless opening where he could make his move. It wouldn't matter that she'd come to the park with others. It couldn't be otherwise. He always made sure he kept away from the watchful eyes of the adults. He tried never to bring attention to himself. Attention wouldn't do. As long as he stayed back, he would go unnoticed, oblivious to everyone because he didn't stand out. Making a mistake at this point would cost him. He couldn't get careless when he was so close to what he wanted. So he sucked in a slow, deep breath, glanced upward, daring to take his eyes off the dark-haired child long enough to get himself under control.

He had only to be patient and watch and wait for his opening, which would come, it always came. If he were persistent, he would be rewarded.

Another fifteen minutes went by before one of the grown-ups, one of the mothers, called to the dad reminding him it was time to start the burgers and dogs. The man watching from the sidelines saw the father bend down to say something to his daughter. The father pointed in the direction of the soccer field where a group of youngsters kicked around a ball.

It became apparent her dad meant for her to go play with the other kids. Perfect, he decided. The dad would be caught up in starting the charcoal grill, maybe lose track for a moment. That's all the time he'd need. He made sure the adult turned his full attention to getting the food going before he focused fully now on the child, no older than twelve as she dutifully trotted off to join her playmates. But when she hung back, for some reason, as if reluctant to join the game, he knew then for certain. Shy. Malleable. Perfect.

It was a sign. He absolutely knew then she was the one. She would be special. This one would never end up where he'd put the bones of others. He'd see to that. This one would be the girl who helped him launch his enterprise, the business venture he'd been thinking about starting. Whitfield's Little Angels. Of course, he couldn't very well use his real name in the company logo. That would be incredibly stupid on his part. But there would be no more wasting time getting his project off the ground. And this little one seemed perfect. He'd definitely made the right choice there. Nobody, he thought now, was better primed and organized than he for what he did. Establishing order upfront meant success later. That's why he'd never been caught.

Now all he had to do was get his hands on the merchandise.

For a good fifteen minutes more he became a spectator. Still as a statue, he waited. After all, patience was a virtue.

When the soccer ball missed the goal and rolled out of bounds in his direction, he recognized his opening had arrived. As the newest member of the team, as if ordained, the little girl darted off to retrieve the loose ball so her friends wouldn't have to.

He had his story ready. He'd had years to prepare his ruse. The lie the child would believe. It had worked before. It would work here again today. As soon as the dark-haired girl veered into his zone, he would work his magic.

From the sidelines, he ran his tongue around his lips in anticipation as the girl got closer, closer to her fate. It was only a matter of time now. The bushes concealed him till that very last moment, that very last precious second when she belonged to her parents.

He spared one glance in the direction of the adults, still absorbed with prepping the food.

But in that last instant, unnoticed by the grown-ups, was all it took. He started talking fast, spinning out the lie quickly, believable to a trusting twelve-year-old.

As he always did he guided the child to his car—and ultimately to his purpose.

CHAPTER ONE

Present day
Friday afternoon, March twenty-sixth
Seattle, Washington

The intermittent chunks of ice spitting from the gray sky pelted the concrete pavement leaving it sloppy and slick. The freezing drizzle probably meant winter would hang around through the weekend at least. Not only did the storm shove spring into the background for another couple of days, the nasty weather made for an early dusk. Nine-to-fivers started eyeing the sky soon after lunch, wanting only for the weekend to finally get here so they could hurry home.

The gloom brought rush hour closer while traffic began to build up and clog the intersection of Fourth and Pike. What with early birds trying to get a jump on everyone else, bumper-to-bumper exhaust hung in the air while SUVs and little hybrids jockeyed for the same going-home space.

The park across the street appeared empty except for the bundled-up homeless pushing their shopping carts along the sidewalk or in between hedges as they already began scouting out the best places to spend the night. A reminder that the brutal cold over the next twenty-four hours would not be kind to either man or beast forced to be out on the streets tonight.

Wind snapped out of the north, the gust causing trash to become airborne and whirl the debris into wet, paper like dust devils.

Street vendors and musicians had packed up right after lunch, as had the panhandlers. Both groups had either wandered into one of the coffee shops to lounge away what was left of the afternoon or had simply retreated to some inner sanctum, someplace else where they could nurse a strong cup of java or an Irish coffee to chase away the chill.

Several streets away, the teen hookers clustered under an overhang of sorts trying to stay dry. A small, anorexic brunette, who already looked as though she'd gone too many rounds with the needle, hung back to the side. Around her bone-thin shoulders a tight-fitting, faux red leather jacket didn't look as though it kept her warm enough—certainly not with the matching red miniskirt that barely came down to her thigh-high, shiny black, plastic-looking, patent leather boots covering her skinny legs.

Visibly shivering from the cold, she danced in place as leaves blew around her feet. She took several shaky drags on a damp cigarette until her eyes darted automatically to the small pickup that pulled up to the curb. Because she was closest, and maybe slightly more desperate than the others, she shot out from under the awning, approaching her customer on the passenger side window, eagerly negotiating her fee quickly with the driver before hopping inside to bask in the warmth of the truck.

Not five hundred yards from where the young prostitute jumped into the truck, the man waited. He wasn't interested in the young hookers even if he often used them as a fallback. The teen streetwalkers were far from his first choice. But there were times a man with certain urges had to make do.

Today wasn't one of those times. Today he had other prey on his mind.

From behind the wheel of his rusted-out blue van he cruised the neighborhood, up and down the streets, circling the block several times in an area he'd been scoping out for more than a week. His eyes lit on the school and he checked his watch. Timing was everything. He hoped he'd get lucky as he pulled the vehicle up to the curb to wait.

Fifteen-year-old Erin Prescott raced across an open field of wet grass adjacent to Jesuit Preparatory Academy, her flame-red shoulder-length hair flowing back in the breeze. Intent on getting to spend a couple of hours with Jason Avery at the mall, her mind fretted about how she looked. She hoped her hair didn't frizz up the way it always did in the predictable damp Seattle weather. She hoped by the time she made it to the mall, her face didn't look like someone had set fire to her cheeks. Why did she have to have such wild red hair and the blotchy skin to go with it anyway? Why couldn't she have silky blonde tresses and gorgeous skin like Mary Jane Pruitt? Mary Jane didn't have to worry about splotches of any kind. Her skin was flawless.

Erin's looks aside, a seventeen-year-old senior with a car had invited her to spend his Friday afternoon with him which pretty much had Erin floating on air. She wasn't sure why Jason had picked her and she didn't care. She knew Jason had his driver's license and drove a sporty little BMW he'd gotten for his last birthday. Although Erin couldn't imagine the reason, she wanted to meet Jason at the mall more than she wanted the next upgrade for her iPhone.

It had all happened right after third-period English class when Jason had approached her in the hallway. He'd stood right there beside her locker and suggested they meet up after school. Erin had tried to play it cool. But the prospect of getting to hook up with the hot-body Jason and spend the afternoon with him had caused her to ditch cheerleading practice. By doing so she not only risked getting into trouble at school but at home as well. If her parents found out about the trip to the mall she'd be grounded. Knowing her parents, it would probably last until she turned sixteen. But to get to spend two hours alone with Jason Avery would be worth every minute she'd spend in trouble.

Checking her watch, the fifteen-year-old decided she had at least until seven before anyone would be home at her house, maybe more if the nasty weather held up her parents in traffic. If luck was with her and she happened to be a measly thirty minutes late she felt sure she could pacify her parents with some bullshit story to keep her out of trouble.

That reasoning gave her hope, enough to enjoy a couple of tacos with Jason, especially if she could talk him into giving her a ride home in his sleek BMW.

As rain dripped from the tips of the swaying evergreens behind her, Erin ignored the sting on her cheeks from the biting wind. Her one-track mind on Jason, she rushed on toward the Central Link, picking up her pace just as the train station came into view. The train would get her to the mall in less than twelve minutes and take her to the boy who made her heart race every time she spotted him in the halls at school.

Without a backward glance at her surroundings, head bent in the rain and wind, she didn't see the man come up behind her.

By the time she did, it was too late.

Spotting the girl dressed in her school uniform, getting all wet in the drizzle, he left his lamppost to tag along behind her. Who would have guessed the miserable weather would have given him such a gift and one as precious as the cute little redhead? She'd be his reward for the lousy week he'd had. Four days earlier he'd tried to snatch another child only to have the kid scream her head off. Because of the racket she'd made, he'd been forced to let her go before he ever got her to the van. He'd been sloppy. He was already in trouble with the boss. Today, failure wasn't an option.

He took a second glimpse at how sweet and young and innocent-eyed this one looked, almost beyond belief. He liked knowing he'd be her first. Just the thought made him realize some things were meant to be.

As the girl quickened her pace, he did as well, enough so that his long legs overtook hers. But he had to act fast. The girl was getting closer to the train with every step she took. He had no intentions of letting his prize slip away.

From the downtown skyscrapers came the working stiffs, pouring through the doors in mass exodus as if someone had opened a giant floodgate and given them their first whiff of freedom in five days.

The sidewalks filled with people, shoulders bunched under umbrellas. They darted to waiting cars or rushed to catch buses or made mad dashes toward Central Link. Still others scurried to a few of the local neighborhood bars hoping to spend the next several hours joined in happy hour solidarity as they kicked off the weekend with friends or co-workers.

The cold rain beat down making it a perfect night to stay huddled indoors. Whether it was keeping warm in front of a crackling fire at home with family or getting sauced with your colleagues at the local pub, it didn't matter. Unwinding, relaxing after a long week was expected, especially when it capped off a harried, stress-filled five days at work.

And because Josh Ander was a creature of habit, he walked among the throng of people on the streets of downtown as if it were a sunny day instead of pouring down rain. Dressed in his everyday garb, jeans, a Polo shirt, and well-worn Nikes, the Seattle native wore his proverbial raincoat like a proud uniform as if the wet were no more than a mild nuisance. He let the water sluice off his long ebony hair that had a tendency to curl up over his collar.

Craving a cold beer, hoping for a couple hours of mindless drinking with his programmers, he was certain happy hour would put him in a better frame of mind. A mood had been nagging at him that he couldn't blame on the wintery weather. He'd spent enough time dwelling on the past of late and looked forward to spending the evening with his employees, drinking at their favorite watering hole, Gull's Pub. He'd learned early on that spending time with his staff in a social gathering was a crucial, even necessary event to keep morale high.

As founder and CEO of Ander All Games, Josh never missed an opportunity to socialize with what he believed was the backbone of his company. His employees deserved more than benefits, more than bonuses, even though they got those as well. He'd discovered that when he took the time to pick up the tab for several rounds of brews every Friday night, his employees appreciated the attention and responded in kind when he had to ask for extra effort on their part.

Josh relished hanging out with his gang. In fact, he enjoyed their company as much as they seemed to enjoy his. On some level the gesture worked both ways. After busting their asses, sometimes putting in a solid seventy-hour work week, the very least Josh could do was buy a few rounds of beers. It was Josh's way of making sure he kept his staff happy—and loose.

That way when he asked them to step up and produce a newer, better version of the game that had put Ander All in the history books, *The Mines of Mars*, they'd do it without question, without fanfare. Because of that, Josh considered his employees nothing short of gold. Simply put, they were some of the best and the brightest people he could find.

By the time he walked through the double doors of the downtown pub, his wire-rims were spotted with raindrops as water dripped from his six-foot, lanky frame and onto the scuffed, hardwood floor. Before he even removed his coat, he began to try and clean off his glasses so he could see. When his programmers gave out a shout to get his attention, his head turned at the greeting. He noted several of the square bar tables had already been pushed together to accommodate their Friday night ritual, which apparently had been underway for some time. Josh's gray eyes took in the tabletop where two pitchers of brew sat half full. It hadn't taken long for his team to start without him.

"Sorry, I'm late," Josh announced as he took a seat at the end of the table. "Had to finish the package design for *Hidden Cities of Mars* before Georgia leaves on vacation next week."

"How's that looking?" Gareth Myer asked.

As one of the newest and youngest members of his team, Gareth perhaps felt the greatest pressure to contribute. At least that was the way Josh saw it. And with Gareth's next comment, Josh was sure of it. "Did you get my suggestions? I emailed them to you last week. There were some improvements I thought we should make so I included a detailed attachment."

Josh smiled, nodded at Gareth's confidence and enthusiasm. "I did. I appreciate your contribution. I added a few of your recommendations to my proposal. Georgia will consider the ones she finds creative and toss out the rest."

"But…it's your company," Gareth pointed out. "You…"

Josh held up a hand, adjusted his glasses. "True. But that's why I hire people who know what they're doing. Georgia knows marketing and you know programming. Since you both seem to be good at your jobs and that makes you both an asset to the company in different areas, Ander All benefits and I'm happy. Georgia tells me we've already created a ton of online interest with help from our savvy marketing team and the sales department backs that up. It seems the preorders for *Hidden Cities* are breaking the records for *Mines* by a wide margin."

"That's because as programmers we're the rock stars of the game world," chipped in Todd Graham, second-in-command and another long-haired geek who thought nothing about wearing his brown hair tied back in a ponytail with a white piece of string.

Josh rolled his eyes. Todd had been with him at the beginning when they'd both taken an idea in a smelly college dormitory at UDub and turned it into a multi-million-dollar company. Even though Todd had been the one to build the platform, it had been Josh who had taken the initiative and scrounged for all the funding. Knowing full well Todd preferred staying in the background and wouldn't walk into a bank to do a pitch if you paid him, Josh relished his front man role, didn't mind the limelight. In fact, as long as Todd didn't like leaving his programming world, their partnership thrived. Plus, Todd's lack of social skills weren't exactly conducive to navigating the financial world. Just one of the reasons Todd was left alone to create code in a fantasy realm while Josh handled people and all the details and responsibilities dealing with the day-to-day issues of running a company.

With another successful launch on the horizon, all eight programmers raised their mugs in mock salute to Josh Ander.

"Here's to *Hidden Cities of Mars* then and working all the bugs out before release. To the best boss in Seattle," Kyle Weaver added, hoping a little kiss ass would go a long way in landing him the promotion he'd been lobbying so hard for over the better part of six months.

"Come on guys, you think I don't know I'm just here to pick up the tab?" Josh teased as he picked up one of the pitchers of dark brew and poured his own first pint of the night.

"True. But we thought we were pretty clever at hiding that," Kyle tossed back good-naturedly.

Josh finally hung his wet coat on the back of his chair and settled down to shoot the bull and swap war stories with these people he considered the heart of his company.

They kicked around new game ideas. You couldn't get programmers and geeks together for any length of time and the talk not turn to planning and designing another type of futuristic game. They all offered input.

"You know," Gareth Myer began, "the Internet's all abuzz over the sightings of a lone wolf on the prowl in urban Seattle. That would make a helluva game."

"I read about that," Todd chipped in. "In the area near the marketplace. Very strange reports. The sightings always occur at night under a full moon."

"Oh come on," Kyle chortled. "They probably saw coyotes. The paper did a story a few months back on how coyotes are hunting pets in King County. Cats and small dogs aren't safe."

But Gareth shook his head stubbornly. "No, these reports are in addition to the coyote sightings. Don't believe me? Here," Gareth said as he pulled out his cell phone to show Kyle all the websites. But it was Josh who took the phone out of his hands and stared at the small screen. He read the articles in fascination.

"Maybe we could design a game around the wolf, trying to avoid humans while at the same time looking for food in an urban setting," Josh suggested.

"Sounds boring," Todd retorted. "We'd need something to spice it up, like a gorgeous female warrior that accompanies the wolf everywhere he goes." With that, the chatter took off to how exactly they could accomplish that.

Two hours later, after doing his part to down two more pitchers, Josh looked up to see Michelle Reardon sidle up to stand beside their table. Michelle, an aggressive five-foot-three-inch blonde annoyance he'd been trying to let down gently for the past three weeks without success, stood a couple of feet away, glaring at him. She'd been a friend of Annabelle's, someone who'd showed up on his doorstep one night four months ago after he'd gone on a drinking binge. In his drunken state, he'd taken Michelle to bed. Huge mistake on his part. Something he had regretted since the morning after. Since the first of the year she'd been doing her damnedest to move in with him, an event he had no intentions of letting take place. The fact that they'd slept together more times since then, only made Josh more aware of what an error in judgment he'd made.

Because over the past three weeks Michelle had upped the ante.

She had taken to showing up uninvited at his office, worming her way into a few social gatherings around town, and like now, popping up unexpectedly at the pub. Gull's was his bar, had been for almost a decade. He'd ordered his first legal pint here. He'd be damned if he'd let Michelle Reardon ruin his only watering hole.

He didn't need a stalker. No surprise she'd followed him here. She somehow always knew his schedule better than he did. He'd made a mistake, a big one, but that didn't mean he was willing to keep making that same slipup over and over again by letting her win each round.

"Hello, Michelle," he managed in a low voice.

"Hi there, Josh. You should have told me you were coming here for happy hour."

Josh had also discovered Michelle could lie with the best of them. "Why? I'm here every Friday night, rain or shine. You know that."

When his developers started to make room for her at the table, it pissed him off. "Michelle, we need to talk."

"Oh, Josh, relax. I'm just having a beer with you guys. No big deal." She looked around the table and said, "Look, there's plenty." To prove her point, she picked up his pint and drank a long sip. "You'll never even know I'm here."

At that moment, Josh realized he was done. He wanted her out of his life and tonight it was now or never. But it wasn't his style to make a scene in a public place and especially in front of his staff. "Fine. We'll talk—later."

Another couple of hours flew by and he did his best to ignore Michelle, tried to concentrate on listening to the guys relate tales from the salt mines. The stories about how they'd managed to put together code, found and fixed bugs over the course of a week, became a series of jokes.

And when Josh glanced Michelle's way, it made him giddy to see that she acted bored with it all. Nothing pleased him more. Maybe she'd leave on her own. But as the evening progressed, she stubbornly stuck.

When the talk turned to spouses, stories about their significant others, their kids, babies, even due dates, Josh saw Michelle's persistence start to falter for real. The conversation had hit the highs and lows, the ins and outs and Michelle showed all the signs of wavering.

After draining his glass, Josh got up to go to the bathroom. Swaying slightly from all the booze, he made his way to the back of the pub and into the men's room. While standing at the urinal, he heard the door open to his right and glancing over his shoulder, saw Michelle enter the restroom.

"Goddamn it, can't I take a piss without you following me in here? Get out!"

"Come on, Josh, how about a quickie?" She moved toward one of the empty stalls. "I know you want me," she offered suggestively as she started undoing the buttons on her dress. "You've proved it to me over these past months."

"Get out of here!" he yelled again. "Get out, now!" he repeated. He quickly finished up his business, flushed the toilet and zipped up his pants. When she simply stood there, he stormed past her and out of the men's room into the small corridor leading to either the front of the pub where his friends waited or the back and the door to the alleyway.

By damn, he wasn't taking this anymore. No way would he go back to the table, not now, not back to where Michelle could latch on and cling like a gnarly vine. He was not going to buckle and take her home with him tonight.

Spotting the back exit and needing the fresh air to cool off, he slipped through the back door. The stench of stale beer and garbage hit him immediately and pissed him off even further.

Damn it, the pub was his place to unwind on a Friday night and be left alone. Michelle had no business coming here, intruding on *his* turf.

Pacing back and forth he drew in deep breaths, sucking in cold, damp, smelly air. He wished he had a cigarette even though he'd given them up after meeting Annabelle. Damn Michelle, anyway. He'd taken her to bed because he'd been lonely. But even having Annabelle in common wasn't enough of a connection for either of them, not by a long shot. Couldn't she see that? In all these months there had been no chemistry between them, not an ounce. Hadn't she seen that, too?

He decided what he needed was a pot of strong coffee to help him get sober before he headed home. But when he turned to go back inside, a noise at the end of the alleyway had him stopping, turning around.

Four men of various sizes appeared from behind a Dumpster. But one stood out, grungy, taller than the rest, taller than Josh with the look of the street about him. In a matter of seconds, the four guys had Josh surrounded.

In his annoyed state, Josh suddenly realized how far he had wandered from the back door.

In the glow from a streetlight, he saw the glint of a knife as the taller man came within three feet. "Hand over your cash," the man demanded quietly as he looked Josh up and down. When he caught sight of the Rolex on Josh's wrist, his lips curved. "Well, well, what have we got here?"

One of the other men added, "See it. Let's have the watch. And that ring. Come on, we don't have all night."

Josh wasn't about to risk his life for eighty bucks and a wristwatch he could easily replace. Nor was he going to fight these guys since he happened to be three sheets to the wind and unsteady on his feet. But damn it, a man had his pride. He brought the cash out of his pockets and undid the clasp on his watch. But when it came to pulling off his wedding ring, he hesitated. "Let me keep this. It has sentimental value."

"Bullshit. That's what they all say."

"No, really," Josh countered, doing his best to explain. "My wife died last year. This is the ring she gave me the day she married me. There's an inscription."

As if to prove a point, one of the other men got tired of listening to the drunk get all sappy. All at once, the thug threw a punch, which Josh took full force on his chin. The blow knocked him back a step. It took Josh a couple more steps backward before he was able to right himself.

Another man chose that moment to try and wrench the ring off his finger. At the same time the man wielding the knife made a jabbing motion toward Josh's chest.

Outnumbered, Josh managed to dodge one jab but saw the men had no plans to leave without getting the ring. Josh watched the knife dart in then out, up and down. The taller mugger seemed determined to scare him. Shit. He was in deep shit, he realized as he finally lost his balance and went down, slamming into the ground butt first.

All at once, *she* came out of nowhere dressed in black and leather.

Josh watched through bleary eyes as the scene before him unfolded.

The woman warrior waded into the street gang armed with nothing more than what looked like a toy lightsaber. But man, could she wield that thing.

Josh looked on as his avenging angel whacked heads with her nightstick, used her long legs to land kicks to the belly, the head, and anywhere else she could reach. She hit like a linebacker, shoved bodies out of the way like a running back.

At one point, her leg swept up in an arc in a perfect karate kick. Her boot made contact with the tall guy's arm. The knife he held in his hand flew through the air. Josh heard the clatter of metal as the blade hit the concrete.

But the warrior seemed too busy to notice. Her next move sent one of the guys airborne. His body met up with the brick wall. She pinged another into the Dumpster like a pinball. Josh watched as the thug slid down in a heap. The last one took a dive toward her and paid for his efforts when she dodged the blow, used her nightstick to whack him in the back and then shoved him with a foot, sending him head first against a concrete abutment guarding the garbage bins.

Her arms never stopped moving, neither did her legs until the bad guys lay groaning in pain around her. Cautiously she approached each one and sent a series of jabs and punches to their heads and ribs until she was sure they were down for the count.

As Josh's assailants lay beaten to a pulp by a long-legged, baton-wielding female, he finally picked himself up and did his best to stand.

"Get out of here," she yelled in Josh's direction. "Go back inside." When he remained motionless as if still mesmerized by the turn of events, she rolled her eyes and screamed, "You in shock or something? Go! I've got this."

It was true. He seemed unable to move, wondering whether he'd conjured her up. She was like the female hero in one of his games come to life right before his eyes in the dark alleyway. He finally found his voice. "I'll say. Who are you?"

"This isn't the time for a get-to-know-you social. Get the fuck out of here. Now!"

But Josh stood his ground, at least the ground that wasn't littered with groaning bodies. The bodies began to try to get up which only brought the avenger into a low-crouching, ready-to-fight stance, eager for round two.

"Well, come on then," she challenged. "You want more? Fine by me. I've had a shitty day up to now and you four are the icing on my cake. Come on, let's go another round. What do you say?"

But to Josh's astonishment, instead of fighting back, the leader of the pack simply held his head in his hands and groused, "Shit. This bitch is nuts. I don't need all this trouble for a lousy eighty bucks. I'm outta here." The tall guy, who no longer held a sharp knife in his fist, was the first one to gain his feet. With an incredulous look on his bleeding face, the man who'd had the biggest mouth, all but ran out of the alley, leaving his buddies to fend for themselves even though they were still laid out flat on the cement.

The avenging angel went over and kicked at a shoe. "You guys playing dead or something? You gonna get out of here or what?" she demanded in the direction of the prone body count.

But sensing their leader had turned tail, one by one, each bad guy began picking himself up off the pavement. Eventually, Josh's assailants all followed suit and fled. They didn't even bother to stop to pick up the switchblade.

But Josh's avenging hero did.

In awe, Josh watched as she tossed the six-inch blade back and forth from hand to hand as if determining its weight and value before tucking it neatly away inside her boot. Because she no longer held the baton-slash lightsaber, he realized she'd already slipped that away inside the long, black leather coat she wore.

It was about that time Josh felt the burn in his left shoulder, saw the blood soaking through his Polo and running down his shirtsleeve before trickling down to his bare arm. The woman saw it too, She gawked while the red ooze dropped into a muddy puddle at his feet. She followed the track with her eyes, narrow as slits, up his body until she located the source.

"Damn. Got you in the shoulder, didn't they?"

"Looks like. I didn't feel it though."

"Should've been quicker. Sorry about that. Thought maybe they'd just take the cash and go. Leave you unharmed and standing at least." She shook her head. "Should've known better. Street gangs always try to jab you to make a point. Pun intended."

"What the hell are you doing out here this time of night behind Gull's?" Josh asked, right before he started to sway. This time he didn't think it was from the alcohol.

She inched closer to inspect the gash.

"Isn't squirting, so he didn't nick an artery. You should be fine until you get to the ER." She threw an arm around his good shoulder. "Lean on me. I'll take you as far as the back door then you're on your own. Someone inside will get you to a doctor."

"No." He couldn't say why, but he didn't want her to leave him. "Take me home. I don't live that far. Walking distance."

"You're kidding?" She narrowed her eyes, this time taking a closer look at the guy. His long black hair was mussed up. He had after all just survived an altercation with four thugs. He wore a pair of wire-rims that even now sat on his nose at a slightly skewed angle. Behind the glasses he had eyes so gray they looked almost silver. Gentle. Kind. Soft. And they were glazed over. She liked to think she could judge a man by his eyes. And at the moment his eyes told her, he was sauced.

"Why don't you tell me your name?"

"Bleeding in an alley and you want my name?" she asked in disbelief. "You're a strange one, aren't you?" But willing to indulge the drunk, she replied, "Skye. Cree."

"Sky? Like—?" He pointed a thumb upward. "Like that?"

She rolled her eyes for the second time and tapped his chest for emphasis. "Yeah. No stupid jokes about my name though. I've heard all the lame ones."

"It's beautiful."

She smirked at the wobbly man. "From where you're standing, I guess it is."

Even though she was several inches shorter than he was, he leaned heavier on her just because he could. "*You're* beautiful. My beautiful avenging angel, Skye Cree."

She snorted—her lips curving somewhat—and the small gesture transformed her face. "Skye. Just Skye. Don't go making it out to be something more than it is. Four lowlifes armed with a switchblade thought they'd found an easy mark, nothing to it."

His shoulder might be hurting like a son of a bitch and he was more than slightly sloshed but he recognized irritation and beauty when he saw them come together in one gorgeous female face.

Plus that narrow, Native American face with its high cheekbones had his libido ramping up, even in his inebriated state. Her wide Julia Roberts mouth showed no evidence of lipstick or gloss. Not a hint of makeup covered her cinnamon skin. But the cold coupled with the fight had pinkened her cheeks with a natural glow that made him want to reach out and touch. But her demeanor told him that might be a very bad idea.

It was hard to tell how tall she stood, especially with the pair of military-style boots she wore, or how much they added to her height. Slim. Fit. Athletic. If he wasn't hallucinating she had violet eyes. Violet. No hint of eye shadow could improve on those dazzling Elizabeth Taylor eyes. Probably contacts, he decided as he studied the mass of hair stuffed under a dark purple watch cap. Her hair reminded him of soft, midnight silk. Raven black, it offset the bright-colored hat. But when the glimmer of light hit her bangs just so and with the loose strands twisting carelessly out every which way, it looked as though that raven black glistened around her face.

Josh thought his avenging angel fairly glowed.

"So, I'm the easy mark?" he tossed out with the same cheerful tone as any grateful victim might who had survived an altercation with four muggers. "You saved my life, Skye. Where did you learn those moves? You were fucking awesome."

This time she chuckled. "You *are* in shock." Or plastered, she decided. Just what she needed, a drunken frat boy who had to have a nursemaid in order to get home. Suddenly, she pulled the knife back out from her boot. She yanked up his fancy shirt and cut off a hunk to use to wrap up his shoulder to try to stop the bleeding. "There, that should do till we get you home, although you may leave a blood trail. You sure you can walk? You pass out on me and it's gonna piss me off."

"No, I can make it. My place is close. I'm Josh. Josh Ander. I've never seen anyone take on four guys like that before—and win."

"You want to stand here and go over the play by play? Socialize later," she hissed. "We need to get that wound patched up. You're bleeding like a stuck pig." As she threw his good arm around her shoulder and took on some of his weight, she muttered. "Getting you there's gonna be a problem. Your place better be close, else I might just decide to drop you in the nearest doorway and leave you to fend for yourself."

She'd been on the hunt and now it seemed she had to babysit a helpless, wasted schmuck.

CHAPTER TWO

It took almost twenty minutes for them to walk six blocks to the Pike tri-area. But in the cold and damp chill of midnight it seemed to take a lot longer. They didn't say another word to each other mainly because it took everything in Josh to keep from passing out. And Skye, Skye didn't seem the chatty type, especially with most of his weight draped heavily onto her.

While the pain was bearable, the blood loss got to him. He wasn't going to pretend it didn't. As they made the trek through the empty streets, like an idiot Josh suddenly recalled how once upon a time his mother had set her heart on his becoming a doctor, specifically a surgeon. Now that the sight of his own blood made him feel woozy, the idea of dealing with anyone else's on a daily basis seemed fairly ridiculous. He found that incredibly funny and started chuckling.

But his mirth only earned a snarl from his avenger. It occurred to him then that she knew he was drunk. She'd known all along, and knew that's why he hadn't been able to help her fight.

In the way of the very intoxicated, he started laughing even harder.

When Skye simply shot him another daggered, infuriated look, Josh wondered aloud, "What? No sense of humor?"

"Maybe when you share the joke," she snapped. It wouldn't take much more of this doofus for her to lose patience entirely, she decided. Her sympathy was stretched already about as far as it would go before it erupted into full-blown temper. If the man weren't bleeding from a knife wound…

Josh abruptly stopped walking. As one, they stood in front of a converted building built in 1909. Skye knew the date because a plaque attached to the edifice said so. She realized the structure wasn't just a historical landmark—but very fancy digs.

While he attempted to pull a card key from his pocket, Josh leaned even further into Skye. "Damn, I left my raincoat back at the pub. No wonder I'm so fucking cold."

"You're fucking freezing because you're more than likely going into shock. And I'm sure your damn raincoat will still be there tomorrow," she puffed out as resentment bubbled up inside. Despite his injury, empathy was dwindling to a good case of hostility. The man obviously couldn't take care of himself if you spotted him a flamethrower.

She didn't have a whole lot of tolerance with numbskulls who were too timid or too drunk to defend themselves. On top of that, his expensive loft gave her pause. The place made her tiny dot of an apartment look like a dump.

"I should have thrown you through the back door of the pub when I had the chance and let your friends deal with you," she barked. "What were *you* doing in that alley without your coat on, obviously drunk, and all but wearing a sign that you were waiting to get mugged?"

"Fresh air," he grumbled. "It seemed like a good idea at the time." That brought on another round of drunken laughter.

In response, Skye jerked the card key out of his hand and ran it through the reader, handed it back to him in a snit. She heard the lock click open. They stepped into a stylish lobby decorated with a rectangular mahogany sofa table and a couple of French provincial wing chairs on either side. Proof once again, the digs were upscale. Very. The rich, tan-colored wall adorned with paintings by local artists, along with crown molding, and a regal collection of bric-a-brac told Skye the place reeked of money.

She let out a low, muffled humph. She couldn't stand French provincial or anything with bric-a-brac or crown molding.

As they made their way to the elevator on the left, Skye swallowed down more bitterness. Once she got him into the car, aggravated at getting pulled into this entire situation, out of patience, Skye, once again, jerked the card key from his trembling hand and swiped it through the slot to get the thing moving. The sooner she got the drunk into his apartment, the sooner she could doctor his shoulder, dump his ass, and be done with Josh Ander.

"Which floor?"

"Eight. Penthouse."

Should've known, she thought sourly as she pushed the button. So typical.

When the door slid open, she half dragged him into a stylish open layout with polished oak-planked wood floors. Compared to her five-hundred-square-foot hole-in-the-wall, the place looked like the fucking lobby at the Four Seasons.

A wall of windows flanked one side of the living room with what she was sure during daylight hours was a high-rise view of the harbor. The other wall held a bank of electronic gadgets and enough stereo equipment to stock a small appliance outlet, not to mention the biggest flat-screen TV she'd ever seen in her life.

Skye might not know firsthand her way around a tastefully decorated home but she knew an Aubusson rug when she saw one. Several were scattered over the hardwood flooring. She bypassed the masculine brown leather couch, and headed straight for the matching plush, cushiony side chair, immediately dropping his butt down into it.

"Got a first aid kit? Where's the bathroom?"

By this time Josh was more than a little ready to get off his feet. Groggy, he slumped and fell back on the chair, pointing the way to the bathroom without so much as turning his spinning head. "There. Down the hall. You'll find whatever you need there."

Skye took off in that direction.

He shut his eyes, tried to set the pain aside. As he listened to her footsteps retreat, he absently wondered if the woman ever did anything leisurely. She seemed to have so much nervous energy she all but hummed whenever she moved.

His warrior came back carrying the first aid kit, rubbing alcohol, peroxide, and a pair of scissors. She dumped everything on the coffee table and knelt in front of him. On bended knees, she ordered, none too gently, "Take off your shirt."

"I've been waiting six blocks for you to say that."

"And you can wait another six years," she returned flatly. "Want me to cut off what's left of the Polo? It might be less painful," she pointed out.

"Sure."

With that, she snipped the material from the ragged edge the knife had made at the tail up to the buttons at the neck. She stretched the blood-soaked fabric back to get a better idea of how bad it was. A closer look at the pain on his face though had her using a gentler hand as she helped him sit up so she could get rid of the shirt altogether. After studying the wound, she headed back to the bathroom. A few minutes later she returned with several hand towels, and a sewing kit she'd found inside a very tidily arranged drawer that looked as if an obsessive-compulsive had directed everything line up just exactly so.

She inspected the open gash again. The knife had carved about four inches of tender flesh. It looked jagged but not that deep. Good thing this wasn't the first time she'd had to stitch up a cut or play doctor to someone who'd been stabbed with a knife. She could handle a little slice to the shoulder.

Digging into the kit, she pulled out white tape and a roll of gauze. She threw open the sewing kit and selected the longest needle at least three inches in length, an ugly-looking thing she would use only as a last resort.

But when Josh's eyes zeroed in on the needle, he blanched and a wave of nausea hit him. Since he'd already felt like a wuss once tonight back in the alley the moment he'd been rescued by a woman, he sucked it up.

It didn't go unnoticed by Skye. "You feel like puking, let me know now. We'll do this in the bathroom."

"I'm fine," he gritted out. Since he had no intentions of appearing even weaker, he kept his head back and his eyes closed and hoped like hell his angel knew what she was doing.

As if reading his mind, she told him, "Don't worry, I've done this before. Got nicked with a blade once myself when I got a little too close to a wino going through the DTs. Anyway, I'll use the butterflies before I resort to the needle. How's that? It just depends on whether or not I can get it closed without too much trouble. The needle's just for backup. How much alcohol have you had?"

"Not enough for stitches."

"Where do you keep the liquor? And I need something to hold tap water."

"Scotch. I want Scotch. Cabinet. Kitchen. You'll find bottled water in the fridge."

She shook her head and patted his knee. "Tap water will do just fine for cleaning out the wound."

"Shouldn't you use peroxide for that?"

"Plain water's better for now. With a deep gash peroxide can sometimes trigger gas bubbles in the bloodstream." She grinned when she saw him go a little paler.

"Really?" The wave of nausea hit him again. He swallowed down bile and wondered if maybe he should have opted for the ER after all.

"Don't be such a baby, Ander. I'll find what I need."

Something told him she would. She seemed more than capable of taking care of herself. She'd certainly taken care of him along with four guys in an alleyway. He still wasn't sure of what he'd witnessed. His avenger, his warrior goddess, could be a dream. It might *all* be a dream, except for the bloody gash in his shoulder made by a six-inch switchblade knife that hurt like someone stuck him with glass shards. The searing pain made this all too real.

As soon as Skye hit the kitchen light, she blinked in admiration. What French provincial couldn't manage to do in his lobby, Ander's shiny stainless steel appliances did in spades. She couldn't help it. She wanted to live in the man's kitchen and never leave. The room was the size of her entire apartment with rich oak wood cabinets that made her drool as no fancy dress ever had.

What would it be like to cook a meal in this kind of setting? she wondered. Her fingers automatically reached out to skim the sleek marble countertop. She itched to open every drawer, explore every nook and cranny, to peek through his walk-in pantry.

When her eyes landed on a state-of-the-art coffee machine, she all but purred with envy. If she didn't have a man bleeding in the other room, she would have loved to spend several hours in here seeing what kind of meal she could whip up in this professional, chef-inspired kitchen.

She had to force herself to hunt down the Scotch. Grabbing the bottle, she poured a generous amount of the liquid into a goblet then ran tap water into a stainless steel mixing bowl she found in one of the cabinets. After loading up a tray with all of it, she took one last reluctant look around the room before flicking off the light.

The minute she got back to the living room, she handed Josh the crystal with the booze.

"Down this."

He didn't need to be told twice. What the hell had taken her so long anyway? He took the glass and drained it. On top of what he'd already consumed the Scotch didn't take long to work.

As soon as the alcohol kicked in and his eyes glazed over, Skye kneeled down and went to work. Using gauze and the plain old tap water in the bowl, she began methodically to dab the skin to clean the wound and surrounding area.

At the pain of having his shoulder worked on, Josh stirred again, looking down to check the gaping wound.

Knowing he needed a distraction, she used her voice to walk him through it. "I'm only cleaning out the dirt, checking to see how much damage the blade did, making sure I have everything I need to get the job done. Relax. Trust me."

He tried to focus on her. It wasn't difficult. She'd taken off her cap. To his surprise her black mane fell into a straight blunt cut that swung down neatly at her shoulders. When their eyes locked, he hadn't been hallucinating. Violet eyes speared his. He knew now there were no contacts, just striking, purplish-blue orbs.

Before she started applying the butterflies to stitch him up, she had to know, "Last chance, Ander, to head to the ER, let a pro handle this."

He shook his head. For some reason he had confidence in her.

"I'm going to use peroxide now to disinfect because it isn't that deep, not seeing layers and layers of tissue damage here which means you're lucky. No muscle injury, either. Looks like it didn't tear up too much cartilage at the joint. Didn't reach the bone."

She measured the gap, decided she could work with what she had. "I should be able to close using the butterflies. That's good. You've lost some blood. It'll probably make you weak for the next couple of days. And you're gonna want to get a tetanus shot, especially if it's been longer than five years. If I were you I'd call your doctor first thing in the morning and get him to prescribe some antibiotics."

She glanced up at the sound of Josh snoring softly. She merely shook her head and for the first time since she'd met the guy—laughed out loud. "Well, you're a mellow drunk, aren't you, Josh Ander? You're gonna be sore in the morning though."

After getting the bleeding to stop, she secured the butterflies in place. She finished wrapping his shoulder, taped the gauze together. She hoped he was right-handed because it would take a couple of days before he'd feel like using his left arm again.

She cleaned up the mess, gathered up the supplies and carried them back to the bathroom where she'd found them. She even took the glass, bowl and tray back into the kitchen, and washed everything out in the sink.

Twenty minutes later, she exited the building, stepping into the frigid night air. It had stopped drizzling for the first time all day.

She pulled gloves from her pocket, tugged them on before glancing down to check the time on her watch. Two-fifty. Not even three yet, early for her. She had cut short her night to come to the aid of the wealthy boozehound. After the hours she'd wasted saving Josh Ander tonight the trail of the man she hunted had gone cold. She cursed softly under her breath. Okay, so it had been awhile since she'd seen a man so in need of getting out of a jam. She supposed it wasn't his fault he'd chosen that alley to…what…get some fresh air to sober up? Why had the guy been out there in the dark without his buddies in the first place? she wondered. After all, didn't Friday night happy hour go hand-in-hand with friends? She sniffed the damp air, grateful Josh Ander was no longer her problem.

And just like that, she turned her attention back to the task at hand. She'd been so sure she had spotted him near Gull's Pub. But she'd been sure before only to be disappointed—and wrong. How many times was that now? How did the man always manage to dodge and evade her?

"I hope to hell your life was worth the one that may have been lost tonight, Ander. I hope to hell you were worth it," she muttered as she struck out for home on foot.

Without a sound she strode past the long string of parked cars lining the curbs. Several alleyways later, a dog started barking at the stray cat that sat taunting him on top of a fence post, knowing perfectly well it was safe from the canine that yapped below it. Out of the corner of her eye, she watched as a homeless person went through the garbage bin behind the Chinese restaurant east of Olive Way, foraging through the contents for something to satisfy his empty belly.

As her senses filled with the familiar sounds of the night, the blue fog rose and began to edge up out of the ground, thick as smoke. She'd gone no more than two hundred feet or so when that same mist took shape and began to swirl bluer, thicker around her. While the haze encircled her like a warm embrace, she felt the energy flow through her veins. The eyes came first, a wolf's eyes, a deep violet like her own, glaring out from the gray plume. They sought hers through the vapor and locked.

Skye never got tired of watching it happen even if her sanity sometimes battled with the mystic side of her forefathers. She had long ago accepted the reality of Kiya, her wolf, her spirit guide as much a part of herself as the color of her own hair and eyes. If she hadn't she no doubt would have ended up in a padded room somewhere, locked away from the general public.

Silver and sleek, once the wolf's majestic body shivered into its finished shape, Kiya raised her regal head to sample the heavy air. The wolf flicked her ears back in recognition. It was that simple gesture that offered Skye the comfort she needed, the drive, the light. Despite the lateness of the hour, the presence of the wolf gave Skye that boost of inner strength. The piercing gaze had a calming effect. Her frustration at the way the evening had ended fell away. Her black mood lifted.

The silver wolf matched her step for step as they walked together in the gloom, the wolf ever vigilant, ever watchful, ever protective. Without Kiya to guide her, Skye doubted she'd have made it this far. Without Kiya's knowledge, her essence, her presence, Skye Cree's life would have turned out far different, if she had lived at all. No doubt she would have died thirteen years earlier at the hands of a predatory monster.

Kiya's spirit had saved her.

All this time the wolf had always been there when Skye needed her the most. Unlike those who had purposely turned away from her, Kiya had not.

Maybe because after so many years there were still lessons yet to learn, doubts to deal with, demons of the human variety to take down.

For that reason the funk tried to slap back at her. But Kiya's voice inside her head came through strong and clear and snapped Skye back from the nagging hopeless feeling.

Remember, Skye Cree, the hunt isn't always successful. There will be another night, another hunt, you must never give up. The wolf is a patient hunter. Your path in life was set long before you were ever born. Find those that need you. They cry out in fear and pain. They are bound, kept hidden, locked away. Seek them. Set them free, Skye Cree.

The bastard was out there somewhere, snatching the innocent. Skye knew it, she just had to find some way to prove it. And she would. But now the trail had gone cold—again. If anyone knew firsthand what the man was capable of doing to a young victim, it was Skye Cree.

Cold now, Skye pulled the collar up on her long black coat while Kiya, the wolf, the hunter, her mother spirit, the one she'd counted on for years, steered her homeward. Together they headed farther west toward the harbor in the dark mist of predawn.

If she intended to find the bastard, she needed to catch some Zs to be ready for what she had to do tomorrow.

Because sadly for Skye, the quest was never really over, not as long as there were sex offenders walking the streets who made it their life's work to prey on little kids.

CHAPTER THREE

Erin Prescott couldn't stop crying. Her stomach hurt. In fact everything hurt, even her hair. He'd jerked her hair even though now the man lay next to her with his big hands stroking her mane of red locks. He seemed fascinated with her hair. She knew he was talking to her because she heard his voice, his words, but she couldn't distinguish anything coherent in them.

She didn't want to listen to anything he had to say anyway. But having to be this close to him on the bed, she had no choice.

She'd bled when he'd pushed himself inside her. And the second time had hurt just as badly as the first. Erin couldn't help it, her thoughts flew to Jason Avery. What would he think of her now, here in this bed with this creepy man with the greasy blond hair?

Would Jason ever again ask her to go with him to the mall?

Erin cried softly as the man turned her over to face him. If he started kissing her again she was sure she'd vomit. As the bile rose up in her throat, she shook her head and started trying to get up off the bed. When he protested, she screamed, "I'm going to barf. I need the bathroom or I'm going to throw up all over you!"

He relinquished her allowing her to move unfettered into the restroom, an extension of what looked like it had once been some corporate executive's office. The bathroom had no tub, just an enclosed shower stall along with a toilet and sink. All of which hadn't seen a good scrubbing in a decade or more. Even though she made a mad dash, her captor was right on her heels. When she tried to shut the door in his face, he yelled at her. "No, you don't. Leave the door open, so I can watch you."

But there was no place for Erin to go. She had to find a way out of this place. As she lost the contents of her stomach in the toilet again, she slumped down to the battered linoleum.

Erin eyed her abductor, still terrified of what he might do, and noted he'd momentarily stepped away from the door. She looked around for a way out. When her eyes landed on the window about six feet off the floor, she made herself get up and go over to the glass. It was dirty like everything else in the place. Not an hour earlier, she'd seen a rat scurrying into a hole in the woodwork. But oh, how she wished that rat could somehow lead her out of there.

With one hand she tried to wipe off some of the grime but even standing on tiptoes she couldn't peer out into darkness. She'd never felt so alone and lost in the whole of her fifteen years. Why? Why had she ditched practice to meet Jason? And why hadn't Jason offered to drive her to the mall with him? Stupid. She'd been incredibly stupid.

When she heard a noise in the other room, she turned back to make certain he wasn't watching her. As her hands shook, she stood on tiptoes again and with everything she had left inside, she did her best to lift up the glass, one inch, then two. Even if it was just a crack, the wintry night air drifted inside. She could smell the fishy smells from the harbor. She leaned her head on the wall, held her stomach, and dissolved into tears again. *Please. Please someone come for me. I have to get out of here. Please don't leave me here. Help me find a way out.*

Skye accepted the images and the sounds for what they were. The dreams always came strong and fast. To Skye they were almost as much the enemy as the despicable men who hunted children. She'd been a child the last time she'd slept without dreams and the voices that haunted her. Awake now after only a scant three hours sleep, Skye rolled over and knew it would be another gray and dreary morning before she even lifted her head from the pillow.

There were nights she didn't sleep that much and still dreams had a tendency to dominate her waking moments, especially when a child called out to her for help. There had been a time when she'd tried to shut them all out, close herself off to the message of each one. But most nights that was damned near impossible. So over the years she'd learned to use what she could, to gain insight into how she might be able to help those she saw and heard—and find them.

Tonight she thought she could make out the girl's face, certainly her voice, even though she had no idea of the girl's name. Wherever she was, she hadn't been there for very long. She hadn't been a captive for more than a couple of days, maybe even less than twenty-four hours. The girl's speech, the tone of her voice, told Skye a lot.

That voice might've held terror as it quivered and pitched but it had also held hope, hope that someone might come and save her.

The hope is what drove Skye Cree.

There was never any doubt in Skye's mind that the girl wanted her to hear—needed to make sure someone heard—and do something. There were parents out there frantic with worry who could do nothing but rely on law enforcement to bring their child back to them, safe and sound.

The girl was out there, locked up, held against her will, sick, scared, hurting. And no one knew better than Skye Cree the thoughts that had to be running through her head. That familiar mindset of wanting to run, to get away, to have someone, anyone, walk through the door and set them free, rescue them from their bonds. Perhaps that was the link, what the wolf spirit picked up on, what the heart of the hunter connected to.

How could she get any sleep now with the image of the girl in her head, with the heaviness weighing on her heart?

Skye crawled out of bed, threw on a robe, and went to the window. Drawing back the vertical blinds so she could peer out, she stared beyond her little balcony and out into the city not yet fully awake below with all its warts and meanness.

Because monsters were real—they might not have horns and red eyes or fangs or razor-sharp teeth—but they didn't need demon-like qualities to be able to inflict heartache and pain, injury or death. They were out there and Skye intended to put an end to those she could get her hands on.

It had been that way for years.

But first she had to get to the girl, the girl with the red hair, the one who had pounded on her door figuratively, at such an early hour, albeit in her mind, to get her attention. The girl had accomplished that much, Skye thought as she leaned her face against the cold glass, watched her breath fog the pane. There was a time to sleep and a time to act. The girl needed help. There were so many out there that did, too many to count, too many for one person to find alone. But alone is what she had been for too many years. And alone is all she knew. Tonight wasn't about her anyway. It was about the girl with the red hair, the one had reached out and begged for help.

Skye went to her laptop and booted up her computer. The girl didn't just need action, she needed a miracle. And for anyone else a miracle might be hard to come by.

Lucky for the little redhead, Skye Cree knew something about making the impossible happen.

CHAPTER FOUR

Josh came awake in the same chair where he'd fallen asleep. Even without his wire-rims he could make out the soft morning light drifting through the window. He could tell it was still overcast and drizzling. He patted his pocket, then looked around for his glasses and found them on the table next to the chair. He didn't remember taking them off and wondered briefly if his avenging angel had done so for him.

He'd slept like the dead except for the images he'd had of a certain scantily clad raven-haired goddess warrior with violet eyes flitting through his head in his dreams. The scantily clad part had been his own making, his personal touch enhancing the imagery. After all, his gaming background required a more detailed fantasy. Besides, it was his dream, wasn't it?

Just when he began to think last night had never happened, he started to rise and felt the sharp slap of pain in his left shoulder. Not only that, his head rumbled with a hangover the size of Mount St. Helens.

Slowly he eased out of the chair. There was no sign of the first aid kit, or his bloody shirt from the night before.

And no sign of said warrior goddess.

He went to the hall bathroom in search of aspirin for his pounding brain and found the remnants of his tan Polo scrubbed out like a rag still holding onto a reddish stain and tossed over the side of the tub to dry. She'd put away the first aid kit along with all the other supplies. To satisfy his curiosity that she was really gone, he did a quick walk-through of his bedroom and the guest room, and then headed to the kitchen.

When he didn't find her there, disappointment gave way to resentment. Using his good hand, he got out coffee beans and dumped them into the grinder.

As he ran water for the carafe, he wondered what the hell was wrong with him. And what had he expected anyway? That a woman like that would stick around waiting for a drunk to wake up from his stupor?

Maybe in the movies things like that were written into cleverly crafted scripts but in real life, they just didn't happen.

While he waited for the coffee to finish he thought back to what he knew about his avenging savior.

Other than the fact that she had the most incredible eyes he'd ever seen, she had to be a professionally trained martial arts expert. He'd never seen anyone fight like that least of all a woman. And that he decided he would keep to himself since he was pretty sure she would take offense at his phrasing, might even find it sexist.

At the moment, he didn't care.

Last night in the alley it hadn't been a smoothly choreographed movie set but a real life event. He'd seen her take on four tough guys, single-handed, and come out on top. That didn't happen every day. But she certainly seemed comfortable in the role.

Maybe she'd been a cop. He hadn't thought of that. But she hadn't identified herself as one. The way she fought made her an expert in…what? A black belt? Karate? Kickboxing? Aikido? Taekwondo? Jiujitsu? Wing chun? Was there a difference?

As a self-described geek, Josh didn't know squat about self-defense except what he'd seen and learned from the movies and some of the moves he had translated into graphics for his games, specifically those from Bruce Lee movies. After pouring a mug full of coffee, he sweetened it with enough sugar for two people and went to boot up his laptop.

He decided to Google martial arts to find out what he needed to know.

After thirty minutes he'd ruled out aikido because it taught that the safety of the attacker comes first. During the rounds last night Skye hadn't seemed overly concerned with the bad guys getting the worst of the deal or taking their well-earned lumps.

He considered karate, discovered it was Japanese while taekwondo originated in Korea. Watching a video from YouTube convinced him the two were similar yet the knowledge didn't bring him any closer to learning Skye's specific training.

Nothing stood out about which particular skill she'd used since she could have practiced a combo of all of them, especially kickboxing. Whatever it was, it sure as hell had gotten the job done.

Josh's shoulder still throbbed like it was on fire. He got up to dig around in several drawers and kitchen cabinets looking for a bottle of Tramadol left over from his last root canal. When he found the bottle, he uncapped it, swallowed two pills with a glass of water and went back to his laptop.

He let his fingers fly above the keyboard until he hunted through what he needed trying to remember what she'd said was her last name. If he had her name, he might be able to coax out a few personal deets from the Internet.

Dee. See. Cree. Yeah, that was it, Cree. Skye Cree. He smiled remembering she'd made an concerted effort to make sure he knew not to make fun of her first name.

Didn't she know her name, her face, conjured up an ancient goddess of war, replete with sword and shield? He could see it now, her standing along the majestic shores of some distant land waging battle against an invading army.

The gamer in him went one step further and painted in those images of regal castles standing tall and stately in the background while Skye Cree went head-to-head slaying the enemy, one by one. Somehow he knew he had to make that picture in his head come to life in a role-playing combat situation. Just as many artists had been inspired to paint their masterpieces, the savvy gamer slash programmer in Josh wanted to make Skye or rather the image of Skye Cree come to life inside one of his games.

Skye Cree. The majestic, ancient warrior goddess, defender of the weak and vulnerable.

He chuckled to himself. Cop or not, he doubted the woman from last night would appreciate his enthusiasm for plastering her face on one of his cleverly designed plastic packages.

But there was one question he could settle with a phone call. If she was a cop, that much could be determined by asking the right people.

If Skye had known Josh was checking up on her, she would have been livid because at that moment, Josh Ander wasn't even an afterthought to her.

Six blocks from his ritzy loft, she was holed up in her tiny, one-room studio apartment still on her laptop—sitting cross-legged on her bed—trying to sort through reams of statistics and information on the area's sex offenders.

The room cast a few shadows from the grudging light that peeped through the blinds and did nothing to help her wake up. So she picked up the television remote, flicked on her little twenty-six-inch flat-screen at the foot of the bed. Even though it was Saturday and early still, she flipped through the channels until she got to local news.

She set her MacBook off to the side, crawling off the bed with the intention of starting a second pot of coffee. Her feet hit the floor about the same time the perky, chipper anchorwoman began relating the news of the last twenty-four hours.

Another girl had gone missing. After listening less than sixty seconds, Skye recognized that face with the spattering of freckles, the red hair from her dream. And now she had a name. Erin Prescott had disappeared from outside her Catholic school yesterday afternoon in the rain. The fifteen-year-old hadn't been seen since her last-period class. The girl hadn't shown up for cheerleading practice nor had she made it home.

Skye's throat went dry. In her mind's eye she saw Ronny Wayne Whitfield. He had to be the one who had abducted Erin. It couldn't be a coincidence that she thought she'd spotted him near Gull's Pub last night. That was what...three streets over?

She looked around for the phone. She should call Harry Drummond. Even though she was certain he wouldn't have anymore answers for her today than he had yesterday or the day before or last year.

She decided bugging him would get her nowhere.

She'd have to hit the streets again, check out the places Whitfield frequented on her own. She sighed. And that had gotten her what in five years? Absolutely nothing. Nada. Zip. Zilch. Mainly because the info she had on him was so old it was no longer pertinent.

Coffee, she needed more caffeine to think. After getting another pot started, she flicked through the channels to get the full court press. Sure enough, Erin's disappearance flooded the Saturday morning newscasts. Skye watched with sadness and revulsion as the station cut to live feed where Erin's frantic parents stood outside their house, looking as though they hadn't slept at all and begged the public for any help in locating their missing daughter.

Familiar, it was all so familiar. Just seeing the anguish on their faces drowned Skye with memories from the past, a past she had never quite been able to put behind her. In fact, she was pretty sure she'd never be completely normal because of it.

She chewed her thumbnail, realized she had to do *something*. To hell with this, she thought. She tossed the remote on the bed and picked up the phone again, pushed in a few buttons she knew by heart. She wouldn't catch him at his desk, not when he was on a case this high profile but she hoped he had forwarded his calls to his cell.

Not every private citizen had a cop on speed dial. There were times Skye wished she didn't. But sure enough, the minute Harry Drummond answered, Skye went into her spiel. "Harry, this is Skye Cree. I'm ninety-nine percent sure the guy who took Erin Prescott yesterday was Whitfield."

On the other end of the line, patient as a priest, Seattle detective Harry Drummond bit his tongue. Since the minute he'd been handed the Erin Prescott case last night he'd been expecting Skye's phone call.

"I'm surprised you waited until eight-fifteen, Skye." No other person, not even his own wife, would have found him so willing to talk in the middle of a case. But this was Skye Cree; for Skye he had always made exceptions.

"Okay, so lay it on me."

She blew air into the phone and looked around her apartment. In the smidgen of space she considered her kitchen, she began to pace. "Look, Harry, I spotted him yesterday, a block from Fifth and Cherry. I'm certain it was him. That's less than half a mile from Jesuit Preparatory. And then last night—"

"Skye, a block from Fifth and Cherry would put him in front of the police station."

"I'm aware of that, Harry. But I know what I saw." If it hadn't been for getting sidetracked last night with Josh Ander, she might have gotten lucky and caught Whitfield in the act. Okay, maybe not exactly in the act but at least in close proximity to where Erin had last been seen. After all, she knew this predator's habits as well as her own.

Skye heard Harry's sigh into the phone.

"Skye, honey, I'll check Whitfield out, again, run him through the computer again and see what it shoots out—but you know as well as I do, he's been gone from Seattle for some time now."

More than once Harry had tried to keep tabs on the man to no avail and more than once he'd tried to convince Skye of that very thing only to fail miserably on both counts. If only he could get her to move past her obsession with Whitfield. "You've got to understand I have nothing on him, haven't since he walked out of prison five years ago. He served his four years and the system cut him loose. If he's out there he's kept his nose clean." And Harry didn't buy that any more than Skye did. Harry wasn't convinced the guy, once a child molester, could change his ways, much less keep away from young, innocent girls. "Whitfield hasn't been seen in all that time."

At least not by anyone but Skye Cree, Harry wanted to add. But he held his tongue and bit his lip instead. If anyone had the right to judge Ronny Whitfield it was Skye Cree, at least in Harry's book. "I haven't even been able to verify he's back in Seattle—at all."

Skye had heard it before. "Which means you can't discount he's here. He comes and goes right under our noses at will. I can feel it. I'm telling you I saw him yesterday big as life not a block from the police station. You know he has an aunt and uncle who live in Tacoma. They have seventy-five acres of land out there. He's living somewhere on that property. Tacoma is only forty minutes from Seattle, Harry. I know it was Whitfield yesterday. Same skinny build. His hair's a little thinner but it's still dirty blond. It's him."

She waited a beat trying to let that sink in before she told him the rest. Even though she couldn't tell him how she knew, her mouth went suddenly dry at what she was about to say. Details were something a cop needed to hear. "Harry, Ronny probably approached her from behind, asked for directions, maybe got her attention away from the fact a stranger was talking to her and then he stuck a needle in her arm or anyplace else he could reach. It was cold yesterday. Erin probably had on a coat, or wore something with long sleeves. Ronny more than likely went for the neck. It all happened fast before he dragged her into his vehicle, which he left waiting nearby, parked on the street." She heard Harry's impatient sigh through the phone and added quickly, "You have to believe me..."

"How is it you can speculate on that kind of detail, Skye? Tell me."

"The cops come up with theories all the time, why can't a private citizen do it, especially one who knows this guy's routine?"

"*Did* know his routine." At least part of that was true. Part of him wanted Skye to be right for her sake. Something about the way she always tried to keep him in the loop every time she thought she had spotted Ronny Whitfield tugged at his heart. "But I can't hunt him down every time a girl goes missing. Surely even you understand that, Skye."

"Sure, Harry. I get that. But..."

"No. I don't think you do. No one would be happier if I could connect Whitfield to every missing girl in Seattle. But it doesn't work that way. Now, I said I'll check him out, and I will. If I can track him down I promise I'll find out where the son of a bitch has been hiding once and for all."

With a sigh she finally plopped down in the chair at her little drop-leaf table. "That's all you can do then I guess. Thanks Harry, I appreciate it."

Reluctantly, Skye hung up the phone. She went to the coffeemaker, poured another cup. Chewing at her bottom lip, she knew what she had to do, what she always had to do.

She didn't intend to let Ronny Whitfield roam the streets of Seattle preying on little girls or anyone else for that matter. Not when Skye Cree could draw a breath.

Frowning suddenly when she spotted a brown leaf hanging on her dieffenbachia, never one to rein in her ADD, she grabbed her watering can to give the plant a long drink. As she buzzed from cane plant to schefflera to spider plant, she went back over her Ronny Wayne sighting the day before. Even from a distance of sixty feet she'd glimpsed the predatory look. He'd been on the hunt. She was sure of it.

As she tended her potted begonias, snapping off deadheads, her mind flew to Erin Prescott. She considered what the fifteen-year-old had endured over the past sixteen hours and fought off the anger. She needed to focus on the kidnapped girl. She was alive in the dream last night, which meant Whitfield had been the one to snatch her. That was the man's MO.

She knew very well Ronny would play with her for at least two days, maybe more before he either passed her on to someone else in the network—for a price—or got rid of her via his connections in the underground sex trade. Didn't she know that firsthand? That's what Whitfield had planned to do with her, wasn't it? If he could sell a twelve-year-old girl and get top dollar for her thirteen years ago, why would Whitfield leave making that kind of money in the dust for a career stocking shelves at the discount store?

No, he was still out there and active. Just because Harry couldn't find him didn't mean he wasn't still picking out little girls in the park. He would set his own pace, take the time to scare the poor girl into doing whatever he wanted. That was the way Ronny worked. Hell, who was she kidding? Any child molester would know how to frighten his young victim into complete compliance, use any method he could find that worked.

But Erin was alive. Skye could feel it in her bones.

Would Kiya lead her to Erin? Because her spirit guide had never let her down before, Skye had to believe that once again she'd find the answers she needed. It was the only way her brain could work at the moment.

Even though she could trust Harry, he didn't really understand the way she felt; maybe he never had.

After she made sure the soil in her mother's two-decade-old, four-foot-tall ivy hadn't dried out, she drizzled water over the Boston fern. Thinking of soaking rain from yesterday, she charged outside to check on the rosemary and sweet basil she had growing in a plastic tub she'd found at the Dollar Store. Her sliver of a balcony served as her garden, a treasured space that always reminded her of her parents and their love for growing things.

Maybe one day she'd have a real garden where she could actually dig in the dirt as her father had once loved doing, and take care of plants that actually had their roots in the ground.

Thinking about her father made her feel nostalgic, sentimental even.

She sighed, remembering how Daniel Cree had loved nothing better than to put a seed in the soil and watch it sprout. He'd been an excellent cook, who had loved going out and picking his own herbs for the dishes he came up with. She looked around at her sad little substitute, her poor excuse for the patch of green she craved.

For now her fourth-floor, tiny walkup would have to do.

After all, Skye had done everything she could to keep the one-room space from feeling like the oblong rectangular box that it was. She had a two-cushion sofa, a love seat really, she'd found at a thrift store for twenty-five bucks and recovered with slipcovers.

She used it to separate what she thought of as her living room from her bedroom. The "bedroom" consisted of a full-sized antique bed that sat in the corner of one wall at an angle almost touching the sofa, with a mere six inches to spare. But as long as she could maneuver through the space, and she could, it was like another room to her.

She had a sunny yellow bookshelf she'd painted herself sitting beside the bed. She'd filled it with classic novels like *Little Women, Beloved,* and *Pride and Prejudice* along with all her music CDs, everything from Pearl Jam and Nirvana to David Cohen's acoustical guitar masterpieces to Smashing Pumpkins and Teddy Thompson.

Her "kitchen" was on the opposite wall, a wall that held a sink and a set of overhead cabinets stuffed with a colorful collection of antique Fiestaware she treasured. A narrow slice of shelf space acted as her pantry. The bins beside the sink and stove she used for pots and pans. Those too, she'd picked up at the Goodwill store for a song. A two-burner stove, a microwave, and a compact-sized refrigerator rounded out the rest of her kitchenette.

Living in such small quarters, Skye had a place for everything and strategic positions for her few precious pieces of furniture. Like the cherrywood drop-leaf, a fifteen-dollar garage sale find she'd parked in front of the window so she could look out while she drank her morning coffee or ate her supper in the evening.

For the first time since last night, the garish size of Josh Ander's loft popped into her head, especially that gigantic kitchen.

Just thinking about all that wonderful space and how great it would be to prepare a meal there with every utensil known to mankind at her fingertips had her daydreaming about a bigger place.

She had to shake those thoughts back from fantasy land. She wasn't destitute.

There were reasons she lived as frugally as she did. Living on the inheritance from her parents, Daniel and Jodi Cree, such as it had been at the time, kept her from having to go out and get a regular nine-to-five job.

The money was hardly a fortune, far from it. The fact that she'd managed to stretch such a small amount since the day seven years ago when she'd finally reached eighteen was a testament to Doug Jenkins.

Doug had been her parents' lawyer and a good family friend. Doug had done everything he could to make sure Daniel and Jodi's only daughter had been well taken care of by investing her inheritance so that if Skye watched her pennies, she could live off the estate for several years to come without having to go to work for anyone.

And at this stage of her life, Skye seriously doubted she could exist in a regular job environment where she might be forced to put up with nosy co-workers who would surely get around to asking about her past and then pestering her about details. For her, curiosity from strangers never ended well.

No, a regular job wouldn't do.

Plus, she had never been very good with authority, which brought her right back to why she lived as cheaply as she did.

In fact, Skye refuted the word cheap.

She had no problems spending money on a decent laptop when necessary. Her MacBook, for example, had a seven-hour battery and had been well worth every penny she'd paid for it.

Then there was her car, a used Subaru she'd purchased less than two years ago after driving the fifteen-year-old Honda Civic she'd bought from Velma and Bill Gentry until it had fallen apart on the side of the I-5 Freeway. Even now the sporty little gray Subaru still had less than twenty-thousand miles on it. Because instead of driving every time she went out the door, she preferred to either walk or bike wherever she went.

She had, after all, picked up her Cannondale mountain bike for a song from an ad on Craigslist, bought barely-used from a woman who had been divorcing her two-timing husband and was shedding every reminder of him to start a new life in San Francisco. Lucky for Skye, that included the man's four-thousand-dollar bike.

As Skye checked off the mental list of things splurge-worthy, she didn't hesitate to add her stash of state-of-the-art surveillance equipment, equipment essential to her—work.

She couldn't do without her police scanner, her night vision goggles, or her weapons. They all fell into the same category as her laptop. In order to chase down perverts who preyed on little girls you needed the finest gear. It was as simple as that.

Buying things like pricey seven-figure lofts, on the other hand, fell into the extravagant I-don't-really-need category.

No matter how she tried, Skye couldn't relate to anyone having as much money as Josh Ander. How could she? Middle class is what her parents had been and middle class is all she knew. Those roots enabled her to live on a budget, made stretching her dollars more of a habit than a choice.

After all, she cooked her own meals regularly, save for the occasional cheeseburger at the golden arches or the times she splurged on espresso at her favorite coffee shop.

Was it a crime to want the money her parents had left her to go where it would do the most good? Her parents would've wanted it that way.

She had all the basic comforts. And that's all anyone needed, all she needed. She didn't require an excessive lifestyle. Her rent was cheap and the studio came with utilities. She kept a small storage unit with some of her most cherished keepsakes, things that had belonged to her parents, possessions from childhood she couldn't stand to part with or sell.

The fact that she didn't have room inside her tiny living space to keep any of it close at hand, Skye disregarded as simply not the point.

Besides, she liked to think her parents would have approved of how she spent the money they'd left her.

She put on gloves, wrapped a scarf around her neck and threw on a jacket over her robe. For a change of pace, she retrieved her laptop from the bed where she'd left it and took it outside to the little plastic deck chair. Once again she got busy trying to pull down as much information as she could regarding likely locations Whitfield might use to hold a young girl hostage over several days.

She didn't think he'd be stupid enough to bring her out to the land owned by his aunt and uncle. But to cover all the possibilities she decided she'd need to make a trip out to Tacoma just to be on the safe side and see for herself.

CHAPTER FIVE

So Skye Cree wasn't a cop, undercover or otherwise.

It had taken a few phone calls, four to be exact, to the right people to find out she wasn't in law enforcement. Even a gamer like Josh Ander had his connections. A local business owner usually did. And by tweaking an official state database, Josh had even pegged her address. That is, if she hadn't moved recently and if the info he'd pulled from the website was up-to-date.

Finding out that her apartment was only six blocks from his loft was nothing compared to the information he'd discovered about his warrior goddess when he had Googled her name.

He'd hit a gold mine full of data there. No one could accuse Josh of not knowing how to use a search engine.

Now, he stood staring out the window at the fog. He wished he'd left well enough alone, that he'd let the image of goddess remain steadfast in his mind.

No wonder she could defend herself with such zeal, he thought bitterly as he paced the length of his living room.

He had to be insane for thinking about paying her a visit, an impromptu visit. What would she do if he did? She would freak out for sure.

There was, however, any number of excuses he could use for showing up uninvited at her front door. Gratitude topped the list.

He would simply convince her he had felt the need to thank her one more time for saving his life. Crazy, it sounded stalker-crazy showing up at her door, though. But he had to see her again, it was as simple as that, especially after what he'd found out.

Josh got up from the table and headed to the bathroom to shower and shave. If he was going to make an ass out of himself, by damn he would do it cleaned up and not looking like he had the hangover from hell.

The rain had finally stopped, but dark clouds still hovered low to the ground.

Josh walked the six blocks to First Avenue in the cold all the while thinking about what he would say. When he finally looked up and found himself in front of Skye's building, a four-story vintage brownstone two blocks east of the harbor, he paused only briefly before walking up the steps to the front door.

He went over the master plan one more time, determined to sound grateful. He was just about to push the buzzer when to his amazement the door flew open and Skye Cree stepped outside right into his chest.

Dressed in a black ski jacket, well-worn jeans so faded they were almost white, with a deep blue scarf wrapped around her neck that came close to matching her eyes, she dazzled his senses. Her hair was tied back into a sleek ponytail. The strap of a satchel of some sort stretched across her chest.

"I was just coming to see you," Josh admitted all in one quick blurt.

With degrees of alarm on her face and in angry clipped tones, she huffed out in exasperation, "How did you find me and—more importantly—why did you feel the need to?"

By the wary glaze in her eyes he could tell the woman did not like finding him standing outside her door. He held up both hands in front of him. "I'm not stalking you or anything like that. I just...I wanted to thank you again...for saving me in that alley...for fixing my shoulder—for everything you did last night."

Still suspicious, Skye countered, "Okay. You've thanked me. Now what?"

"How about a cup of coffee?" He saw another layer of unease creep back into those violet eyes. "Coffee, Skye. That's all. Public place. Your choice."

"Okay. There's a place around the corner, Coffee & Cakes. They make terrific apple muffins."

They started down the steps together. "You never answered my question, Ander. How did you find me?"

Lying to her wasn't an option. "Computer. Search engines are a computer geek's best friend."

Skye frowned. And just like that people could find her. It made her cringe knowing how easy it was. It took a few more minutes before the rest dawned on her. "Which database did you crack? You're a hacker," she accused.

"I'm a business owner," he corrected and tried for glib. "A gamer."

"What else? Wait a minute." She stopped walking and grabbed his arm. "Ander? Ander All Games. That's you?"

He smiled and adjusted his glasses. "Just a little gaming company I started about ten years ago with a friend when we were in our first years of college and neither one of us found particular success at impressing our professors."

"I see. You didn't mention who you were last night." But she should've known. There had been indicators. The fancy address. The furniture. The Aubusson rugs. She'd ignored them all because of his injury. She picked up her pace again. "You didn't really come here to thank me, did you? What is it you want, Ander?"

As if sensing a vibe, she stopped in her tracks, turned to face him full-on again. "If you found where I live then you know all about me, don't you? That's it, isn't it?" She threw out her arms wide, raised her voice an octave in frustration. "Nothing to see here, Ander. I'm not some freak show waiting for a crowd to gather so they can snap pictures for chrissakes. I deserve my privacy!"

It didn't escape Josh how truly enraged she was. "Yes, you do. No argument there. I was curious about the woman who came to my rescue, that's all. And yes, I found out who you are and what happened to you but—I had no idea. This morning I decided you were a cop. I wanted verification." He didn't think she wanted to hear how much he respected what she'd gone through which he intended to mention as soon as she calmed down.

But by the time they reached the coffee shop, he'd already made a decision. He threw open the door for her and offered, "I want to help you with—your mission. I owe you that much."

"My mission?" Despite her irritation with him, she looked up into his eyes. Those slate gray eyes held such understanding that she wanted to trust him. But trust had to be earned. "You don't owe me anything. Right place. Right time. I got to kick some ass last night, side benefit, so I'm not complaining. And I'm pretty good at it."

"No argument there. But...I think I have an idea how I might be able to help you with your—work." When she started to protest, he quickly added, "Before you say no, hear me out."

They placed their orders for coffee and apple muffins and found a table in the back where they could talk.

"What exactly do you think you know, Ander?"

"Could you call me Josh?"

"No."

He sighed. "Okay. I got curious. I Googled you. Thirteen years ago when you were twelve years old, a pedophile named Ronny Wayne Whitfield kidnapped you in broad daylight from a park where you were playing within forty feet of a bunch of other kids your own age. They said you disappeared into the bushes after you went to retrieve a soccer ball and never came back out. In fact, your family was within a hundred feet and never heard or saw him abduct you.

"But within the hour, he'd taken you back to his apartment and raped you. He held you for three days, during which time he also negotiated with a couple of guys in the sex trade business, human traffickers, to take you off his hands after he got finished with you and sell you to the highest bidder, where they in turn would ship you out of the country, somewhere overseas.

"But somehow you managed to escape your bonds, got out of his place, and run for help. The detective who handled your case was a guy named Harry Drummond, who did everything he could to make sure Whitfield was prosecuted to the fullest extent of the law. You were scheduled to testify against the son of a bitch in court. Everything was fine for the eighteen months it took his case to work its way through the legal system. Everyone was confident they could put him away for at least fifty years.

"But then one day your parents were killed by a drunk driver in a car accident. Your mother's sister, your aunt, became your legal guardian, and for whatever reason, she refused to cooperate with the district attorney to allow you to testify. Because the prosecutor didn't have your testimony, it left the door open for Ronny Wayne to plead out to a lesser charge, which he jumped at. He only served four measly years for what he did to you."

"So? Just because you can use the Internet doesn't mean you know a damn thing about me."

"You might possibly be the strongest person I've ever met," Josh said with absolute conviction in his voice.

When she merely rolled her eyes at that assessment, he decided to go on, "This guy, this Whitfield, got out of jail five years ago. The first couple of years he had to register as a sex offender on parole, he used an address in Tacoma, a trailer belonging to his aunt and uncle. But after his parole ended, for some reason, he's been able to disappear off the radar. My guess is you've been chasing him ever since because you don't believe for a minute he's given up his habits. That would make you around eighteen or nineteen when you first started the hunt, just out of high school. Instead of moving on with your life, you've made Whitfield and anyone like him your mission in life. I think that's what you were doing patrolling that alleyway in the middle of the night. You were on the trail of some predator, maybe even Whitfield."

Despite the go-to-hell look she gave him he ignored her. "Your business, not mine. My guess is you think he's here, Whitfield that is, back here in Seattle. Skye, you understand him better than any cop ever could. You know he isn't ever going to stop his…predilection. You're after him. You've trained for years, physically, mentally, for the time you'll—for lack of a better word—encounter him again. It's how and why you're able to do a combination of martial arts techniques in your sleep."

Skye leaned closer so no one else could hear. "Are you done? You do a helluva lot of guessing, assuming, for someone who should know better, certainly someone who doesn't know squat about me. It's a helluva theory. That's all."

"What if I could find him for you?"

She grunted at that. "Are you crazy? What makes you think you could find the low-life son of a bitch when the cops can't?" She didn't mention the obstacles she'd faced over the years in trying without success to pick up the guy's trail.

"Let's just say, I have certain skills, certain resources, and I'm willing to use them to go where the cops can't or won't," said Josh.

"Why? Why would a guy like you who owns a company worth millions, risk everything he has to break a few laws so you could find a two-bit sex offender who can't keep his hands off little girls?"

"Because I wouldn't be sitting here if it weren't for you."

"That's ridiculous."

"Is it? Those guys were willing to kill me last night for some change and a piece of jewelry I wouldn't give up. I pay my debts."

"I'm sure you do." She grabbed her satchel and stood up. "Thanks for the coffee, Ander. Consider your debt paid. But I work alone."

Before she'd taken two steps, Josh was on his feet.

"Really? Tell me, Skye, do you think Whitfield could've been the one responsible for snatching Erin Prescott?" He saw the answer come into her eyes, saw the way the pain lingered, the way the anger kept her focused. "I watch the news, too."

"Fine. Come with me then."

It looked like the woman could use reason and logic when she wanted to. Even though he would have preferred to stay in the cozy coffee shop, she led the way outside in a huff.

Once they were standing on the sidewalk, she gave him both barrels, poking him in his chest with her finger for emphasis. "You listen to me. Just because you have the money doesn't mean you have the control. I'm in charge. Always. You don't agree to that right now, the deal's off."

"Fine."

"And you aren't the only one who can work a keyboard. It just might be the time to mention I've spent years going over databases from the state parole board. I've gone through countless statistics, addresses, updates from that agency and through all of it, I haven't found so much as a toenail clipping from Whitfield. It's as if he's fallen off the face of the earth. And you have the nerve to think you can find him because you're some big time gamer who might possibly be able to hack a database?"

"Okay, we'll coordinate our efforts. By the way how much did I get right back there?"

"Enough. You do a lot of guessing though—that's unnecessary. From this point forward, I'll tell you everything I've found out…whatever you need to know…about Whitfield. We'll compare and share our information. But my private life is just that, Ander. Private. Off limits. No matter what you goddamn well found out on the Internet. Understand?"

And with that, Skye Cree turned and left him standing there as the rain began to spit from the clouds again.

CHAPTER SIX

Skye gritted her teeth all the way to the market where she picked up milk and eggs, some fresh fruit. She usually enjoyed the outing but today she couldn't let go of the scene at the coffee shop—or the look in Josh Ander's eyes.

Pity. Those gray slits had burst with it.

Damn the Internet anyway, she thought miserably. And damn it to hell with snooping busybodies who couldn't keep their noses out of her past. Just because someone had the ability to log on and find out every aspect of a person's life—not to mention all kinds of personal information one might not want the entire world privy to—didn't make it right.

On the walk back to her apartment, she tried to lose the attitude and calm down. By the time she reached her front door, she'd achieved a somewhat Zen approach to Josh Ander. She didn't completely want to bash in his head.

Why couldn't everyone just leave what happened to her in the dust? Why couldn't they just let it be and leave her the hell alone? This is what always happened whenever she tried to get close to anyone or even when she didn't. As soon as they found out what had happened, people invariably judged her for something that occurred a dozen years ago.

Wasn't this the reason she did her best to avoid people? Wasn't this the reason she'd given up trying to date? This was at the core of why she loved her solitude, her late-night walks through the city.

Damn it, she'd rather ignore total strangers than have to dredge up sordid details, especially with someone trying so hard to get to know her.

She'd been a child for chrissakes. But whenever people found out about the infamous Skye Cree, they invariably treated her differently. Maybe they didn't do it intentionally, but still, you could see it in their eyes, in their demeanor. Okay, maybe judging her was a little too harsh a word. But they customarily exhibited sympathy. Empathy. Pity. Concern.

Christ, some even wanted to know what it had been like.

Sickened at that thought, remembering those kinds of questions, she did her best not to grind her back teeth down to dust.

She had to admit, though, the only thing she'd seen on Josh's face had been the pity, a big old slice of it the size of Mount Rainier.

It didn't matter she reminded herself.

The dozen years since Ronny Wayne Whitfield had been difficult to live through. She'd gone to therapy, of course. She had been doing better, improving every day at putting it behind her—and then her parents had died in that stupid car accident. A drunk driver, not paying a damned bit of attention to what he was doing, ran a red light—and with that one act ended right then and there what was left of her childhood.

She'd lost her parents at thirteen. After that, she'd been forced to live with her aunt and uncle. Religious fanatics, her mother had called them. And that was only a slight brushstroke of what Aunt Ginny and Uncle Bob had really been like.

Moving in with her mother's only sister and her husband immediately after the funeral had been sheer culture shock. It hadn't taken two days before Skye figured out the couple hadn't really wanted her at all. Or better still, they hadn't known what to do with her.

As she let herself back into her apartment, she remembered how dear old Ginny and Bob had treated her as if she had some sort of disease. At twelve their niece had been kidnapped and raped by a pedophile. Yet they had acted as if Skye was the one who should be exiled away from society, someone who should be shunned, closeted away from other decent folks.

It hadn't taken long for Skye to realize her aunt and uncle had been humiliated at what had happened to her. Well, join the club. She'd been plenty embarrassed about it herself at how everyone seemed to know. So much so they hadn't wanted her to talk about it—least of all to anyone in a public forum—like in a courtroom setting in front of all to see and hear. So as the court date had gotten closer, Aunt Ginny had simply refused to let her cooperate with the district attorney's office. And since good old Aunt Ginny was her legal guardian, there was nothing Skye could do about it. At one point Ginny had even threatened to take her niece and disappear, anything to keep the girl from testifying in public so that Ginny wouldn't have to suffer public shame and listen as her niece rehashed what had happened in front of the whole world.

Maybe if Skye had been allowed to put the whole episode behind her then and there, she wouldn't feel this weight of responsibility now. No matter how Skye worked it out in her head, because of her, Ronny Wayne Whitfield hadn't gotten fifty years but rather was out, still walking the streets. He'd been paroled after serving only four years in prison and spent a short two years in the parole system. Once that ended, Whitfield had been able to vanish without a trace, a sex offender that the public no longer kept track of or cared about, except maybe for Skye Cree.

Inside her tiny galley she put on a fresh pot of coffee before setting out the makings for a cheese omelet. By the time she sat down at the table with her food, her anger had diminished to a slow simmer and burn along with resignation.

She couldn't change the past.

After mulling over the entire exchange back in the coffee shop, she wondered if she should have simply opened up to Josh Ander, maybe told him about seeing Whitfield yesterday near Fourth and Cherry. Should she have told him everything, bared her soul so to speak?

The Internet didn't tell the whole story, not by a long shot. Despite her existence as a loner, she wondered what it would be like to have someone to confide in, really open up and share things with, heartfelt things.

And could a man like Josh, with his wealth and contacts, really help her find scuzzy Whitfield?

She drew in a deep breath. Questions blasted her. Trust was something she didn't take lightly. At some point, if she worked with him, she'd have to remedy that—and tell him the whole story—eventually. For now, she continued eating her eggs and thought about what the night ahead might yield.

Hopeful, she hurriedly finished her food and cleaned up her mess. To get ready to hit the streets, she decided what she needed was to clear her brain entirely of Josh Ander and let go of her fury. Steeling her mind, shutting away everything else might open up channels so that with Kiya's help she could focus enough to find Erin Prescott.

According to what she'd seen in the dream, the girl was being held in a rat-infested empty building nearby, which didn't provide her with a lot of info to work with. Because of the downturn in the economy, there were more vacant buildings in Seattle than she could shake a stick at. It annoyed her on many levels that if she had to dream she didn't understand why those same dreams couldn't provide her with addresses, the kind that were front and center, in big bold letters on the sides of buildings that gave her something definitive. That would make her life so much easier, she mused.

There was always a chance she'd get lucky and the likes of Ronny Wayne would make a mistake. Skye had to believe that.

For months now she'd been working on something she hadn't even shared with Harry. Erin wasn't the only young girl who had turned up missing in the Seattle area, just the most recent. But for now, Erin was out there somewhere, hurting and scared.

And it was up to Skye Cree and Kiya to find her.

In the misting rain, darkness shielded Skye as she moved away from the lamppost on Columbia and headed toward Cherry via Third. Even though she loved the night, valued the smells that often drifted on the heavy Seattle air, she practiced an eagle-eyed vigil, one a sentry might recognize as obsessive, maybe even anal retentive. But to Skye, details were meant to be paid attention to, scrutinized until you found holes or weaknesses.

Over the distant sound of traffic several blocks away, Skye could make out a party just getting started in one of the neighborhood row houses. Probably college kids, she decided.

A whiff of seafood drifted from the harbor area and reminded her she hadn't eaten since the omelet that afternoon. She silently promised herself that once she'd made the rounds, she would treat herself to a stack of pancakes at Country Kitchen on Grove. Just the thought made her stomach rumble.

Next to her, as if sensing that, the wolf sniffed the air. As long as Kiya hunted beside her, Skye believed her parents would always be nearby. And the spirit guide would always be a link to her father's people. Even though Daniel and Jodi lived strong in her heart, Native custom dictated that long after the mortal body died, the spirit still walked the earth in various forms of their choosing. Skye liked to think her connection with Kiya had grown stronger after their deaths. Invisible to others? Absolutely. No one could see the wolf but her. That alone made her different, a freak.

But Skye Cree didn't give a rat's ass what anyone thought of her. At least not since middle school, not since Whitfield, and not since her parents had been taken from her too soon.

When the woman and the wolf reached Fairfax, Kiya cut through an alley heading west and Skye trailed after. She overheard a fight ramp up between a man and woman about whose turn it was to take out the trash. From that point, Skye began trying to retrace her steps from Friday night and the area where she was certain she'd spotted Whitfield.

Heading down yet another back street, she took a shortcut to Fourth Avenue, and didn't stop until she was within a few steps of Jesuit Preparatory Academy. She looked across the empty campus and did her best to visualize how Ronny Wayne might have gotten Erin into his car.

Flashes, hard and fast, came at her in a series of snapshots first, then like a video, it all played again.

Summer. July twenty-second. A Sunday. A picture-perfect day for children to enjoy the open spaces of a city park with family. The sun was out, the temperature in the mid-eighties. For Seattle, it was almost a heat wave. Her parents were enjoying the afternoon with two other couples on a picnic, cooking burgers for themselves and hotdogs for the kids. The adults had formed a circle with their lawn chairs and drank beer from the cooler they'd filled with ice-cold drinks. The talk turned to playing a game of softball later.

Not thirty minutes earlier, her dad had played Frisbee with her and some of the other kids right before her mother had reminded him it was time to start the grill.

Skye had been about to join a group of kids in a game of soccer. She'd been watching them kick the ball around an open field, playing, laughing, and occasionally arguing good-naturedly about calling fouls. She remembered she'd chased after the ball. She'd gone into some bushes to retrieve the thing when it had rolled beyond the cardboard box the other kids had set up as their goal.

The moment she'd stepped into the hedges, a young, rangy man with blond hair had blocked her path. He'd told her he had a little girl who was new in town, who wanted to join the other kids in the game, to play with the other children. But his daughter was shy. Could Skye walk with him to the car and talk her into joining their game?

He'd known her name. Didn't that mean it was safe to follow?

She remembered getting to the dark green car, remembered looking for the little girl he'd mentioned inside, and not being able to see her. Where was she? Thinking she was perhaps in the backseat, Skye remembered the panic that had begun in her throat, locked there, when she hadn't seen the child sitting where she was supposed to be, waiting, waiting for the strange man to open the door and introduce her to a new friend.

In the next moment, a huge hand had covered her mouth. Just as she'd been about to scream, she'd felt the prick of a needle in her arm, and before she knew what was happening, he'd thrown her into the backseat of the car.

After that, there had been nothing but blackness.

Skye sucked in a breath remembering that terror-stricken, twelve-year-old girl. She forced the memory away.

Concentrate. Focus. Flashbacks wouldn't do her any good tonight.

Skye knew as well as anyone that the likelihood Ronny Wayne would leave his prize to go out on a Saturday night in the rain was virtually nonexistent. But she had to try. Sitting at home wasn't an option. It was never an option.

Plus, Skye had nothing better to occupy her time anyway.

God knew it had been more than three years since she'd been out on what any normal person would consider a date. And look how that had turned out? It had ended with the guy—Derek Pierce was his name—wanting to get closer to the woman he'd been attracted to, had taken out to dinner—something most women her age did all the time and thought of as second nature.

All Derek had wanted to do was touch her after their kiss and move to the bedroom to show her how he felt. The kiss she could handle. It was what came next she had a tough time with. When she'd pushed him away, he'd left confused and angry. Her fault. She'd sent out too many mixed signals. Skye couldn't blame Derek. It wasn't his fault she couldn't deal with the touching beyond a certain point.

Any therapist worth his salt would be more than happy to explain all the whys. She didn't want or appreciate a bunch of psycho-buzzwords at this point in her life trying to figure out why she couldn't connect with the opposite sex. She knew why.

After the disastrous experience with Derek, she'd decided dating wasn't worth her time.

Maybe one day…

About that time Skye caught sight of Dee Dee, a sixteen-year-old hooker with a fondness for crystal meth, leaning up against a brick building between Blanchard and Bell. In spite of her habit, Dee Dee was a wealth of information and liked to talk. And lately talk on the street had Skye convinced that someone had himself a lucrative business trafficking young girls in the sex trade.

Dee Dee might be young, might be a speed freak, but if you could catch her at the right point in time, she was more reliable than a neighborhood crime watch commander.

"How's it going tonight, Dee Dee? You look cold."

"Hey, Skye, I'm fucking freezing. Where you headin' anyway? Don't you ever stay in at night? Ever? I had me a nice home, that's where I'd be right about now, curled up reading a good book."

"You know me, Dee Dee. I'm a night owl."

"Shit, Skye. You're a hunter, everybody knows that. You been lucky lately? You caught anybody I might know?"

Skye shook her head. "What've you got for me tonight?"

Dee Dee bounced in place, either from being cold or high, and blew a breath into her hands to try to warm them up. "I seen that stringy-haired man hanging around the school again. That's three times. You know the one, hanging around that private school. You're right. That asshole's creepy-looking. He's losing his hair...fast."

Skye pulled out a twenty from her pocket, handed it off to Dee Dee. Even though she was pretty sure she knew exactly what the cash would be used for, Skye didn't hesitate to offer the girl something in exchange for information. "When? Exactly when, Dee Dee, don't hold back. Think. You spoke to him?"

"Yep. He was on foot. Two days ago. He was cruising, looking for a redhead."

"What time of day?"

"Afternoon. I told him about Lucy but he wasn't lookin' for my kind, Skye. He wanted fresh, if you get my drift."

When a rusted-out, ten-year-old sedan pulled up to the curb, Skye knew she'd lost Dee Dee as soon as the girl's eyes drifted to the potential john. Sure enough, Dee Dee darted off the wall hoping to score the trick before anyone else beat her to it. Over her shoulder, Dee Dee yelled, "Go get him, Skye. Get that bastard!"

Skye watched Dee Dee haggle for her fee before hopping into the Ford. She watched the vehicle make the right turn at the corner, and Dee Dee was gone.

The reality of life on the streets for a teenager who'd run away from home, Skye thought now. A kid with a major drug problem before she'd even turned fourteen.

Sadly, she couldn't spend the rest of the night dwelling on Dee Dee's lot in life.

For now, she turned her attention back to the wolf. It circled the school for a second time, trying to pick up Erin's scent from the day before.

The wolf must've picked up something because Kiya left the grounds and headed down another side street, following a trail to a part of town that was more industrial than commercial.

There were plenty of ancient manufacturing buildings. Some Skye was certain hadn't seen any type of life except for rats and the occasional stray cat or dog in more than thirty years. She should know, since she'd taken the time to explore some of the more isolated ones a time or two.

She continued to walk, scanning the dark, a lamppost in the distance her only means of light. Cautiously gauging her surroundings, she moved from shadow to shadow until she reached into her pocket, took out a penlight, and shone it to be able to see a stingy three feet in front of her face.

She covered another half mile down yet another back street until she lost sight of Kiya. The dead end came upon her suddenly littered with debris along with uneven and broken concrete. This was new terrain, rocky, difficult to maneuver in the dark. She was almost certain she had never made it down to this particular spot before. It was too secluded. The nearest residence or store had to be at least six blocks away.

At the sound of a low growl, Skye turned and spotted the wolf standing some twenty-five feet away, refusing to give ground. Standing stubbornly next to the side of a building, Skye waited for the wolf to decide to yield. But when that didn't happen and she saw Kiya begin pacing back and forth with no intention of budging, their eyes met in the dark. Skye homed in on the wolf's instincts. Trust. Skye backtracked, and heard it then, a low moan coming from—somewhere, an open window maybe.

Skye glanced up. It was then Skye spotted the small open window above them about twelve feet off the ground.

Even though her long black coat was plenty warm, chills formed along the nape of her neck. She stopped dead still to listen, heard it again. She started moving closer toward Kiya and the source. The wolf hadn't moved.

Someone was hurting and in trouble.

Like the night before.

Not knowing what she was dealing with, every sense in her body went on alert. She watched now as Kiya began to stalk back and forth, back and forth along the side of the building. Just like Ali Crandon. Just like Hailey Strickland.

Finally Kiya raised her head, those eyes locked with Skye's.

"Nice work," Skye said aloud as she stroked Kiya's head and thick fur. After several long minutes, she heard it again, a low guttural whine and then a voice. Words croaked out, "Is anyone out there? Help me, oh God, please help me."

Kiya let out another low growl.

"Yeah, yeah, definitely female and in trouble," Skye reasoned. She looked around for something she could use to boost herself up far enough and onto the narrow ledge, enough to get a look in the window. Eyeing several crates near a Dumpster, she darted over and grabbed one, emptied the contents out on the ground; they looked and smelled like something undefinable and rotting.

Moving back to the brick wall, she set the box in place and hoisted herself up. The ledge was wet and slick from the rain. Damn it, why hadn't she thought to bring a pair of gloves?

She began to try to pull herself up where she could peer inside.

It took three tries but she finally managed to apply enough pressure with her arms to leverage far enough up to see inside the room. Thank goodness for all that time she'd spent training. She pushed up with her elbows. And saw a girl lying on her side, naked, stretched out on the filthy tile floor of a dirty bathroom.

Skye swallowed hard. The girl had red hair. Erin Prescott had red hair. Skye's first thought was that maybe the girl was dead. Was she too late? No, she'd heard moaning several minutes earlier. Skye's heart did a double time in her chest. She slowed down her breathing, tamped down the adrenaline. She forced her mind to clear.

The girl was *not* dead. Skye pushed everything out of her mind but that one fact.

She raised the window enough so she could get inside. With all her might she swung her leg up and over the ledge and through the open window. At that moment, the girl turned her head to look wide-eyed at Skye.

In a hoarse, gravelly voice as if the she had spent the last twenty-four hours crying, the girl begged, "Help me, please. He's coming back. He's…going to kill me. I know he is. He says he won't, that he has plans for me but…" The girl hiccoughed.

"Erin?" Skye asked in a whisper while at the same time she held a finger up to her lips in a signal to be quiet.

As if understanding, Erin nodded, and in a low voice exclaimed, "Oh God, yes. Please…help me. I want to get out of here."

Teetering on the window sill, Skye quickly pulled her other leg through the frame and into the small space of the bathroom. On one knee, she leaned down to the girl and put a hand on her forehead. Erin's body burned with fever. "My name's Skye. Where is he, Erin? Is he in the next room?" she murmured.

The girl shook her head. "The store…I think. He went to get…food and some medicine…for my stomach. I've been sick…throwing up ever since last night. He…he…raped me."

"He's a bastard," Skye replied. "Now listen to me, you're going to be okay. I know. I've been right here where you are now."

Erin blinked at that with wide green eyes staring back in wonder. "You're just saying that. All I wanted to do was spend some time at the mall with Jason Avery. That's all. Now, he won't want to have anything to do with me."

"No, I'm not just saying it, Erin. But right now isn't the time for my life story. You listen to me, if this Jason doesn't want to talk to you at school, the guy isn't worth your time. But right now, the priority is to get you the hell out of here. Got it?"

"Got it."

From that moment on, Skye forced herself not to react to the bruised and battered face, nor to the blood she saw on the girl's legs and torso. Skye moved with one purpose. She stepped to the bathroom door, opened it just a little, and peered out. The adjoining room was empty except for one soiled and stained mattress on the floor and an ugly side chair. Tousled sheets covered the bed. With no heat, the place was freezing cold.

The place looked exactly as it had in Skye's dream.

"How long have you been in here by yourself, Erin? Try to think now, tell me how long he's been gone?"

A trembling Erin began to stir and try to sit up. "I...I don't know...maybe ten minutes, I guess. He...took my...clothes. He said...I...I couldn't run without my...clothes."

"We'll see about that." Skye slipped off her coat and put it around Erin's shoulders. "Stick your arms through here. Listen, here's what we're going to do. Can you walk?"

Teeth chattering, Erin replied, "I can run...if it will get me...out...of here."

"Good girl. I want you to stay behind me the entire time. No matter what happens, stay behind me. Understand?"

"I...I...don't have any...shoes."

"It's okay. We'll get you some. You follow me, okay?"

"Okay. What if he sees us?"

"I'll kick his ass." Skye took Erin by the arm and dragged her along past the nasty room and into a hallway. In the lead, Skye listened for any sound of movement.

When she heard nothing but an empty shell of a building, she tugged Erin further away from that room.

"Do you have a gun? He has a gun."

"Good to know." Skye didn't want Erin to think about that right now. Half of her wanted to run into the son of a bitch, the other half wanted to get Erin out of there as quickly as she could and away from that room. But either way, Erin needed some reassurance.

Skye reached inside the coat Erin now wore and pulled out her baton just in case. She withdrew a knife from her boot and handed it to Erin. "Listen to me. I know you're scared but I won't let him anywhere near you, Erin. Do you understand? He'll have to come through me to get to you. I guarantee you the man's a chicken shit bastard when it comes to taking on an adult, even a female grown-up will scare the crap out of him. I won't let him anywhere near you. If the worst happens and he gets past me though, use the knife. Go for the gut when you slash out. For some reason it seems to hurt the most. Okay?"

When Erin nodded in agreement, Skye grinned for the first time at the shorter girl. "But he won't get past me. You ready? Now let's get the hell out of here."

Skye found a back staircase and led Erin down one floor to ground level. When she spotted an exit door she pushed it open a fraction, peered out into the misty night. Seeing no one in the alley, she pulled Erin through the doorway and out into the darkness.

Skye spotted the wolf almost immediately. Their eyes met again. *Get us out of here, Kiya.*

The wolf looked away, sniffed the ground and took off.

It wasn't easy to maneuver in the dark. The nearest streetlight was a half a mile back. Did she dare turn on the penlight in case Erin's abductor came back and spotted the light? Remembering the rocky condition of the parking lot, Skye decided to hell with it. She took out the penlight. She deliberately kept them next to the building for cover until they were out of the alleyway.

She glanced up ahead, made sure she kept Kiya in view until the wolf picked up her pace.

Skye did the same as she and Erin broke into a run across the dilapidated asphalt, filled with potholes and crumbling blacktop.

They stopped only once when Erin stumbled and cut her foot, but Skye dragged the girl upright, making sure they kept up the dash to freedom. She continued pulling Erin away from the area heading in the opposite direction from the nearest grocery store, or at least the only grocery store Skye knew anything about that was open this time of night.

At the sound of a car engine, Skye ushered Erin behind a row of hedges where they waited and listened. When Skye determined that the car was headed away from them, she tugged Erin back onto the pavement. Rock strewn as it was, moving across the stretch of concrete was better than staying in one place and risking that the asshole might come back at any moment.

For what seemed like an eternity, they continued to sprint, cold and wet with Skye in the lead and encouraging Erin to keep pace behind her. It was a good two more blocks before Kiya stopped and Skye heard the sounds of boats in the harbor and felt they were far enough away to rest and make the call for help.

Even then, Skye knew that in Erin's mind they had not gone far enough to put distance from that nasty room and what had happened there with the goddamned pervert.

It would never be enough distance.

By the time the two stopped near another abandoned building, Erin's feet were bleeding and freezing and she was out of breath. Up to now they had not exchanged a word, not since they'd left the confines of Erin's prison as if they were both afraid to utter a sound.

But now, Skye looked around for an address, some identifiable landmark to give the cops. When she spotted a restaurant in the distance, she pulled out her cell phone and dialed Harry's home phone number, a number she'd dialed many times in the past but never more urgently than at this moment.

While she waited for an answer, she pushed Erin down on what was left of a concrete loading dock and said, "Rest. You'll be home before you know it."

Even wearing Skye's coat, a shivering Erin never let go of Skye's hand. "Don't…don't leave me, okay?"

"Not a chance."

"Did this same thing really happen to you?"

"Oh yeah. And I survived. If I survived, you will, too."

"Th…thank you."

As Skye kept Erin's hand clutched in an iron grip, the minute Harry answered his phone, Skye's words tumbled out in a flurry so fast she hoped he got it all.

She needn't have worried.

Harry Drummond had known Skye Cree for more than a dozen years. And never had he moved as fast as he did now.

CHAPTER SEVEN

In the ER, Harry sat in the waiting room with Skye while the doctors worked on and examined Erin Prescott. Her condition was good, her spirits better now that she'd gotten out of that miserable place and away from her captor.

The police had informed the Prescotts that Erin had been found alive and even now they were en route to the hospital to be reunited with their daughter.

While Harry waited for the girl's parents to show up, he held on to Skye's hand in a death grip.

"If I live to be a hundred, I'll never understand how the hell it is you do what you do. This is the third girl in as many years. You are an amazing young woman, Skye Cree, absolutely amazing. Have I told you that lately?"

"That's not what you said when I was eighteen," Skye grumbled as she sipped from a Styrofoam cup half-full of bad-tasting vending machine coffee.

"Yeah? Well, sue me. It was my attempt at fatherly concern. I didn't want to see you patrolling the streets in the dark of night with no hope of ever rescuing anyone let alone ever stumbling upon Ronny Whitfield's whereabouts. Shows you what I know. I still want you to tell me how it is you find them…when—"

Skye decided she needed to do a little tap-dancing to get Harry off that subject. "Back then you thought I was in need of a team of psychiatrists," Skye said, reaching up to pat his cheek. "And maybe I was, still am. It was appreciated, Harry."

When Harry scoffed at that, she added, "Okay, maybe appreciate is stretching it but I was only eighteen, too young to realize you were worried about me. I didn't care. I didn't think I had anything to lose. You were such a pain in the ass back then anyway, worse than you are now."

There were reasons she cared for this man like she did, but there was only so much she was willing to share, even with him. A police officer tended to ask way too many questions. "I know what you thought back then and how troubled you were that I couldn't take care of myself. But Harry, now you know I can." She squeezed his hand. "Is there any word?"

He shook his head. "He must have heard the sirens and hightailed it out of the area. The place was empty when my men got there. They waited for him to come back. So far, he hasn't."

"Look, I tried to get her as far away from the building as I could before I called you. We must've walked a half mile. She was scared to death. So you don't know yet if it was Whitfield or not?"

"Prints are all over that place. It's just a matter of time. And we have her exam with the perp's DNA. I'll know by morning if it was Whitfield. You didn't ask her?"

"Come on, Harry, give me some credit. No, I didn't whip out a picture of Whitfield from my back pocket and ask her right then and there before I got her out of that goddamned filthy hellhole."

Harry stood up. "Well, I can and will. I'm just waiting for the docs to give me the go ahead to talk to her. I've got patrolmen crawling all over that area right now within a twenty block radius. Got uniforms off-shift volunteering to go door-to-door for another twenty-four hours to cover the neighborhood. If he's anywhere near there, we'll find him. And if it was Whitfield, we'll know it."

Skye sighed. "I'll bet a twenty he's gone, Harry."

He shrugged. "Maybe. But thanks to you, Erin is safe and I've got men combing the area. We might get lucky."

At that moment, an anxious couple in their mid-forties walked up to the nurses' station. Skye stood up and crossed to Harry. "I guess there's no way for you to keep me out of this. Maybe you could just say you found her."

Harry shook his head. "No way, kiddo. It doesn't work that way. Besides, the media was on the story five minutes after the police scanners went nuts. And one of them brought you into the picture not long after. Just like before."

As Harry watched Susan and Jay Prescott's approach, he leaned over and whispered, "Buck up. You've been through this in the past. Because of you Ali Crandon and Hailey Strickland are somewhere safe and sound tonight with their parents. Think of that. And now, you can add Erin Prescott to that list."

Skye mentally braced for the harried couple who rushed over in three quick strides. It was the woman who asked, "Are you the one who found our baby?"

Harry rocked on his heels and nodded. "This is Skye Cree. She's the one who found your daughter."

Skye stuck out her hand but before she knew what was happening, Susan Prescott had wrapped her up in a huge bear hug. "Thank you. We're so grateful. How can we ever repay you?"

Next, Jay Prescott took his turn giving her another bear hug in gratitude, but Erin's father was all questions. "How? How did you ever find her? Are you undercover? Are you a cop?"

Skye shook her head and smiled. "Right place. Right time. Look, I need to get going. It was nice meeting both of you. Right now, the important thing is to go take care of your daughter. And remember, she can put this behind her. She just needs to know that both of you are in her corner."

"We are. We will be."

As she headed to the elevators though, a nurse walked up and announced, "The doctor is still in with Erin, but she keeps asking to see the woman who rescued her." The nurse's eyes landed on Skye. "From the way she described her rescuer that must be you. The doctor suggested I come and get you."

"But her parents—"

"Will get to see her in a minute. Right now, Erin's asking for *you*. Come on, this way."

Reluctantly Skye followed. On the walk down the corridor, memories flooded past Skye. She did her best to shut them down and focus on the veteran nurse because the nurse kept up a steady line of chatter. "I've seen hundreds of rape victims, but the young ones tug at my heartstrings. It's something I never get used to. And this one…Erin refuses to settle down and let us sedate her for the exam until she's talked to you, seen her parents. Also, I recognized your name when Erin mentioned it. The girl didn't but I did. I remember what happened to you. And I know this isn't the first girl you've found." The nurse finally took a deep breath and reached out for Skye's hand. "I just want to say how strong I think you are. You're an amazing young woman. That fifteen-year-old is lucky you found her and she knows it."

"Um…thank you," Skye muttered. Why the hell hadn't she left sooner? Fifteen seconds more and she'd have been out of this place. She hated hospitals. They brought back a slice of her life that covered surgeries and painful recoveries.

Inside Erin's exam room, Skye's self-consciousness didn't get any better. She stood back as the doctor made notes in a chart. But the moment the girl spotted her and reached out a hand in her direction, Skye couldn't get to Erin's side fast enough.

"It's okay. I told you it would be okay."

"Please let me have a minute with Skye." At Erin's insistent plea, the fresh-faced doctor turned to Skye and smiled widely. "You're a remarkable woman, Ms. Cree. I'd like to give you a hug but I'll settle for a handshake instead."

After shaking hands, the doctor and the much older nurse left the two of them alone. The minute the door shut behind them, Erin said, "Thank you for getting me out of there. I'll never be able to repay you. I was scared to death of him." When Skye started to speak, Erin went right on, "Tell me again how it won't matter, that I can get past what he did, what he took from me."

"You can either let it destroy you or kick it in the nuts. The girl I saw emerge from that stinking room wouldn't stop at that though. Nope, she'd likely jump any hurdle that got in her way. Look at what you did. You ran through the freezing cold, into the night, cut up your feet to get away from him, to get out of there. You remember that when you feel like giving up. I won't tell you it'll be a walk in the park because it won't be. But you'll talk to a therapist and you'll win."

"Can we talk again, maybe when I get back home?"

"Sure. We're survivors you and I. And survivors stick together."

When the door opened behind them and Erin's eyes landed on her parents, she started crying.

"Thank you," Susan Prescott said to Skye as Susan wrapped her arms around her daughter.

"You need anything Ms. Cree, you have only to ask," Jay Prescott offered as he patted Skye on the back. "We owe you."

Once out in the hallway, Skye had to lean up against the wall for support. She'd known exactly what to say to Erin. She just hoped the fifteen-year-old would be one of the lucky ones and be able to cope with her ordeal. After all, she'd been standing right here before with two other young victims. When she saw Harry approaching, she pushed off the wall, ran a trembling hand through her hair.

"How's she doing?"

"About like you'd expect."

"Go home, Skye. Get some rest. If anyone's earned a breather, it's you."

"A breather? How many others are out there, Harry, out there in seedy rooms at the mercy of degenerates, scared to death, afraid to make a move?"

"Skye, it takes a toll, I know. But get some rest. Okay?" Harry put his arms around her. "I'll have an officer take you home," Harry offered. "I won't take no for an answer."

"You'll call though, right? You'll let me know if it was him?"

"You know I will."

By nine a.m. Sunday morning it was all over the news.

Josh drank his first cup of coffee standing in front of the flat-screen TV listening as the local news anchor described how Saturday night, Skye Cree had found and rescued Erin Prescott, the girl who had spent twenty-four-plus hours with her kidnapper in an abandoned warehouse near the harbor.

If Josh were in awe of that news, he only had to wait for another reporter on a different channel standing outside the hospital to explain how this had been the third time in as many years that Skye Cree had found and rescued an abducted young girl.

The first had been ten-year-old Ali Crandon, who had been kidnapped during an outdoor birthday party, snatched right out of her mother's front yard in broad daylight.

In that case, police had issued an AMBER Alert because they had a description of the girl's abductor. Three hours later, Skye Cree spotted the girl in the company of a known pedophile walking down Western Avenue where she approached a suspicious man with his arms locked tightly around a very frightened little girl.

Witnesses later described, a brief altercation had taken place and Skye Cree had rescued the little girl from her kidnapper.

Josh shook his head at that assessment of the event. If it had been anything like the exchange in the alley, the one he'd personally witnessed, the pervert hadn't stood a chance.

Ten months ago, Hailey Strickland had been the second girl Skye had saved. After snatching Hailey at a bus stop, her abductor had thrown her into his car and headed south to his apartment in Kent. It wasn't clear how Skye had found the thirteen-year-old or what Skye Cree had been doing in Kent.

Right now the details weren't all that important to Josh. What he wanted to know and what the reporters weren't saying was whether or not they'd caught the guy who took Erin Prescott. Was Skye right? Was Erin's abductor Whitfield?

When his buzzer sounded telling him someone was at the front door of the building, he pushed the button on the intercom. A familiar voice came back.

"It's me, Josh. It's Michelle."

At those words, Josh saw red. He couldn't help it. Enough was enough. This had to stop and there was no better time than right now to let her know how he felt. "I'm coming down to the lobby, Michelle. I'll be there in a sec."

"Josh, wait…"

But he was already pushing the Down button for the elevator, fuming all the way to the first floor.

The minute he stepped outside the car, he made his way to the front door. He didn't intend to let Michelle get inside the building. His body blocked her entrance as he stepped further outside forcing her to take a step backward.

Under overcast skies they stood facing each other on the awning-covered portico.

"You disappeared last night from the pub. I brought your raincoat. You left it. I told the others I'd see you got it."

"That's nice of you but…"

"You won't even let me inside?"

"No. It's over, Michelle. I've tried to tell you several times now but you refuse to listen. Every time you show up uninvited, you're simply pissing me off."

"That's mean. What would Annabelle say?"

"Annabelle's gone, Michelle. And she wouldn't want you throwing yourself at anyone, least of all me."

The slap she laid on the side of his face stung but just for a moment. Josh looked into her eyes and saw rage and something else, something he'd ignored up until this minute. Michelle acted more than a little unbalanced. At least the blow had been honest, possibly the first honest emotion they'd shared together in months.

"How dare you? I slept with you…now I know you just took advantage of the situation. I thought we were…"

Rubbing the side of his face, he didn't let her finish. "You thought wrong." When he jerked his raincoat out of her grasp, she turned on her heels and ran toward her Chevy parked on the street.

As he rounded to go back inside, he saw Skye standing three feet away, holding on to a bicycle. She'd overheard the entire exchange.

"Breakups can be so ugly sometimes," Skye reasoned, rocking back on her heels.

"What are you doing here? Shouldn't celebrities get to sleep in?"

"Celebrities? You've been watching too much TV, Ander. I'm just out getting my exercise, seeing how the other half lives on a Sunday morning. Got a cup of wake-up coffee?"

"Sure, come on up. You can leave your bike in the lobby."

"So you trust your neighbors?"

"I don't know. Now that I look at it they may not be able to resist a Cannondale."

"Got a good deal on it from a woman selling off everything that belonged to her cheating bastard of a husband."

Once in the elevator, she wanted to know, "How's the shoulder? Following doctor's orders?"

"You mean the hack that tried to fix me up?"

"You never even paid the hack. You got my best surgical skills for gratis."

"As I recall, I bought her a decent cup of coffee and a muffin and she bit my head off."

"That's 'cause you're a nosy bastard who couldn't mind his own business for a lousy twelve hours."

"I'm sorry, Skye. For all of it."

It was the sincerity that kept her comeback light. "Oh great, so now you're apologizing for something you had nothing to do with? That bites."

As they stepped into his loft, he took her by the arm. "You're the most incredible woman to have gone through so much at such an early age. To come out of it able to help others the way you do is nothing short of—incredible."

"Yeah, sure." Determined to downplay her part in the rescues, the ones the media were going nuts about, she pointed out, "Look, if you're planning to make a big deal out of Erin and Hailey and Ali, think of it this way. Those girls aren't the only ones out there suffering in that kind of environment. Besides, do you have any idea how many miles I walked, how many blind alleys I went down, how many blocks I covered, how many pairs of boots I wore out before I got lucky? That's all it is, Josh, blind luck. I could go another couple of years before I so much as locate another kidnapped girl in distress."

He wasn't so sure about that but kept his opinion to himself for now. "You have a knack."

She snickered. "My knack consists of insomnia, excess energy that borders on ADD, an innate stubbornness, and knowing I'm the reason Whitfield is walking the streets."

"What?" Josh turned to stare. "You aren't serious? You were a child for God's sake. Your aunt refused to let you testify. How is that *your* fault?"

"What do you know about it anyway?" Frustrated, she took a deep breath in, let it slowly out. "Look, back off, okay? It's early and this is a touchy subject for me."

"How'd you get so stubborn?"

"It's embedded in the gene pool. I mostly take after my dad."

He nodded knowingly. "The Nez Perce side of the family where the Native American look comes from. I found that on the Internet, too. But where do you get those eyes of yours?"

"Geez, Ander. You really are a piece of work." When he continued to stare at her, she shrugged one shoulder. "My mother, okay? She had these large violet eyes, gorgeous chestnut hair, a brunette who happened to hook up with a dark Native American. Do you have that coffee or not? And just so you know, I wouldn't turn down a stack of pancakes either."

"Okay. There's a café two blocks over that makes terrific light-as-air pancakes."

"What? How about you throw together some pancake batter in your fancy gourmet kitchen? What about that?"

"Pancake batter? You mean…I'm not sure I have…" He trailed off, his gray eyes looking genuinely perplexed.

"You have flour, some Bisquick maybe?" She pushed past him on the way to the kitchen. She couldn't believe he didn't use this beautiful room to prepare meals. She turned in a circle. "You mean you have all this and don't even bother to boil water here every now and then? That's—criminal."

Josh started opening cupboards. To him the kitchen was just another room where he could store stuff he rarely used. "I make coffee. Sometimes I get desperate and scramble an egg in the microwave." He refused to admit how rarely that occurred. "That's about the extent of my culinary skills."

She shook her head. "That's pitiful. Out of my way, Ander, this kitchen was meant to create masterpieces, not stagnate at the hands of the inept. Wait until you taste my pancakes."

In one fluid motion, she tossed her jacket over a chair and started opening drawers and cabinets, trying to locate what she needed.

Josh stood back out of her way. And realized that just like her athletic body, she moved as if she knew her way around food prep.

"Fortunately for you I take my whipping up pancake batter very seriously. I consider the person who created waffles, pancakes, or crêpes nothing short of a virtuoso in the kitchen. Crêpes are an art form. But today, for simplicity's sake, we'll go with the basic pancake."

He didn't much care if she popped bread in the toaster. Right then he was too busy considering and admiring *her* art form.

Once she got down bowls and found a whisk, she went in search of ingredients. He didn't have Bisquick but she found flour and sugar in canisters filled to the top as if they'd been sitting there waiting for someone to discover their potential. She dug out spices, baking powder, and even unearthed a bottle of pure vanilla. She located a bowl and did her best to re-create her mother's recipe she remembered from childhood. It had been a while since she'd made them from scratch but she was confident she could come close.

She turned up bacon hiding behind eggs in the refrigerator and set it to sizzling and popping in a skillet. A second tour through the pantry gave up bottles of syrup, even honey. While the cakes browned she got down the plates and napkins and set the table.

Twenty minutes later, Josh's eyes feasted on the bounty of food. He took a seat at the table, waited until she'd sat down, and dug in to his stack of fluffy pancakes. "Mmmm, these are fantastic. All this was in my kitchen?"

Used to cooking meals for one, it gave her belly a strange sense of pleasure to watch the man enjoy the breakfast she'd thrown together. "I opened the pantry, the refrigerator, and miraculously it all came together on that six-burner commercial wonder called a stove. It's known among the common folk as cooking, something we have to do at home to save money rather than spend it on eating out."

Josh ignored the dig. "Not to be difficult but I heard the microwave ding a couple of times. I can microwave stuff."

"Defrosting frozen pizza into a manageable glob is *not* cooking. I found your stash of boxes in the freezer." She took a bite of yummy pancake. "You need to make a trip to the market. How is it you have pure vanilla but no lemons or fresh fruit? I was forced to substitute freshly squeezed lemon juice with lime that I poured from a green bottle I found buried in the back of the fridge. The contents expired two months ago."

"Lime juice in pancake batter?" He shook his head in wonder. "The citrus must make it fluffier, right?"

"Ginger ale works, too, but you didn't have that either and I didn't want to use beer which you have in abundance."

"Really? Hmm, well, I have a woman who comes in once a week to clean the house. For an extra twenty-five she'll do the grocery shopping. Sometimes she gets this idea in her head that if she brings in…actual food like bacon or sausage, I might get the hint and turn on the stove."

Just then Skye's cell phone rang. Glancing at the readout told her it was Harry. "Hello."

"The prints came back. It wasn't Whitfield in that warehouse, Skye."

"What? No, no Harry, it was him. I know it was."

"Look, this is an ongoing investigation. You know very well my captain would have my ass if I divulge too many specifics even to you. But I can confirm Whitfield didn't grab Erin Prescott."

Disappointment fell across Skye's face before she said into the phone, "Then who did?"

Harry could tell her because they had already put out an APB for the man and put feelers out from Canada to Mexico. "Sex offender named Brandon Randle Hiller, age thirty-six. Served six-and-a-half years in Clallam Bay for molesting his girlfriend's twelve-year-old daughter. Got out almost five months ago."

Curious now, she stared at Josh as she asked Harry, "Does he look anything like Whitfield?"

Harry lost the tether on his patience. "Skye, this fixation has got to stop." He didn't want to mention that Hiller and Whitfield looked enough alike to be brothers. "Right now, I have to run. The higher-ups are close to having a conniption. How about I stop by your apartment later this afternoon, if that's okay—and we can finish this. And just so you know, the Prescotts want to meet with you again."

"What on earth for?"

"Gratitude. It's a powerful emotion. They have their daughter back because of you. They'd like to be able to tell you again how much they appreciate what you did."

"They did that already, several times in fact."

"And it may be a dozen times more. I gotta go."

At the disconnecting click of the phone call, Skye's shoulders sagged. She'd been so sure she'd seen Whitfield near the Catholic school. "It wasn't Whitfield. I don't understand that at all. I guess I must have been hallucinating. Again."

"What?" Josh sat up straighter. "You thought you saw Whitfield? Yesterday? Near Erin's school? That's—probably not a coincidence."

After blurting that out, she felt embarrassed. "My eyes must be playing tricks on me. Either that or maybe I need glasses."

"How'd you find the Prescott girl, Skye? And the others? It wasn't blind luck."

"Well, that came out of nowhere." She took a bite of pancake even though she'd lost her appetite. "Right place. Right time."

He wasn't buying it. The look on her face told him there was something she didn't want to say, something she had no intentions of sharing with him. "Maybe. How'd you escape from him anyway?"

"Are you always this nosy over breakfast?"

"My point is you have excellent survival instincts, as well as reflexes. If you think you saw Whitfield yesterday I believe you did."

Skye simply stared at him. No one, not even Harry, had ever really believed her. She leaned across the table slightly and stated, "You really want to know how I got away from the bastard that day? I got lucky. He went out to buy cigarettes and beer. The minute I heard the door close, I started trying to loosen my ropes. I'd been working on them for most of the night anyway. When I finally got my hands free, I booked. That's it. There's no mysterious element involved, no cryptic aspect to understand, no secret to reveal. Now, could we talk about something else?"

He smiled at her even though he knew there had to be more. "Sure. I have myself an incredible partner."

She frowned. "Geez Ander, you're easily impressed. And we haven't even discussed collaborating on the other stuff." She had to change the subject away from herself, away from Whitfield.

As if Josh understood, he decided he needed to change direction. When he opened his mouth to speak, so did she. He waved his hand for her to go first.

"How exactly did you come up with *Mines of Mars* anyway?"

"Everyone wants to know that. Have you ever played it?"

"You're kidding, right? Hasn't everyone played the most popular video game that outsold *Halo*?"

He grinned. "It has taken off. The whole thing was pretty much a joint effort with my best friend, Todd Graham."

"Right, the friend from UDub."

"Actually we go all the way back to middle school. Todd's a little awkward around people."

"Shy?"

"No, not that, more like socially stunted. He has Asperger's syndrome."

"I can relate. I know a little something about being different."

"Your ADD?"

She nodded. "I don't think I had it as a child, it sort of evolved once I had to go live with Ginny and Bob. I'm pretty sure it was the culture shock thing along with the loneliness. I didn't make friends once I got there. It seems no one wanted anything to do with the likes of me." She met his eyes, shook her head. "There's no explaining some people's small-mindedness. But that wasn't the only reason. Most people had a tendency to give my aunt and uncle a wide berth. It seems even among religious devotees they stood out for their bizarre beliefs."

"Like what? That's a lot of lonely years from thirteen to eighteen." And his heart went out to the outcast she'd been. His own middle school years hadn't been all that different as a nerdy gameplayer. But then he hadn't been forced to go live with a weird aunt and uncle.

"For one thing, I wasn't allowed to listen to music, any music. And I loved music. When my parents were alive they took me to concerts in the park. We'd dance like fools in the living room to old Stones songs or to Springsteen. That all ended with everything else. Ginny and Bob thought music was the work of the devil. So was makeup, and short skirts, for that matter. I had to wear outfits Ginny had hand-sewn. They dressed me in stuff right out of the fifties." She shook her head. "You know what's weird though?"

"What?"

"Those four years Whitfield spent in prison, he probably had more freedom than I had. Ginny and Bob watched me like a hawk. I got to go to school five days a week wearing those ugly dresses, then to church Sunday mornings. Wednesdays and Fridays were for fellowship but still church-oriented stuff filled with prayer. I'm pretty sure Ronny Wayne had it better in jail than I did."

He reached out, covered her hand.

"That's why I couldn't wait to get out of there once I got that high school diploma in my hand. The day after I graduated, I packed up my stuff and hitchhiked the hundred and fifty miles into Seattle, got a job at the Country Kitchen. By this time my dad's best friend had bought the place. Travis needed a line cook, third shift, and I could flip burgers, fry potatoes."

She shrugged. "It worked for both of us. A couple of months later, this lawyer friend of my parents named Doug Jenkins walks into the place, sits down at the counter, tells me that since turning eighteen I'm entitled to my inheritance. I didn't know what the hell he was talking about. He had to convince me."

"You didn't know about it?"

"No one had ever mentioned my parents had life insurance or a little money put aside. Turns out, the money was a little investment account my mom and dad started and had been sitting in the bank for five years collecting interest. And thanks to this honest lawyer, I could have access to my trust, such as it was. By that time, I'd rented a room at Lena Bower's house, a woman I'd met through one of the waitresses. About three months later, I got my own place. It's nothing like this." She waved her arms at the size of the room. "But it's all mine and I can listen to music anytime I want. And dance around the room in my underwear if I want."

He'd have to remember to take her dancing and to concerts. "I wouldn't mind seeing the underwear."

"I believe you've made that abundantly clear." Her stomach jumped with nerves at the idea of that. To break the flow of the conversation, she got up to refill her coffee cup. "I want your kitchen. And maybe this fancy coffee machine. Sheesh, I have a Mr. Coffee I bought at a garage sale for five bucks. Has to be fifteen years old if it's a day." She laughed as she generously poured more half-and-half into her brew. "And it still works like a top. Well, except for the weird noises it makes."

"Anytime you want to come here fix a meal, be my guest. Since you made breakfast the least I can do is cleanup." He got up to rinse off their plates before loading the dishwasher.

"The least? Good thing you can find the appliance. Who was the cute little blonde-haired beauty you broke up with earlier?"

"Ah, that was…a friend of my late wife's. We umm…I didn't exactly...we were never really—"

"I get the picture, although I'm pretty sure the blonde thought she'd ventured into a long term scenario, maybe hit the lottery all the way to the love department, while you were thinking more along the lines of fuck-buddy. She's smitten. Am I right?" She took a sip of coffee and looked at him over the rim.

He didn't care for her assessment, but she was right on the money about Michelle, even he recognized that much. "I hate to admit it but, yeah. She's been a bit of a stalker lately."

When he said nothing else, she prodded, "So you were married?" At the look of surprise on his face, she tossed in, "You aren't the only one who can use a search engine. Depending on which website you hit you can obtain almost any number of personal facts about Joshua Sebastian Ander, age thirty. Sebastian? Where the hell did that come from?"

"It was my Polish grandfather's name from my father's side of the family. Which brings me to a question about you. What middle name goes with Skye?"

"We aren't talking about me."

"Sure we are. We could postpone talking about me while I try and guess your middle name."

"Oh for God's sakes. Fine. Skye Melody Cree."

He busted out laughing. "Melody? And I thought Sebastian was bad."

"Oh shut up. Now, back to those websites I found. Almost all of them mentioned you are one of Seattle's youngest and brightest entrepreneurs. That's a given. But…one of the city's most eligible bachelors? I guess women go for those little glasses and the long black hair, huh? Look, you might as well spill your guts because otherwise I'll just keep badgering you, returning the favor, in spades of course."

He gave her a prolonged, disdainful look. "Okay. But I don't see how dredging up the past is relevant here."

"Your wife died."

He snarled low in his throat. "About a year ago I came home from work one evening, found her lying on the floor in the bathroom. She wasn't breathing. She didn't have a mark on her body, no bruises, no gaping wounds, nothing. The coroner said she died from a heart attack."

"I'm sorry, Josh."

Their eyes met. This was the first time she'd actually used his first name without the usual mocking, scornful bent she usually took. "So was I. So was I," he repeated.

"You loved her."

"I did. We were only together for two short years. She was only twenty-eight years old. How does a woman that young die from a heart attack, and not know she had anything wrong with her heart beforehand? Her parents told me she'd never even so much as had an attack of indigestion let alone any type of heart ailment."

"Life is a mystery. People die young. My parents were only thirty-eight when they were coming home one day from the grocery store and stopped at a red light. They were sitting in a left-turn lane at two-thirty-eight in the afternoon when a drunk driver ran through the intersection from the opposite side and ended up crashing his car on top of theirs. That was the exact time on the clock in the car, which was pretty much totaled. They both died instantly while the drunk driver, a guy in his mid-fifties with several DUIs under his belt already, lived. Go figure."

"I'm sorry, Skye. Thirty-eight is way too young. And way too young for you, at thirteen, to be left alone without your mom and dad."

"So...we agree the past, for both of us, is something we..."

"Take off the table? Sure."

"Agreed."

"Good. Now that we've settled that, let's stay with subjects that interest both of us like Ronny Whitfield."

"How do we find him? I know he's out there...somewhere—stalking young girls. He may not have been the one to grab Erin Prescott—this time—but you can bet your sweet ass he's someplace else targeting other Erins."

Josh went to his laptop, booted it up. "On that we agree. What exactly do you intend to do when you find this guy?"

Skye rocked back on her heels, took another sip of coffee. "Observe. Follow. Find out what he's up to." She told him about her theory that he lived near Tacoma on land that belonged to a relative. When she took in the look on his face, she said, "And yeah, I've already been out there. Four times. Just as a concerned citizen, of course, taking a nice long drive in the country to see the sights, who just happened to end up near his crappy mobile home. It's time to take another road trip out there to see if all's as it should be."

Josh narrowed his eyes. "When were you planning to do *that*?" He reached out, grabbed her arm. "You shouldn't go out there alone."

Maybe she should delve into these feelings he kept stirring up inside her every time she got close to him, or like now, whenever he touched her.

"What would you have done if you'd spotted Whitfield on any of those sojourns you took?"

She shrugged, batted her lashes and tried to look innocent. "Concerned citizen, right place, right time. Maybe."

But Josh wasn't quite that naïve. "Okay, we'll assume you won't take the passive route. Did you ever want to be a cop, make it official?"

She tipped her head to one side, cocked a brow and glared at him. Damn it, how did this guy read her so well when he didn't really *know* that much about her? "Did you get that off the Internet, too? Because yeah, I did, for about five seconds, but I had this one little problem."

"And that was?"

"I couldn't pass the psychological profile."

He spit out some of his coffee. That was the last thing he had expected her to say. "Really?"

"Really. I have an attitude problem when it comes to perverts that use little kids for sex. I want to crush them into little pieces before kicking the shit out of them." She laughed at the look he gave her and added, "Contrary to popular belief they don't actually give out commendations to those kinds of police officers."

"I don't have a problem with that."

"Then you, Mr. Ander, would probably have a problem passing the psych exam, too. Look, I have a high school diploma, didn't want to waste time in college. The only time I've ever really held down a job with pay is the six months I put in at Country Kitchen right out of high school. But I'm not stupid."

"No one said you were. I went to college, briefly. My mother hoped I'd become a surgeon but I have this little issue dealing with the sight of blood, much to my mother's disappointment."

Amusement flicked in her eyes. "Ah, Friday night. That's what you found so funny in your inebriated state. The irony. It's a good thing I didn't know that at the time. You could've passed out on me."

"Exactly." He made a face just thinking about dealing with blood on a daily basis. "The first two years at UDub, I found I could put my C++ skills to work creating games and apps. Hey, IDE was my life back then." When he saw her puzzled look, he added, "IDE, integrated development environment. I've always been good with code. Plus, I love games, puzzles, solving mysteries even. My roommate and I created a computer game, got lucky marketing it. In the last twenty-four hours, I seem to find myself thinking about how Whitfield the predator, is just a different kind of puzzle or mystery that needs solving. Where'd he go when he got out of the joint? How'd he disappear?"

"Listen to you. The joint? Did you talk like that two days ago? I'm pretty sure you didn't."

He smiled before telling her, "I'm mesmerized by your eyes." When she didn't say anything, when she just kept staring at him he added, "But then I'm probably not the first person that's ever told you that."

She shook her head. "Are you coming on to me? You dump one woman and then half an hour later you're putting the moves on me. I'm not in the market, Ander. Got it?"

Josh nodded. "Got it. Sorry. You have issues you haven't gotten past. I understand that."

Skye strode out of the kitchen before turning around and heading right back in, getting in Josh's face. She slapped one hand on his chest. "You don't know me. You don't know my *issues*. Just because you looked me up on the Internet and found a couple of ancient newspaper articles about me, does not in any way mean shit. But I'll tell you what I know about you and it took me less than twenty-four hours to figure it out, mainly because I'm *very* observant when it comes to sizing people up."

She ticked off the points on her fingers. "One, you have a major drinking problem. Two, I'm not the only one who hasn't moved past their *issues*. *You* haven't gotten over your wife's death. Three, *you* are lousy at confrontation unless of course, it's dumping a five-foot-three-inch woman. So, do not think you know me, do not presume or assume you know anything about *my* issues."

With that, Skye stormed out of his kitchen, hopped on his goddamn personal elevator and went to retrieve her bike.

CHAPTER EIGHT

Skye spotted Harry Drummond the minute she turned the corner, pacing back and forth on the sidewalk outside her apartment building.

"Where've you been? I was starting to think you'd stood me up."

"Nah, I took my bike and rode off a mood, had to drop it off at the storage unit. Come on up."

"Why do you keep the bike there?"

"No room at my place. When was the last time you were here? I've added a few things," Skye explained as she took out her key and unlocked the front door of the building. Once inside the tiny vestibule, she studied Harry's body language, the slump of his shoulders. She hadn't known the man for thirteen years without recognizing his temperament. "You aren't here for small talk. What's up?" The two started making the climb up the stairs to Skye's fourth-floor walkup.

"Erin's started talking. She said Hiller kidnapped her, used her, and planned on selling her to someone else."

Skye arched a brow. "Human trafficking? I told you so. That confirms the MO. You know damn well that fits Whitfield's past to a tee." She lifted a hand in peace. "Don't even bother denying it."

"I wasn't going to. But…"

"Come on, Harry! Ronny keeps them around for a couple of days, three at the max, gets his jollies and then passes off the girls to his friends in the underground sex trade. We both know Ronny gets his cash, his asking price, which is probably in the neighborhood of fifty grand, maybe more depending on the girl. It's a win-win for the pervert community."

The detective sighed. "Now, you're making things up. You know I don't have a shred of evidence that points to Whitfield for running so much as a red light let alone connecting the bastard to human trafficking. But…"

Once again, she didn't let him finish. "Why didn't you mention this on the phone earlier?"

When they reached the door to her apartment she turned to stick the key in the lock and decided Harry definitely had something else on his mind.

"How long have we known each other?"

After walking inside, she tossed her keys into the bowl on the little table and wheeled on the man she'd known for so long. "What exactly do you want from me, Harry?"

"Level with me. Tell me how you found Erin. I want the truth. And don't give me any bullshit about being in the right place at the right time. I might've bought that story two years ago with Ali and the second time with Hailey, but not now, not with Erin, not 'third time's a charm' crap either. I want to know the truth."

For the second time in a little more than an hour, someone wanted details she had no intentions of revealing. For one thing, no one would believe her. And for another Kiya was a Nez Perce tradition, a private, personal belief from her father's people. She would share Kiya with no one else. Ever.

"Geez, you'd think I had some mystical creature leading me down a blind alleyway to the kidnapper's lair." She rolled her eyes for better effect and snapped her fingers. "Next time a reporter sticks a camera in my face, maybe I'll try that out and see how many look at me like

I've lost my mind or need to be committed to a safe place without any sharp scissors lying around."

Harry cocked a brow in frustration. "Skye. You are the most secretive person I know. You always have been even when you were thirteen." He held up his hands in peace and stared at the stubborn set of the woman's jaw. "Not that you don't have a right to your privacy but—" he scrubbed a hand over his tired face. "You don't share with me, I don't share details with you about my cases, which means stalemate because you have no intention of telling me anything. Am I right?"

She lifted a shoulder in a show of nonchalance. "There's nothing to tell." He wouldn't believe her about Ronny Whitfield so why in the hell would he listen to her if she told him about her mythical spirit guide? Her father had cautioned her not six months before his death that telling anyone about Kiya was not a good idea. Looking back, Skye took that as something akin to Daniel Cree's premonition, something her father had felt, compelled him to warn her about disclosure. Just because the Nez Perce were fierce in their beliefs, it didn't mean anything to Harry. Or anyone else for that matter. Just because her father's people believed that part of getting through life meant staying true to your spirit guide, staying on your path, a path destined before birth, didn't mean a cop wouldn't laugh his ass off.

And she'd been laughed at for many things.

She sent Harry a sharp look, recalled the very first time she'd ever set eyes on the man in the hospital. He'd been standing there beside her bed wanting to know if she was okay. The hardcore questions he asked came later, things like how exactly had she gotten loose? How had she snuck away from her abductor without detection? The inquisition then wasn't that much different than today's. But back then he'd taken the word of a little girl and accepted it. These days it seemed to be a little tougher to swallow.

Harry Drummond would never in a million years believe that during her three days of captivity with Ronny

Wayne, Kiya had been the one to get her through the entire ordeal. Her spirit guide had told her what to do to escape and when exactly to do it. Even at twelve Skye had known that no one outside of her parents would believe that.

Skye didn't think remembering her father's warning now was a coincidence. As far as she was concerned, Daniel Cree's words were etched in stone. Besides, the only people who had ever known about Kiya had been her parents—and they were gone.

To change the subject, she offered, "How about some coffee?"

"Sure," Harry said as he took a seat at her little kitchen table. "I know there's something you're keeping from me. If it's illegal...we'll start from scratch, start over from this point forward. I didn't like it when I found out you were prowling the streets at night. I thought then that it would only lead to disaster. But I accepted it because it was you and I knew that deep down it was something you had to do."

Skye reached out, put a hand over his. "If prowling the streets at night is illegal then I'm guilty. But that's all I'm doing, Harry. Stop worrying about me."

"I'm fairly certain that ship has sailed."

Skye huffed out a laugh and tried for a casual demeanor. She kept her eyes diverted to the task at hand, filling the coffeemaker with water, measuring out beans for the grinder. "Aw, you know, I've always liked you, too."

But Harry continued frowning and got serious. "Up to now I think I've been reasonable in looking the other way during what I considered your very unorthodox method of going out at night—which also covers how exactly you find...these girls but—"

"It isn't a crime to walk the streets at night, Harry," she reminded him, putting her hands on her narrow hips as the Mr. Coffee began to sputter and brew. Harry wasn't the only one that could dig in.

"How did you find Erin—specifically?"

Okay, she would play the game. "I went on my rounds as usual, past the prep school, ended up near the docks. I heard her crying out for help. The window was open about an inch. I boosted myself up, raised the window, and climbed in. There she was in the bathroom, not a stitch of clothes on. She was burning up with fever. I threw my coat around her and we booked, called you. That's it, Harry. Just a lucky turn of events, no different than walking past Ali Crandon and realizing that sick bastard, Chad Rossi, had his hands on her. No different than going antique hunting that day in Kent and stumbling across Hailey getting out of that asshole's car in the parking lot of his apartment complex. What was his name?"

"Perry Duncan."

"Yeah, Duncan. He's serving twenty-five years to life for that."

"And Rossi's locked up in Aberdeen. You know the public might buy this lucky shit stuff, Skye. Maybe because when the media puts a nice feel-good spin on the rescue angle story, the general public eats it up. I know two years ago I even bought into it because I wanted to believe you. The second time—" he waved his hand back and forth indicating an iffy gesture. "But after last night, not a chance. I'm a cop, Skye. A pretty damn good one at that. You tell me it was luck, fine, we'll leave it at that—for now. But I plan to keep asking you until you bend, let me in on exactly how you get so lucky. I've never seen anyone as good at evading as you are. And that's probably my fault because when it comes to you I've been lenient. I talk to you when I shouldn't. I tell you stuff I shouldn't."

"Oh please." Skye got down mugs for their java and turned to face him. "Fine. You keep asking and I'll keep telling you the same thing. Now, what else did Erin tell you? I don't mean the dirty details, those you get to keep to yourself. I want stuff like what the perp looked like, what kind of car he drove…that sort of thing."

"Stop it! You are not a member of law enforcement. This is an ongoing investigation. Mine at that. Weren't you

. You don't share with me. I don't share with

'Blah, blah, blah. I get it." She'd been stonewalled oefore. "But I get results and you can't argue with that."

"Look, I share too much with you as it is. If Captain Wallace ever finds that out, I'll be walking a beat or taking early retirement for good and that won't help either one of us. I don't want you crossing a line, Skye. I might not be able to pull you back if you do."

"So you came by to grill me about the how, and to insist I'm doing something illegal to find these girls? I have news for you, Harry. Accusations aren't going to make me tell you anything," Skye grumbled.

"Maybe so, but we've always had honesty between us, or at least I thought we had. You could at least come clean with me."

"Nice try. You haven't used that approach in a while."

With that, as if in defeat, Harry ran a hand through his thinning, once-brown hair turning gray all over. "Skye, you try me, you really do."

She grinned and threw an arm over his shoulder. "But you love me anyway."

"Yeah, but I'm beginning to wonder why. This Whitfield preoccupation has to come to an end sometime. I just hope you know what you're doing. Because damn it, I really don't see this obsession of yours ending well."

CHAPTER NINE

Brandon Randle Hiller wasn't just a pedophile five months out of Clallam Bay Correctional; he was also a reformed meth addict. He'd had the better part of seven years to kick his habit. Even though he might've been forced to give up the drug behind bars—mainly because he didn't have anyone on the outside to smuggle it into jail for him with any reliability—the blue acid had long since left its mark on his mouth and skin. His teeth were brownish and had a tendency to chip when he ate nuts or other hard food, which meant he was badly in need of a dentist most of the time. His pockmarked complexion was often a source of embarrassment and turned off a lot of people at first glance.

He'd started losing his hair during his first two years locked up which caused him to have to shave his head. A fact he wasn't happy about. When he'd been younger he'd thought his blond hair was his best feature. Now that he'd been off the meth, he'd been doing everything he could to grow it out again. As a result it grew mostly on the sides and the back of his head but not on the top. But he discovered that if he wore a ball cap whenever he went out, it looked like he had more hair than he actually did.

Hiller's looks were the least of his problems. Unfortunately, he couldn't keep his mind from wandering to little girls. Underage girls were his daily bread. A fix he couldn't live without.

Today was no exception.

He'd found another one, cute and wandering down the street by herself. An easy mark to be sure. This time though, he intended to take care of that sticky problem of leaving a witness behind by making sure he didn't leave anyone around who could identify him. No one could finger him using a DNA match if they couldn't find a body. That's why he planned to take care of this one—afterward. No more kidnapping a mouthy teenager either. He'd learned his lesson there, too. In spades.

He knew he'd made a huge mistake the night before with Erin. Leaving her alone to go get the little bitch some medicine for her puking stomach had been an attempt at being a nice guy. No more of that kind of thing, either, ever again. No more Mr. Nice Guy.

Brandon pulled the van, which also acted as his primary place of residence, to the side of the curb. He'd spotted the girl, who looked to be about twelve, some forty-five minutes earlier picking up snacks at the convenience store. He'd followed her through the blue collar neighborhood and now watched her with eagle eyes from his side mirror as the little golden-haired blonde took her sweet time walking home. At least he assumed that's where she was headed. All he had to do was approach her, get her to talking and get close enough to jab her with the needle and pull her into his vehicle.

Brandon drummed his hands on the steering wheel while the little girl drew closer. Once she got even with his van, he crawled into the passenger seat, flipped the door handle and hopped out onto the grassy curb.

About that time a male stuck his head out of the house two doors down and bellowed in the direction of the child. "What took you so long? Did you get the can of soup? You know I have to leave for work soon and I still have to fix dinner. Come on, hurry up, I haven't got all day."

At the sound of the voice, Brandon slunk down like he was checking the front tire on his van. Out of the corner of his eye, he made sure he memorized the house number where the little girl disappeared through the front door.

In his warped mind, a plan took shape.

Skye worked off the mood Harry had left her in by hitting the gym, a place that was little more than a dingy basement. Even though the underground space had a locker-room feel about it and wasn't much to look at, it sported a fancy treadmill she used for bad weather running, a decent weight bench, a state-of-the-art elliptical, and a not-so-fancy, old-fashioned punching bag that hung from the bare-bones rafters.

Well-worn indoor/outdoor carpet covered the concrete floor beneath her feet but had never been tacked down with any permanence except for the duct tape in spots. Which meant you could trip and stumble if you weren't used to all the little indicators. Skye was familiar with every mismatched seam, with every bump and bubble.

She ought to be since she'd been coming to this little out-of-the-way, hole in the wall for more than seven years.

Because she knew the proprietor, Travis Nakota, the guy who also owned the Country Kitchen where she'd once worked, Travis willingly let her use the equipment free of charge.

Over the years Travis had proved to be someone she could turn to. After all, he'd been her father's oldest and dearest friend.

In life, Travis and Daniel Cree had grown up like brothers, both sharing shaman duties in the same tribe. Daniel's and Jodi's deaths had hit Travis almost as hard as they had hit Skye. He'd wanted to take her in after the accident left her without parents. But the courts said with Skye's history, a family friend, especially a male one, would never do. So Skye packed up and went to live with her blood relatives, Ginny and Bob.

As she pummeled the bag with her gloved fists, she had to admit Travis was as close to family as she had left. Besides Harry, and one or two others, Travis was probably her dearest friend in the world and one that knew every one of her quirks.

Because quirk was one way to describe Kiya, Travis hadn't exactly "seen" the wolf firsthand. And no, Skye hadn't spoken to him about it, specifically. Even when she reconnected with Travis once she found her way back to Seattle, she kept her father's decree first and foremost in her mind. She shared Kiya with no one, not even Travis. But since Travis and Daniel did share a link to the Nez Perce, Skye knew Travis believed in spirit guides. He couldn't be shaman and not. Whether Daniel had ever discussed his daughter's specific Native path with Travis wasn't something she ever asked Travis about—and since he never mentioned it—she didn't either.

That was fine with Skye. Having a spirit guide made her different. She accepted that. But having so few friends she could count on set her apart in another way entirely.

And wasn't that fact just sad she thought now as she sent another series of jabs into the leather. Practicing kicks now, she threw out a leg, brought her foot up and into the side of the bag with a thud. She rotated, angled again, and threw out the other leg in a wide arc.

As it so often happened, Ronny Wayne's face appeared on the bag, which had her bashing and thumping the target even harder with hands and feet.

For the next twenty minutes, Skye continued to work up a sweat. In her mind she always won the battle with Ronny Wayne. Today was no exception. She just wished that one day she'd get the chance to deliver the blows to his sneering mug up close and personal. One day, she reasoned, as she sent another round of punches to Ronny Wayne's likeness.

She knew for a fact that monsters existed. She'd had the misfortune of crossing paths with one at the age of twelve. Yes, she'd gotten away from him. But not before the damage had taken its toll. As always, she didn't intend to let Ronny Wayne win though. That she would never do. Not when she was twelve. Certainly not now that she was an adult. Not ever.

Seven blocks away, Josh did his best to get some work done. He replied to emails, approved another marketing campaign for a different game they were working on still in the design phase, went over sales reports, and checked the status of other projects in the pipeline. He did all of it with the pain growing worse in his shoulder. It wasn't easy. Hunting and pecking the keyboard gave him a headache.

He ignored several calls from his best friend and business partner, Todd Graham, asking why he hadn't come back to the table Friday night, why he'd disappeared. Up to now, Josh hadn't shared his involvement with Michelle with anyone else and he had no intentions of doing so at this point. He hoped like hell though, he'd finally gotten through to the woman.

When the discomfort in his shoulder became a steady throbbing pain and made him feel feverish and weak, he allowed a little self-pity to creep in—and shook his head at his own stupidity. Hadn't that been the very reason he'd reached out to Michelle Reardon in the first place? And look how that had turned out. He wished he had never touched Michelle. No, that was regret, and a lesson learned. Now, he wished like hell he hadn't pissed off Skye Cree.

He'd stewed about her blowup for hours. Even tried to do some sketches with her in mind as the female heroine in the game he planned to design. But when it became more difficult to concentrate he went back to brooding.

Because if she'd hung around the loft, he might've been able to coax her into spending some quality time with him—relaxing, maybe watch a movie, maybe have a decent conversation. It didn't seem to him like the woman ever took the time to unwind. In Josh's mind, no one needed to chill out more than Skye Cree.

There were all kinds of questions rattling around in his head about the woman. If he wrote them all down, he'd probably get writer's cramp. That's how much he wanted to know about her.

Besides that, every time he was around her, something inside him wanted to shout out a long list of praises, most of which he knew she didn't want to hear and wouldn't believe anyway. How did a man convince a woman she was one strong-willed, independent, beautiful super female? And that, he had to admit sounded corny—and phony.

Because he had to be burning up with fever to come up with such clichéd sentiments, he dug in his desk drawer and took out a bottle of aspirin, dumped three into his palm. After getting them down, he let his head rest on the back of his desk chair. Closing his eyes he drifted off to sleep and dreamed about a video game where his warrior goddess continued to kick serious ass in a made-up distant fantasyland.

When he heard a continuous buzzing in his head, Josh's nap came to an abrupt end. It took him a minute but he finally realized it was the damn buzzer from downstairs. He hoped to Christ it wasn't Michelle.

After stumbling on his own two feet to reach the intercom, once he got there, Josh yelled into the speaker, "What?"

"Hey Josh, it's me, Tate."

Josh rubbed his forehead. Even though he felt like crap, he couldn't very well turn away Annabelle's little brother, even if the guy almost matched him in height. "Come on up."

Once the elevator doors dinged open. Tate strolled in, all smiles, wearing jeans and a purple UDub sweatshirt, wet tennis shoes on his feet, slick with rain. "Hey man, how you been? How come you don't return phone calls anymore?"

"You know how it is with work. Oh wait. You don't know. How come you aren't in class?"

"You need to get out more. It's Sunday, Josh. And spring break started Friday."

"Ah. Right." Still trying to wake from his nap, Josh adjusted his glasses, stared at Tate, long and hard. "You ever gonna graduate, kid?"

"Two years," Tate answered, shaking his head. "You look like crap by the way. How about a beer?"

"Not until you turn twenty-one."

Tate sent him a puzzled look. "Josh, my birthday was two months ago. I'm legal."

"Oh. Sorry." Josh scratched his chin. "I guess I must've missed that. You should've said something. I've been a little out of it lately," Josh said as he walked into the kitchen to get a bottle of Steelhead out of the fridge.

"Yeah? Try a year." Tate bent his head to get a better look at Josh. "You don't look so good, bro."

"I don't feel so good," Josh admitted as he twisted off the cap, handed the beer to the man he would always consider his brother-in-law. Even that small motion had Josh wincing in pain and Tate caught the expression on his face.

After taking a slug from the bottle, Tate asked, "What's with you? You sick or something?"

"I had a little run-in Friday night with four muggers outside Gull's. One of them cut me."

"No shit. What happened?"

Josh related the incident blow-by-blow. When he was done, Tate's eyes got wide. "Wow! The woman saved your ass from four guys? How often does that happen? Is she...you know...like a wrestler or something?"

"You're such a schmuck, you know that? No." The image of Skye had his fever spiking. "In fact, the woman's hot."

"Really? How hot?"

"Too hot for a lowly college sophomore like you. How are the grades?"

Tate ran a hand through his hair. "Oh man. They're fine. I guess. It's just that I'm thinking of chucking school once I get this semester over and done with and taking some time off."

"Why?"

"'Cause I'm sick of school! Dad's on my case about grades all the time. Since Annabelle died—" Tate blew out a frustrated breath. "Because I'm all he's got now, he just won't get off my back…about anything."

"Do you want me to talk to him?"

Tate shook his head. "It won't do any good. I tried to tell him you didn't graduate and you did all right for yourself."

Josh could relate to the kid's dilemma. After all, his parents hadn't exactly been overjoyed that he'd bypassed finishing college for working out of a basement on video games. "My guess is that didn't go over very well."

"Yeah, he was pissed. We argued. That's all we seem to do lately."

"Surely you can understand your dad's stance on school, Tate? Years after the fact, I wish I had that degree hanging on my wall."

"Why is he so mad at you anyway?"

"Short answer? His only daughter is gone and I'm still around. He's not too happy about that."

"Like that's your fault."

"In his eyes, I guess it is."

"Look, I just wanted to come over and…I don't know…talk, play a video game, or something."

Josh slapped Tate on the back. "Sure. How about some beta games we're considering marketing next year? You could try them out, tell us what you think."

"Awesome. I was hoping you'd say that. You know, maybe I could go to work for you or something…you know…down the road…like maybe this summer."

"I already told you, Tate, learn source code, especially 3D graphics and I'll put you to work in development. Even if it will more than likely piss off your father so much he may never speak to me again."

Tate pumped a fist in the air. "Yes! I've already been practicing with a variety of text editors. I even created an app. Here, let me show you." Tate took out his cell phone.

Josh rubbed his forehead again. The aspirin hadn't even put a dent in his aching head. But being the supportive and exemplary brother-in-law Tate had grown used to while Annabelle was alive, Josh simply said, "Come on, I'll get you set up on the laptop." And with that, Josh prepared to spend the afternoon listening to another fervent gamer extol the virtues of all the new characters he'd come up with over the last few months.

That night, alone and jumpy, Brandon Hiller had driven around the residential streets until well past dark. He'd already made sure the man of the house had left for work. Now all he had to do was make certain the little girl he'd followed home was in there alone. He circled around to the backyard, noted there was no yippy dog to deal with. From the fence line he moved to the door, trying the knob. Locked. He took out his burglar tools and set to work cutting the glass out of the nearest window, which happened to be to the left of the back door. When the cutter scored a perfect circle, he pushed gently on the cut until it gave way. He reached his hand inside and released the catch mechanism. Lifting the window, Hiller deftly crawled over the sill and through the frame. He found himself in a small laundry room.

He opened the door and was immediately drawn to flickering lights indicating a television set was on in the front room. He drew the knife from his back pocket, something that would definitely put him back in prison if he ever got stopped, not to mention the rape kit he kept in the van.

The girl was sprawled on the sofa, mesmerized by the scene unfolding on the screen. Because of that she didn't hear his approach. In the shadowy room, he came up behind her, stuck the blade to her throat. "Do exactly what I tell you and I won't hurt you. Are you the only one in the house?" He already knew the answer to that because he'd been watching and waiting.

When the girl nodded, he demanded, "Get up! You're coming with me."

"Where?"

"We're going for a ride." As he led her out the back door to his van, he asked, "By the way, what's your name?"

"Jenna. Jenna Donofrio."

CHAPTER TEN

Skye moved through the cold and fog toward the Pike/Pine corridor. Even though she could see her breath in the crisp night air, it felt good to be out and about. It always did whenever she walked the streets. What might have given any other female pause as she patrolled her neighborhood at such a late time of night had the opposite effect on Skye Cree. She felt completely at ease in her element.

Perhaps it was her hunter instinct, the Kiya influence, or something else. She didn't really know the how or why of it, only that she loved everything about the wee hours around midnight, including their contrasting sounds. She appreciated the noisy side of the streets, as well as the peaceful quiet.

Every once in a while she could catch music, sometimes heavy metal, often times classic rock or even folk music on occasion depending on which street she walked down or whatever tavern she happened to pass. She could make out the laughter and the conversations drifting from the local bars. Some stayed with her and lingered while others reminded her there were people having fun, people with normal lives who didn't wander up and down the streets in the middle of the night.

If someone had bothered asking, she couldn't have come up with an answer, only that this is what she was destined to do. Long ago, she'd given up trying to explain the whole thing to Harry or anyone else. He hadn't understood why she felt compelled to go out every night, searching, hunting. All she knew was she couldn't very well sit on her ass while monsters roamed her turf preying on children. Boy or girl, it didn't matter. Children were vulnerable. She couldn't live with the non-doing.

She supposed that was really the bottom line. Night would fall and she had to do—something. No one could possibly understand that or identify with it. But she didn't much care whether people understood her.

Melody and merriment echoed out and broke into that mindset, reaffirming to Skye that despite the meanness in the world, there were any number of people on any given night sharing their good times with friends or family.

Had she ever had that, experienced it with such a casual refrain that she could taste the warmth of companionship, of friendship?

She didn't think so. Certainly not since her parents died. All day she'd been pondering that missing element to her life. Friends. There were a few, a handful really. Acquaintances. Sure, people she'd met on the streets, people she spoke to at the market, the bakery, the coffee shop on a regular basis. They all impacted her like a brushstroke.

But boyfriends. Now that was the missing piece. Someone to share a closeness, a bond. No, she'd never had that as an adult and probably never would.

The whimper of a sleepy infant coming from one of the row houses she passed caused her mind to blink reluctantly in another direction. More personal thoughts, she mused. Things she liked to call her what-ifs. What-ifs were indulgences she usually didn't bother lingering on for too long. She couldn't. What-ifs couldn't be changed so why spend time there in frustration and sadness?

A resignation came with the chilly wind that rustled the leaves at her feet and brought her full circle. No point in dwelling on thoughts about a life she'd never have no matter how often they wandered into her brain. Ah, but when those little dings came fast and hard, like tonight, and tried to take root, she had to bat them away into another realm. No, it wouldn't do to stay there long, mired in what-ifs.

What was wrong with her? she wondered. Why these nostalgic moods today? She refused to even consider that Josh Ander might be the reason because he'd stirred up things inside her. There was no harm in admitting she was attracted. If she couldn't be honest with herself...what was the point? So she'd admit the nerd in him pulled at her belly. It had to be those wire-rims and the soft gray eyes behind them.

She was just about to turn the corner onto Denny when she heard someone call her name.

"Skye! Skye! Wait up!"

Skye turned, saw Dee Dee run up, breathless. "Dee Dee. How's it going?"

Dee Dee grabbed her arm. "Skye, I'm so glad I saw you. It's Lucy. You have to help me find her."

Skye's brow furrowed before she remembered which one of the girls was Lucy. "You mean the redhead you mentioned last night?"

"Yeah, that's the one. Nobody's seen Lucy all day. Skye, you gotta help me find her. The cops won't do nothin' to help. And you found that schoolgirl just last night, the one that was on the news. You're better than the cops at finding people anyway. Help me, Skye, Lucy wouldn't go off by herself."

Skye blew out a frosty breath, watched it evaporate before she spoke. After all, it wasn't that unusual for a hooker to go missing for a couple of days then resurface when she was good and ready. But noting the concern on Dee Dee's face, Skye didn't have the heart to say that. Lucy might've been a hooker, but the girl deserved to have someone give a shit enough to care if something had happened to her. "Has Lucy ever talked to you about going off on her own maybe leaving the streets behind?"

Dee Dee sent Skye a look of disbelief. "All the time, but Lucy's pretty much like the rest of us, Skye. She's got nowhere else to go. Besides, I'm telling you, Lucy wouldn't just leave without letting me know where she was going. We look out for each other. You know that."

Because Skye did, she asked, "Do you have a recent photo of Lucy, Dee Dee? And I'll need her last name, date of birth if you have it and anything else you think might be important."

"I don't have her picture with me. But I'll get it to you. Lucy's last name is Border. Lucy Border. She's originally from Portland."

"How old?"

"Sixteen. Same as me."

"Then bring the photo tomorrow to the Country Kitchen. If I'm not there, leave it with Velma, okay?"

Dee Dee nodded. "I'll be there. And thanks, Skye. I knew I could count on you to care."

"Yeah, well...I haven't done anything yet. Save the thanks for after I've found her."

While Skye continued on her way, something nagged inside her. Was it a coincidence that Erin had been a redhead who had gotten away? Did Brandon Hiller have a penchant for redheads? If the man was desperate enough, would he settle for a young prostitute in lieu of a schoolgirl?

The first indication that Skye had someone dogging her was when Kiya lowered her head and let out a low, throaty growl in warning. It was then Skye heard the soft footsteps behind her on the pavement. She reeled around just in time to avoid a blow in the back. Her feet kicked out in rapid succession, sending the pipe wrench flying and her assailant stumbling to the ground.

She took a long gaze at the body sprawled on the sidewalk. A frail young teen looked up at her, a stunned realization on his face that his attack had been thwarted. The kid didn't look strong enough to take down a wet noodle let alone a physically fit, in-shape female.

Even in the dim light from a streetlamp, Skye recognized the boy had the wariness in his huge brown eyes that came from living on the streets. She watched as he immediately put his hands up then curled into a ball. The shaggy-haired adolescent yelled in a high-pitched voice, "Don't hurt me! I just wanted a few bucks for something to eat. That's all, I swear."

"And your way is to try and knock me out with a rusty pipe, take my money because you're hungry? How about asking next time?" Skye bellowed back.

About that time, Kiya snarled again.

Out of the corner of her eye Skye caught more movement, this time from her right. She whirled around expecting to see one of the kid's pals coming to his defense from the bushes. Instead Josh Ander made his way out of a crop of dense hedges before running up to them in a huff.

"Are you okay?" he wanted to know, his eyes transfixed on the silver wolf that stood a few feet away. "Do you see that? Do you see that silver wolf over there? It growled just before the kid here tried to attack you and just now at me. A wolf sighting right here in Seattle." For the first time Josh glanced down at the teen still prone on the ground. It was then he asked, "What's his deal?"

"We were just getting to that," Skye grumbled, still glowering at the teenager. "Petty thievery will get you killed in this neighborhood," she stated stubbornly. "Okay, let's have it." Once again, she sized the kid up and waited for what she was sure would be a smartass reply. He didn't look like he weighed more than a hundred pounds soaking wet. This was no tough guy persona hiding behind those warm brown eyes. "Well?" she prodded, waiting for his reply.

The boy started blabbing. "I got kicked out of my house two weeks ago. My mother's new boyfriend took an instant dislike to me, a lot more than some of her others. The bastard sent me packing."

"He kicked you out and your mother let him?" Josh asked in astonishment.

Skye threw the grown man a disbelieving stare. Was he really that unfamiliar with what went on in the real world? She took a step closer, eyeing the yellow-purplish bruises on the teen's face and around his eyes, some still in the healing stages. "These bumps a gift from your mother's boyfriend?" she demanded.

"Yeah."

"You aren't selling yourself on the streets, are you?" Skye wanted to know.

The kid's eyes went wide. "Not yet."

"How old are you?"

"Sixteen," he replied quickly.

A little too quickly for Skye, as she assessed the boy as much as the lie. "So you've resorted to mugging people to eat?"

"No, you're the first one. You looked alone and I thought I might be able to knock you down, maybe knock you out and take whatever money you had in your pocket, since, you know, you're a girl."

Josh couldn't help it, he laughed outright. "Wow, did you ever pick the wrong woman, kid!"

From the ground the boy looked up at the two adults, acting as though he needed to confess even more. "I've been stealing stuff though to survive."

"Define stuff?" Skye queried, resting her hands on her hips.

"Purses, wallets, jewelry, anything of value I can lay my hands on. I broke into a couple of houses, took some rings and pearls then pawned the stash down at Slade's on Twelfth."

Skye sighed. "What's your name?"

"Zeke Hollis. Are you guys cops?"

"Nope. Want a job, Zeke Hollis?"

"You got one?" The teen shot back, clearly skeptical about the offer of anything from anyone.

Skye pointed to Josh. "Any chance you could use a gofer down at your fancy gaming place?"

Clearly taken aback by the question, Josh tried to think of a reason not to make this wayward youth part of his company. But after several long, strained seconds of silence, he changed his mind, recognizing the look on Skye's face. He could tell she'd already been suckered in. "He'd have to take a shower and put on some clean clothes first."

Skye reached out a gloved hand to the filthy teenager to help him to his feet. Up to this point Zeke had been sitting on the ground, wary. His clothes were soiled as though they hadn't seen a laundromat in weeks which might've been why the kid reeked. Reluctantly, Zeke finally grasped her gloved fingers and pulled himself to a standing position.

Skye tilted her head, stared at the guy's small stature. He didn't even come up to her shoulders. If this kid was a day over sixteen, then she'd have to be forty.

"Is that agreeable to you, Zeke Hollis?"

"It's kind of hard to get in a shower at McDonald's or anyplace else for that matter. And I'm not wasting money washing clothes. I gotta eat," Zeke admitted.

From two feet away, Skye heard the kid's stomach rumble. "Yeah, that is a problem," she reasoned. "We'll get you a place to stay. How's that? But first we get some food in you. Good thing Country Kitchen's open twenty-four."

"My car's parked one street over," Josh disclosed, pointing down the street.

"That's okay, CK is two blocks up." She turned back to Zeke. "How does eggs and bacon sound?"

It sounded fantastic to Zeke. But he hadn't been born yesterday. Two weeks surviving on the streets had made him a lot savvier. When someone did something for you, they wanted something in return. Nothing was free. He needed to know the terms upfront. "Why would you do that?" Zeke asked, clearly stupefied at the offer. He looked

Josh up and down. "I'm not blowing anyone not even for a breakfast."

It was Josh who answered. "Good, because we aren't really into kids."

For the time being, Skye ignored the boy's crudeness. She couldn't blame his suspicious nature or his hard outlook on life. She lightly took hold of his thin shoulders and turned him around, pointed to head back the other way. "Food's that way. Let's go. Where've you been sleeping for the past two weeks, Zeke?"

"Since they ran us off the Viaduct, I find any place where there isn't a crowd—or drunks, or people that want to fight all the time. I avoid the Jungle. I spend the night in the doorways of empty buildings, mostly, or sometimes I sleep in the park in the bushes, can't sleep out in the open without attracting unwanted attention. And if you're too obvious the cops will hassle you."

That assessment had Skye taking in another quick gulp of night air. The kid did indeed have a bleak take on life. She threw a subtle look at Josh, who looked like he needed to be in bed at the moment recovering from his knife wound instead of walking down Dearborn. Jesus, the man looked downright ill. But as they rounded the corner at the end of the block, she decided the Zeke issue needed to be handled before anything else.

Without a word between them, she sent another knowing look at Josh that clearly meant, "This kid needs a hand and we're it."

With a slight nod of his head in agreement, Josh cleared his throat, and said, "Sounds like you know a little too much about the streets for a kid your age."

"What do you know about it? Besides I'm no kid," Zeke snapped back.

"You're right." Skye took the time to meet Zeke's eyes. "You aren't a kid anymore. But we do know this. You need a place to stay instead of trying to make it on the streets—alone. A thirteen-year-old has no business dodging street bullies and going hungry."

"You mean sixteen?"

"No, I mean thirteen, Zeke," Skye challenged, as she directed him down an alleyway, a shortcut to get to the restaurant. "Is that your real name? Be straight with me."

"It's my real name," Zeke acknowledged, albeit reluctantly. It didn't matter he thought. He intended to take off right after he scored the meal.

"When's the last time you ate?"

"This morning."

"Sure, whatever you say," Skye muttered, noting the rumbling coming from the kid's stomach. She opened the door to the all-night diner and heard the jingle announcing a customer. They stepped inside a retro eatery with dated décor. Every booth, every table, every stool was either blue-green or some shade thereof. Even the well-worn, off-white linoleum floor had flecks of green speckling in the pattern.

Skye nudged Zeke toward a booth in the back so their happy little trio could have a heart-to-heart. She waved to the waitress taking orders at another table.

Velma Gentry had probably worked third shift at Country Kitchen close to three decades, certainly longer than Skye had been coming in here either to work or stuff her face.

When Velma sauntered over, her graying auburn hair bunched up in a tight bun, Skye looked up into the face of the woman she considered an honorary aunt. "How's Bill?" Bill was Velma's second husband of twenty-five years and a bit of a slacker.

"He'd be fine if he'd ever get his lazy ass up off the damned couch long enough to take me to a movie. I ask you, is a night out, once every two years, too much to ask?"

Skye chuckled at the same complaint she'd heard over and over again for no less than seven years. "Next time I see him I'll plant that idea in his head for you. How's that?"

"Good luck with that," Velma grumbled. "What can I get you kids to drink?"

"Milk for the boy. And I'll take a coffee. What about you, Josh?"

"Orange juice for me," he mumbled. He desperately needed to load up on vitamin C, maybe any other vitamins that might give him an extra kick because the pain in his shoulder kept up a steady burn. The discomfort reminded him how much energy it took for him to remain upright. No way would he pass out in front of the starving kid.

Thirty minutes later, over scrambled eggs, bacon, and a stack of pancakes, Josh and Skye did their best to prod reluctant information out of the sulky street kid.

They watched in fascination as Zeke devoured every bite of the food put in front of him. The poor guy ate like he hadn't seen food in two days.

But when Zeke started peeling off napkins from the dispenser then wrapping up the extra pieces of toast and flapjacks from Josh and Skye's plates and shoving the food down into his dirty jacket pockets, Skye stilled his hand. "That isn't necessary. Where I'm taking you, you'll have breakfast in the morning and three squares a day. But you'll have to go to school, Zeke."

"No way," the teen replied stubbornly. "School's almost as bad as the streets."

"Yes, way," Josh declared as emphatic as Skye. "School is a non-negotiable part of the deal."

The boy eyed them both. Now that his belly was full, he intended to set them straight. "I got news for you guys, you two can't make me do shit. I made that whole story up. And you guys bought it. Suckers."

"I see." And because she did, she steepled her fingers, sat back. Without raising her voice, she leaned in closer to Zeke. "So you played us to get a meal, is that it?"

The kid jiggled his knees up and down in a nervous twitch. "It worked, didn't it?"

"You're a real pro at this stuff, huh?" Skye tossed back getting into the game. She took out her cell phone for effect. "How about I make a call to the cops? Right now, right here."

The boy paled. "Okay. Okay. No need to do that. But you don't got a right to tell me what to do or where to go. Nothing."

"So you prefer what happened tonight to keep on happening? Let me ask you something, Zeke. What if I'd pulled a knife on you? What if someone else had? What would you have done then? What if I'd told you I was taking you to get a meal, but led you down that dark alleyway, took out a knife and..." She hit the table with the palm of her hand to get Zeke's attention. "Then bam! I slit your throat."

Even Josh's eyes grew wide.

"I'd've run like hell. I'm pretty fast," Zeke said, keeping his cool.

"You can't avoid the mean that's out there forever, Zeke. It will eventually catch up to you. It may not be tonight. It may take months, maybe even years. Is that what you want? To spend what's left of your childhood on the streets?"

"I'm not going to some foster care *home*." Zeke spit out the word 'home' as though it offended his senses. "You put me there, I'll run off first chance I get. You can't make me stay."

Skye held up her hand and ticked off points with her fingers. "First fact, I don't have the authority to send you into the system without a court order from a judge. No one does. Second fact, I certainly know someone who could get it done though—tonight—with one phone call, a court order in thirty minutes or less. Third, I do know something about the system as I lost both my parents when I was about your age and had to go live with relatives. No one gave me a choice in the matter, either. And I hated that. But the fourth thing, Zeke, you won't survive on the streets. How do I know? You can't even take down a woman, let alone a stronger, bigger male. You've been out there two weeks already and look at yourself. I'd think going to school would be a small price to pay for getting fed and having a roof over your head without having to resort to mugging poor innocent women on a dark street corner to begin your life of crime where the cops will eventually catch you and lock you up. You'll spend the next five years either in juvie or worse, sent to prison. And don't think it can't happen. There are fifteen-year-old kids not five miles from this spot locked up in county because they started out on the wrong track. And Zeke, do you have any idea what they'll do to a kid your size in prison? Hell, even in juvie, you'll be at risk for the same thing. Do I have to spell it out for you? Because I can—and will."

She hoped to hell she got his attention. When she saw him swallow hard and grow even paler than he had been before, when it looked like his food wanted to come back up, she knew her words had made an impact.

"Where did you have in mind?" Josh nodded in Zeke's direction. "To send him? Maybe if you shared a few details about the amenities there it might make ol' Zeke here a little more enthusiastic."

"I'm not without people I know, friends that owe me a favor every now and again." Maybe there were so few that Skye could count them on only one hand, but they were steadfast and loyal, those few. Travis she'd known the longest. But Velma Gentry had been solid gold at taking her under her wing in those early years, making sure she got a decent place to live and plenty of food to eat. Velma had been the one to introduce her to Lena Bowers, a lady customer who came in to the restaurant at least twice a week and always ordered the same dish, tuna on wheat toast with French fries. Lena was like an honorary aunt, without all the fanatical pontificating.

When she noticed the panic in Zeke's brown eyes, Skye added, "Don't look so scared, Zeke. It's a nice place. I can attest to that. At least check it out, spend the night tonight. If you don't like it, I won't force you to stay there and tomorrow we'll reassess your situation. But rest assured I'll get you off the streets one way or another. If not tonight, a month from now. If I have to go on a quest to find you, next time I won't be so quick to—be this reasonable."

"What does that mean?" Zeke wanted to know, clearly curious about what she intended to do.

"It means, Zeke, I'll notify the court in a heartbeat." She quickly added, "But I don't want to do that. I want you to give Lena Bowers a chance. I know Lena, personally. I rented a room from Lena for almost six months after high school. She's a nice lady, a good person." Which was an understatement, the woman was a saint in Skye's book. Lena had been like family for years.

But there were a couple of things she needed to make Zeke understand. "Nice doesn't mean Lena's a pushover. She's not. Like a lot of other people, Lena's had a rough time of it lately. And I will not bring a thief into her house, someone who plans to steal from her and take off at the first opportunity."

"Why can't I go home with you? Or you?" A sullen Zeke asked them both.

Skye glanced at Josh and noticed he looked even more out of it so she did the explaining. "Because I don't have the room and Josh here has to get up and go to work tomorrow morning. Look, Lena's a good friend but she's no easy mark. You hurt Lena, Zeke, you hurt me. You hurt me, I'll hunt you down and payback will be severe. Count on it. So before you decide here and now that you'll pacify my face at the moment and then take it out on Lena later, reconsider. I'm cautioning you to think long and hard about any decision that would bring trouble to Lena. Do we understand each other?"

"Yeah, I guess."

"Good." Skye stretched out her hand. "Your word now, Zeke, that you won't hurt my friend in any way."

Zeke sat up straighter and put his hand in Skye's.

She stood up then, pulled out her cell phone, and said, "I'll make the call to let Lena know we'll be dropping by.

This time of night the least I can do is give her a heads up. I'll be right back."

The minute she stepped away from the table, the boy stared at Josh. "She never intended for me to go to work for you, did she?"

"Smart kid. No. She never bought the age thing. And no one else will either. Did you lie to her just now? Is Zeke Hollis really your name? Level with me now, man-to-man. Because if she finds out you haven't been truthful, she'll be furious. You don't want Skye Cree angry with you. Trust me on that."

All of a sudden the boy looked worried. Jittery, his leg shook even more. "That's my name. I'm kinda glad I told her the truth on that. She's kinda scary."

That brought a laugh out of Josh. "You have no idea. Be glad she put you on your ass right away and didn't beat the crap out of you in the process."

"Really? She could do that?"

"Really. And yes, she could do that."

Finally Josh got an idea. "I tell you what. Do you play video games, xBox, Playstation, that sort of thing?"

Zeke moved one slim shoulder. "Sure. Who doesn't?"

"You give this place a chance, a real chance, and you can spend your afternoons with me after school—here." He took a business card from his coat pocket, handed it to the boy.

"Ander All Games? You're kidding? You're Ander All Games? *The Mines of Mars* kicks ass. When's the second update due out?"

Josh chuckled. "Soon. And yes, I'm Ander All Games. And that woman you tried to mug is—"

"Your girlfriend. I got it," Zeke finished.

Josh grinned in the way of male bonding. "Not yet, but I'm working on it."

They'd walked back to Josh's little hybrid and in less than twenty minutes Josh had them parked at the curb in front of a Victorian with Tudor revival features.

Lena Bowers had left the porch light on. At the sound of three car doors slamming shut, a woman dressed in jeans and a bright lavender button-down blouse, appeared in the open doorway. She hesitated only briefly before stepping outside.

The moment she spied Skye though, the forty-nine-year-old Lena rushed down the steps and met Skye on the walkway. The two women hugged before Skye announced, "I'm afraid I brought you another stray, Lena." Skye left her arms around Lena as she leaned in and whispered. "This one needs a bath as soon as you get him settled in. He stinks."

"Won't be the first one," Lena muttered back. "Might as well get the awkwardness out of the way now."

With that, the women broke apart and Skye made the introductions. An unwilling Zeke moved forward.

Lena studied the newest arrival and noted he looked scared to death as though maybe he'd just been delivered into the hands of the cruel stepmother. Lena immediately set about to make the boy feel more comfortable. "I've got a room I think you'll like. It's all yours for the duration of the time you're here. It belonged to my son, Jason. He didn't make it back from Afghanistan."

Zeke's eyes went wide. "He's dead?"

"He is," Lena said sadly as she led the trio into her living room. "Skye says you've already eaten so that only leaves getting cleaned up and getting into bed. It's almost two, way past time for even a worldly sort to hit the sack. We'll forego talking about school until the morning. But if you stay here, you'll have to go to school. Understand?" Lena emphasized.

"We already covered that," Skye advised, meeting Zeke's brown eyes in warning. "Didn't we?"

"Fine," Zeke grumbled.

"Let me show you the room," Lena offered, leading Zeke out into the hallway. "I put clean towels in the bathroom. You'll take a shower before crawling into bed. Clean sheets there, too. No negotiation or arguing about the shower."

"Okay," Zeke said a little overwhelmed at the woman's no-nonsense style. He had to admit it was better than a cold piece of concrete.

Back in the living room Josh looked around for a place to sit before he fell down. Using the arm of the sofa he dropped down and then reached a hand out to Skye. "You never answered my question. Did you get a load of that wolf? I've never seen one except in pictures until tonight."

"What wolf?" she asked casually trying to hide her annoyed state at that line of conversation. Doing her best to downplay the entire incident, she purposely looked away and said, "You mean the dog?"

"No. It was right there in plain sight, right there on the street. It growled right before Zeke jumped you. You know there have been coyote sightings up near Thirteenth and Cloverdale. It's been all over the news," he added, noting her upset demeanor. "And just recently it's been all over the Internet about wolf sightings in urban Seattle, especially near the marketplace. In fact I think—"

"Josh, get real. It was a dog," Skye repeated this time more forcefully.

Josh narrowed his eyes. "I know the difference between a dog and a wolf, Skye. Besides, I've never seen a dog that fierce. That was a silver wolf. Come on, how could you miss seeing a silver wolf with huge blue eyes in the middle of inner-city Seattle? They were so blue they almost matched yours."

"Are you delusional?" she huffed out. She decided to shift gears. Instead of arguing about it, she needed to sound a lot more convincing. "You mean that white dog? Oh that. Sure, I saw the dog. Looked just like one of those Australian shepherds. They have blue eyes you know," Skye explained.

She took a long look at his face to see if he bought it. Then she realized something else. For the third time in a span of a few hours, she noticed how flushed his face looked. "Josh, are you ill?" She reached out automatically, laid a bare hand on his forehead. The guy looked positively feverish. "My God, you're burning up. That cut must be on the road to an infection. We need to get you in to see a doctor. The sooner, the better." And preferably not talking about seeing a silver wolf with blue eyes.

"But what about the wolf?"

"I'm sure the *dog* will be fine. I think I saw a collar with tags," she lied. "What were you doing out there anyway?"

"I was worried about you, so once you left your apartment, I followed you."

Skye frowned. "Should I be concerned with this stalker side to you?"

About that time Lena came back into the living room carrying bottles of water for both of them. Handing one to Josh, Lena told him, "This one isn't used to having anyone worry over her." Lena shot Skye a knowing look. "You know it's true. Every one of the people who love and care about you expressed our concerns about your...unorthodox habit of walking the streets, patrolling that beat of yours every single night, rain or shine." Lena turned her attention to Josh. "Voicing our fear didn't do a bit of good."

"That isn't true," Skye argued. "I listened to all of you, took your concerns under advisement. When Harry offered suggestions I paid attention. Same as I did with Travis who got me into training every day. Even though you and Velma told me it was a bad idea, I told you both it's something I still have to do."

Skye pointed her finger at Josh. "But that isn't the issue here. You must be out of your mind walking around in that neighborhood at night, especially after what happened behind Gull's Pub, and with only one good arm, and running enough of a high fever that you're hallucinating. Remember you have a knife wound to your shoulder."

"I haven't forgotten. But...you were pissed off at me this morning and I wanted to make sure you were okay."

Skye couldn't help it, his worry made her heart flutter just like it had in the ninth grade when Gage Martin became her lab partner in third-period biology class. Come to think of it, Gage had looked at her with that same shade of gray eyes, so gray they appeared silver.

"Is that why his shirt is seeping with blood?" Lena asked. "Looks like his bandage needs to be changed, too."

"He's also burning up with fever," Skye railed and shook her head. "That's it. I'm taking you to the ER. Now! No argument."

Josh stood up and swayed. "That's probably an excellent idea because...as it turns out...I don't feel too good." And with that, before Skye knew what was happening, Josh collapsed in a heap on Lena's living room rug.

CHAPTER ELEVEN

"**F**unny, when you called tonight you didn't say a thing about bringing a hunk along."

Skye eyed the older woman with an air of scorn. "I thought I could ditch him after the restaurant," she explained. "But ever since I saved his ass, he seems determined to…annoy me."

"He followed you tonight out of concern. When my late husband, Brock Bowers, was alive he used to do things like that all the time. I think it's sweet. And if you had any romance about you, you'd feel the same."

"Don't go making it out to be something it's not. I've known the guy forty-eight hours and it's apparent, he's lousy at taking care of himself. Trust me about that. Just look at him."

"Oh I have. He looks pretty good to me. I'm a sucker for all that long black hair. And those sexy gray eyes. If I were twenty years younger I'd fight you for him."

"You would not."

"Would, too. And you know what? I'd win." Lena winked and handed her a bottle of peroxide.

Skye snorted and peered down at Josh, now shirtless, lying on the couch. For the second time in as many days she had to treat the guy's wound, which also meant she got another excellent view of the man's bare chest which just pissed her off because it told her, once again, there wasn't a thing wrong with the man's physique.

"I need to get some antibiotics into him. I bet he didn't even call his doctor this weekend like he was supposed to do and get a tetanus shot. See?" Skye began to work herself into a rant. "He can't even take care of himself. All he had to do was stop into a clinic or an urgent care facility and get one simple shot. But did he do that? No. What kind of a guy refuses to look after himself like that?"

Knowing Skye Cree wasn't the most patient of individuals at the best of times, Lena pointed out, "Maybe he's just a regular guy who doesn't routinely have a lot of stab wounds to deal with, Skye. He designs games for a living. He doesn't know a thing about the kind of world you see on the streets. It's obvious Josh Ander lives in another world from us entirely."

Skye blew out a frustrated breath. "Well, anyone that can think up war games on Mars ought to be able to know when you get stabbed with a nasty knife here on earth, you take care of it. Just because he conjures up fantasy for a living doesn't mean he has to live there. I will agree with you though that he doesn't seem to know anything about the real world. And that's just—pathetic."

"Oh my God, you're worried about him?"

"Of course, I'm worried about him. I stitched up that gash and he's walking around like it's no big deal. The guy's bleeding, the wound's festering. The man's a mess. Having millions in the bank doesn't make him immune to infection."

"You can stop yelling at me now," a weak voice said from the sofa. "There's nothing wrong with my ears."

She knelt down next to him, laid a hand on his cheek. "Good. Then hear this. Emergency room. Now. Antibiotics."

"You win," Josh muttered.

"Wise man," Lena said. "I'm going upstairs to check on Zeke, make sure he's washing some of the street off and I'll be right back down. Then we'll get this big guy into the car."

Fifteen minutes went by before Lena returned. With her help Skye got a weak Josh into his Ford Fusion and drove to the nearest ER just off Cherry. Once there, she struggled to remove him from the hybrid and drag his ever-increasing dead weight into the standing-room-only waiting area.

A dour-looking woman disguised as a nurse stood behind the reception desk. Skye glanced at her nametag. Marcie Kellerman. Marcie's brusque greeting told Skye everything she needed to say to get Josh treated before morning. And she wasted no time going into her pitch. "This is Josh Ander, one of Seattle's most influential and wealthy software designers. He's already passed out once tonight and is likely to do so again if he has to sit out here on one of your incredibly hard, uncomfortable plastic chairs for three hours."

Skye could tell recognition flashed across Marcie's face at the name. She noted the nurse's gaze studied Josh's features, the flush of his cheeks. Skye checked Josh's color herself. The guy did not look well at all.

"Josh Ander? I saw his bio on television. Flipped through his photo spread inside *Addicted to Games Magazine* last Christmas. My sons own every game he's designed. They play his stuff all the time. Their favorite though is his first one, *Zombies on Mars*," Marcie confessed.

"Believe me, if he could he'd tell you himself how happy he is to hear that," Skye said. "But I'm afraid he's going to fall flat on this linoleum floor in about ten seconds if he doesn't get off his feet."

"Bring him on back then."

Skye wasted no time pulling Josh along doing her best to follow Marcie.

"Okay, Mr. Ander. What seems to be the problem this morning?"

Now to the tricky part, Skye mused. "Friday night he encountered a mugger. He took a knife to the shoulder. I tried to treat it at home but…now it's infected. He's been running a fever." She shot Josh a dangerous glare and added, "Probably all day."

"Oh. My. Well, let's get you checked out then. Did you report the incident to the police? Because if you didn't…"

Just as Skye had surmised, dedicated Marcie looked like a stickler for detail. "Of course we did. But you know the cops. They'll get right on it maybe in about two weeks." It didn't hurt that Skye gave her an adorable show of dimples to offset the lie.

"Yep, that sounds like them." Marcie got out the blood pressure cuff, wrapped it around Josh's arm, jotted down his reading and other vitals and stuck a thermometer in his mouth. "Oh my, yes, he's at a hundred-and-four. As you could tell, the staff is pretty busy this morning since they're piled up out there higher than a cord of firewood. This is the only urgent care facility within ten blocks. The rest of them have closed their doors. But the doctor will get to you as soon as he can."

Soon turned out to be a forty-five minute wait, during which time Skye listened as Josh rambled on about a silver wolf. When he wasn't talking about Kiya, he teetered on the fringes of a romantic poet who couldn't keep his hands to himself.

He reached out, clasped her hand in his. "She smiled and that transfigured me and left me but a lout, maundering here, and maundering there, emptier of thought than the heavenly circuit of its stars when the moon sails out," Josh quoted.

"Yeats?"

"You need to smile more often, Skye Cree. You've got the cutest dimples when you do." He raised his head a fraction and whispered, "Why don't we head to your place after this? It's much closer than mine." The minute she sat down next to him, he began to toy with strands of her hair.

Since the guy was practically out of his head with fever, mumbling poetry one minute before turning into an octopus the next with what seemed like eight busy hands, Skye decided to cut him some slack and humor him. "My place might be closer but it isn't nearly as swanky as yours."

"What's that got to do with anything? A bed's a bed. You're really hung up on fancy and ritzy. You know that?"

"Oh really? Which one of us owns a loft that sells for seven figures?"

"See, that's exactly what I'm talking about. You're hung up on...stuff. I want to see where you live, Skye. Because I want to take you to bed. My place, your place, it really doesn't matter as long as we end up between the sheets."

That had her heart doing a little lurch while her belly dropped as if on a rollercoaster. "You are talking serious nonsense now."

"Hey, it's the truth. Lean over here a minute."

"Why?"

"I want to see your eyes better. Why do you think?"

"You're flat on your back and you want to make out?" She inched closer just to see if he had the strength to follow through.

But Josh surprised her.

He took that moment to snake his good arm up behind her neck to pull her down to his level. Her hair fanned out across his face. When she lifted a hand to push it back, he nipped at her bottom lip. His mouth meshed with hers in a heated flash. Instant lust spiked between them. He drew the kiss out, took them both deeper into the flame. She tasted like the sweet maple syrup she'd poured over her pancakes. He had one short moment of lucidity when he felt her pulse pick up and realized she'd finally yielded completely.

Any other time her hesitation, that reluctance would have tipped him off, but he was too far gone into the kiss to have reality move in and set up house.

Skye had to remember to breathe. She felt his beard where he hadn't bothered to shave. It wasn't just his skin that was rougher than she imagined, she felt the hunger in him biting at the fringes. Despite that, she sunk into the kiss as butterflies gathered in her stomach.

So this was what it was like to simply drop, to free fall from the top of an eighteen-story building, she decided. Her descent took her as close to lust as she'd ever gotten. How anyone could survive the assault of his mouth on hers she didn't know. This was like no kiss ever, certainly nothing like the last time when Derek had merely stuck his tongue down her throat. This time, she wanted...

At the brief knock on the door before it burst open, Skye jerked upward. As if entering a wind tunnel she had to fight her way to the end. She heard the doctor clear his throat right along with Josh's weak voice. But both sounded like they came from a distance.

"You have lousy timing, Doc," Josh uttered.

But for Skye, she had to take a step back to replay the whole thing in slow motion. Josh possessed skills that were light years beyond anything she'd known firsthand. She'd felt a measure of longing before—been attracted to other men—before putting up a barrier. Albeit briefly. She wasn't immune to desire for what she could never have. Up to now she'd avoided taking that step toward intimacy, toward the physical—on purpose.

But Josh was slowly changing all that.

And she didn't like what she was feeling for him, not one bit.

She made the mistake of looking over at him lying vulnerable on the table while the doctor treated and sutured the nasty gash. Josh's face told her that he was in various amounts of pain. And she hated seeing anyone hurting. She steeled herself against the conflicting mood knowing full well she desperately needed to protect herself from falling headlong into a relationship with a man like Josh Ander.

But while the head buzzed with all manner of rational advice, the heart longed for that wild ride she'd never taken.

Driving through the streets of Seattle on the way back to Josh's loft, Skye had time to use reason and logic to her advantage. She looked over in the passenger seat where he dozed from the two shots the nurse had given him. When she came to a stop at the light on Seventh Avenue, her fingers itched to reach out and comb through his long, ebony hair.

What was happening to her anyway? Where was that woman who'd sworn off men for life?

Forever was a long time, she concluded. Just thinking about his mouth on hers had her lower belly...longing for something she'd decided wasn't for her. No, she wasn't a virgin. She'd never be that. But she was inexperienced in developing relationships while Josh Ander ran through them like water through a sieve. His wife had been dead less than a year and he'd moved on to the blonde without a backward glance. Is that what people did? Move from one sexual relationship to the next?

Josh could equate sex with love and kindness while she could not. He'd been married and had a sexual history while she had nothing except—pain and horror.

Something about that wasn't fair.

She thought of the petite woman he'd broken up with less than twenty-four hours earlier. A spurt of jealousy sprouted. And that was ridiculous. But she had to admit she did not want to think about Josh and the blonde spending time horizontal.

The power-punch of that kiss back at the hospital had made her want something she couldn't have. And that was when he'd been weak, flat on his back. What sort of kick would he manage when he was a hundred percent?

She couldn't let that happen again. She'd get him home, tuck him in for the night and that had to be the end of it.

The minute Skye pulled the little Fusion into Josh's parking garage and found the space labeled "Josh Ander," she cut the engine. In the silence he popped up like a Jack-in-the-Box and scrubbed a hand down his face.

"I must've hit the snooze button."

"You needed it. Look, I need to shove off. You're plenty capable of getting inside on your own."

He reached over, did what she hadn't had the nerve to do. He combed his fingers through her silky black hair. "Skye?"

"What?"

"Don't go."

Those two words melted her icy resolve into slush. "Josh—"

He trailed a finger down her jawline. "Look, as soon as I hit the door, I'm getting shuteye. I'm asking you to be with me. No fooling around just lie down beside me. That's all...for now anyway."

"You mean you don't want to..."

Because she couldn't even say the words, he knew then for certain what he'd suspected back at the hospital. He'd denied his suspicions because he'd been too rocked by the kiss to admit it to himself. His warrior goddess wasn't so tough. No one had ever made love to Skye Cree. And he reveled in the idea he would be the first.

But not tonight.

"Of course, I do. But not right this second. I need to recharge." It wasn't a total lie but he had to ease her into thinking about being with him, letting him touch her, eventually enough to make love to her. "I want you with me while I do."

She puffed out a breath. "Okay." It was just that simple, she decided. Why make it out to be complicated. Attraction, sex, desire, all natural elements to life. She just needed to get used to the idea she was attracted to Josh Ander and he might really, eventually, touch her.

Pleased with her answer, Josh crawled out of the car.

When they headed to the elevator, a good two feet separating them, Josh changed that once the doors dinged open. His good arm winged out and took her hand. He tugged her to him and kissed the palm. Again, he heard her suck in a deep breath.

"No need to be nervous."

"Easy for you to say."

"Skye?" When those violet orbs finally looked up, met his eyes, he said, "As much as I love the idea of making love with you, relax. I'm not going to try to get you out of your clothes right this minute."

"Really?"

His grin spread. "I told you, at least not yet." The door to the penthouse slid open and Josh pulled her out into the loft and down the hall.

Once they got to the bedroom, though, a set of nerves hit Skye. She wasn't sure what to do with her hands. While Josh flicked on the bedside light and began to undress, Skye could do nothing more than blink at the room, at the pale blue painted walls with creamy crown molding.

The space itself reminded her of marshmallow clouds and gray-blue skies coming together in the middle of a spring day. Soothing. One wall held nothing but books from floor to ceiling. The furniture spoke male in that it was sturdy, deep chestnut, and bold. Good thing his decorator had gone with soft beiges and baby blues to accessorize and offset the dark wood. A thick cream-colored textured rug settled in under the bed, leaving the edges a trove of cherry hardwood.

One glance at Josh and she noted he'd already started tossing an assortment of pillows into a handy blanket box at the foot of the king-sized bed.

While she continued to stare, Josh got busy stripping out of his clothes. His jacket came off first before his tennis shoes and socks. He wrestled out of his shirt by awkwardly pulling it over his head. He unbuttoned the snap of his jeans.

All of a sudden, Skye wanted to move from her spot but couldn't make her feet work. She wanted to be the one to lower that zipper. But she'd waited too late. The minute he got down to his boxers, he simply threw back the covers and crawled between the sheets just as he'd promised.

She stood there another minute feeling silly and childish. She shrugged out of her coat, tossed it and her scarf onto the nearest chair. She toed off her boots, but left on her socks, shed her jeans and sweater, padded over wearing her bra and panties to flick off the light. In the dark, she made her way around to the other side of the bed and slid under the covers.

Josh did his best not to stare at his warrior goddess. He found himself struggling for the control he'd vowed on the ride up in the elevator. He took a steady breath, refusing to blow it now.

"Cold?" Josh asked, patting the space between them. "It's chilly in here. Scoot over and I'll warm you up."

Without a word, Skye slid over and turned into his arms. He settled her down beside him by placing a tender kiss in her hair and wrapping her up. "Now close your eyes and watch the cowboy ride off into the sunset. Watch him until he disappears completely, okay?"

"Does that really work for you?" she finally muttered, inhaling his scent. He smelled like rain and fresh air.

"Most of the time."

"Josh?"

"Yeah?"

"Thanks."

He kissed her hair again and said, "Now go to sleep."

And with that, she snuggled into his chest.

In less than two minutes, they were both dead to the world.

CHAPTER TWELVE

For two days now sixteen-year-old Heather Moore had been kept in the same dank windowless room, shot up with enough drugs to make sure she remained complacent. Confined in a ten-by-ten chamber of horrors with no heat and a concrete floor, the high school drill team captain had been beaten over most of her body from her chest down to her ankles. They never left a mark on her face. But because of the bruises along her ribs and butt and legs, she found it difficult to stand up.

For the first three days, she'd been used repeatedly by several different men, one of whom had to be as old as her father. The other two had been younger but equally gross and disgusting. They'd taken her clothes, her shoes—her innocence.

Her kidnappers had locked her away in a storage unit of some kind with orange doors. She knew that because whenever they opened it she got a peek out into the hallway. The orange doors were the roll-up variety that were raised and lowered on tracks.

Over and over again, she kept hearing the sounds of water lapping against the side of the building, especially at night if the tide came in. She'd heard a foghorn several times which meant they had to be holding her close to the docks.

If she ever got out of here alive she vowed never again to go into an online chat room. She'd never again agree to meet up with a total stranger she'd met there either. "Ron" was supposed to have been another student her own age attending a neighboring high school. How was she supposed to know that in real life he was a middle-aged man past forty?

Times like this, when she woke from her lethargy, she thought she heard crying and the moans of others coming from outside her cell. They were faint, weak, but if she wasn't dreaming or hallucinating, the sounds meant she wasn't alone in her prison. That's what she thought of this place, locked in, unable to get out of the dungeon. The place stank with the odor of mold and mildew, of sweat and body odor reeking from the urine-stained mattress she lay on. This morning someone to the right of her had gone to the bathroom, she was pretty sure it was number two. But then someone in the unit to the left of hers had puked. The awful smells were enough to make her stomach hurt.

It took everything she had just to roll over and plant her feet on the floor. Naked, she forced herself to stand up. The room spun in layers of constant motion. Once she steadied herself and her equilibrium returned somewhat, she made herself take that first step to the door. The six feet seemed to take forever. There was no knob, so she kicked at the metal roll-up door. Just as she already knew, she was locked in.

When she heard male voices, she crept back to the filthy bed and pretended to be asleep. Maybe if they thought she was still out, they wouldn't give her anymore drugs. Maybe if she were lucid for longer than five damn minutes, she could find a way out.

They kept talking about shipping her out of the country in two days. If that happened, she'd leave this place and never see her parents again. She'd never see her friends at school, never see her little brother celebrate his thirteenth birthday. Tears filled her eyes. She squeezed them shut tightly to keep from letting the bastards know she was awake and crying.

When a key rattled against the padlock, she went dead still, determined to make them think she was still out of it. She purposely slowed her breathing, tried to stop shaking—and prayed. She prayed her act would fool them and they would leave her alone. She prayed someone would come for her. She prayed and bargained. If she ever got out of this filthy place she'd never log into another chat room as long as she lived. She'd be good. She'd never stay out late again. She'd do exactly what her parents wanted her to do. In fact, she promised she'd never do anything wrong ever again.

But first, Heather had to think of a way out of her tiny metal cell and past her kidnappers.

Being sound asleep in a strange bed didn't stop the dreams or the voices from finding Skye Cree. She might've been burrowed under covers next to Josh from the sheer exhaustion of the last two days, but it didn't seem to matter.

Even though this image didn't seem to have the same punch or clarity as the one that had featured Erin, it still made her restless. The terror of seeing someone locked in a small cell, bruised and battered and chained to a metal cot unable to move around took its toll on the sleeping Skye.

Stirring from the dregs of slumber, she didn't fully come awake. But the dreadful sounds she heard refused to let up. Cries, pleading, moans of torture pulled her down deeper into the abyss. Instead of fighting it, Skye surrendered to the images, allowed them to bombard her. They rushed past her defenses in black and white until she saw the brilliant color orange burst through vivid and clear. From there she felt like drowning in hues of red and purple.

Soon the kaleidoscope changed to dull tones and then turned to gray before fading completely into black.

And just as she already knew, the pictures in her head confirmed the demons were all too human.

CHAPTER THIRTEEN

By four-thirty that morning, Brandon Hiller had finished with Jenna Donofrio. Now he just needed to find a place to dump the girl's body. There were any number of locations he could use, but he already had a perfect site in mind.

Nervous, he glanced in the back and decided it wouldn't do to get stopped by the cops. He eased off the gas and headed toward the I-5 ramp going south.

Thanks to his boss, he knew a place near Tacoma, a place out in the country, miles from anywhere or anyone, where he could take all the time he needed to dig a grave. He knew the guy that owned the land would be none too happy if he found out Brandon hadn't shared the girl with the others. Or traded or sold her to them for that matter.

That was the agreement he'd made. He always had to share what he'd snared. But sometimes a guy had to do what he had to do.

As Brandon drove past Sea-Tac Airport in the misty fog of early morning, as a jumbo jet rumbled overhead about to land from some unknown destination, he worked on his story. He didn't doubt for a minute that the group would want an accounting of how he'd spent his time tonight. He'd failed them already by not bringing them the redhead. Because of that, he'd had to suffer their wrath. Not only that, he'd lost his cut of the take. Ten grand would've kept him from having to get a job. Now, he might have to go to his brother-in-law and beg for a spot on his third-shift roster loading smelly fish onto trucks. Having to get a job would definitely cut into the time he spent roaming, hunting down his next quarry.

But even if the group gave him a rough time, there was no way he could go back and undo what he'd done. He'd taken matters into his own hands—again. His constituents couldn't find out about Jenna. If they did, he'd suffer their retaliation and have to go on the run. He liked Seattle. This was his home. He was familiar with the streets, knew where to find what he needed. Why should he leave it just because his boss had issues with the way he did things?

Just because the guy called all the shots didn't mean he owned Brandon Randle Hiller. No sir, no one owned him. He'd had enough of that in prison.

But he'd better come up with a good story, one that would keep them from knowing he'd taken the twelve-year-old on his own, done with her what he wanted without so much as thinking of sharing her with the others. Because if they found out he had done anything to bring the cops sniffing around, he already knew the consequences. He'd been warned by the head guy not four months earlier and by some of the others along the way not to get greedy.

If they found out, they'd get rid of him—for good.

Remembering the threat and how exactly it had been delivered by the boss man himself, Brandon started working on his alibi, going over several scenarios in his head that offered the best account of how he'd spent his night.

When nothing came to mind right away, he decided he'd have to think on it some more while he was digging Jenna's grave.

Once he reached Edgewood he took a back road into Tacoma and headed toward Commencement Bay. He left traffic and streetlights behind as he turned down a darkened, gravel road.

As the blue van rumbled along the unlit path, he hoped he was doing the right thing. Some people might think it was stupid on his part to bury the girl here right under the boss's nose. But sometimes the obvious was the best solution. Whitfield would never think to look in his own backyard, not in a million years. No one would.

It didn't make sense to Brandon that the guy acted like he hated his own woods. If the place had been Brandon's he'd have made the most of living out here, secluded and remote. A person could do what they wanted living so far away from busybodies. In Brandon's mind, some people just didn't appreciate how lucky they had it.

Because this wasn't Brandon's first time to the Tacoma property, once he got his bearings in the dark, he made a left turn next to a rundown mobile home. He came to a stop, making sure there were no lights on in the trailer. When he figured it was safe and he'd waited long enough to see if anyone looked out the window at the sound of an engine, he kept going, past the tree line until he left the gravel altogether and hit a dirt road.

When he reached the gate, he knew for certain it wasn't locked, but it was closed. Damn it, he'd have to get out and trudge in the mud to get the damn thing opened. He didn't want to get stuck out here in the muck and bog in the dark. With the headlights to help him see, he pulled the gate back wide enough so the van could move through.

After getting his shoes filthy, he crawled back into the van, and knew he still had a good half mile to go before he reached the place where he'd been part of digging a couple of graves before. Brandon had been here on two different occasions with other members of the group when they had needed a place to dispose of bodies, specifically girls who had up and died on them. Because of his familiarity with the area, he knew where the best place to dig was and he intended on making this quick.

At least the girl was small for her age and wouldn't require the hole to be that deep. Good thing she wouldn't take up much space.

The van had to go through a shallow stream and past a thicket of naked hickory and maple that looked like the trees had forgotten to bud several seasons ago. As soon as his headlights landed on the clearing, an area of recently turned earth came into view. He cut the engine, got out and went to the back. Before opening the doors, he glanced around, checking for any hint that someone might have spotted him. When he saw nothing out of the ordinary, he got to work, getting out the shovel he'd brought.

He had to admit the area was more than a little spooky this time of night. When he'd done this kind of thing before, it had been in broad daylight with the sun shining bright on his shoulders and he'd been in the company of others. Now, alone, he considered every noise—the hoot of an owl, each snap of a twig, each chirp of a cricket—a possible sign his activity had been discovered.

Brandon shook off the cold along with the chill crawling up his back. He had to remind himself there was nothing out here but the bones of others, certainly nothing that could hurt him.

He let his adrenaline spike when he started digging through the wet earth, the mire and the muck until he had to stop to clean off the mud that stuck to his shovel. While he flicked spade after spade of topsoil into another pile, he considered how he should get major points for already taking the initiative and coming up with a substitute to please the boss. He might've already lost the redhead, but hadn't he given the group a replacement in record time? Knowing he might still have amends to make, Brandon realized that keeping the boss happy had to be priority one. Because of that he began to dig faster. Maybe if he hurried he'd get to reap the rewards of his creativity.

CHAPTER FOURTEEN

Josh woke to the sound of rain batting the glass. Gray light filtered through the stingy slice of open curtain covering the floor-to-ceiling windows. Because he'd taken his watch off he couldn't tell what time it was. Late morning, he decided, after doing his best to twist around to see the time on the alarm clock only to realize that if he moved too much he'd wake up Skye.

Since his shoulder still bothered him some but felt better than it had in two days, and because he had a beautiful woman nestled up against him, Josh decided work on this Monday morning would have to wait. Out of habit though, he began mentally going over his schedule for the day.

But just as he was getting into his mental to-do list, a sleepy, sexy voice mumbled in his ear and interrupted his train of thought. "Do we have to get up? It's so nice right here."

He'd take this distraction any day of the week and twice on Sundays. Skye looked tousled and rumpled. He couldn't quite bank his lust. But he did his best to throttle back. "Not at all. You can stay and sleep as long as you like. I should probably get up though, take a shower, check my emails, contact the office, let them know I haven't died since Friday night."

She rubbed the sleep out of her eyes with the heel of her free hand, the one that wasn't tucked into Josh's rump.

She blinked at her surroundings and did her best to ignore the bare chest she found herself snuggled up against. "What time is it?"

He rolled to his back, taking her with him to glance at the time on the clock. "Almost nine. We got less than five hours sleep. Why don't you…?" He made the mistake of gazing down at that face, those eyes. Even with tangled hair and a mussed-up look, the woman bordered on stunning. There ought to be a law against anyone having eyes that mesmerizing who didn't get her eight hours of beauty sleep. He had an overwhelming urge to run his hands in all that hair.

Lying half atop his chest, Skye found that free hand drifting down to the distinctive hard lump under the cover. Like a magnet it seemed to draw her there.

"Don't play with fire," Josh cautioned, stilling her hand. "I'm only human, Skye." This time he did run his fingers through her hair, smoothing out some of the knots as he went. "God, you take my breath away though."

She cleared her throat. "Josh, there's something you should know. This is exactly the kind of thing I've avoided—" She took a long, deep breath.

"What kind of thing?" he asked, trying to put a casual tone in his voice, hoping that maybe if she opened up about it…

Skye chewed her lip. How could a grown woman be so nervous and so reluctant to admit she hadn't been with a man before other than the sleaze ball who'd taken her virginity? Clearly uneasy, she cleared her throat again. "I tried to date a couple of times in high school. It didn't…go well. A couple of years later I tried again after meeting this guy in the coffee shop on Pike. I guess I was about twenty. That time we tried kissing…then…when…things…when he wanted to take it to the next level—" She shook her head. "I liked him just fine. It wasn't that at all, I just couldn't…bring myself…to…go there."

"We'll take it slow. It doesn't have to be right this minute."

She let out a huge puff of air. That meant he got it, there was no need to draw him a better picture, Skye decided. "That's just it. I don't want to take it slow. I'm twenty-five, Josh, which means I'm practically dead in the water, sexually. It isn't fair. I want to stop letting that bastard win this part of my life, too. I've let him win far too much as it is. I want to move past this—for good. It's time, don't you think?"

"Now's not a good time to expect objectivity on my part."

In a whisper, she added, "But...you could help me with this? Please."

Josh saw her lick her lips, not in a suggestive way, but more like a nervous habit. And it was that little gesture that had him swallowing hard right before he raked his hands through her hair again. He drew her up until their eyes met. "If you're sure it's what you want."

When she nodded, he murmured in her ear, "Then don't think of anyone else but me, Skye. No other time or place, just right now, right here with me. Put everything out of your head and think of me, hold on to me."

"You'll show me what to do? I mean...I don't—"

"Shh. Beautiful Skye," he murmured and ran a finger across her cheek, noted her eyes were as big as saucers. That look told him she needed seduction with a taste of the reward yet to come. Because she didn't have a clue of the possibilities and because he wanted to be the one to show her, he covered her mouth, gently, trying for easy and tender.

As she clung to him, the kiss spun out like molten flares streaking brightly across a warm summer sky in June. For the first time in her life Skye understood desire, its power, its energy, its flavor. She felt like Josie Geller in *Never Been Kissed*, standing on that pitcher's mound on a warm spring day as Sam Coulson planted the big one on her lips.

Josh knew it was up to him to set the pace. He tugged on all that hair again, moved his mouth to her ear. He lingered, brushing and grazing before skimming along her cinnamon skin to her shoulder. But when he came back to her mouth—fiery need had him sinking in—and drowning.

He banked that, and chewed lightly on tender flesh, another shoulder, an upper arm. Her short intake of breath urged him on. His hands skated along her back, unhooked the no-nonsense bra she'd worn to bed. Firm, small breasts stood at attention, nipples erect. Leaving a slick wet trail downward, Josh licked the tender tip to a rock hard bead before taking it into his mouth. Sampling, tasting, he feasted.

She'd never felt anything so glorious. Pleasure rippled through her wave by lapping wave. Greed—pure and simple—had her wanting his mouth—everywhere. "Don't stop," she cried out. To make sure he understood she cupped both sides of his head and latched on.

When she burst in climax, no one was more surprised than Josh. He'd barely gotten started, hadn't even touched her yet, not really. But he reveled in his success and ran with it. His hands glided along her body until he reached the equally plain white panties. Breaching the cotton, it felt as if he'd stirred the embers in a roaring blaze.

Fingers teased and got him a series of oh Gods along with a chain of ripples and quakes. Twice more, she came. To hell with slow, Josh thought and guided her hands to his shorts.

Taking the hint, Skye slid them along his skin until he simply kicked out of them. Rolling her to her back, in one thrust, he dived in, the joining taut and tight. As incredibly overpowering as it was for him, he wanted her first time to be exceptional. He urged her legs to lock around his waist. A feral hunger rose up between them. Rhythm built. Pace quickened. Fierce need won out as they each came in a rush of shimmering light.

And with it, the face of Skye's past was erasing. A chunk of fear fell away.

They lay there, wrapped, still bundled.

He looked down into violet eyes. She looked up into his gray.

"That was—" she puffed out a breath. "Is it always like that?"

What was he supposed to say? He'd never been with a woman who'd ever popped before he'd even gotten to— the main event. "No. You're very orgasmic."

"I am?"

He chuckled and tucked a strand of hair behind her ear. "You are."

"Was I okay?"

"Skye, if you'd been any better, I'm pretty sure I'd be dead."

A giggle snuck out of her throat. "That was—amazing. You were…" She searched for a word, just the right compliment. She might have been a novice at making love but she'd read as much as she could about it online and in books. According to articles she'd skimmed on the Internet, men needed a certain bump to the ego afterward. Josh Ander had certainly earned a few accolades. "Do you design games like you make love?" Without waiting for an answer she whooshed out, "That was fairly brilliant, wonderful!"

At the praise, he shook his head and finally rolled off. "If you're trying to dish out kudos, I'll take as many as I can get." He tugged her up to a sitting position, took a long look at the view, eyeing her firm breasts. "What do you say we get wet?"

Her lips bowed up into a wide grin, revealing a pair of delicious dimples, something he hadn't noticed before maybe because since he'd met her she hadn't done a whole lot of smiling. If it were possible, the toothy grin added even more beauty to her face.

"Is that where we do it again, in the shower?"

"Morning sex. Shower sex." He wiggled his eyebrows. "Two for two makes for the perfect start to a rainy day. Come on." Grabbing her hand, he tugged her into the bathroom.

She wasn't prepared for the arched entryway or the lavish size of the room. This was definitely not the same place where she'd retrieved the first aid kit. "Ohmygod. This is like something out of a rainforest," Skye uttered, clearly taken aback by the size of the shower stall.

"It's an energy efficient body shower with rain jets," Josh explained, reaching around her to turn on the spray and push several buttons on a control panel.

"It's like that famous waterfall in Hawaii or maybe someplace just as tropical." Gray tiled slate, in various shades, formed the three-sided enclosure. Four lighted showerheads rained down from the seven-foot ceiling while three more generously angled from the side. There was no annoying shower curtain to deal with or door to slide off its track. She'd never seen a shower with its own floor-to-ceiling window wide enough to let in all manner of light or one with music piped in. If she wasn't mistaken Tchaikovsky's *Seventh Symphony* poured from the speakers. There was even a place to park your butt while the water spilled over your tired muscles and worked out the kinks.

Once under the steam, Josh lifted up her chin and said, "Your mouth is still gaped open. If you don't close it, you're gonna drown." As if Josh read the expression on her face, he squeezed out peachy-smelling gel, rubbed it between his hands and began working it over her shoulders and back. "And if you drown," he continued, "we might not be able to do this."

Spreading his hands over silky skin and smoothing the foamy bubbles up and down her torso, he drew her against him, brushed her wet hair out of the way so he could nibble her neck. "I didn't hurt you, did I? I got a little carried away."

"You did?" She shook her head and turned into his chest, elated at the idea of it. "I thought it would be uncomfortable but—I wanted you so much, I didn't even think about how it might hurt."

"How about now? You'll be sore."

"Really? I don't feel sore. I feel energized, like there's a new me. It was way past time, Josh. There's no need to baby me."

Oh but he thought there was. He just had to find his control. "Mmm," he muttered against her ear. "I don't want you hurt, ever again."

She felt his hardness against her belly and went with instinct. No spectator this time while he did all the work, she touched. She explored. "Hmm, I promise I won't be such a dud and let you do everything this time." To prove it her mouth found his. It was a wondrous thing just to be able to run her hands over the strength in his shoulders, the defined chest, over lean hips and belly. But she didn't stop there. She used her fingers to travel downward to stroke and caress.

Two steps and Josh had her backed to the wall. Mist and heat carried him into the blistering kiss. Teeth gnawed at tongues. But hunger for her drove him to stake a claim and take. Need had him bringing her legs up and locking around him—to plunge deeper.

Having him inside her was like wet silk. Skye wasn't sure she could ever get enough. She let her head fall back and rode him full out, fast and hard until they both shuddered in fiery release.

Back in the bedroom she pulled on her pair of jeans, and looked over at Josh, who stood butt-naked, his back to her while he dug through his dresser drawer for underwear and socks. "How come I don't feel self-conscious or awkward? I thought I would. It seems so—natural now, watching you stand there in the buff."

Pulling out his own fresh clothes, he glanced over and realized she had to put the same things on from the night before. "You just answered your own question. What happened between us is a natural step between consenting adults." He slipped one leg, then the other into freshly laundered jeans and looped his belt around his waist, zipped up his pants. "You know, it wouldn't take much extra time to stop by your apartment, pick up some clean clothes—to bring here—for later."

"Later? Why? I have my own place. You always move this fast?"

He frowned, realizing she was taking that step back and closing off right before his eyes. Mixed signals he recognized. He ran a hand through his still damp hair and said, "Look, I just thought…it seems a little unfair that I'm at home around my own things and you…never mind." It seemed to him she really did not want him setting foot inside her studio. Maybe that was all it was. But it bugged him. How was it she didn't feel uncomfortable now after they'd just shared the intimate act of making love, but he'd hit a nerve at suggesting they go pick up a few of her belongings and bring them back here? Maybe he *was* out of line. Maybe he *did* need to put on the brakes.

When he saw Skye pick up her coat to leave the room or rather storm out, he nipped her around the waist. "You have to know this is the best morning I've had in a really long time. I just want you comfortable here, all the way relaxed."

"If I were any more relaxed, I'd be boneless." She smiled, ran her fingers down his cheek in a tender gesture. "I'm glad to hear you don't have regrets. I know I don't. Now, I'll go get the coffee started," she offered and abruptly left the room.

He told himself she needed some space and he would give it to her. After all, she'd made progress by leaps and bounds letting him touch her, make love to her. He knew she still had issues. But he was willing to work through them slowly if that's what it took. He wasn't exactly sure what it was about the woman that had him feeling things this strong, this quick. To hell with this, he thought. He had to get to work anyway.

Later in the kitchen, after pouring a much-needed mug of caffeine, he was sweetening the contents when Josh stated, "Maybe now isn't the best time to talk about this since you seemed to be in a mood—"

"Oh for God's sake, I'm not moving in with you. You're still not over your wife."

"When did I ask you to move in? Just because I suggested you pick up a few things for later is not—"

She rubbed her fingers back and forth on her forehead. "Okay, okay. Maybe I misread you. My fault. This is all totally new for me."

"Then we're...on the same page?"

"Sure."

"Then I want you to show me how to fight the way you do." He'd already thought about this several times over the weekend. It seemed like the most efficient way to learn from the person he considered the best.

Skye's mouth dropped open. "What? You're kidding?" She stared at the man who had just done all manner of spectacularly dirty things to her body—twice.

"Train me, Skye. I have to be ready if I encounter someone like I did Friday night. Not only that, I want to help you get Ronny Whitfield. You might need backup when that happens, especially if you're thinking about making a trip out to Tacoma."

Unbelievably touched that he'd used the word 'when' in the same phrase referring to Whitfield, Skye fumbled for a reply. She tossed her still wet hair back off her face. "Josh...that's..." She tried to think of the right way to convey what she wanted to say. After several long seconds though, staring at the eagerness in his eyes, she went with her gut. "Actually that isn't a bad idea. Although it is kinda crazy."

"Yes, I guess it is. But I've done crazy things before."

"This might be the craziest. Don't get me wrong, anyone can work on strengthening muscles, making sure they're able to run a mile to keep in shape. But when it comes to defending yourself, you have to be willing to take someone out. You can't hesitate. You hesitate and..."

"I'm aware of that. But we'll hash that out later. First, you should know I discovered some info you might be interested in. I happened upon a porn site yesterday morning."

Skye automatically wrinkled her nose. "Okay."

"I found an old username Ronny Wayne used five years ago when he signed up. That was a couple of months after he got out of prison."

"Ah. Now you've got my attention. You can go back that far online?"

"You bet. Anyway, from the old username I followed his online trail to another porn site, a private one." He adjusted his glasses and continued, "Which I hacked."

Now she smiled. "That's very clever of you."

"It is. He belongs to a group that spans the globe. I think the man's into sex-trafficking."

"Tell me something I don't already know. Of course he is."

"No, I don't think you understand. Tracking the private site, I think I can prove it."

"Really?"

Before he went any further, he wanted to know more. "But you might explain to me how it plays out for him. Exactly."

"He grabs the girl, or has someone else do it these days, then keeps her around to share with his friends—for a price or as part of the deal, part of the perks. Either way, they use the girl until they're done and then sell her to the highest online bidder. There's a very active group in South America, Venezuela to be exact. Then there's another group, active in Europe, Bosnia to be more specific."

Josh narrowed his eyes. "How do you know that? Specifically."

She'd walked right into that one. She bluffed. "You aren't the only one that can use a computer."

Josh wasn't sure he believed that explanation. It had taken everything he knew as a hacker, everything he'd learned about software applications to get him through site after site of complex firewalls. "I trudged through several intricate mazes yesterday to get that far and believe me it wasn't a walk in the park."

She went back to the topic. "Did you save any of this data?"

Josh sent her an incredulous look. "I saved it all to its own flash drive."

"Something we could give to Harry then."

Josh picked up on an undertone. "When you told him about the trafficking, Drummond didn't believe Whitfield was part of it." It wasn't a question.

"Not exactly. He's a cop. Cops usually need hard proof before they can get on board with anything."

"I can get more."

"Really?"

"What I found was tip of the iceberg stuff. I have a feeling there are many layers in his tangled web. Look, there's something else. I want to put you in a game, or rather your likeness."

"No."

"Come on, Skye. It would be a rendition. It would have a graphics comic book feel to it, nothing more than a cartoon likeness really."

"No. There is no negotiation on this, Josh. I do not want Whitfield stumbling on that kind of thing and getting off on it."

He held up his hands. "Okay, I get it. You're right. I'll adjust the face and the hair so it doesn't resemble you at all. How's that?"

"You'd do that?"

"Yeah. I'm sorry I even considered...I wasn't thinking."

"Make her a blonde, will you? I always envied the golden-haired cheerleaders in school."

"Why? You have beautiful hair. The blonde doesn't work for me, maybe a redhead."

"Since when? I thought most men loved blondes."

He picked up a few strands of her hair. "Not me, I love all this black."

"Yeah, so you said about a dozen times since Friday." She grinned and started to get out the makings for breakfast when her cell phone chimed. Skye looked at the number, still riding the afterglow from two bouts of morning sex, and piped up, "It's Harry. Hey, Harry, what's up?"

"Skye, we have another missing girl. Jenna Donofrio, twelve years old. Her father got home from his third-shift job at Gordham Press this morning around seven-thirty, only to find an empty house, his daughter gone. Looks like someone cut the glass on a back window to get inside."

"Hmm, back-to-back abductions? Could Brandon Hiller be responsible or do you think it's an unknown?"

"I don't know, Skye. I just don't know at this point. What I do know is that the girl didn't take a glass cutter to get out of her own house. She's not a runaway."

She picked up on the frustration in his voice, even though he'd only been on the case for a couple of hours. "What do you want me to do, Harry?"

"The media's already on the story. Wanted to keep you in the loop. And whatever it is you do, you might want to do it now, if you get my drift. Unofficially."

Even though rain still poured down outside, she didn't hesitate. "I'm on it. Have they issued an AMBER Alert?"

"I'm afraid it doesn't meet the criteria. We don't have a description of the captor, no make or model of a vehicle. There's nothing we can use for an alert."

"But the media has her picture out?"

"Oh yeah. That we did immediately. Look, I've got to go. You find anything, call me."

The minute she clicked off, Josh pressed the remote on the TV in the kitchen. "Missing girl? Might as well get the details. You go out in this, I'm going with you."

"Josh, I'm used to doing this on my own."

He ignored the stubborn lock of her jaw. His eyes focused on the screen and the exploding news story. His stomach dropped. "Jenna Donofrio is only twelve."

"According to Harry he got into the house through a back window by cutting the glass. Ronny Wayne usually abducts his victims from the outdoors, parks, around schools, that sort of thing. Never once, that I know of, has he ever gone into a house and taken a child out that way."

"What about the Hiller guy?"

"Same MO as Whitfield as far as I know. Doesn't have a history of going inside a house to rape or abduct from a residence. Unless of course, he amped up, got desperate because of what happened Saturday night, leaving Erin alone, letting her get away. Urges, predilections don't disappear because of failure. They just keep trying, ramping up their efforts until bingo, one way or another they have success."

"So it's possible. Let's say the rain keeps the kids inside. A perp gets desperate enough he'll do anything for his fix, especially when his fix is kids."

"Exactly." When the phone rang a second time, Skye groaned. "Crap, it's Lena. What do you suppose Zeke's managed to do in a measly seven hours?" She pushed. Answer with all the eagerness of a woman desperately trying to maintain her cool. "Hi, Lena, what's up?"

"You might've told me that your Zeke is in fact, a Zoe."

"What are you talking about? How the heck did I miss that?"

"You heard me. Zeke is a girl. Zoe Hollister is her real name."

"Well, for God's sakes." Skye thumped her head. "He, or rather she, certainly had me fooled. And that might explain a lot about why she's on the streets hiding as a boy."

"I'm sure it does because her mother's boyfriend got a little too friendly, hence the leaving home."

"How'd you find that out anyway?"

"I raised sons, Skye. There were several indications. First, I laundered what little clothes she peeled off after she finally agreed to take that shower. They weren't boy things. Then I got a better look at her coming out of the bathroom. After a good night's sleep, I confronted her this morning and she 'fessed up."

"So she didn't get thrown out of the house, she's a runaway? Damn, that makes it a sticky situation."

"Not from where I'm standing. That child is not going back home as long as the mother lets her boyfriend live there. If I have to get my own attorney on this, Skye Cree, I'm determined."

"Okay, okay, calm down. I agree with you, Lena, but we can't hide a runaway."

"Then I'll get an attorney."

"We'll talk about this later. Look, there's a girl gone missing."

"I know. It's all over the news. You go do what it is you do. For now, I've got Zoe handled."

"You sure?"

"Yes, I'm sure. Now go."

Within the hour, she'd hit the streets with Kiya in the drizzle and biting wind. She'd persuaded a reluctant Josh to keep to his Monday work routine, which included a mandatory afternoon staff meeting with his department heads. She'd pushed every button, used every cliché to get him *not* to tag along with her.

The man wasn't nearly ready to sit down and listen to a long-drawn-out explanation about Native American customs and folklore that covered her personal belief in spirit guides and a wolf that only she could see. The fact that she and Kiya had conversations was probably not something a man like Josh would ever understand anyway and certainly couldn't fully accept without a good deal of rationalization.

That pretty much covered the reason Kiya, the wolf, belonged to her and her alone and always would. She'd been born connected to the spirit of the wolf. The hunter.

Just because she'd had mutually satisfying, mind-numbing sex didn't mean she shared the knowledge of Kiya with anyone. That especially included Josh Ander. He may have thought he'd seen a silver wolf—she was pretty sure she'd nipped that delusion in the bud—but how he'd managed to see Kiya in the first place when no one else ever had, nagged at the back of her mind.

She wasn't sure what Josh's sighting meant exactly.

The answer to that came from Kiya.

It means you have a strong connection to the man. He's your destiny.

"Destiny with a multi-millionaire? That's bullshit. That doesn't even sound like me."

Your destiny isn't up to you, not entirely. Remember, the threads of your life and your future are intertwined.

"Since when? Come on. It's all over the Internet people have reported seeing a lone silver wolf hanging around urban Seattle. No way all of those sightings could be my destiny."

Destiny means many things, Skye Cree. This city is your home, your community, part of your tribe. The people in it, all the people you interact with will eventually play a part in your future. There is a place in your future for Josh Ander whether you accept it or not.

"We need to put this aside for now and concentrate on finding Jenna Donofrio."

Sadly, I sense Jenna's spirit is no longer with us.

Skye stopped walking. She looked down at Kiya, met the wolf's eyes. Violet locked into violet. Anger blocked the familiar instinct. "You might've mentioned that an hour ago. Jenna's gone?"

She is. You needed this time for reflection before exploding into rage. Rage works against you. Fury and anger will get you nowhere.

Skye took deep breaths, tried for calm. "Tell me who is responsible."

You already know that.

"Do not talk to me in riddles! Not now, not today. I want a name!"

Brandon Hiller followed her home from the grocery store. She went to get a can of soup. After her father left for work, he went back in the night and took her.

"What did he do with her body?"

You know I don't see everything, Skye Cree.

"Damn it!" Skye yelled out loud to no one. It never occurred to her that the wolf was wrong. She'd trusted Kiya with her life too many times to question the knowledge that came with it. She suddenly remembered the vague dream from the night before. Her exhaustion had caused her to drop into a deeper sleep than usual. Did the red and purple have anything to do with Jenna?

Don't confuse the images, Skye Cree.

"Are you certain?"

I am.

"Could I have done anything to prevent Jenna—?"

You could have done nothing to prevent her death.

Skye was still trying to calm down when she glanced up and noticed she'd walked all the way to the corner of Eighth and Stewart. Low hanging clouds drifted along the pavement. More rain would be coming through within the hour, she decided. She wanted desperately to lash out, to hit something.

Would she ever be able to stop the monsters out there from hurting kids?

Instead of smashing her fists into the likes of Hiller, whom she had to catch first, she drew out her cell phone. How the hell did she intend to explain details to a member of law enforcement and convince him she wasn't crazy and in need of years in therapy?

What a mess, she decided, rubbing her aching head. Helluva note, after her first morning bout of incredible sex with one of Seattle's hottest hunks, she had to come face-to-face with this. Confronting her deepest fears at being labeled a flake, a freak, and cracked hadn't exactly been on her Monday morning to-do list.

One thing she knew for certain. Over the past several years, she'd already pushed Harry's innate cop radar to the limit with Ali and Hailey and Erin. What the hell would he think of her once she told him there was no chance Jenna Donofrio was coming home alive? What cop wouldn't want the specifics of that and how the hell she knew them?

That's okay, Harry, she thought. *I sure as hell wouldn't believe me either.*

But because she had to try, she punched in Harry's number.

CHAPTER FIFTEEN

Sitting in the conference room at Ander All Games surrounded by his staff, Josh couldn't concentrate. For one thing, his mind kept replaying the morning spent with Skye. He'd never believed in love at first sight. After all, it had taken him months to fall in love with his wife, Annabelle.

She'd been a cute brunette, who'd caught his attention at Comic-Con in San Diego where she'd been working one of the booths. She'd been decked out in some kind of sexy red costume that had showed plenty of leg and cleavage. Within hours of meeting, they'd gone back to his hotel room and hadn't surfaced till noon the next day. But that had been more about sex than any deeper feelings on his part. Love hadn't entered the equation until almost a year later. They'd shared a lot of common ground when it came to the same interests, games, music, movies, food, even politics. But having a lot in common was a far cry from rocking each other's world in the sack. Surely they'd done that on some level at some point since they'd spent several years together. At least he hoped they had. He had to wonder now if he'd ever rocked Annabelle's world.

Because he didn't like admitting that his own hadn't shaken quite that much with Annabelle, certainly not the way it had with Skye. He hadn't wanted to devour Annabelle. Skye on the other hand, he wanted to eat from head to toe until he thought he might explode. It didn't seem he could ever get enough.

Like right now. Instead of taking care of business, what was he doing? He couldn't seem to stop thinking about Skye Melody Cree. Hell, Friday night when he'd left the office for happy hour he'd never even heard of the woman. And now...he didn't want to wait six hours until he saw her again. He wanted to make sure she never got hurt again or suffered pain or...he scrubbed a hand over his face.

He didn't believe in love at first sight. But by God if she had to face Ronny Wayne Whitfield on her terms, he wanted to be there with her when she did.

Embroiled in the disappearance of a child, Harry didn't have time to waste on half-baked ideas or theories. But when they came out of the mouth of Skye Cree, he decided to give her fifteen minutes of face time. Instead of delivering the news about Jenna to him over the phone, the two had agreed to meet at Country Kitchen.

He'd just sat down when Skye went into her spiel by prefacing things with her usual "don't ask me how I know" routine. She mentioned the Brandon Hiller angle before leading Harry into the bad news that he was no longer looking for a kidnapped victim but a murdered one.

It didn't take long for Skye to get an earful from Harry. And the seasoned detective wasn't buying it for a minute. "So, in addition to your other skills, you've now developed psychic abilities? Do I have that right? Since when?"

"You really can be an ass sometimes, you know that?"

"Unless you can be more specific, a lot more, you're way out of line here, Skye. The way I figure it, that girl's been gone less than twelve hours. She still has a chance..."

"You know the statistics as well as I do. No, actually better than I do. Every hour that passes increases the likelihood that she won't be found alive. Be realistic."

"Only if you come clean. Now!"

Skye understood the fury, expected it. Anytime a child was involved, hurt, it took a toll on everyone involved. But in her effort to get him to listen she moved past the rage. "Hiller probably waited until he was sure the father wasn't coming back right away before he made his move. By the way, have you checked out Hiller's connection to Whitfield? The one I mentioned yesterday. I found some information on the Internet that clearly…"

Harry had heard enough. "Goddamn it, Skye! Not all child abductions in this city revolve around Ronny Wayne Whitfield."

"Says you. I know what I know."

"And won't disclose how."

"I'm trying to help. You wanted my help. *You* called *me*."

"A bad decision I'm now regretting. Look, I checked out Hiller after our conversation yesterday, couldn't find a single time he'd ever crossed paths with Whitfield. Hiller did his time in Clallam Bay, Ronny at Walla Walla. Five hundred miles apart, Skye. And years apart. So, yeah, I looked into it. Now what? I don't have time for this. I'd hoped when you called that you had something solid, verifiable. I see now—" he pointed his finger at her and cautioned, "You need to move on, or whatever, get past this goddamned fixation on Whitfield. I know he ruined your life, took a part of you you'll never be able to get back, but you need to stop this obsession and let it go."

"Harry, why didn't you ever mention that there have been five other girls reported missing since Hiller got out of prison?"

"Where the hell did you get that kind of information? Who the hell told you that? If I find out anyone's been leaking—" he rubbed at his throbbing temple. "I'm wasting my breath."

"That's what the Internet's for right along with SEO. I can use a computer, Harry."

"You know damn well, I'm not at liberty to discuss an open case, Skye. Besides, I'm only one detective. I don't handle all the missing persons cases in town. You know that."

"Hmm, something to consider. Who does? I mean which detectives specifically get assigned to missing persons?"

"You don't need to know that." He slammed his fist on the table in frustration. "What's gotten into you? This preoccupation of yours has got to stop! Now you're taking it up a notch by telling me the Donofrio girl's dead. Damn it, I want you to tell me how you know that."

About the time Skye was about to go head to head with Harry over those words, Josh walked up to the table.

"And you need to ease off, Drummond," Josh demanded, although he too was curious as to how exactly Skye knew Jenna Donofrio wasn't coming home.

Skye's eyes went wide at the way Josh spoke to the cop. This combative side to him was different than the geeky nerd she'd come to—care about.

Harry stared at Josh. "Who the hell are you? On second thought, I don't care. Right now, I've got a little girl to find." Harry threw some bills on the table and stood up. "I'd love to blame this on you," he told Josh. "But I know better. She's pretty much been like this since she was sixteen. God knows I've tried to get her to give up this notion that she sees Ronny Wayne hiding behind every tree or building or park in Seattle, especially now that Hiller is involved. I give up!"

"Can you blame her after what the bastard…?"

"Oh great. She's turned you into a fanatic believer as well. Ronny Wayne is a monster, no question about that. But Whitfield is not the answer to every child abduction that occurs within a seventy-mile radius of Seattle. The sooner you get that through your thick head and hers, the better off you'll both be." With that, Harry stalked off leaving Josh staring down at Skye.

"He's under a lot of stress," Skye said.

"That's no excuse to rail on you like that."

"True. It isn't the first time we've yelled at each other. I doubt it'll be the last."

"How do you know Jenna Donofrio is dead?"

Her loud sigh indicated to Josh getting any information would require a certain amount of patience and a lot of motivation to open up. So he slid into the booth across from her, signaled Velma over. "Hey, Velma. How's it going? You working a double shift or something? You were here less than twelve hours ago."

"Thanks for noticing. I often work a double when lazy-good-for-nothing waitresses don't show up for their own shift. And it's going fine now that Bill's out of my hair." She leaned in for effect and added, "Went fishing for two days. I'm gonna be dead on my feet by two this afternoon. But you know what? I'm determined to have me one of those girls' nights out with my sister this very evening while he's gone. Going to the movies, see that new gangster movie starring that little hottie Ryan Gosling. I don't mind a bit admitting that's one man that flat out gets my blood pumping. Listen to me go on, I know you didn't come in here to get a great big ol' status update on my life. Now, what can I get you two for chow?"

"A tuna on wheat toast with fries and an iced tea for me. Skye?"

"The breakfast special and another coffee will be fine."

"English muffin, right?"

Skye nodded and Velma left them alone.

"Okay. I'll ask again. How do you know the Donofrio girl is already deceased?"

"What makes you think I'll tell you when I've known Harry more than a dozen years and won't open up to him? If it's because I...slept with you, think again."

"Please. You'll tell me because I won't stop asking until you do. Does it have anything to do with the silver wolf with violet eyes I saw on the streets last night?"

"You mean the white Australian shepherd?"

"Save it. This morning during my staff meeting, which should've held my interest and had me deeply engrossed in the status reports from each of my department heads, I got curious. While I listened to my crew go over the bugs in the new code, and all manner of other issues, I went on the Internet and searched Native American folklore and customs. Guess what? I got about two million hits on varying tales covering all kinds of different spirit guides. It's a fairly common belief among most Native Americans that from the time a person is born some type of animal or bird is reported to guide the child from adolescence through adulthood and beyond, most notably appearing to the youth around the age of twelve or thirteen. The wolf is an extremely popular symbol. I'd say the silver wolf I saw is yours and is the reason you were able to ditch Whitfield that day. I'm surprised Harry hasn't figured it out, seeing as how he's known you so much longer than I have."

Sarcasm aside, Skye blinked at the realization Josh not only accepted the wolf's existence as reality but that he seemed to take it in stride.

He studied the stunned look on her face before adding, "I still say I could design one helluva game featuring you and the wolf."

That brought her back to reality. "How many times do I have to say it? My private life is not an open book laid out for someone to play on a stupid game console. It isn't. I've had enough people looking at me as though I carried around some disease to last a lifetime. I'm not willing to be the object of snickering idiots who figure out it's me in your world of game fantasy. Got that?"

"Loud and clear. But you shouldn't deny me my fantasies."

Velma approached, set down their plates, eyed the tension between the two and decided to make it quick. "Refills?"

"Sure," Josh replied jovially as he watched Velma pour coffee and tea in a flurry. He waited until she took off before he said, "You didn't exactly deny that it's a Nez Perce fable."

"How can I deny what you found on the Internet? It's there. It's enjoyable, fanciful reading. It offers a reasonable explanation of the legend. My grandmother used to spin tales all the time like that. But...that's all they were." She picked up her coffee, sipped. And made the mistake of looking directly into his eyes. Something, she wasn't sure what, made her want to let go of the burden once and for all. But with the next breath, she came to her senses. She cut into her eggs, forked up hash browns to go with it and declared, "But the silver wolf's a nice touch."

He munched on his sandwich, leaned back, took a long slow drink of his iced tea, set down his glass. "It's probably a coincidence then that the wolf is a hunter—like you."

She stewed over his reasoning while the food she tried to swallow all but lodged in her throat. Finally she blurted out, "You think you want to know. But really...you're better off keeping your distance from me."

It was like a slap in the face but he wasn't going to let her know she'd struck a nerve. If she wanted to play that game he wasn't going to let her evade any longer either. "Why? Because you don't want to discuss and share things that are important to you? That's fine, I get that. But you're really lousy at bluffing. Do you really want me to do that, to keep my distance?"

"I can't have children," she blurted out.

Josh blinked. Now it was his turn for shock to register. "Son of a bitch."

He got up, slid into her side of the booth. He took her chin, snatched up her hand from the table, worked his fingers into hers and held on. He tilted her head up so her eyes were forced to look into his. "Remember when I told you that I thought you were the strongest person I'd ever met? I meant that. It wasn't just a line. If you think this makes a difference in how I feel? It doesn't. Why'd you tell me anyway...here...now...like this?"

She shrugged. "I don't know…I thought…you deserved to know because…I…I don't want you to keep your distance."

"Like that was going to happen," he confessed before bending his head so he could take her mouth. At the touch of lips, the flame caught, crackled to life in blazing white.

"Really?"

"Yeah. When do we have our first training session?"

"You still want to go through with that?"

And knowing what Whitfield had done to her, what she'd suffered at the bastard's hands, he was more determined than ever. "Of course, I want to put my many moves into practice."

She snickered. "Okay. But it's your body. How about we start tonight?"

"Fine by me."

"Let's hope you still feel that way after I'm done with you."

After forty-five minutes of lifting weights with Skye in her so-called gym, Josh was out of breath and realized that he was woefully out of shape, more so than he'd thought. Funny how inactivity like sitting in front of a keyboard all day could cause the muscles to forget what they'd been meant for in the first place. He tried to finish running the two miles on the treadmill before he dropped.

"How you doing over there?" Skye asked with a bit of a smirk on her face.

"Peachy thanks," he huffed out. "Is there any particular reason you don't belong to a regular gym?"

"Missing ogling the women already, huh?"

"I'm missing beverages mostly," he returned, wiping sweat from his face with the tail of his T-shirt.

"There's water," she said and pointed to a tiny mini-fridge under the stairs.

Josh pushed the Stop button on the machine, waited for it to finish its cycle and then stepped down. The old cooler held nothing but water bottles. He uncapped one and guzzled the contents. But as he stood there something caught his eye. The door to an area no bigger than a broom closet stood open, allowing him to get a look inside. His eyes zeroed in on an ancient metal desk. Above it hung a large paper street map of Seattle with various stickpins strategically placed dotting the points of interest. But the pins were coordinated with colored yarn, which in turn had a photograph of a young teen or child attached to it. He pointed to the makeshift office. "What is this?"

"It's what I like to call my war room," she explained as she took the bottle of water out of his hands and drank generously.

"All these pins represent missing children?"

"Sadly, yes. Some recent, some go back years. But all have one thing in common. They all disappeared without a trace and the cases remain unsolved."

"That's…horrific. Don't they usually form a task force when so many go missing?"

She let out a loud sigh. "You'd think. But in this case the missing come from several different jurisdictions, not Seattle specifically. That itself poses a problem and makes for a lack of continuity between police departments, a lack of a combined effort. And then there's the problem of teen runaways, and yes, including preteen children. Kids *do* run away. Just look at Zoe. She took off apparently because of her mother's boyfriend. Some of these kids have difficulties at home so they're likely to storm out for a variety of reasons, and not want to go back. But the problem compounds itself when the police tend to lump missing teens into one category, mostly chalk up the disappearance to teen rebellion. Once they decide the kids booked simply because they got mad after a fight with mom or dad, or got a burr up their butt, and took off, it's a major problem with the case. You have no one actively looking for those considered runaways. Big gap there.

Kids do take off on their own but they're eventually found or come back. That doesn't account for the ones on that map, the exceptions. The ones that had no reason to take off on their own, the ones where communication likely broke down between agencies, that's why I put them on my map. People like Whitfield count on that. Advantage Whitfield."

"That's reason enough to organize this thing."

"Organize? I'm not sure what you mean. I just don't want these kids forgotten."

"With you, I don't think that's possible." Josh noted the sad look that settled in her eyes so he changed the subject. He pulled her to him, nibbled on her lower lip to work his tongue inside.

She ran her hand up his chest, felt his heart pounding with the effort to cap off the run he'd just finished. "You're awfully sweaty. How much longer do you want to…workout?"

"How much privacy do we have down here?"

Her answer came by tugging off his T-shirt, running her tongue along his bare shoulders, licking at the drops of sweat sticking there. "Maybe you could show me again what I'm supposed to do? I'm a real fast learner, but kind of like training for battle, I believe in—lots of practice."

"Plenty of repetition? Not a bad belief system." When she started to back him up against the wall, he muttered, "Now we're talking."

Hours later, they made a stop at Lena's house to assess the Zoe situation for themselves. It wasn't every day that Skye found herself taken in by a street brat. But that's exactly what had happened.

Curiosity about how she'd been fooled had Skye staring at Zoe as the girl sat across the living room slumped in a chair holding Lena's Kindle Fire in her lap.

"Zoe likes to read. She's rediscovered *Harry Potter and the Sorcerer's Stone*," Lena explained when she saw Skye glaring at the girl.

But Skye could hardly believe it was the same person they'd dropped off the night before because the young male had somehow morphed into a teen girl. Even with her hair cut short like a boy's, Skye should've been able to pick up on the fact that Zeke was a Zoe.

Now that Skye really looked into the huge doe eyes that were way too big for the face, she could see that face had a few too many female traits. For one, it was more rounded than square-shaped. The nose turned up slightly at the end. The eyebrows were more arched. The forehead more vertical. But Skye had to give it to the kid. Zoe had certainly done an excellent job with her disguise.

Dressed in an oversized but clean T-shirt and freshly laundered jeans, the girl looked almost content.

"Are you mad?" Zoe asked, finally taking her attention away from Harry Potter. "Josh said you'd be furious if you found out I lied."

"Why did you?"

"You can't be a girl on the streets without men trying to mess with you!" Zoe bellowed in return. "I had to make sure they thought I was a boy. I chopped off my hair in the restroom at the convenience store after the second day when I almost got raped by two old guys who kept trying to grab me so I'd sleep with them in their box."

Skye tilted her head, studied the uneven layers. Because she knew what it was like on the streets for a female, any age female, she shook her head. "No, I'm not mad. But you could've told me, us, the truth. Did Josh and I look like we were on the verge of doing away with little kids, Zoe?"

Zoe looked away, dropped her gaze to the floor. "Don't send me to a foster home, Skye, please."

Skye met Lena's pleading eyes as well. "We'll work something out."

That made Zoe smile. And then as if thinking of something else, she turned to Josh. "If I start school, do I still get to visit you at Ander All like you promised?"

"You start school you're welcome there anytime. In fact, you keep your grades up and I guarantee we could use that energetic gofer Skye mentioned. How does six bucks an hour sound to work as our tester?"

"Testing games? Sweet!" Zoe exclaimed. "But if I go to school, I want the secrets of how to get from Level 12 to 16."

"In *Mines*?" Josh asked. "Deal. But you have to really try at school."

"Sure," Zoe agreed.

Josh and Skye stayed for supper. And over Lena's fried chicken and mashed potatoes they learned more disturbing details about Zoe's situation at her mother's house. The boyfriend had moved in and within days had set his sights on the teenage girl.

Skye knew it happened all too often. It was just one of the reasons there were so many teen hookers living day to day in a chasm of drugs on the streets. They were sometimes forced out to escape bad situations at home. But it wasn't only that which contributed to their dire circumstances. Sometimes the reality of it all made her sick at her stomach. So she kept her comments brief over dinner. But afterward, while Zoe and Josh loaded the dishwasher and worked at cleanup, Skye pulled Lena into the living room for a chat.

But it was Lena who got things going. "You contact the system and I'll lose her. You know I will. I see you want to in the way you acted at dinner. This is different than any other time you've brought me someone from the streets. I've never turned away a single soul you've brought me, Skye Cree. And they were all a lot older than Zoe Hollister. That girl still has a chance, a future, and I'm willing to give it to her. You have to…"

Skye had heard enough and held up a hand to stop. "I just want to be sure you're certain Zoe really doesn't want to live with her mother? At all?"

"Skye, her mother is a biker chick with a slew of drug problems."

"You know that for a fact?"

"Yes. Zoe and I made a trip over to the address she gave me."

"I don't want you to get played here, Lena. I'm trying to protect you. Do you know what you're getting into with Zoe? You take on the responsibility at her age and you're looking at those difficult high school years you'll have to deal with all over again. Is that really what you want to do…at…this stage of your life when you could be…I don't know…traveling?"

"Go ahead and say it. At my age? I don't want to travel. I have a nice home here. And yes, that's exactly what I want. I lost one son and that ripped my heart out. My other has a busy life away at college in California. He comes home for four days at Christmas. That's it except for a few emails he sends when he feels like it. He has his own life and although I might be his mother, he doesn't seem inclined to stay in touch. I still have the ability to love something, Skye. I don't want to see a girl this young trying to make it on the streets. You send her back with her mother and that's exactly where she'll end up again."

Skye sucked in a breath and let it out. "Okay, okay. I'm on your side already. But do you know what a fight you're in for? Her mother will likely take you to court, biker chick or not, and she'll likely win."

"Then I'll just have to find me a kickass lawyer. Do you know one?"

"The only attorney I know is Doug Jenkins. He knows his stuff. But the man's the antithesis of kickass. In fact, he's more laid-back than that guy in that movie, what was it? Ah, *The Big Lebowski*, minus the long hair and the mismatched clothes."

"That's a shame. I mean I really need a hard-nosed advocate who knows something about kids living on the streets and their awful situations back at home."

Skye knitted her brow as if considering. "Hmm, Doug's certainly a stand-up kind of guy." Skye thought a few minutes more before saying, "You know what?"

"What?"

"He might be laid-back, but Doug is a big believer in kids, any kids, and he loves the underdog. It's worth a shot. He certainly watched over me when it counted and worked a few miracles when it came to my future finances. Without Doug I'd still be flipping burgers at Country Kitchen. Not that there's anything wrong with that."

"Doug sounds like he might be just the man I'm looking for after all. Give him a call, will you? Zoe needs as many believers watching over her as she can get because I'm not sending that child back to live with her mother as long as that boyfriend is still in the house."

CHAPTER SIXTEEN

Susan and Jay Prescott lived in a restored Tudor revival in the Phinney Ridge section of Seattle. Both had good jobs, a mortgage to deal with each month, bills that had to be paid on time, and the occasional marital spats about those everyday issues that went along with any busy household of five.

Susan worked as a paralegal while Jay had been an architect for almost fifteen years. They attended dance recitals, paid for piano lessons, spent their Saturdays at Little League games, along with every other event associated with their kids. Basically, they were the typical American family trying to deal with the stress of ordinary life the best way they knew how.

They had two other kids besides Erin, one boy, one girl. But Erin was their oldest. Susan and Jay Prescott had decided to send Erin to the private preparatory academy after she'd gotten in trouble in her spring semester of middle school for cutting class. Erin had started trying to impress the wrong crowd. At least her parents believed that since their daughter had shown a rebellious streak in the past. In order to nip that kind of behavior in the bud, Susan and Jay thought the change of scenery at the more disciplined Catholic school would keep Erin on the straight and narrow and therefore out of trouble.

They hadn't counted on the likes of Brandon Hiller entering their daughter's little world. But then what parent wanted to consider that their child might one day decide to ditch school—even if that child had been heading someplace she wasn't supposed to—only to have the misfortune of crossing paths with a rapist? Little did they know rapist was Hiller's side career and that he'd already promoted himself to killer?

Both Jay and Susan knew they were lucky to have Erin back at all. Like any parent they watched the news and were aware of the dangers out there. So they were fortunate Skye Cree had somehow been able to locate and rescue their daughter so soon after she'd been taken. Otherwise...

Jay and Susan wanted to do something to show their gratitude.

As much as Skye understood that, she didn't like the idea of meeting with the parents. Parents invariably asked questions. Number one and foremost on their minds, they wanted to know how she'd been able to stumble upon their daughter. And wasn't that the niggling little bugger she couldn't afford to divulge? In the past, Ali Crandon's parents had wanted specifics, so had Hailey Strickland's. Skye could share her determination, her obsessive nature, even that feeling that compelled her to go out every night in search of the missing. But anything beyond that like dreams that came in the dark of night, voices she couldn't get rid of, or a wolf no one but she could see had to be held back.

They wouldn't have believed her anyway.

And now, after being ushered into the Prescott's living room, after peeling off her coat and handing it to Susan Prescott, her eyes settled on Joshua Sebastian Ander. Skye couldn't help it, she gaped, open mouth and all. The man sat comfortably on the sofa, as if he owned the place, with a cup of tea in one hand and, if she wasn't mistaken, a homemade sugar cookie in the other.

They hadn't seen each other in two days. Skye had spent that time steeped in details, pouring over the list of girls reported missing within a hundred-mile radius of

Seattle while Josh had been bogged down in the grind of running a multi-million-dollar company.

They hadn't exactly found common ground yet. After all, they needn't be joined at the hip just because they'd slept together. But seeing Josh at the Prescotts had her wondering what was going on. "What is he doing here?"

Josh's face creased into a smile when Susan answered for him. "Josh called to tell us about the idea you both had. We think it's not only brilliant but doable so when you agreed to meet with us, we invited him along, too. We want to help the cause anyway we can—that means monetarily as well as helping get things going."

"The cause?" Skye asked and shot Josh a lethal glare. Her first impulse was to storm out, get the hell out of there. She didn't like being kept in the dark. Not only that, she felt cornered, trapped. Since she had no idea what Susan was talking about and didn't want to cause a scene, Skye simply went with a benign comment. "Ah, that is good news."

Josh knew it was unfair to blindside Skye like this. But he believed in her even when the woman didn't always believe in herself. He'd wanted to be here—and now that he was, he'd just have to deal with her temper. The extra perk was a godsend. Skye Cree wore a snug-fitting, flowing white dress that showed off her cinnamon skin which of course included a look at her long legs. She'd added high heels with straps that wrapped around her ankles. The shoes made him want to start nibbling at her toes and work his way up. She had feathery-like dangles hanging from her ears that glittered all the way down to her shoulders. The woman absolutely took his breath away.

When he realized Jay Prescott was in the middle of a dialogue, Josh had to slide his fantasies into another drawer to deal with later.

"After what you did for our daughter, we wanted to show you how grateful we were. We'd already talked to Detective Drummond about offering you a monetary reward but he explained to us you wouldn't take it. Then when Josh called us with your idea about starting a private foundation to help find missing kids here in Seattle, we didn't have to think twice about it before we realized it was a fantastic way to pay you back and help other kidnapped children at the same time."

Josh cleared his throat, turned his focus to Skye. It was time he entered the fray. "Any donations would be used to help you with expenses as you continue to have the same kind of success in the future that you've had in the past locating children like Ali and Hailey and now Erin. We want to make sure that goes on."

Jay took it from there. "I've asked a number of my clients from work to donate money to the foundation already. They jumped at the opportunity to get in on the ground floor of such an enterprise, one that would take an active role in helping you find the missing, kids that have been kidnapped by the likes of Hiller, especially when Skye Cree is personally involved in the foundation's day-to-day operation. I already have pledges in excess of twenty thousand dollars."

Skye put her hands on her hips, ready for battle. "Let me get this straight. Your donors want to give this so-called foundation twenty grand to pay expenses to do what I already do on my own every single night anyway?"

"That's right. We could name it The Skye Cree…"

"No," Skye said emphatically, her voice steely in its resolve. "I'm only going to say this one time. I do not want anything named after me. That's non-negotiable. The only way I'll be involved in this thing at all is if you call it something else."

Prepared for that pigheadedness he'd seen so often before, Josh calmly set his teacup in its saucer and offered, "How about calling it The Artemis Foundation then?" When he noted the puzzled look on Skye's face, he went on, "Artemis, Greek goddess of the hunt, adored for her devotion to animals, protector of children and the vulnerable."

"You're kidding?" Skye tossed back, ready to argue with that description. That is, until she looked over at the Prescotts who were beaming from ear to ear. Their dazzling smiles told her they were voting in Josh's favor on this half-baked idea. Outnumbered three to one, Skye retorted, "Now wait a minute...that's a corny name and this is moving way too fast...I'm not ready to have a foundation..."

But Susan didn't let her finish. "Perfect assessment of our Skye, I especially like the protector of children," Susan said, putting an arm around Skye's shoulder just as a mother might do. "That's exactly what you are." Susan put her own hand over her heart. "This mother is so thankful. Because of you, I have my daughter back. She'll need counseling of course but that's minor compared to...getting her back alive. I want you to do this for other children, Skye. Please. For me. For Jay. For Erin and the others out there who need your help."

And just in case Skye wanted to debate further, Josh was ready to enhance his position. "In mythology Artemis was often depicted carrying a bow and arrow. The hunter, Artemis could be the logo. I'll design it."

"Great," Jay decided. "I'll work up the non-profit setup and tax exemption angle with the federal government so we'll have all the legal stuff clearly defined and covered."

"Is this really happening?" Skye asked, obviously uneasy with the high profile aspect of it all. "I feel like I've stepped through the looking glass. I really don't want...this."

But Josh bulldozed over any of her objections to point out, "It's a great way to make sure the work you do is funded so there's never a chance a kid might fall through the cracks. You wouldn't want that to ever happen, would you?"

"Of course not, but..."

"Then it's settled," Jay stated quickly. "Let's open a bottle of champagne to celebrate."

While he disappeared to get champagne, Skye asked Susan, "How is Erin?"

"They released her yesterday from the hospital. She and my other two children have gone to spend the rest of the week with their grandparents on their farm in Eastern Washington. We're headed there right after this meeting. Jay and I are taking time off from work until we see that she's okay. I don't know what you said to her in the hospital but…it helped. Since then she's determined to be just like Skye." Susan smiled.

"You let me know if she ever needs to talk."

"I'm sure she will," Susan said. "But right now, she's trying to recover both physically as well as mentally."

"Believe me, I know," Skye said, reaching out to take Susan's hand.

Later behind the wheel of her Subaru as she headed over the Aurora Bridge and back to her apartment, Skye turned to Josh and commented, "That might be the sneakiest thing I've ever seen anyone do. But then I don't suppose I really know you all that well. Trusting one minute, stab me in the back the next."

"Come on. You know this is a great way to continue doing the work you do and get help from the citizens of Seattle," Josh said, resting his hand over hers as it gripped the gear shift. "And getting to know each other better will come over time. But as stubborn as you are I decided I needed to be a helluva lot more clever and crafty to get around your obstinate streak."

"Because you of all people knew how I'd feel and yet…you did it anyway."

"Skye, you're good at what you do—better than anyone I've ever seen. Who else finds three missing girls?"

At least he wasn't asking how she did it. Yet. "When did you cook up all this foundation stuff?"

"You make it sound like a scam. It's not. I got to thinking about it the first day I found out about the three-for-three saves. Skye Cree walks the Seattle streets at night, patrols them really for the good of its citizens. And I should know because I'm one of those citizens who benefited firsthand. She's like a cop but isn't. She doesn't get paid for what she does which is saving people. She's committed to finding kids who've been abducted and taken, snatched right out of their safety zones. She should have resources at her disposal, financial backing to get the job done on a grander scale. People want to get involved but they don't know how. They want to help, Skye, but don't know how to do it. They can't exactly go out every night like you do. But they still want to be a part of it. Donations to the cause are the answer."

"Money," she harrumphed and added, "So you're sitting on the Board of Directors. You, Jay and Susan Prescott and Ali Crandon's parents are welcome to use the fancy titles. One of you can take care of the money that comes in, because I don't want to deal with that. I don't want to be some figurehead—"

"It isn't why you do it. I get that and believe it or not, they do, too. Jay volunteered to keep track of the money, at least initially. Bill Strickland, Hailey's father is an accountant. He's agreed to act as treasurer down the road. These parents are indebted to you, Skye, and want you to have the financial help to find as many as you can, anyway you can."

"You really think so?"

"I know so."

She sighed with the realization things were about to change and probably not for the better. But she didn't intend to stand in the way of change if it could help find a single missing kid. "I'm not wearing a suit."

"Why would you want to put on a suit? That dress by the way is kickass. You look fantastic. The heels are a great touch. So why would you need to wear a suit?"

"Because that's what people expect of someone who runs a foundation…"

"I'm the owner of my own company, Skye, and I'm rarely forced to wear a suit."

"We'll probably have difficulty getting donors."

Josh grinned, realizing the white flag of surrender from the other side signifying he'd won the skirmish. "I disagree. There are parents out there who've discovered a nasty side to Seattle. I think they'll want to do something about it."

She tapped the steering wheel as she drove. "Were you aware when you got this going that our state was the first in the nation to criminalize sex trafficking?"

"I didn't know that. See, you're the right person to do this, Skye. I know you don't like publicity or recognition but this needs to be dealt with by someone…"

"Who's lived it?" Skye finished his thought. "I suppose you're right, although I'm uncomfortable in the spotlight. The focus needs to be on finding the victims, saving as many of these kids as possible from the sex trade, putting an end to the trafficking aspect."

"There you go."

"By the way, how the hell did you get out to the Prescott's house in Phinney Ridge anyway? I didn't see your car when I pulled up. You're on foot."

"There's this thing called public transportation."

Skye snorted. "Come on get real. I'm serious. How'd you get out to their place?"

"I took a cab hoping you'd be in a better frame of mind after we ganged up on you and I lowered the boom with the news when they told you about the foundation idea. But hey, I've used public transportation before."

"Sure you have."

"Of course I have. I didn't always have my brilliant mind to fall back on. I had to develop a highly popular game before I made a dime. I lived in a friend's basement for six months tweaking the graphics. Why is it you give me such a hard time about my…success, my loft?"

Skye snickered. "Wait until you see my tiny cracker box and then we'll talk."

"Okay, let's stop by now. I've wanted to see your place since that Saturday morning I dropped in and you were so pissed off at me. We'll pick up a few of your things while we're there, toothbrush, a change of clothes. We could even spend the night there."

Skye sighed. "Sure, why not? You might as well see how the other half lives. Just don't expect too much."

She found a place to park the Subaru on the street and walked a block to the front door of her four-story building. Caught up in the give and take of the conversation about the foundation, neither one noticed someone had followed them.

Skye unlocked the door of her walk-up and stepped inside. Flicking the wall switch, light flooded the one room.

She watched self-consciously as Josh looked around, considered her things, cringing a little at the way he studied the shabby chic furniture that wasn't fit to occupy the sidewalk outside his building let alone his posh loft.

Or the way he looked at her slice of kitchen that wasn't really a kitchen at all but more like the tiny galley on a boat. It didn't even have a window over the sink to gaze out of while doing dishes.

Or the way his eyes landed on her books and the few items she considered her treasures, like her colorful Fiestaware displayed on the open shelves for all to see because she didn't have regular cabinets.

Or her mother's stained-glass work that her aunt Ginny had somehow managed to save and pass on to her without too much of a fuss.

Each of these bits and pieces of her life Skye felt reflected the links to the past, her childhood. Her mementos revealed her quirky persona, her wide-ranging tastes in color, which she'd inherited from her mother. Each of her cherished possessions was its own little memory. They represented a special event or celebration she'd had with her mom and dad. Or times when she'd shopped and enjoyed the outing, searching for that terrific bargain or that perfect piece, the joy of selecting and adding knick-knacks here and there to what she already owned.

Despite that, she chewed on her thumb, the whole time watching as Josh continued to study and judge her things. Why wasn't he saying anything?

Josh took in the tiny five-hundred-square-foot studio. Not an inch of the room remained available. The pathway from the front door looped its way around the small sofa and bed like a rallying point.

She'd stuffed everything she could into the space. In fact, it was wall–to-wall furniture. Although the condo was crammed, it was also colorful, charming, and eclectic. A couple of homemade quilts covered the old iron bed. More than a dozen intricate stained-glass designs decorated three of the four walls.

And then there were plants of all kinds that blocked part of a sliding glass door so they could get whatever light came through the vertical blinds. He assumed the door led outside to her balcony, and a place designated to hold whatever leftover plants she couldn't get to grow inside. Along with all of her other talents, it seemed Skye had a green thumb.

When he heard what he thought were bells tinkling together, he cocked his head to listen and realized the sound came from beyond that glass door. Wind chimes, he realized—and smiled at the whimsical touch. This was the side of the woman he'd been trying to pinpoint, the side that told him she was anything but tough as nails twenty-four-seven.

After he took a little too long to comment though, Skye was just about ready to rip into him and tell him what exactly he could do with his opinion, when Josh finally spoke up.

"Is there anything you don't grow? What is this?" he asked, rubbing a leaf between his finger and thumb. It looked like some sort of gigantic ivy, spreading out everywhere; at least he thought that's what it was. The plant came up to his chest. Did household ivy even grow to such heights?

"I…I like to grow things. That was my mother's marble queen ivy. She got it as a wedding present. It was one of the few things of hers my Aunt Ginny let me keep." Skye looked around the packed room and had to admit how stuffed to the gills the place was. "I know it's silly and ridiculous to try and grow plants in such a tiny space…but…both my parents loved to garden. And this is all I've got."

Unbelievably moved at knowing she'd had such a difficult time holding on to the simple things such as a plant belonging to her mother, his heart felt like it turned over in his chest. "It isn't…ridiculous…at all. Your plants are thriving. Like so many other things, you're obviously good at it. What else do you grow?"

"Herbs mostly, for cooking. Things like rosemary, sage, basil, some oregano for sauces, I grow outside on the balcony. You know the usual."

He chuckled. "Sure, the usual. The Fiestaware brightens up your kitchen. Did you make those slipcovers?" he asked, running his hands over the fabric on the sofa.

"I did. Lena lets me use her sewing machine."

"You've got a domestic side to you, Skye." And he never would've believed that if he hadn't seen it for himself. "Who did the stained glass?"

"They belonged to my mother. A friend of the family salvaged them for me before they could be tossed out. My mother was an artist."

"A good one, it seems. What was her name?" He suddenly wanted to know everything about the mystery that was Skye Cree. The woman's depth of talents simply fascinated him.

"Jodi. Jodi Cree. For a while she owned her own ceramics shop in an old brick building over on Fairfax."

"So that's where you get your artistic side."

"I don't have an artistic side."

"Sure you do. Making slipcovers, growing things, an eye for color. Someone loves their antiques. Nice Wheatland."

"Wheatland?"

"That bed isn't a replica. I'd say circa 1910. It's worth about a grand, Skye."

"You're kidding? It cost me twenty bucks."

He ran his hand over the little table where she ate. "This cherrywood drop-leaf is in mint condition. You have excellent taste in furniture."

"I was about to tell you to stuff it."

His arms went around her waist. "You really need to drop the attitude." He backed her up against the bed and flopped down on top of her when she collapsed on the mattress. "I've always wanted to make love on a Wheatland."

"You have not."

"How do you know?"

"Because I know."

"Skye Cree doesn't know everything," he pointed out as he nibbled her throat.

"I don't?"

"You didn't know I purposefully got you up here so I could get you out of that dress, did you? Your place had the nearest bed where I could get you out of your clothes." He started working the outfit off her shoulders, little nips and bites with tongue and teeth.

She giggled and tilted her head down to meet his eyes. "You know I'm still upset with you and you're trying to distract me."

"I'm trying to seduce you. How'm I doing?"

"Mmm, you need to try harder. After all, I'm not a woman to be trifled with."

"I would never trifle. I might cavort. On second thought, we should both cavort."

When he heard her giggle again, he pressed his lips to hers. He rolled to reverse their positions so he could lower the zipper in the back. He pushed the dress the rest of the way down, and the strapless bra came with it, exposing her breasts.

He rolled again so his body covered hers, dragged her arms above her head and started a slow deliberate assault of senses. There was the soft stroking along skin, the savoring of each tender spot he found where she responded the most. He used lips and tongue to feast on each nipple and curve before moving lower where the flare of her hips enticed him all the way in. Sampling and teasing, he felt her tremors as they built into aftershocks, felt the quiver in her belly when she came again.

Toeing off his shoes and socks, he shed pants and shirt as clothing littered the small space of floor. He pushed her back into pillows and plundered again until she was breathless. Arching her back, she rose up and met him, slide for glorious slide. She wrapped around him while nails dug into his back, urging him on. In rippling need, he took them both up and over—and together they dropped off the cliff to soar higher—and higher still.

CHAPTER SEVENTEEN

Since his release six years earlier from Walla Walla, Ronny Wayne Whitfield had gotten a whole lot smarter. Just because he'd been caught in the trap once didn't mean he was stupid. Because he had to consider how much more he'd gotten away with that no one knew about, he slept just fine at night knowing his hands were clean. He'd never get caught in the act ever again. He couldn't. They couldn't touch him as long as he wasn't the one who did the dirty work. So far, he'd kept that pledge and made it his mantra. He'd found a way, a clever way, to get others to do his bidding. Not only that but he had a lucrative business that said he'd been successful at it. Ronny had perfected his network so much from Vancouver to Tijuana that he pretty much ruled the West Coast.

No one offered a better product than ol' Ronny Wayne. He concentrated on the very young, those girls between the ages of eleven and fifteen were his meat and potatoes. He kept ten like-minded individuals on his payroll at all times, people he'd met during his prison stint, people he could trust personally or those that came highly recommended to him by close associates. For five years now they'd been able to maintain a "professional" organization that others envied.

It was a simple operation really.

Ronny received online orders from all over the world. He sent his associates out to fill those orders. In the meantime, he and his friends got to have their fun and when they were done, the product albeit slightly used, was then shipped out to their destinations, some as far away as Bosnia and Thailand. But since South America was a hot spot right now for trade, business was booming.

Since he'd left Walla Walla in his rearview mirror, he'd learned to make the best use of the Internet. Chat rooms as well as all the social media outlets were his best tools. In fact, he was almost a guru when it came to establishing phony online personas that were adept at luring young girls into innocent conversation. Pretending to be their own age, he could usually lend a sympathetic ear about the pressures of turning in homework, or how putting up with so many parental rules was unfair. He'd get them to talk about a boyfriend if they had one or if they didn't glean information he could use for later. That method led to find out whether or not they were happy at home, and if they were willing to meet with him. Ronny seemed to possess an innate charm that translated well to attracting young girls. But then his associates weren't bad either. As good as they were though they didn't have Ronny Wayne's style or his motivation. That's why it was left to him to oversee the entire operation. He usually found plenty of girls online who were unhappy at home about some stupid little teenage girl thing. He'd play on that, play it up, and then once he got her to trust him, he'd start talking about meeting her face-to-face in order to offer an even better shoulder to cry on. Of course, that was only one lure he used. There were others depending on the circumstances. He also had contacts that liked to find their own favorite commodity, a certain type of product, and stick to it.

Ronny had his hands in marketing, sales, and advertising, but he had to admit his favorite was the testing, testing the product before shipping and delivery was the icing on the cake.

Expenses weren't a problem. His aunt and uncle let him live in a cabin at the edge of a wooded area that backed up to his own stream. He had his own satellite dish, and his own network for distributing the videos that were necessary to solicit business. His remote location worked because he'd been left alone by the authorities. His last known address was on file in some state database that indicated he lived in a rundown trailer. He chuckled at that. If you were clever enough you could fool even the cops.

When his second-in-command came through the door, he alone could see the irony. If being clever didn't get the job done, then enough cash surely did.

"Talbot."

"Whitfield. You have my money?"

"Right here." Ronny pushed a fat, zippered bank bag across the desk. "But I want assurance that the docks will be clear and the manifest will pass customs."

"Yeah, yeah. You got it. Have I ever let you down?"

Whitfield stared at the cop, who was starting to go gray at the temples. Four years earlier Ronny had discovered Talbot's fondness for little girls in a chat room. From there, he had been blackmailing the fifteen-year veteran detective to make sure the cargo ships they used for transporting the girls could be loaded and sent on their way without a hitch from the authorities. So far it had worked like a charm. "There's always a first time."

"You just keep a tight rein on that loose cannon Hiller. The grapevine tells me the crime scene investigator in Seattle found the guy's fingerprints all over the warehouse where Skye Cree managed to free the Prescott girl. That makes three she's managed to steal from you. Having Hiller directly involved in an active case isn't part of the deal. And there's nothing I can do about keeping this one low key, so don't even ask. It's a different jurisdiction. You keep a watch on that sick bastard, Whitfield, or I'll have to—"

"To what?" Ronny pulled open a desk drawer. "That cash in your hand isn't the only perk you're getting out of this deal." Ronny threw a stack of photos on the desk and cautioned, "Unless you want your wife to see these in her mailbox tomorrow morning, or your chief to get an email with several attachments from an anonymous source, I'd stuff the threats if I were you."

"Fine, fine, but Hiller is a problem. If you don't take care of him, he's going to blow this thing wide open. I'm telling you, he's a hot item right now. That's all I'm saying."

Ronny had already decided that Hiller was a good bet for the missing Donofrio girl, too. But he said nothing to Talbot about that. He didn't tolerate any of his associates holding out. Ever. Especially someone so new to his operation. That's exactly what he thought Hiller had done. The man hadn't been able to account for his whereabouts or his time with any believability. Ronny knew a liar when he saw one. And because of that Ronny Wayne readily agreed to deal with the matter, personally.

After all, Ronny Wayne Whitfield wasn't the same man who'd picked up a twelve-year-old Skye Cree that day in the park. Now, he was a businessman who ran his own multi-million-dollar enterprise that regularly brought a crapload of money into the local economy. He wasn't about to let the likes of Hiller put a kink in his well-oiled machine.

They always met up at the warehouse district near the port, mainly because that's where most of the action took place. Over the course of the last several months though, Brandon had discovered something about himself. He didn't really like sharing the bounty.

He'd originally met Whitfield in an online chat room. Once the two men had established a trust that only comes from having served time in prison, once they'd checked out each other's history and could rely on that information as solid, they moved on to their shared interest and ultimately their mutual goal. Whitfield had offered him the job of a lifetime. Hiller would be on the lookout and solicit "new girls" to fill the "product" pipeline, all the while getting to sample the wares and Whitfield would give him a cut of the take when the product sold and shipped.

For five months it had worked. But now as Hiller pulled his van into the bumpy asphalt parking lot a few minutes early for his meeting with the others, Hiller was more than a little jumpy. He'd known for several days that Whitfield hadn't believed his story about where and how he'd spent his time the night Jenna Donofrio went missing.

Brandon came to a stop and shoved the gear into Park. He realized he was in trouble the moment he looked up and saw the boss himself waiting for him outside the doorway.

In the five months since he'd hooked up with this outfit, one thing was certain. Whitfield almost never took care of anything himself. That's what the lackeys were for. But when Whitfield did decide to get involved with settling disputes, it never ended well. Because Hiller was one of those lackeys, a funny feeling crawled up his spine.

Even from where he sat behind the wheel of his van, Hiller could tell Whitfield was pissed. When he spotted one of the other men move to take up a position next to the boss, Hiller panicked. He threw the van into Reverse, hit the gas and screeched backward out of the lot.

Hiller slid the gear into Drive and floored the accelerator. All the while Whitfield and his men ran after the van.

In a quick sweep, Hiller saw all three men scurry to a black luxury SUV and then heard the screech of tires as the trio peeled out after him.

The chase was on as Hiller quickly took a right on Surrey before taking a left on Ninth. Because he'd grown up here, he knew every roadway, every back alleyway, and every trick to maneuvering through the traffic-clogged streets.

It took all that and more to shake the determined men inside the Mercedes M-class that tried to catch him. Good thing he had a head start. He avoided the Magnolia Bridge altogether, kept to Fifteenth Avenue at speeds that reached well past eighty-five.

As the businesses whirled past him in a blur, he made a right into where more industrial buildings sat mostly vacant at this time of night until he took a side street to Taylor. At Taylor, he fishtailed once before circling back through a parking lot, jumped the curb to head southeast in the opposite direction on Elliott Avenue. Once he got to the split, he gunned the van taking Mercer east all the way to the 99. Once on the 99 he headed due south.

It was then and only then that he allowed himself a glance up and studied the rearview mirror, knew he was home free. Fancy driving had allowed Hiller to leave Ronny Wayne Whitfield and his henchmen in the dust. This time. Now he just had to figure out how he intended to avoid the man from here on out.

CHAPTER EIGHTEEN

Josh had to accept the fact that Skye felt compelled to go out every night to roam the streets. It wasn't something he was keen about despite what he'd said. Having the woman he cared about put herself in harm's way every night took some getting used to. So he supported her effort and understood the why of it. He wished he could go with her. But he couldn't patrol Seattle until the wee hours of the morning and run his company during the day on four hours of sleep.

Besides, the woman had a rock-hard head when it came to discussing anything that hinted she'd make a change to her routine. Even the mention of taking her out of her element simply pissed her off. She'd already reminded him no less than a dozen times she'd been doing this for several years without any input from him.

While that might've been true, it didn't make watching her sail out the door every night and into some of the meanest neighborhoods Seattle had to offer any less worrisome.

Some nights all he did was toss and turn, restless, edgy, stressing every minute she was out there alone. But he'd seen her in action firsthand and had to believe she could handle herself because thinking otherwise would get him exactly squat.

Because arguing with Skye Cree was a waste of time and energy.

After some discussion though, he *had* gotten her to agree to cut back on her time so that she'd leave the loft at around nine p.m. and be back by three and in bed with him. It wasn't an ideal arrangement by any means, but Josh considered it a small victory she had agreed to it at all.

They took turns sleeping at each other's places. And every day they made slow and steady progress toward building trust and getting to know each other a little better. There were still things she held back. He didn't worry about it too much. At times he thought he was on the verge of getting her to open up only to get right to the brink and before he knew what was happening, she'd shut down again. He supposed it was her nature. Add in the fact she hadn't had anyone since her parents to talk to on a deep, emotional level and he could understand why she kept her distance.

That's one of the reasons they made the most of every minute they got to spend together.

Saturday mornings and getting to sleep late went hand in hand. But when you hadn't really gotten off to sleep until four a.m., it was a must. Then when your stomach wouldn't stop rumbling with hunger, it was time to get up and refuel, take care of the basics.

"I'm starving," Skye muttered still half asleep.

He smoothed back her hair from her face and said, "How about you snuggle back down, get some more shuteye while I run out and get us some breakfast burritos from Juan's down on the corner. How does that sound?"

"It sounds wonderful."

"It does. Because no one makes big, fat, breakfast burritos with everything on them better than Juan's. Plus, I can call in the order before I leave and they'll have it ready for pickup."

"Juan's should really consider adding delivery."

Looking over at her, he couldn't resist it and ran a hand down her thigh. "How about in exchange for picking up breakfast, we spend the rest of the day snuggled between the sheets. Not leave the house at all for any reason."

"Hmm, burrow for a burrito. I could get on board with that. You make the run to Juan's, I'll start the coffee. How's that?"

As Josh started to throw on a shirt and jeans, she added, "I want the sunrise special with guacamole. And plenty of salsa. Don't forget the salsa."

He slipped on his tennis shoes, grabbed up his keys off the nightstand. "Be back in a flash," he added as he walked out of the bedroom and was gone.

She heard the elevator ding open and close behind him and wondered if she had time for a quick shower. Reluctantly she threw back the covers, crawled out of the cocoon, and headed into the closest thing to a rainforest she'd ever get to see. She didn't understand how anyone could spend a scant five minutes in that shower and not want to set up camp. But she'd give it her best shot. She played with the buttons on the panel to set the water temp a tad hotter. As Pearl Jam battered the senses through the speakers, she closed her eyes and did her best to imagine standing naked under a waterfall in a green and balmy rainforest.

Michelle Reardon waited until she saw Josh get into his Fusion hybrid and leave the parking garage. Once she watched the car disappear out of sight, she took out the key to Josh's building she'd pilfered from Annabelle just two short days before the woman's death, and made her way to the elevator, pushed the button for the penthouse.

On the ride up, Michelle formulated her plan of action. If the bitch was upstairs in Josh's bed—and she was pretty sure Skye was there—Michelle would take out Skye Cree the same way she'd dealt with Annabelle. How dare the slut attach herself so quickly to Josh Ander after everything she and Josh had been to each other since last

Thanksgiving? With Annabelle out of the picture, the two of them had been free to share their feelings and innermost thoughts as well as sex. Michelle knew sex was a powerful bond men couldn't resist. As long as she gave Josh hot and sweaty sex, he would be at her beck and call. At least that had been true before the whore scum had shown up.

Michelle intended to make Skye Cree pay for that. Making a move on Josh had been a major blunder on Skye's part. And the stupid man had fallen for it. Stupid man would have to be dealt with as well, Michelle decided as she stepped off the car and into the open area of the loft. The moment she stepped into the entryway, she knew instantly Josh had been screwing the black-haired bitch. The smell of sex emanated all the way from the bedroom. Seething, Michelle made a decision. She'd have to take more drastic measures than she had with the timid, mousy-haired Annabelle.

Having made up her mind, she tromped into the kitchen to get the knife she'd need.

Skye had just finished drying off when she thought she heard the floor creak out in the hallway. She hung the towel on the rack, checked out her image in the mirror and decided to put off turning on the blow dryer to deal with the long-drawn-out process of drying her massive hair until after she got dressed. So she headed into the bedroom to pull on a pair of yoga pants and a top. But she hadn't even reached the dresser when she heard a noise beyond the bedroom door as far away as the kitchen.

Since her shower had taken all of ten minutes, she wondered how Josh had gotten back so quick from Juan's when the place was usually packed this time of the morning, especially on a weekend.

When the sound became more pronounced, when she heard the opening and closing of what sounded like drawers in the kitchen, Skye decided to check it out.

Before she'd even opened the bedroom door though, Skye heard Kiya's growl in warning along with that voice inside her head that all but screamed out a threat—nearby.

Skye threw back the bedroom door, expecting to see a bold, daylight burglar. Instead she spotted the cute blonde Michelle Reardon making her way from the kitchen into Josh's living room, an eight-inch carving knife gripped in her fist.

The two women locked eyes.

"You sure you want to start this because I'll take that big-assed knife away from you and kick your bony tail end all the way back across Lake Washington," Skye cautioned. "How the hell did you get in here?"

"I used my key. *My key*," Michelle repeated. "Doesn't that tell you anything?"

"Yeah, it tells me you're one part liar and another part thief. Josh never gave you a key. If he had he'd have asked for it back that day out on the sidewalk when he told you to get lost. Apparently Blondie, you're as dense as a stump."

"You stay away from Josh Ander. He belongs to me!"

"Uh, really? I must've missed that part. I'm pretty sure I was standing three feet away when I heard him kick your ass to the curb." But the look on the blonde's face told Skye the woman might not be playing with a full deck. She'd seen that look on the streets in the eyes of some of the homeless women who suffered from dementia. But Skye didn't think Michelle was suffering so much from dementia as much as delusions, big ones.

"You did no such thing. Josh was in a mood, a snit. That's all it was. He gets that way from time to time. If you'd been with him longer than two weeks, you'd know about his dark side."

"Josh has a dark side? Maybe you should clarify that for me."

"I think he did something to Annabelle, made it look like a heart attack. The authorities let him get away with it."

Oh Josh, thought Skye, you've been dealing with an unhinged woman for months and didn't even know it. But Skye kept her face bland when she demanded, "How do you know it wasn't a heart attack? Maybe Annabelle's heart just gave out."

When the woman just stood there, Skye figured she needed to get Michelle talking by any method that worked. "People have heart murmurs, weak hearts run in families, it can be genetic. Maybe Annabelle had rheumatic fever when she was a kid. That weakens the heart muscle some. Any number of things could've happened to her. Why don't you tell me what you think Josh did to her…exactly."

Stony silence.

Okay, thought Skye, she'd already surmised Michelle's ulterior motive. She needed to ruffle a few of the woman's unhinged feathers. "So how long before Annabelle died did you want Josh for yourself? Did Annabelle know you had a thing for her husband? How did she feel about a friend jonesing for her hubby?"

Just as she hoped would happen, she hit Michelle's crazy button. "Shut up! You stupid bitch, shut up! You have no idea what you're talking about. Josh wanted to be with me. We had to get rid of Annabelle because she was in the way of us being together."

"What the fuck are you talking about?" Josh yelled from the other side of the room. He stood frozen just inside the entry, holding a sack which Skye assumed held the breakfast feast he'd gone out to get. "What the fuck did you do to Annabelle?"

Michelle started tugging on her hair with one hand, wrapping it around her own fingers while she still clutched the knife in the other. "I…I…did it for us."

Josh threw the bag on the hall table and advanced on Michelle. "Us? There was never any us. You were supposed to be Annabelle's friend, Michelle. You hung out with both of us. From the moment Annabelle met you in the bookstore, a couple of months after we got married, she felt sorry for you. That's why she always invited you over here."

"I...I...no, no...that isn't right. It wasn't that way at all. We watched movies together. We popped popcorn. You wanted to be with me, not Annabelle."

"I was fucking nice to you because you were a friend of Annabelle's! Nothing more than that! Answer me, Michelle, what did you to Annabelle?"

Michelle's eyes glazed over even more than they had been. "I...I might've given her a few sleeping pills before giving her...a shot. I shot her up with succinylcholine. I used to be a nurse."

"Succinylcholine? That paralyzes," Skye stated.

But it was the wrong voice for Michelle to hear right at that particular moment. At the sound of Skye's words, Michelle went into a rage, moving on Skye with all the finesse of Norman Bates's mommy in *Psycho*, the knife raised to do the most damage.

It all happened in under a minute.

Skye pivoted, blocked the blade and took out Michelle's legs from under her. The woman did indeed land on her bony ass.

By that time Josh had rushed over, planted his shoe on the wrist that held the knife. He reached down, jerked it out of Michelle's grip. "Call the cops," Josh directed. "I want this piece of shit out of my house and locked the hell away for good."

"Already on it," Skye told him as she punched in Harry's number.

"Didn't they do an autopsy?" Harry Drummond wondered several hours later after joining Skye and Josh at the kitchen table where they sat, drinking coffee. So far, he'd taken them both through Michelle's arrest and interrogation, replayed what the lead investigator, Brad Jones, had told him about the woman's statements once they'd gotten her into a downtown interview room. As far as Harry knew, the woman was still confessing and acting Baby-Jane-Hudson-crazy.

"There was, but I don't know if they did a toxicology screen. They just called me a couple of days after she died and told me her heart had given out, stopped." Josh snapped his fingers. "And just like that she was gone."

"Doesn't sound like they submitted toxicology tests for analysis. But you're welcome to contact Brad to get the specifics of your wife's case, Mr. Ander. This belongs to Brad now. I do know succinylcholine has been known to mask a heart attack so you might want to prepare yourself for an exhumation of the body. After the statements this Reardon woman's made so far, if this were my case, that's what I'd do, an exhumation to be certain."

Harry picked up his mug, sipped the liquid inside. "I do know this much. Michelle told the lead investigator after they got her to the station that she befriended Annabelle that day in the bookstore because she'd seen you and decided she liked what she saw. In her warped mind, the best way to get to you was to go through Annabelle."

"Get out," Skye exclaimed. But when she looked over and saw that Josh had tears in his eyes she reached over, squeezed his hand. "I'm so sorry, Josh. But at least you know now Michelle murdered Annabelle and why."

"Well, look kids, it's been a blast but I still have a little girl to find. If I were you I'd let Brad finish interviewing Reardon, let him wade through a ton of paperwork after the interrogation and confession is complete before following up. But I'd say a clever defense attorney will probably go for insanity."

"Damn it," Josh said, still holding his head in his hands.

"Yeah. Ain't society grand?" Harry said before disappearing through the door of the kitchen.

After Harry left, Josh continued to sit and stare into his cup and mull over the last two years. "Annabelle was nice to her," Josh muttered. "I couldn't count how many times she invited Michelle over here for dinner, and yeah, to watch movies. The woman hung around like a third wheel. I didn't think a thing about it. I should have."

"Stop it. Maybe all those dinners weren't Annabelle's idea. Think about it. Michelle probably did the 'oh poor me I don't have anything planned tonight routine.' More than likely played on your wife's sympathy. You said it yourself, Annabelle felt sorry for Michelle. The woman obviously used that to her advantage," Skye offered. "Just out of curiosity…and you're under no obligation to come clean here but…"

"What?"

"How long exactly did it take for you and Michelle to…hook up after…?"

Josh swallowed hard and looked away. "Eight months. She showed up one night after I'd finished off a bottle of wine by myself. That's no excuse I know but…you were right the other day when you said I had a problem with alcohol." He ran both hands through his hair. "Plus, I'd been feeling sorry for myself. At times, I still do. Michelle is the reason I was in that damned alleyway that night."

"Ah."

"I was avoiding going back inside. Right before that she'd followed me into the men's room. It pissed me off. I got out of there and left her standing with her dress undone, offering herself up to me in the bathroom. I didn't want to go back to the table, Skye. At the time I thought the back door was my best option. I'd been out there brooding about twenty minutes or so when the gang showed up."

"She's obviously unhinged."

"She is. But you know what? I want her to pay for what she did to Annabelle. I want to see her wearing one of those ugly jumpsuits for life and spending it in a tiny cell."

Skye laid her hand on top of his. "Believe me, Josh. I know exactly how you feel."

Over the next several hours Skye left Josh alone so he could deal with calling Annabelle's parents and telling them what had happened with Michelle before they caught wind of the story from the media.

Their relationship might be new but Skye could tell Josh was hurting. The pain in his eyes, the humiliation in his voice at having to admit to his in-laws that he'd slept with the woman who had killed Annabelle made for an uncomfortable conversation.

But when it was done, Skye went over to where he sat at his home office desk and pressed up against his back.

"Sorry I was on the phone so long."

"Don't be silly. You had to call them. It was necessary. They deserved to know the truth, and to hear it from you."

"Yeah. But that was the hardest call I ever had to make. To get the evidence against Michelle, they're on board with the exhumation. You know what they told me?"

"What?"

"Annabelle brought Michelle along to meet them for lunch one afternoon. It seems her parents warned Annabelle the woman seemed a little unbalanced. Annabelle defended the woman by telling them Michelle was a little eccentric, which was an understatement."

Skye kissed his hair, ran her hands along his back. "Sometimes we overlook the obvious because we're too close to a person to see, really see, their major faults. I'd say Michelle played Annabelle like she played everyone else. I would bet Annabelle had no idea Michelle had a thing for you. Or if she did, she thought it was kinda cute or probably no big deal. Whatever it was, Michelle had a lot of people snowed."

"Sad to say, I fall into that category. I thought the woman was harmless." He took hold of Skye's chin, circled her mouth with his finger. "I guess our day spent in bed will have to wait. I have to let my parents know, too. One more phone call."

"Do what you have to. I've got some work to do anyway. I want to go through my list of missing girls one more time, see if I can come up with a link."

"Use my laptop," he offered. "Give me fifteen minutes and I'll help you."

She watched as he reluctantly picked the phone up again, knowing his heart wasn't really into making the call.

Later as they lay in bed, after they'd made love, Josh asked, "Okay. Something's been bothering you since this morning when Michelle pulled her *Fatal Attraction* stunt. What is it? Level with me."

She sat up, looked long and hard into his face. She'd already made her decision to test their growing intimacy by dipping her toe in unbelievable, fanciful legends. If he balked at knowing, then she'd have her answer to that as well.

But if Josh could be upfront with her about the chapter in his life that covered Michelle, an embarrassing episode for him to be sure, then she could return the favor. Although it hardly seemed like a fair trade comparing a psycho stalker bitch to a beautiful silver wolf with violet eyes named Kiya, Skye had already decided to open up. After all, Josh had claimed to see the wolf himself, something no other person had ever done, not even her parents. Kiya seemed to think that was significant. Skye had to follow her instincts because everything inside said she needed to trust Josh enough to share.

"It's true. Something's bothering me all right. I'm just not sure how you're going to react when I tell you."

A knot of fear tightened his gut. "Just rip off the Band-Aid, quick and fast."

"The night you saw the white Australian shepherd—"

"You mean the silver wolf with eyes that match yours? Yeah, I might have been running a high fever but I know what I saw and heard. Others have seen a wolf matching that description, too."

She inhaled deeply, let it out so she could go on. It was his trusting eyes that kept her from chickening out. "What you heard was...you were right about the Nez Perce legend, about the spirit guide, about all of it. My father's spirit guide was a hawk named Deata."

"Dee-ah-tay," Josh repeated sounding out each syllable. "Tell me all of it. When did you first see yours?"

"I was three or four I guess. It's my first real memory. I was standing in the backyard picking flowers in my mother's garden. Yellow daisies. This dog came up out of nowhere. One minute it was empty space. Then the next, she just walked right up to me. At least that's what I thought it was at the time, a dog. It came over to me and licked my hand. I knew her name then, saw that her spirit matched mine. I don't know how I knew at such an early age, I just—knew."

"The wolf is a hunter. But the legend says it happens during the time when a young person comes into his or her own, adolescence. Surely you couldn't have been—"

She shook her head. "It's different for everyone, not a hard and fast rule. Like me, my father first saw his spirit guide at a young age, four or five, while Travis didn't see his until just after his tenth birthday."

"Travis? The guy that owns the gym knows about your wolf?"

She shook her head. "No one knows. You're the first." She smiled and ran her hands through his hair. "On so many levels, you're the first for me, Josh."

He brought her hand to his lips, placed a kiss on the palm. "Sounds like the age thing might run in the family. So what's your wolf's name?"

"Kiya."

"Kee-ya," Josh repeated. "That explains a lot." And would account for Kiya's presence the day Skye had gotten away from Whitfield at the young age of twelve. But then, so much more made sense. A light dawned.

"Kiya leads you to the girls. Kiya is how you know Jenna Donofrio isn't coming home? Kiya is how you got away from Ronny Wayne." It wasn't a question. "Exactly how close had you been to Kiya before…your abduction…that day…in the park?"

"Not very. Of course I regretted that later. If I had spent those eight years from four to twelve connecting with her on a bigger scale I would've known, I would've listened. But that day, I remember hearing this voice inside my head. It kept saying, 'don't go' over and over again before I went running after that damn soccer ball. 'Don't go' it said. Kiya was trying to warn me. But of course, I didn't listen. There on the other side of the hedges was a blond-haired man telling me he had this little girl who wanted to play with the others but was too shy to join in on her own. Would I go to the car and talk to her about joining the game? I said sure. That's the last thing I remember before waking up in his bedroom…terrified…because I was tied up."

Josh squeezed her hand. "You don't have to do this, Skye, not for me."

"No, I don't. But the point is those bastards will use any lie to gain a kid's trust. That's what they do. And when the ruse or the story doesn't work, they'll snatch them anyway, right off the street. When grabbing them won't work for some reason, maybe because there's a crowd or too many people around, they'll break into houses. Take them right out the fucking front door in the middle of the night."

"That's what makes them monsters." He pulled her closer. "So that's it? That's what was bothering you, weighing you down? You wanted to finally tell me about your spirit guide?"

"It's a huge deal for me. I don't want people thinking I'm some kind of freak, least of all the person I'm sharing a bed with. But I figure since you'd already read about the custom and didn't seem spooked by it—"

"I don't think you're a freak. I'm glad you thought enough of me to finally share it though. I'd figured out most of it the day I looked it up. I just wanted you to tell me."

"Is that why you look so relieved?"

"I was convinced that something about my sleeping with Michelle only eight months after I lost Annabelle had turned you off for some reason, disgusted you. I thought you were ready to walk."

She stroked a finger down his jaw. "Josh, you were lonely. I know something about being alone. There's no set rule on grief and everyone handles the process differently. I spent years without having anyone to talk to. Besides, it'd take a lot more than that psycho bitch Michelle Reardon to make me walk. I'm stronger than that."

"Yes, you certainly are."

CHAPTER NINETEEN

Training with the woman you were sleeping with might not have been the smartest thing Josh had ever suggested. And "training" was stretching it. A more descriptive term might've been "crash dummy" more specifically, Skye's personal crash dummy.

They made a habit of meeting during the lunch hour in the dingy gym to work out. But he was getting his ass kicked on a regular basis by an athletic woman who fought like a fiend even when the entire exercise was supposed to be practice. He was pretty sure Skye didn't recognize it as such.

Skye pivoted, used her body to throw Josh off balance. He went down hard on his butt again hitting the indoor/outdoor, non-padded carpet with a thud.

"I don't know why I bother, I spend more time on my backside than I do upright," Josh grumbled as he got to his feet to circle her again.

With the back of her hand she mopped at her brow, went into a low crouch before sweeping out her feet once more to take him down a second time.

"That's because you're holding back, which isn't doing either one of us any good. Now try to really attack me this time."

When Josh approached her from behind, the minute he put his hands on her, she flipped him neatly over her shoulder. He met the carpet for the hat trick. "How exactly is this teaching me to fight as well as you?" Josh asked from his position on the floor.

She picked up a bottle of water, glugged down half of it before handing the rest to him. "You've got a point. We'll practice your form then, go through the blocks and kicks until you can do them in your sleep. Didn't you ever take karate at some point as a kid?"

"No. I was a nerd even then. I preferred to talk my way out of a situation."

Skye guffawed. "I'll try that next time I come upon three guys that want to stick you and take your money."

"It was four and I was sloshed. How many other people got robbed that night in urban Seattle near a pub? I couldn't have been the only one."

She drilled a finger into his chest. "You weren't…robbed."

He caught the jabbing finger. "Thanks to you."

"We're on the same side here, Josh. I knew this was a bad idea. I have a hard time easing off. It's one of those things that came out in the psych evaluation. I'm too aggressive and we're getting on each other's last nerve."

"Then I guess we're done for the day. I have to shower anyway and head back to work. I have a meeting with marketing. Besides, there are few things we need to go over." He checked his watch. "How about you stop in later, say around three? I'll be done by then."

She tilted her head to study his face. "What's up?"

"I said I'd find Whitfield for you and I intend to do just that. I have a line on the guy." He raised a hand. "Don't get your hopes up, not yet, anyway. It's a lead, nothing concrete…yet. But I've been working on something."

Curious, she ran her hand through his drenched hair, wrapped her arms around him from the back and placed a kiss on his sweaty neck. "Have I told you lately that I find you exceptionally hot when you work out?"

He felt her firm breasts press up against his back. "Keep that up and it'll get you a nooner. And I'm not telling you what I've been working on here. I need to show you."

She sighed and settled for kissing his ear. "That's mean."

He spun her around and patted her butt. "If I didn't have a meeting I'd take you right here."

"Hmm, I guess there's not a single perk to owning the company. It's a damned shame you couldn't be a little late."

He was picking up some bad business habits since he'd met her. But what the hell. Being on time was highly overrated, especially since those firm breasts were already pressing against him.

Josh kept eight people waiting in the conference room for twenty minutes; one of them was Todd Graham.

After spending the obligatory ninety minutes going over brands and strategies with each of his department heads, Josh noticed Todd hanging back when everyone else began making their way back to their cubes. "Something on your mind?" Josh asked.

"What's up with you lately?"

"I don't know what you mean."

"Sure you do. You never once mentioned anything about Michelle even though every one of us in the office knew she'd tipped over the edge sometime last Christmas."

"Really? You knew she was crazy? You might've said something."

Todd shook his head. "Crazy is subjective. People have called me worse. But Michelle was shooting out all kinds of signs that no one paid any attention to, least of all you. And now—"

Josh cocked a brow. "Go on."

"You seem to be involved in something with someone who's very intense…very serious."

"Which is none of your business."

"See, that right there is the very reason I kept my mouth shut about fruitcake Michelle. I thought okay, Josh knows best, he always knows what he's doing. He knows trends, sales and pricing, graphics, was the first one in the industry to offer 3D graphics, but let's face it…when it comes to women…Josh Ander has a tendency to think with his dick."

Josh found himself grinding his jaw. "Are you sure we're discussing me now? You're the one who married some woman you'd known for less than sixty days that you met in a strip club—ended up getting served divorce papers five months later after you found out she was banging the limo driver who had picked you two up at the airport coming back from Fiji—where you'd spent your honeymoon."

Todd stuck his hands in his pockets and jingled his change. He was always jingling something. "Look, after what happened with Michelle, I don't want to see you get hurt. You're like a brother to me. You know I'd do anything for you. And yeah, Angie did a number on me. That's why I don't want to see the same thing happen to you."

Josh took a breath, slapped Todd on the back. "I appreciate the brotherly concern, but I've got it handled."

Todd shook his head. "Then it's worse than I thought. That's what they all say right before they take that plunge off the cliff without the parachute or safety net."

At five minutes to three, Skye made her way past security that would have made most banks envious and strolled into a ritzy reception area.

Things were obviously popping at Ander All Games. Everyone Skye passed seemed bent on crunch time and meeting deadlines, not to mention fixing broken code. But they all seemed to be intent on one thing, coming up with better and grander adventures on Mars.

Without much of a wait, Josh's secretary, a middle-aged woman named Kendra, ushered Skye into a plush corner office where Josh sat behind a modern chrome and glass desk. He didn't look like the same man who had waged a faux attack on her earlier in the gym or the one who'd shown her his own personal kind of adventure six blocks from this very spot. She was pretty sure he hadn't taken her to Mars but she did feel like she'd left earth a couple of times.

In fact, Josh Ander looked exactly like what he was, a sexy geek who had found his place in the business world and ruled his domain with a savvy eye toward the bottom line.

When he glanced up and grinned, her silly heart did another Gage Martin flip in her chest. Only this time it was about a hundred times more potent than ninth grade. "You clean up nice, Ander. But I think I like you better sweaty."

"Funny, I was about to say the same thing about you." He rose, closing the distance between them and pushed his office door shut. He picked up a strand of her hair, pushed it behind her ear, pressed his lips to hers. The kiss was a tender mating, a gentle brush that all but lit a furnace. Hot and steady the flame built. "If we were alone I'd say we take advantage of the desk."

Her eyes went wide. "The desk? Right here?"

His mouth arched up. "Maybe later after everyone goes home for the night."

"Come on, don't keep me in suspense."

"Right to business. Okay, if you're correct and Whitfield is the one behind the sex-trafficking in the area, then he has to have a way to get Internet access in order to keep his business running. That's crucial."

"Why is that significant? He could be using anyone's name. He may have access but the account could be set up with a fake ID. In fact, they probably are. He would use the name of a relative in a heartbeat." But it was a good angle she hadn't thought to pursue.

He sat back down at his desk and laptop. "It's significant because he has to pay a carrier for service and if he does, we can track the billing. True, he might be using a phony account, but there can't be that many accounts near the Tacoma property. It's a process of—"

"Elimination. You're good at this." She leaned on the corner of his desk, peered over his shoulder as he tapped keys in fast strokes.

"I like to solve puzzles. And this one's been bugging me since we met." He continued to talk while his fingers flew. "You have to have a social when you request service, any utility service—whether it's setting up your water, gas, or cable—asks for a social security number. While the info you provide to them might be phony it still leaves a record. There are a number of ways to crack the system." He turned the laptop around so she could check out the screen for herself. "And voilà, this is exactly what I'm talking about. See?"

Could it be that simple, she wondered? Glancing at the records, she saw a list of not one account, but several using the same social in the same zip code as the Whitfield property where the felon was supposed to be living. "What is it I'm looking at?"

"Every utility account that uses the same social within that same zip code. There aren't that many because it's a rural area, not that populated. After you narrow it down to the social, after I got this far, I cross-referenced the aunt and uncle and came up with eight accounts. Interestingly enough, none of them provide a listed service to the trailer, at all, which means it's probably unoccupied. But a satellite view of the area shows a cabin not mentioned in Whitfield's official state parole file. I'm sure the parole board would find that in violation." He tapped more keys and brought the image up on the screen.

"That means the other accounts—"

"Match the cabin on the same Whitfield property."

"Why eight?"

"One for each kind of service they requested for that social security number. You've got electric, gas, water, high-speed Internet and cable, satellite, telephone, and even the bill for sewer service."

"Josh, that's brilliant!" She got up and started pacing his office. "Maybe now might be a good time to mention that since Brandon Hiller left prison several girls have gone missing in the surrounding area of Seattle, which when you think about it, would make sense if Hiller is one of Whitfield's underlings."

Josh sat up straighter in his chair. "You think Hiller is responsible for all the missing girls?"

"Not all, no. But at least the ones in the last five months." She pulled a piece of paper from her coat pocket. "Here's the list I managed to put together on my own. Nine girls in all, ranging in age from ten to sixteen, went missing recently."

"I see I'm not the only one good at solving puzzles. Nine, huh? One's too many."

"True. According to public records, reports filed by his parole officer, Hiller was a follower behind bars, which makes him prime once he's released to seek out his own kind. Otherwise how's he going to have access to young girls on his own? He isn't allowed to be around kids, so somehow, someway he hooks up with Whitfield, maybe uses the Internet to connect in one of those porn chat rooms you discovered. My theory is Hiller's merely an underling. One of several Whitfield pays to do his dirty work."

At the frown that creased her brow, he asked, "What else is troubling you?"

"I'll say one thing for you, Josh. You are observant. I'm beginning to see what Harry might've been trying to tell me all this time. I've been committing a cardinal mistake here in my thinking—with everything. In fact, in less than ten minutes you just proved I might've been able to find Whitfield all this time if I'd bothered checking something as simple as utility accounts in the area. I never even thought of that."

"No one was sure he was in Tacoma, Skye. And even with what I uncovered it still doesn't prove Whitfield himself is anywhere near that property let alone living in that cabin."

"No, but a check of the place will take care of that little detail. Anyway, hear me out. Up to this point, my narrow focus has been on Whitfield instead of trying to figure out how he's running a sex-trafficking ring and keeping such a low profile. That's the big picture here, Josh, the sex ring using underage girls. And the one I've been missing completely. There's no other explanation but…Whitfield has to be sending his minions out to do his dirty work. It's the only thing that makes sense. But that's not the worst part."

"We need to change that. There's a worse part?"

"There is. I think we might be dealing with a cop involved in all of it."

His eyes narrowed. "Wow! You're kidding? No wonder Harry went ballistic that day at the diner and was in such a pissy mood."

"Harry went ballistic over the fact I discovered the information about the missing girls. He didn't share that with me, not once in all these months. I got upset about that. I was ready to knock heads with him over it when you walked up."

"Go on."

"What if—" It was difficult for her to even say it but she'd been thinking about this angle for more than a week now and it might explain a few things. "I'm thinking if…this cop turns a blind eye so he clears the way for Whitfield to get the girls out of the country en masse for parts unknown who would be the wiser? Who would care?"

"I can see why Harry went over the edge. A cop involved changes the game."

"You could say that. But I didn't share this with Harry. He was on edge anyway over the Donofrio girl. It's not like he wanted to accept that she was dead at that moment in time. I made a mistake that day. It was too soon to share that with him. I should've held it back, kept it to myself. I have a tendency to do a quick draw on the phone with Harry when it comes to sharing what I suspect. That upsets him. It has for years. Sharing the first thought in my head after I find out another girl's disappeared isn't the way to go. I should know by now that cops live by a different set of rules. They need hard evidence, a tip from a concerned citizen, something. And that's where it goes south because I certainly can't tell Harry that my spirit guide is the one that gave me the inside track about all of this."

"Those same rules don't apply to us."

"That may be but that list you're holding says nine girls are unaccounted for in five months and that's— unacceptable. As you can see by the list, Elena Palomar is the youngest at ten. Heather Moore and a hooker named Lucy Border are the oldest at sixteen. We have to find those girls, Josh. We have to put a stop to how Whitfield uses these girls, enslaves them, and then ships them out of the country to be used…for years to come."

"And makes a fortune doing so," he finished her thought. "Then we hit the ground running. I think it's time we take a look around the Whitfield property. Together."

"Sounds like a plan, but I'd like to go talk to the Palomar family and stop by Heather Moore's place first.

"Sure we can go talk to the two families but I'd say the sooner we take a look around Whitfield's place, the better. I just have one question."

"What's that?"

"Where do you keep your equipment?"

"Excuse me?"

"Skye? That night in the alley you had an expandable baton made of hardened steel. Where do you keep your other weapons?"

She huffed out a breath. "You saw the war room. There's a faux panel on the side wall."

"And?"

"I have several Colts to choose from. A .45 my dad carried in the military and a lighter, smaller .380 with less kick."

"Good. Then we won't be walking in there unarmed."

Later, while the fingers of Lake Washington rose up in front of them as they crossed over the bridge to Bellevue, Josh voiced his unease.

"Have you ever done this before, gone to the home of a missing child to ask the family questions, to get further details?"

"Yes. I won't lie, it won't be easy. In fact, it's tragic."

"What exactly are you hoping to learn?"

"Anything that isn't already in the public domain. Things like when they were last seen, the time of day, what they were doing last, what activity, any of their habits we can glean out of the conversation, that sort of thing."

"I take it Harry Drummond would be furious if he knew you were doing this."

"Oh yeah. But Harry is in Seattle, we're going outside his jurisdiction."

While their first stop at the Palomar home didn't yield a whole lot of anything new, the parents did verify what Skye had read online, plus offered up a few little-known tidbits.

Elena Palomar had last been seen playing down the street with a neighbor, Tara English, a playmate from the same fifth-grade class. Tara told the police that when her father had called her in to get ready for a family outing that night, Elena had headed home to her house five doors down. The little brown-haired, brown-eyed girl never made it home. Elena had disappeared in broad daylight on a Saturday afternoon, two weeks ago. There were no eyewitnesses, no reports of a stranger in the area, or a car, no leads, nothing.

Elena Palomar had simply vanished off the streets of a middle-class section of Bellevue leaving behind a family, heartbroken and anguished.

In Kirkland, at the upscale home of Heather Moore, the girl's mother, Janie, was more than willing to talk and led them into a spacious living area chock full of photos of her eldest daughter dressed in her snappy blue and gold drill team uniform. Heather hadn't been heard from since the afternoon she'd walked out of school after practice and never made it home. Her car, a light green VW bug, had been found still parked in the school parking lot.

"I'm sorry to bother you like this, Mrs. Moore," Skye began. "And I appreciate your agreeing to talk to us but—"

Heather's mom interrupted her. "It isn't a hardship to get an opportunity to talk about my daughter. If you or you," she said, nodding at Josh, "or anyone else can help bring my daughter back to her family, I'd talk to the devil himself."

"It's just that we're curious about a couple of things."

"Like what?"

"Namely, whether or not Heather's friends reported her walking out of practice by herself? Did they report seeing anyone hanging around the school that day? Hanging around her car maybe? Was she…?"

Again Janie Moore didn't let her finish. "The lot has security. No one can just get into the parking lot unless they're supposed to be there. At least that's what I was told. And before you ask, my Heather doesn't have a wild streak. I'm sure that's what all parents say. But Heather is dependable, calls me if she's going to be late getting in from a date, even calls me from the mall if she's decided to go look in another store for something else. Both my kids are like that. My son, Heather's little brother, got lost in a department store once when he was three. Heather was there. We were frantic for more than an hour before we found him in the women's dressing room, playing with a stack of hangers." Janie dabbed at her eyes. "Heather knows how I worry. She would never do this on purpose."

"What exactly occupies Heather's time? I mean does she spend a lot of time on the computer?" Josh asked.

"What teenage girl these days doesn't spend half her life on the phone texting or sitting in front of that damned desktop," Janie Moore replied. "I should've unplugged that thing a year ago and thrown it in the trash. There was a time her father wanted to, but I intervened. Oh yes, I convinced my husband it wouldn't do a bit of good since Heather has a two-hundred-dollar phone we'd bought her for Christmas when she turned fifteen that she could use for the same thing. How is a parent supposed to make sure every single person their child comes into contact with on a daily basis can be trusted? Answer me that. It's a parent's worst nightmare is what it is."

Skye reached over and placed her hand on top of Janie Moore's. "I know. I'm sorry to have to be here and ask all these questions, dredge it up again but—"

Janie waved her off. "No, no, it's okay. I like keeping her case in front of the media. I don't want them forgetting about her. But as time goes on, the news crews leave and don't come back unless…they find a…" With that thought, Janie's voice trailed off. "As to what my Heather likes to do in her spare time. That girl's wanted to be in drill since she first started taking dance lessons when she was four years old. She never missed a practice. That's all she ever talked about was getting to dance professionally after high school, maybe down in Los Angeles. Now…" Janie wiped tears from her cheeks.

"And none of her friends was able to offer a good explanation as to who she might have left school with? A boyfriend maybe? Someone she'd met online?" Josh ventured.

"Heather goes out off and on with a boy she met last summer. They aren't exclusive and Ryan was questioned extensively. He was at work that afternoon. I made calls to every single one of her friends, so many I made a nuisance out of myself. Heather would not have left on her own, that much I know. Someone took that girl. I know they did. That's what I told the police, too."

"Who is in charge of Heather's case?" Skye wondered.

"Detective Talbot. Allen Talbot. He's been nice enough without really offering us any hope though. He's made up his mind that she ran off, that she's a runaway and she'll come back when she's ready. Poppycock! I tried to convince him how wrong he was. We had words over it. Have you any idea what it's like when a child goes missing?"

Without really waiting for an answer, Janie Moore went on, "It's horrifying. My Heather is a good girl. Heather wouldn't have just up and gone off without letting me know where she was headed. Why? Why would a girl who's reliable all of a sudden decide to leave her car behind?" She started to tear up in earnest and had to reach for a Kleenex from the table. She wiped at her eyes again. "I want my girl back. That's all I want is for Heather to come home. Her brother's birthday is in ten days. She'd already saved her money and bought him a video game he'd begged me for. I want her back home so she can give him his present herself. She's a good girl," Janie repeated.

It broke Skye's heart to have to listen to the same refrain she'd heard from other anguished parents before. Would the heartbreak ever stop?

By the time Janie Moore walked them to the door, it was well after dark.

As they got into the car, Josh speculated, "I don't get it. We talked to two sets of heartbroken parents, understandably upset and worried. What exactly did we learn we didn't already know?"

"For one thing" she ticked off the points using her fingers. "Elena was taken in the afternoon. So was Heather. So was Erin Prescott. Two out of three after school. The only difference being Elena's abduction happened on a Saturday."

"And that means what?"

"The guy has plenty of time on his hands. His afternoons are free, Saturdays are free. Probably means he's unemployed."

"You couldn't get all that from the Internet?"

"It's a theory and validation. Glass half full, half empty kind of thing. Look at it this way, it's more than we knew beforehand."

Once they got underway, Josh admitted, "Talking to the parents took a lot out of me. It makes you respect all they go through and have to deal with when their child goes missing."

"It breaks my heart."

"Your parents went through that same gut-clenching fear."

"For three days they were terrified they'd never see me again. And the guilt…I don't even want to consider how a parent lives with that."

"Your parents felt guilty because Whitfield took you right out from under their noses."

She nodded absently, thinking back to another place, another time.

Josh squeezed her hand to get her attention. "I do have one question, something's been bothering me. Why kill Jenna Donofrio? I mean, that's what you think happened, right?"

"I know that's what happened."

"Then why? Can you tell me that much?"

"My guess is Erin Prescott got away, escaped. I could feel guilty about that but…in saving one, I lost another. He wasn't done with Erin. I broke his rhythm, pissed him off. The urge hadn't completely played out so he had to find another one and this time—"

"He doesn't want to leave a witness behind who would surely ID him the same way Erin did."

"Erin didn't ID him. His DNA, his fingerprints were all over that nasty room. The stupid son of a bitch ramped up because the urge overwhelmed him and he got desperate."

"Look, don't get upset, but I'm not sure making that trip to Tacoma tonight is a good idea."

"Especially when we're both drained. I agree. We need to be at our best."

He linked his fingers with hers, brought the hand to his lips. "Twenty-four hours won't make much difference in the grand scheme of things, Skye. We have to believe that."

Looking out over the Evergreen Point Bridge, a dread moved through her. "I don't know. We should've gone to Whitfield's first maybe. For some of these girls, Josh, tomorrow may be too late."

"We don't know that." He cocked a brow. "Unless you have some…insight…you haven't shared with me."

She shook her head.

"Then at first light tomorrow, rain or shine, we'll head out."

"I just hope it won't be too late."

As soon as they got back to the loft, Josh mapped the area to and from the cabin and because he was a bit obsessive when it came to preparing for the unknown, he went a step further and rechecked the lay of the land thanks to an aerial view he'd blown up as large as he could get. He hit print for a hard copy.

While Skye simmered Bolognese sauce on the stove to toss over pasta, while oregano and other Italian spices floated on the air around them, they familiarized themselves with the terrain.

Peering over his shoulder, Skye had to concede, "Okay, you were right to wait. It's been almost a year since I've been out there last. June to be exact. And I've always made the trip during the daylight hours. I never actually got out of the car. Instead, I waited and watched from the roadway. One day for about three hours I sat there, used my binoculars to keep an eye on that trailer. Took a few photos. There's a gate located right about here," she added, pointing to a small clearing. "Who knows what's beyond it? But my guess is that he doesn't want anyone getting past this point for a reason."

As he considered how remote the property was, he couldn't believe she'd done this alone. He decided it must've taken her a good deal of courage to prepare for the whole thing each time she went. "I'd say that's a fair guess. Did you see anything of significance on your other trips?"

"Nothing. There was no activity around that damned trailer at all. Not a car went by on that dirt road either. I saw nothing out of the ordinary. Just a place that looked deserted. Now that I think about it, I'd forgotten just how wooded and spooky this place would be after dark."

"Even for you?"

"Even for me. Not only that but we'd need my night vision goggles to see our way around."

Josh turned his head to stare. "To think I actually know someone who owns night vision goggles. That is *so* cool. "

"I wouldn't exactly call it cool but they do come in handy when you're walking a dark alleyway at three in the morning. I should've had them with me when I went after Erin."

"I'm surprised you didn't."

She shrugged. "I'm not perfect, Josh. I've made a few mistakes out there on the streets."

"Like what?"

"Like getting pulled into disagreements between two homeless people fighting over a lousy, filthy blanket, or caught in the middle of two rival gangs trying to settle their differences with nine millimeters."

"Well, at least you have the courage to do *something*. That says a lot about the person you are."

She scraped her fingers through his hair. "I'm pretty sure you're biased."

"I know I am. But this time you won't be alone. What about the weapons, which Colt do I get?"

She shook her head. "Have you ever fired a handgun like a .45?"

"Not in real life but I've played simulated shooter games since I was six. I hate to brag but I'm pretty good. From junior high on, I beat Todd Graham two hundred and sixty-three times in a row until he cheated and broke into the code, reprogrammed the game with his own secret moves."

"Simulated shooter games?"

"Hey, I've killed hundreds of thousands of zombies."

"*Zombies on Mars*, your first venture into the dangers in the universe after nuclear war here on earth. It might not have been as successful as *Hidden Cities* but it was damn clever."

He smiled, adjusted his glasses. "Thanks for that."

"No problem. But your impressive zombie statistics aside, even geeks need to spend time at the firing range to hone their accuracy, especially since your skills at hand-to-hand are less than stellar. You'll need to rely on your weapon. There's a place I go to get out of the city."

"Okay. So, after we stuff our faces with spaghetti, we lock and load. Got it. I hate to point it out but my less than stellar skills reflect poorly on my lousy instructor."

"You are such a wiseass, Ander. You know that?" She chewed her lip before admitting, "And unfortunately correct. I am a lousy teacher. But then I tried to warn you."

"I know. At the time, it sounded like a good idea."

"Yeah, sadly, so many things do."

Once they finished dinner they drove thirty miles north of Seattle to the pistol range belonging to none other than Travis Nakota. Turns out, Travis owned forty acres outside Everett that hugged the Washington coastline where he bred and sold American Paint Horses.

As they turned off the main road, the headlights of Skye's Subaru lit up the entrance. They crossed under an impressive iron gate topper which hung across the opening and signified the name of the ranch. The Painted Crow.

Once they crawled out of the car Josh finally got to meet the infamous Travis Nakota. The fifty-year-old man stood about five-feet-ten with a long black ponytail that trailed down his back and not a hint of gray anywhere on his head.

Josh sensed a man carrying a major chip on his shoulder that had everything to do with the man Skye had brought with her. Although Travis did shake hands with Josh, the man did nothing more than grunt in Josh's direction, especially after spotting the wedding ring still prominent on Josh's left hand.

Josh got the distinct impression Travis wasn't all that happy to make his acquaintance. Travis Nakota acted like a disgruntled, over-protective father, who wasn't the least bit glad to see a man in the company of the woman he thought of like a daughter. Or so it seemed to Josh. He looked on as Skye hugged the older man and watched as Travis actually showed a perfect smile when he grinned back. But not at Josh.

Travis pretty much ignored Josh even as he took out his keys and unlocked the barn-like structure that housed the firing range. When Travis hit the lights, Josh noticed the inside stuck to the same no-frills theme as the gym Travis owned. But the place was out in the boonies and secluded and a lot roomier than the place where they worked out. The spacious interior consisted of only four shooting stations but each one had its own front counter to hold extra weapons and ammo. Paper targets dangled from a two-by-four stud at distances between fifty and eighty yards from each enclosure. There was an automatic target retrieval system, which now that Josh took the time to look around meant the place was pretty fancy for a bare-bones setup. He was beginning to think there was a lot more to Travis Nakota than the owner of a greasy spoon diner. Maybe later he'd ask Skye about the guy's background.

"There's also an outside rifle range," Skye told Josh, as she removed both weapons from their casings and placed them on the counter in the first station.

"Doesn't all the noise bother the horses?" Josh asked and earned a glare from the horse breeder.

"What kind of horse owner do you think I am?" Travis barked. "A horse can be trained to ignore to any number of sounds and that includes gunfire."

"Travis, I'm sure Josh didn't mean anything," Skye said.

"It was a stupid question from a city boy who wouldn't know a horse from a donkey," Travis groused right before turning to Skye, all conciliatory. "Take all the time you need, Skye. Just let me know when you're done so I can lock up." And with that, Travis slammed the door as he went out.

"He doesn't like me," Josh complained.

"He does seem to be in a mood. I don't know what's wrong with him tonight."

"Are you in the habit of bringing strange men around him?"

"Don't be ridiculous—"

"There's your answer."

"What? No way." Then the truth started to sink in. "Ah. Oh. Well…hmm."

"Exactly." Josh eyed the weapons on the counter. "They're both Colts," he said as he picked up the smaller .380, weighed it against the larger model, the .45 caliber. "Nice guns. You can handle the kick on this baby?"

She looked insulted. "That's right. It took me awhile to get used to it. But I put in lots of practice. Both Colts belonged to my father."

"He taught you?"

She shook her head. "No. Travis did that once I moved back to Seattle. If you're ready, let's start with the basics. First, check to see if the safety's on and if it's loaded. Next keep the gun pointed in a safe direction until you're ready to fire. Always keep your trigger finger straight and outside the trigger guard until you're ready to shoot. Like this." She picked up the bigger Colt and demonstrated. "And never point the gun at anything you don't intend to shoot. Got it?"

"Got it."

She took him through another walk-through on safety, another demo on loading and unloading before finally telling him, "Now you try." Skye placed the .45 on the shooting table with the clip beside it and stepped aside to let Josh have a go at it. She watched as he repeated the process. "Good. Okay, now put on your ear protectors and let's see how you handle pulling the trigger."

Josh adjusted his glasses right before he dealt with the bulky, but necessary, ear muffs, then slowly pushed the clip into the gun handle until he heard it lock into place. He flipped off the safety and chambered a round.

"Very good," she muttered, clearly impressed with how well he picked up the mechanics. "Show me what you got, Gameboy."

And he did. He was incredibly accurate for his first time at shooting a heavy handgun. As soon as he'd emptied the clip of the big Colt, a thought occurred to her. "Okay, what other firearms have you handled before tonight?"

"Just a rifle, a .22, shot tin cans on my one and only hunting expedition with a group of guys I briefly tried to impress in high school."

"Well, you did good with the .45. Now try the smaller one. See which one handles better."

He changed out Colts, loaded the much lighter .380 himself, took aim and fired. After several rounds he put it down and stated, "Nope, I like the bigger gun, it has a better feel in my hands, smooth, a better all-around firing experience."

She grinned. "You'll have to fight me for it then," she said with a wink.

"That's not fair, you'll win."

She tilted her head. "Guess what, Josh?"

"What?"

"You're a better shot than I am."

"That's hard to believe."

"No, it's true. You were right though. You're a natural. But practice makes perfect." So she took him through the drill again and made him repeat the entire process. They spent the next hour practicing their aim.

They didn't get back to the loft until after midnight and went straight to bed. But once she fell asleep, Skye's dreams came to her in black and gray images. The past wasn't full of pretty pastels. Not for her. Too often, she found herself back in that messy bedroom with Whitfield.

There were details she wished she could block out forever.

At twelve when the young girl had awoken in that strange place for the first time and found herself in an unfamiliar bed, the air around her had been heavy with stale cigarette smoke, leftover beer, and sweat. The sweat might've been her own because she was scared to death.

Beyond the closed door she heard a television blare with some sporting event, baseball maybe, with the announcers deep into the action, the game. Beyond that, she thought she heard children's voices, playing outside—nearby yet too far away to help. The sounds made her realize she was in an apartment complex very close to a playground like the one where he'd snatched her. Stupid. Stupid. She'd been stupid for believing the man's story about his little girl.

If not for the rag stuffed in her mouth, she would have screamed her head off. Her wrists were bound together and tied to the bed post above her head. She wasn't wearing clothes. Her head hurt from what felt like someone had yanked on her hair. One spot on her arm hurt like it did when the nurse at the doctor's office gave her a shot. Then she remembered the man had taken out a needle and stuck it in her arm. That was the last thing she had remembered before coming awake in this awful place.

When the bedroom door flew open, petrified, she thought she might throw up. Her eyes darted to the man's stringy hair, his slim build, the tattoos on his arms, a snake on one, a tiger on the other. Determined to memorize those few details, she cringed at his approach.

"You're awake? Good." He stroked her hair, removing the rubber band that held it back in place as he went. At his touch, she longed for the drug to take her under again to blackness, blackness had to be better than what was about to happen.

Fear wedged in her throat and stomach, and remembering that fear, she started to moan in torment, flailing about. In anger, in defeat, she grabbed the sheet around her in closed fists.

The restlessness of the woman beside him woke Josh. As she wrestled with the air in sleep there was no mistaking the wave of terror drowning her in the past, the way her head went from side-to-side had Josh cautious even in the simple gesture of putting his hand out to touch her.

So he watched and he waited until her eyes finally flew open. As soon as he realized she was awake, he reached out so he could draw her into his arms, placed a kiss on her forehead. "Bad dream?"

"It's nothing. I'm sorry I woke you. Go back to sleep."

Patience, he thought and knew he needed to proceed with care. "You know better than that. Are you okay now that you're awake? Is there anything I can do?"

She smiled and shook her head, then immediately curled into his body. Right now she needed the safe touch of another person. Touching, being with him, having his arms wrapped around her, maybe that was the answer. Before she lost her nerve, in one quick motion, she moved over him, straddled his belly. She found his hands, brought them up to mold her bare breasts. "I want you, Josh. Now! I'm alive. After these many years, I have to be grateful for that. I want you to take that awful memory away once and for all. I want to feel you inside me. You, Josh, only you."

He closed around her with equal measures of heat and need swimming in the depths. He wanted to give her what she needed. It wasn't the time to tell her, to unburden his heart and soul with all he felt for her. So he would give her the now. He had to believe there was power in the moment. That they could love each other this minute and it would be enough to carry them through whatever tomorrow held.

She rode the tide quick and fast, her head spinning with ripples of delight she'd never known were possible. When he rose up to cover her mouth, when their eyes met and held, Skye knew at that moment she'd found her mate— reveled in the knowing.

CHAPTER TWENTY

At first light, a restless Skye crawled naked out of bed to shower and get ready for what would be her fifth trip in as many years to Tacoma. Funny how such a short forty-five-minute jaunt could create such dread and heaviness around her heart.

Could it be a bad idea to go out there again? She felt the overwhelming burden of worry all the way to her bones. But she'd been out there before and nothing bad had ever happened. Of course, that had been before she'd known about the cabin, before Josh had discovered all the utility accounts for service. Whitfield had to be living in that damned cabin.

She had to clear her mind of everything except finding those girls and learning whether or not Whitfield was the definitive link. Harry would want proof and she was determined to get that.

When Josh joined her in the shower, the rest of her angst drained away completely. Having his hands on her again was the thrill, the exhilaration she needed. As they started soaping each other, she had to admit she couldn't get enough of the man. Who knew sex with Josh Ander would be so addictive?

She looked up into those gray eyes that always managed to draw her in and said flatly, "We could postpone this."

Josh didn't think she was talking about making love. He set her away from him long enough to search her eyes. "Is that what you want? I can go alone, you know. I started to suggest that very thing last night but you seemed so determined then. What's changed?"

"I don't know. A gut feeling. Maybe I'm getting cold feet. But don't worry. I'm not letting you go by yourself. I know we're doing this because of me. If anything happens…"

"It's my choice, Skye."

"That's just it, Josh. You don't have to do this for me."

"I admit I'm not much backup in a fight, but two has to be better than one. You aren't going out there alone."

As they dried off and went out to the bedroom to get dressed, she had to hope that two would indeed be enough if they did encounter Whitfield. She had no idea what had happened to the woman who'd been gunning for the dipshit ever since she turned eighteen and came back to Seattle to live. Now she wasn't even certain that woman existed. Was Josh responsible for that as well?

Pulling on her jeans, she decided she had to get out of this funk. She had less than an hour to get her act together.

As she made her way to the kitchen to start a pot of much-needed coffee for her already jittery stomach, she decided the son of a bitch was more than likely two thousand miles away from Tacoma tucked into some obscure community doing God knows what to its youth.

And she wasn't exactly sure how she'd feel if she had to come away from Tacoma empty-handed again.

Two hours later as the sun tried to break through a low-hanging marine layer hugging along the ground, Josh and Skye looked down from the same ridge where they'd left the car. They stared across the treetops at Commencement Bay, and ultimately to the seventy-five acres that belonged to Fred and Millicent Whitfield.

Fred and Millie had no children of their own. But from what Skye had been able to ascertain from public records, the couple had taken their nephew in after Ronny's young mother died of a drug overdose before celebrating her twenty-first birthday. Whoever had fathered young Ronny had apparently never been a part of his son's life. So when the authorities were on the brink of drumming the four-year-old into the system, Fred and Millie stepped forward to see that didn't happen.

That meant Ronny had grown up here among a smattering of tide flats and a strip of beachfront before it wove back into a stretch of timberland full of Douglas fir, cedar, and spruce.

Skimming the treetops, Josh thought the entire place smelled like a gigantic Christmas tree lot. He had to remind himself that this might be the lair of a sexual predator.

Because they approached from the back side of the property, they had to trek a good half mile through a copse of trees and riparian vegetation to reach the cabin.

Isolated and rugged, the terrain along the way was chock full of slender waterleaf just beginning to flower with their little purplish blossoms and the lily-like red trillium. The Pacific willow hadn't yet budded out, but it would. Come summer, its yellow catkins would make a contrast to the white parsley that grew companionably beside it. Even Skye had to convince herself that such a beautiful stretch of land could belong to the home of her nemesis. Surely the monster didn't exist in such a pristine setting.

They hiked past a variety of sedges where hardhack grew in abundance before making their way up a hillside covered with wild gooseberry and blueberry vines. She could smell Canada mint and recognized its pinkish-purple clumps on the stems. If the land had belonged to anyone else, Skye would've loved to spend her time doing nothing more than exploring the habitat, maybe gathering some cuttings to take back home to transplant in her ugly, cheap plastic tub.

But she hadn't come here to sight-see or collect foliage.

The ground beneath their feet was uneven and muddy, the going slow until they crossed into a small clearing. Here they could pick up their pace, save for the bits of loose rocks and stones littering the earth that hampered their footing.

When Kiya appeared out of the mist, Josh bumped Skye's arm. "You may be used to that, but it still takes some getting used to."

Skye's lips curved up and it was the first time since they'd left Seattle that she seemed less nervous. "It does take a leap of faith I know. But she isn't corporeal. Sometimes it's difficult for me to think of her as simply a spirit, an inner life force guiding me on the path I was meant to take."

"For a wolf that isn't real, she's magnificent in size and color. I still can't get over the eyes. I'd say you hit the jackpot in the spirit guide department. If I'd had one, I like to think mine would've been a ferocious saber-toothed tiger." He thought for a moment before adding, "Or maybe a modern-day panther, sleek, fast and black. Yeah, the panther would be ideal."

"What about the cheetah? It's fast."

"That too. But I'd definitely take the cat family. Imagine following the magnificent jaguar, leopard, maybe even a cougar. Any of those would be fierce."

"Trouble with spirit guides is you don't get to pick yours. Remember Travis? His was the crow. You know, like that movie *The Crow* with Brandon Lee."

"I loved that movie. As I recall the crow brings Eric Draven back to life to avenge the murder of his fiancée then guides him along the way in the process."

"The ultimate role of the spirit guide is to put their life force into the body of another so that person can live." She smiled again. "Just one of the many thousand-year-old legends of the Nez Perce."

When Josh spotted the wolf taking another path, he pointed that way. "Over there, she's heading for that ridgeline straight through the low scrub."

"Come on, we need to keep up."

"I brought a portable GPS just in case." He drew it out of his pocket.

"Good thinking."

The well-worn path was littered with a carpet of fallen leaves in vivid shades of golds and greens. They both stood back and watched as the wolf stopped, sniffed the air, before taking another track farther in. They trudged on past low brush laden with brambles and burrs and a lodgepole pine shedding its needles.

Skye and Josh followed but when they got to a drop off, they had to scramble down a slope where they could peer below to what they hoped was Whitfield's residence. Sure enough from up above they saw a valley, and in the middle of a clearing was a stunning house of glass and angles.

"That's a cabin? Looks more like a luxury resort," Skye muttered.

"Or a fancy ski lodge. That's gotta be at least twenty-five hundred square feet," Josh proffered as rain started to spit from the heavy clouds.

Through prickly shrubs and hedges, Skye crouched, sat on her heels. Doing her best to gauge the distance to reach the back door, she turned to Josh and whispered, "I don't like it. It's too quiet."

"I keep forgetting your wolf instincts are stronger with Kiya around. Whitfield's gotta be inside, right? Why wouldn't it be this quiet?" Josh wanted to know in a soft voice as he bent down even with her level.

"I don't know. In all the times I've been coming out here, though, I never once got this eerie feeling crawling up my spine."

"Probably because you were never this close to the cabin," Josh reasoned.

"True. I only got as far as driving down that dirt road on the other side and past where that stupid trailer sits. Which obviously he wanted people to think was his primary place of residence, while he hung out in his palatial digs hidden back here, surrounded by nature. It's just that—" Her voice trailed off as she thought she heard something. She put her finger to her mouth to shush Josh. But the guy just kept talking.

"I gotta say I'd trust your eerie feelings with my life. What do you want to do now?"

About that time Skye heard Kiya snarl in warning. Branches crackled and crunched to life behind them. At the sound, Josh looked up in time to see a swipe of iron pipe cross his line of vision in a blur.

The thud of metal hitting bone caused Skye to whirl then pivot to avoid the same fate. She came face-to-face with the monster from her past. His hair had thinned. He'd gained a few pounds. His face might've shown a few lines, but he still had those same cold, blue eyes that sent paralyzing terror running through her body. She spared one shaky glance over at Josh's form crumpled on the ground, blood trickling along the side of his head, his glasses knocked off, broken in two.

Whitfield was too close and it was too late to pull out the Colt from under her jacket. Doing her best to focus on Whitfield rather than Josh lying still, not moving, Skye shrieked, "Same old coward, chicken-shit bastard to the core. Ronny Wayne has to come up from behind a man to take him out."

"As I recall you like it like that. From behind, that is. Who is that son of a bitch? If you brought the cops to my door, little girl, I'm going to make you pay."

"Go to hell."

Ronny licked his lips. "Man, you've grown up to be a real looker." He whistled through his teeth before rubbing a hand over his crotch. "But I'd know you anywhere. Let's have us some fun for old time's sake. What do you say?"

"Not in my lifetime. I'll die first." And with that, in one motion Skye reached down and pulled the knife from her boot. "Let's see what you can do with a grown woman this time and not a little kid."

"My pleasure," Ronny sneered as he lunged at her swinging the pipe again. But Skye dodged and sent the knife into the only thing she could reach, Ronny's forearm. The blade grazed a ribbon of skin, deep enough that he screamed in pain and rage. "You bitch! You're gonna pay for that!"

To prove his point, he swung the pipe a third time. Skye avoided the blow and jammed the knife into Ronny's thigh, slicing open more flesh through the jeans he wore.

She had the satisfaction of seeing him writhe in pain before he struck. This time the pipe connected with the knife. Metal clashed with metal. Skye held her own for about fifteen seconds, but Ronny's sheer strength forced the blade to fall from her hand.

Skye staggered back two steps, tried to gain her balance. A quick scan told her the knife was well out of reach. She had no choice but to try to reach the .380 inside her jacket.

But when Ronny spotted the gun, before she could take aim and fire, he kicked it out of her hand. The Colt went airborne and landed in the underbrush, a good ten feet away. He tried to snatch her arm but Skye swept out a leg, cutting Ronny's out from under him. He buckled. She kicked and punched with a series of jabs into his face, connecting with his nose before smacking him in the gut. But with the last blow Ronny managed to grab her arm. From his knees, he pulled her down and began hitting her torso and any other place he could reach.

They slammed into the ground and rolled, giving Ronny the advantage when he came out on top. Skye took each punch until she rammed her fingers into his eyes then into the cut on his arm. Each time she tried to wrestle out of his grip the flow of blood from the gash seemed to make each attempt a slippery mess.

Skye bucked, and did her best to fight back. Clawing and kicking, it became hand-to-hand combat as her nails dug into skin. But despite her efforts, Whitfield's hands finally reached around her throat. Fingers locked, putting pressure on her neck, slowly cutting off her air.

Kiya kept a keen eye on the fight as it ramped up. Snarling, the wolf paced with fury building inside knowing there was nothing she could do physically to help her charge. Trotting over to the unconscious body of Josh, Kiya sniffed his face. The wolf howled in rage trying to force the man to wake up, nudging him with her mind to help her human. But after several seconds, it became clear Josh was fading away. In fact, he was almost gone.

It was then Kiya knew what she had to do. It hadn't been done in a thousand years. But there was no other way. It would cost her. Dearly. But she would gladly pay the price. Skye had to be saved whatever the sacrifice.

Kiya began to shake and shiver.

With all the energy she could muster, the wolf shoved into Josh, forcing her spirit into his lifeless form. Seconds ticked off before the transformation took hold and the merge became complete. Once the crux of her life-force finished running through the man, his eyes fluttered, then opened.

For several long seconds, Josh saw nothing but bright, white light. The headache from hell felt like a migraine with a force ten surge. Everything inside him burned hot about the same time a flash of energy spread through his body.

His vision became crystal clear. So did his hearing. The sound of grunts and fists pummeling flesh made him aware someone was in trouble.

Skye.

Josh got to his feet. His eyes immediately settled on Whitfield where the bastard sat atop Skye, straddling her, his hands clutching her neck.

The need to protect his mate was instant and fierce.

The merge of man and beast had Josh pouncing. The force knocked Whitfield off Skye. Razor-sharp teeth and claws dug in, tore open flesh. Whitfield's throat became Josh's feast. His first taste of blood caused him to raise his head long enough to howl at the drizzle spitting down from above. But that only lasted a few seconds before Josh began lapping at the man's blood again. His teeth shredded more when they moved to the man's chest.

Bruised and battered, Skye finally managed to gain her feet. It took three tries before she could pull Josh off what was left of Whitfield just as a misty fog rose up out of the ground shrouding them in a dark haze.

The earth shook and rumbled. The wind picked up, swirled in angry gusts.

So did the rain. It batted down in sheets.

Skye tried to make her feet move again but when they wouldn't budge as if they were stuck in a bucket of cement, she simply dropped down where she stood. She rested her head on Josh's shoulder, stroked a finger down his bloody face along his jawline. Her voice raspy from having Whitfield's hands trying to force the life out of her, she shrieked, "I thought you were dead! I thought he'd killed you!" She reached behind Josh's neck, brought him into her. "I've never been so scared."

It was then through the gloom, Skye spotted Kiya's body lying in the mud several feet away and realized for the first time the sacrifice her wolf had made. Grief had her sobbing out, "She gave her spirit...to you...to save me. She's gone."

Her eyes filled with tears. Fat drops rolled down her cheeks and mixed with the steady downpour hitting her face. Her breath hitched in unbelievable heartache for the wolf she'd known for a lifetime. "Nez Perce legend speaks of what happened here today but until now, I didn't believe it was possible."

Josh shook his head as if coming out of a daze. He wiped Whitfield's blood from his mouth with the back of his hand before running the other through his dripping hair. He spit out blood and worked his jaw back and forth in an attempt to speak. Slowly, with each word an effort, he declared. "No, Skye, Kiya isn't gone. I feel her heart still beats. But she grows weaker. Her strength is almost gone after what she did. Somehow, not sure exactly, I just *know*. We seem to be...connected now. If she were dead I'd sense it. She isn't."

"Really? I have to check for myself." She started to rise but about that time a sapped Kiya lifted her head in acknowledgement. "Well, look at you, both of you. You seem to be able to read each other, in sync with each other."

"Even with the throb in my head I can hear what she's thinking," Josh stated flatly. "Your wolf is weak but grateful you're alive." He looked into Skye's violet eyes, the bruises beginning to form on her swollen, beaten face. He reached out, took her chin, and examined the damage. "You never have to think about that son of a bitch ever again."

"I know."

Leaning on each other for support, together they went over to the wolf, ran their linked hands through Kiya's thick coat of fur.

"If you truly hear each other's thoughts, then it's true. That was the most incredible thing I've ever seen." Skye rested one hand on the top of Kiya's head, the other in Josh's hair, ran her fingers along the open gash at his temple. The metal pipe had left that side matted with blood mixed with bits of twigs and dirt. "I was so afraid you were dead, Josh. You were so still. And I couldn't get to you."

"Not with that bastard beating on you, you couldn't. I think I was. Dead that is. Not sure yet. Kiya brought me—back from somewhere."

"You didn't move after he hit you—here, on the temple. Not a muscle."

"Tell me about it. My head's still pounding like a freight train's roaring inside. Last thing I remember was that pipe connecting to bone. Lights out. Next thing I know I'm looking down at this piece of shit and I've ripped out his throat."

"Where are your glasses, Josh? I remember they were knocked off your face, broken, in bits. The pieces are around here somewhere. I'll look for them."

"Don't bother. I can see just fine, thanks. In fact, I can pick out that caterpillar crawling up the bark of that tree over there from twenty yards away, make out its shape, its size, even the way it wiggles. Plus, I hear the rustle of leaves, hear animals foraging for food." He lifted his head, sniffed the air. "And mating. Two bobcats about half a mile back. That way." He pointed to the woods behind them.

Skye's eyes went wide. "I suppose that explains how you went primal. I've never seen anyone so—fierce before."

"Yeah? I'm pretty sure I said the same thing about you the first night I saw you back in that alley when the odds weren't in your favor."

Skye shook her head, spared a quick glance over at Whitfield's body, or rather what was left of it and said, "Oh no. He had me dead to rights. If it weren't for you…you were magnificent, Josh. I'm still trying to absorb the fact you were dead. Whitfield killed you. And here you are—"

For the first time, his eyes homed in on her face and the glazed look in her eyes. If she wasn't already in shock, she was definitely heading there. After rubbing her arms up and down through the jacket she wore to get her warm, he took hold of her trembling chin again. "Hey, you okay?"

"I am now. In fact, I'm wonderful. But…are you okay with what happened here, Josh? I mean…" She inhaled a shaky breath, glanced up into his eyes. "Whitfield's dead."

He nodded, pursed his lips. "Sure. What else could we have done? Think of it this way. The bastard will never again have the chance to put his filthy hands on another kid."

"Thank God for that."

"We need to get out of here, but first we need to make sure…" Josh's voice trailed off as he scanned what was now a crime scene. "We cover our tracks; leave nothing that can be tied back to us."

"He kicked the .380 out of my hand and it went into those bushes over there. The knife's around here somewhere."

"You look for the knife, I'll retrieve the gun."

"There's not much we can do about the tracks or the sign of a fight."

Josh stared up at the sky and the rain beginning to pick up. "I don't think that'll be a problem. Mother Nature seems to be on our side. "

It took them ten minutes to gather up what they needed. Once they'd collected everything, once they started heading back the way they'd come, the rain began to pour down in sheets, covering whatever tracks they had left behind.

CHAPTER TWENTY-ONE

That night when Ronny Wayne failed to show up for supper at the main house, the man's aunt and uncle went looking for their nephew in the pouring rain. They'd gone about three hundred yards from the cabin before they discovered his body on a hillside above his house. His throat had been ripped out, his chest torn to shreds.

It took two days for the medical examiner in Pierce County, where the body had been found, to rule on Whitfield's exact cause of death. The man died as a result of a vicious animal attack.

Because of bureaucratic red tape and a stack of other cases piling up, it took another two days for that information to reach Detective Harry Drummond in Seattle. Harry had to read the report a second time for it to actually sink in. He didn't buy it. But he was a man who lived by autopsies and facts and DNA results.

The DNA had been a slam dunk for a wolf bite. Mostly. According to that same Tacoma coroner the test had also indicated traces of human blood in the saliva. The doctor's explanation was that the wolf in question had simply bitten another human before biting Ronny Wayne.

A bite was one thing, but the guy's shredded throat indicated in the autopsy, was a different game entirely.

But after what the Pierce County authorities had discovered in Ronny Wayne's cabin, Harry wasn't sure anyone cared too much about how Whitfield had met his demise. For starters, they'd discovered the registered sex offender had in his possession expensive video, camera, and editing equipment. All of which Whitfield had used to make his own films. His home computer contained in excess of three hundred thousand images of child pornography, and enough trophies to indicate there were a slew of underage victims. It would more than likely take months to sort through both the digital and still formats to assess and identify all the young girls involved. Then there was the inventory list of what appeared to be a thriving sex-trafficking trade between Whitfield and a group of like-minded individuals strung across the world from South America to Europe to Asia.

Harry was pretty sure few people, other than maybe Ronny Wayne's aunt and uncle, cared a great deal about how a wolf had taken down Whitfield. But even the mysterious death of scum piqued Harry's curiosity because none of it felt right to him.

For now though, Harry intended to pursue the sex-trafficking angle because King County and Pierce had formed a joint task force. Harry had known it existed. Hadn't Skye mentioned it to him during countless conversations? How many times had she tried to get him to do more than talk about the active groups in Venezuela and beyond? But with actual evidence on record in another county now, Harry could follow and track Whitfield's paper trail and digital connection to other sex offenders, starting with the man's most recent emails to people in places like South America and Thailand and anywhere else Whitfield had made a connection.

After all, he still had a missing twelve-year-old to find, which had to come first. For all he knew, Jenna Donofrio could have already been whisked off to any number of foreign destinations. Of course, Harry had no proof of that. And until he did, he didn't intend to give up his search to find out what happened to Jenna.

Brandon Hiller had been on the run for the better part of a week, dodging Ronny Wayne and his associates. He'd taken turns parking his van in various neighborhoods, from Ballard to Roosevelt and any place in between. The area couldn't be too upscale otherwise his rusty paint-deprived van would raise suspicions and might be targeted by a crime watch enthusiast or two. He couldn't afford to draw the attention of cops because he hadn't checked in with his parole officer in more than a week which meant if he ever crossed paths with a member of law enforcement they'd send him back to Clallam Bay for good.

All this stress was making him crazy. He needed a release. He checked the time on his thirty-five-dollar Timex. Two-thirty. He decided it was the perfect time to take another pass around the nearest elementary school. If he didn't have any success there, he'd try the park at Town Center Drive and Lawson.

Suddenly feeling better about his prospects, Brandon Hiller made a right at the next corner, and turned into the residential area near Westlake. Pulling up to the curb to wait, he immediately began to tap the steering wheel in a nervous habit as he scouted for what he needed to calm himself down.

He didn't have to wait long before kids burst out of the school in a mass exodus, streaming along the sidewalks and over the rolling grass. Taking in as many choices as he could, soon his eyes lit on the little blonde, the one walking alone, probably a third or fourth grader. He turned the key on the van.

There really was no time for finesse, so he'd have to follow her for a few blocks, wait for his opportunity to grab her and get her into the vehicle. He'd have to get rid of her body someplace else though since he couldn't very well take her back to Tacoma.

About that time, Hiller looked up to check his rearview mirror. His heart almost stuttered in his chest when he spotted the familiar blue shade of a police unit several car lengths back. As soon as the van reached the end of the block, at the corner, Hiller took a left at the four-way stop. When the cop made the same turn, Hiller decided he needed to play it cool. But he also knew he had to get the hell out of the neighborhood. He took a quick right on Madison, realized the cop car hadn't made the same turn. But he took his close call as a sign that he still needed to lie low—and lie low was exactly what he intended to do— at least until it was safe to go on the hunt again.

He couldn't go to his sister's place. He had to find somewhere to keep off the radar, some deep, dark hole where he could hide.

Josh's headache lingered for two days. But even after his head stopped hammering, there were changes. His sense of smell had increased a hundred-fold. He could now distinguish between fear and calm, between friend and foe. Not only that, he could also bench press three times his weight and since yesterday morning, could take Skye down in a sparring match, something he hadn't been able to do before.

He had his same body mass. His muscles were still the same size they'd been since college. It wasn't like he'd gained weight or took on a bodybuilder's physique overnight. He hadn't. But now the strength he possessed seemed...innate, almost otherworldly.

He'd learned a valuable lesson though. Never again would he underestimate the enemy, not the likes of Whitfield or anyone else. He'd been careless. He'd allowed the man to sneak up on both of them and put Skye in jeopardy—again.

Josh had to face the truth. His sloppiness could've allowed Whitfield to kill Skye. If not for Kiya…

He glanced over at Skye, took in the bruises on her face. He could still make out the purplish traces of fingerprints along her neck from the man who had tried to strangle her. Despite two cracked ribs and a wrenched knee, she was getting around remarkably well. Every time Josh looked at her, every time he thought about how close he'd come to losing her and his own life in the process, he could only consider how lucky they'd both been to survive despite their own stupidity. Josh could still see that monster trying to choke the life out of her with his bare hands. No, Josh would take that image to his grave. He would learn from the lesson. He'd never again be quite that stupid.

In the kitchen in his loft, Josh watched Skye as she worked on yet another one of Daniel Cree's remedies to get both man and wolf back to the way they'd been before the merge. Of course nothing in her father's notes covered the actual joining between breeds. Shamans might've sung about it, legends may have been retold around the lodge fires, but no one had ever experienced such a transformation in reality.

"I give up," Skye announced as she pushed her father's leather-bound journal across the table. "I've tried everything, bought every healing herb mentioned in that book, mixed it with all the right things, in the correct measurements and dosage, and not one of them has even come close."

For days the house had smelled of sage, rosemary, and thyme along with a blend of nettle, aloe, and sweet grass. One would've thought Thanksgiving turkey roasted in the oven instead of cooking up an antidote to a thousand-year-old myth.

"I'm not taking peyote again," Josh said flatly. "I admit it was a kick at first to meditate and get in touch with my feminine wolf side, but once should've been enough."

Skye snickered, then sighed. "Josh, I'm no good at this. After this much time has passed the aftereffects of the merge should have diminished by now. They haven't. I've tried every cleanse listed in that book."

"I know you have since I've been your lab rat."

"I should probably call Travis."

"We've talked about this, Skye. I thought we agreed. It's better if we're the only two who know what happened out there."

She looked insulted. "Not now, nor do you ever have to worry about me telling anyone what happened to that despicable excuse for a human being. I'll swear it on the graves of my parents if that's what it takes for you to believe me. No one will know—from me. Ever. And that includes Travis."

Josh rose, went to her, framed her face. "I'm not worried about that, Skye. But Travis is bound to get curious how this all came to be, especially when you start bringing up the legend out of the blue. Don't you think Travis will wonder why you're asking? And besides, I don't think he'll be as supportive as you seem to think since I'm involved. Need I remind you of his less than lukewarm reception the other night? And that was before all this took place."

"Maybe. But he doesn't have to know details. I'm telling you Travis can be trusted. Besides, my knowledge is simply...too limited for something this huge. His is better. And dad's remedies don't exactly cover this type of...ailment. I've read through the entire set of journals...twice."

"How exactly did you get to keep your father's books? The way you described your Aunt Ginny and Uncle Bob, I'd think they would've wanted to burn them at the first available opportunity."

"Oh I'm sure they did. But Travis went in after the accident and boxed up my parents' possessions, kept what he could for me in storage. That included all of my father's books, my mother's artwork. Travis held onto the stuff even though he had to pay storage for years until I could go through the contents and figure out what I wanted to keep."

Josh ran a hand through his hair. He didn't think it was a good idea for them to get a case of loose lips now but

Skye seemed to want to trust the guy. This certainly hadn't been the first time she'd brought him into the conversation over the past several days. "Then what you're saying is this Travis is your only family but not. Maybe that's why he acts like your overprotective father."

She harrumphed at that. "He's never had to worry about that before."

"Until now."

Their eyes met. That pull in the belly had her puffing out a breath. "I'll talk to him. Okay? Travis is like my only real family without being blood. And Ginny and Bob don't count. Travis is genuine. He likes me for me, unconditionally."

Josh wrapped a hand around hers. "I'd say he loves you, Skye. Like a father."

"I won't argue with that assessment. He's been incredibly supportive over the years. And that's why I think there's a chance he'll be able to come up with just the right dose of—something—to help you get back—"

"I don't think this is going away with an herbal remedy. Nor do I think letting anyone in on what happened is the answer. I'm willing to ride it out but...if you want to let Travis in on this deal because he's someone you think you can trust and believe he'll be able to come up with something that might help then I won't stop you. But I don't think it's a good idea."

"You have to trust me." She ran a nervous hand through her hair feeling anything but confident that she was making the right decision for both of them. "I know you're willing to ride it out but I'd feel better if Travis looked at you. We need to know if this is permanent. What if it's permanent, Josh? Have you considered the ramifications of that?" She reached for her phone. "No, it never hurts to call in reinforcements or backup when we're in way over our heads."

"I'm certain that horse has already left the barn, in fact it's probably well into the next county by now," he muttered as he listened to Skye try to explain their situation to a man who did not like him. As the conversation progressed, Josh felt mounting unease with each word out of Skye's mouth. And when Travis suggested that he go get a blood test, Josh knew for certain that getting Travis involved was a very bad idea.

CHAPTER TWENTY-TWO

The next morning Josh's apprehension only increased during the long, traffic-congested drive north out to The Painted Crow. Because Travis Nakota was the last person he wanted to see at the moment. But as the car approached the main gate, Josh got a look at the guy's property in broad daylight and saw what he'd missed the other night. Amid the majestic beauty of thick evergreens and rolling pastureland, the ranch sat on a forest of cliff and peak before it dropped down a good hundred feet onto a narrow inlet of rocky coastline dotted with a variety of conifers.

From inside the Subaru you could smell the unmistakable aroma of salt and sea mixed with Douglas fir and pine. Today the mist of gray rolling in on the horizon met headlong with the blue-green waves that slammed up against the wedge of shore. To Josh it looked like something out of a dark and moody painting.

Maybe it was an omen, he thought as he walked into the lion's den or rather into Travis's living room, a traditional man's room filled with soft black leather furniture, chrome accents, and mahogany wood. Josh expected to see the heads of animals decorating the walls. Instead of that though, there were several large oil paintings done by a local Native American artist named Ty Moon. Josh immediately recognized the style and bold use of color the man was known to use in his landscapes and Native scenes.

As Josh stood five feet away, Travis Nakota never spared him a glance. His demeanor all business, Travis got right down to the reason they were there in the first place. He sat behind a massive desk styled with western carvings and studied the piece of paper with the test results before finally looking up at Josh then at Skye. He scratched his chin. "The bloodwork confirms some of Kiya the wolf is in Ander. Is that what you wanted to know? Does it help knowing the man is an anomaly?"

"By any chance, could you call the man Josh?" Skye requested in a tight voice.

"Why?"

"Because he's going to be around awhile."

Travis twisted up his mouth. "How about if I refer to him as paleface, how would that be?"

"Stereotype much?" Josh asked with an undercurrent of resentment. He was pretty much fed up with the man's attitude. "I'd settle for kemosabe."

"I'll kemosabe your ass," Travis shot back.

"What is wrong with you?" Skye demanded when she turned to face Travis head on. "You've been acting weird lately."

"I'll tell you what's wrong with him. You brought a man here. Twice. Me. And he doesn't like it very much," Josh reasoned. "Isn't that right, Mr. Nakota? Why don't you tell her how you really feel about me?"

"Travis?" Skye asked truly bewildered at his attitude. She'd never seen him act quite so rude and distant before.

Travis let out an exasperated sigh before turning to the woman he considered his surrogate daughter and had since the day the thirteen-year-old girl had lost her parents. During that time he'd had to sit by and do nothing but watch, as she was forced to go live with people, Jodi Cree had described as mean-spirited hiding behind a religious façade. The courts back then might've tied his hands, but now he refused to sit idly by and watch Skye make an error in judgment that might affect the rest of her life. "I knew one day it would happen. I knew one day you'd find some scruffy piece of shit on the streets as you made your nightly rounds and drag him here and force me to be nice to him. Well, it won't work."

"I told you this was a bad idea," Josh tossed back to Skye.

Skye's shoulders slumped. She ran a hand through her hair. "Travis, when I called you, you assured me you could be open-minded and reasonable where Josh was concerned. This is a serious issue and you're making it much more difficult. We need your help—not your anger over my choice in men."

"Fine," Travis managed through gritted teeth. "But I think I've been incredibly generous in the fact that I haven't asked a lot of questions up to this point about your relationship and why in the hell you're with this guy in the first place. Let alone not inquiring as to how this all came about. And why the hell didn't you tell me about Whitfield? Tell me that. Why the hell did I have to read it in the newspaper? Did it occur to you I might want to rejoice at knowing that son of a bitch finally met his demise? They listed his cause of death as an animal attack. Do you think I'm stupid? Do you think I don't know this mysterious ailment Josh has isn't somehow connected to what happened to Whitfield? I may look stupid—"

"Stop it!" Skye bellowed. "I'm sorry. Okay? You're right. I should've told you about Whitfield myself. But we've been dealing with a great deal of stress ever since it happened. Just please do not ask for details. Please."

"Don't ask for details? Your spirit guide has set you upon a path that only you should know about. That's tradition, part of your heritage. And yet, Ander knows. An outsider knows. Someone who makes fun of our beliefs every chance they get." Travis pointed an accusatory finger at Josh and went on, "You may have disturbed her path, altered it, weakened it, and put her on a different course entirely than the one she was destined to walk. Now the path is not clear, clouded even, one that might get her killed."

"Wait a minute. Not now, nor have I ever made fun of Skye's beliefs," Josh avowed. "Kiya is sacred to her. I wouldn't do that. And besides—"

Skye tried for calm. "Travis, there's no point in blaming Josh. It was Kiya's decision, her action is the reason we're here." She turned to Josh. "We might as well level with him otherwise he's only going to jump to conclusions that simply aren't true."

She turned back to Travis. "I've known you my entire life. You were my father's best friend. I need you now. No, that's not entirely accurate. We need your expertise now more than ever. Josh did nothing to bring this on. Nothing. He was trying to help me. You just gave us the test results. What do you think they mean, Travis? That piece of paper doesn't lie. It shows Josh has Kiya's blood running through him. How do you think that came to be? Josh did nothing," she repeated. Except die, thought Skye. "Kiya brought the legend to life on her own. I've heard stories about the spirit-dominated transformation—" Skye's steam trailed off as she dropped down into one of the leather chairs. "And we don't know how to reverse it. Or if it's permanent."

Travis's eyes narrowed at the realization of what she'd admitted. "Kiya...did this? She sacrificed herself for this—?"

"Outsider? Yes," Josh finished.

"What could possibly have happened—?" Travis stopped, deliberately considered Josh, long and hard. He puffed out a breath. "Kiya must have felt you were deserving of this...power then." Travis rubbed at his throbbing temple before steepling his fingers, while sinking back into his chair. His shoulders appeared to slump as his irritation finally reached its finish line. "I might not fathom the why, but then sometimes the spirit guide senses and feels things we do not and cannot understand."

"It was dire circumstances," Josh explained as he began to stride, animal-like, back and forth, back and forth. "But the bottom line is this. We either can count on your help or we can't. Which is it?"

Several seconds went by before Travis spoke. "All right, all right, but let's back up here a minute, take it one step at a time." He shuffled the paper, turned the page to read the rest of the results he held in his hand. For a long time he said nothing, thinking, weighing what he wanted to say. Finally, he spoke in calm tones. "Okay, I'd say at this point, Josh's blood has to be about ten percent Kiya while Kiya is more than likely made up of about that same percent of Josh. At least. That's a guess by the way, a rough estimate. Could be higher, it's tough to tell with any accuracy. That number's preventing both of them from returning to the way they were—in spite of what you've tried—before their uniting of spirit, merging of instincts."

"But it's only ten percent," Skye pointed out. "Surely that small amount wouldn't make that much of a difference. Would it?"

Travis scrubbed a hand over his face. "Wrong. According to what brought you here, what you told me over the phone yesterday traits have merged, remained steadfast for days now. After this much time's gone by the behavior should have diminished. That much I *do* know. It's—significant that it hasn't. And telling."

On some level Josh had already figured that much out for himself. He and Skye had talked about it. There were just too many changes to his norm. He'd always loved steak, but lately meat had become a must, the rarer the better. His senses were off the charts, all of them. He no longer needed his wire-rims to see distance. He could pick up noise from three blocks away—and that was in the city—in the country it was twice that far. But hearing someone with Native American roots and knowledge of the legend confirm what he'd suspected for days took some getting used to.

Skye misread the look on Josh's face for something else. "I understand you're upset but you were dead, Josh.

This…merge, for lack of a better word, brought you back to me. I know you aren't the same as you were but—"

"I wouldn't be standing here if Kiya hadn't done what she did." Josh met Travis's brown eyes and noted they'd warmed some. But then, he saw the curiosity peak in them. "I told you the situation was dire, life or death, a desperate set of circumstances."

Travis nodded. "Life or death, I'd say that tops everything." He'd known when Skye called him something major had happened days earlier to the geeky gamer, so he held up his hands. "I'm getting the picture. It's okay. I don't need to know more details in case anyone comes knocking at my door. Which they won't," he added before looking Josh in the eye. "But I won't lie to you. This could be life-changing. You do know that?"

"I know that. I feel it. But I've been a hardcore gamer since I was old enough to pick up a joystick. It's kind of difficult to be angry when this is probably the most exciting thing that's ever happened to me in my life. I'm part wolfman. On some level, how cool is that?"

But Travis shook his head. "No. It's scary that the youth of our time is so—misguided and uninformed, obviously from the influence of games like yours and Hollywood wolfman movies. I would expect that kind of smugness though. What you are Josh Ander is more like a mutt with wolf *tendencies*. Huge difference. If the percentages were higher, say upward to fifteen or twenty, you might be running wild in the forest right about now." He cocked a brow. "Consider that before you start thinking wolfman or that this could be an extension to one of your clever games."

"So Skye told you about my idea."

"Your incredibly brainless idea? Yes. To suggest a victim might let you use her likeness—"

"I'm not a victim," Skye piped up. "And I haven't been for a very long time. I understand you're pissed off, but don't take your frustration out on Josh. You barely know the man."

"And you do?" Travis shot back. "Just because you're sharing his bed—"

"Watch it," Josh warned, stepping closer to Travis. "My good nature has been recently tested and I'm not above going to the mat for Skye."

Travis gave him a quick nod of his head in approval. "Now, that's a first step and exactly what I wanted to hear—if it's an honest declaration."

"Oh really?" Skye retorted. "He's already gone to the mat for me, Travis. There's nothing else he has to prove to me…nothing."

"I'm aware of that…now. But it means a great deal to me to know this man cares for my—" Travis quickly caught himself and stopped short.

"Yeah, well, Skye means a great deal to me, too," Josh reaffirmed.

"Then are we done shouting at each other? Because we still don't have a lot of answers here," Skye reasoned.

"I don't know. Are we?" asked Josh.

"I guess I am," Travis admitted. "But I reserve the right to shout if he hurts you—in any way."

Skye went over to Travis then, gave him a hug. "I've never dated, Travis, not until Josh."

"I know. I guess I'm relieved at that."

"Then you're taking this awfully well, considering. I appreciate the fact you care if I'm happy or not, alive or not," Skye commented. "You too," she said to Josh. "But we really don't have much choice, now do we?"

"Not when the alternative is pretty lame," Josh countered.

"Not when the alternative might've been death for both of you," Travis surmised, holding up his hand. "I don't even want to know how Whitfield got the drop on both of you."

"We were sloppy, distracted, talking too much," Josh acknowledged. "There's no prettying it up. But I promise you, it won't happen again."

"Good. It's done then. But there's something else you need to know. In times of danger or high stress, I suspect the wolf tendencies may take over entirely, which is what you've already experienced firsthand. You'll feel it when it begins to happen. You'll have to learn to control that part of you. Otherwise, it could take over and you'll be at the mercy of instinct rather than relying on your brain, your human intelligence. Try to think of it as a gift though. Kiya has given you the opportunity to sense things that other humans cannot. But if you don't learn to control the wolf's innate characteristics, it could take over at an inopportune time and cost you your life."

"So much for having super-hero powers," Josh cracked. "I should probably avoid kryptonite."

But Skye didn't see the humor at all. "And Kiya? What happens to her? I sense she's simply a very weak spirit now because her energy is gone, zapped. She isn't strong like she used to be."

Travis nodded. "Her senses have been diminished by mingling with Josh's human traits. Her spirit will take some time to recover if at all. Right now, Josh's influence is too strong. The wolf's spirit may never be the same."

"How is it possible Kiya didn't get any of my smarts that might compensate for what she's given to me?" Josh wanted to know.

"Oh she did, but her own instincts have dropped so much because she gave her all to you, draining hers. All in all, I'd say this is actually textbook spirit guide stuff. Let me guess, Skye was in trouble when Kiya made the leap?"

Josh chewed the inside of his jaw, said nothing.

Travis glanced over at Skye who also remained silent. "Very well, I'll take your silence as a yes. In the future, I suspect the wolf will have to be close to Josh in order for her spirit to ever be completely whole."

"How close?"

"I have no idea. This is all conjecture on my part. According to our legend though, the human could move between both worlds, either that of being a man or a wolf at his choosing. He had to occupy one or the other, not both. You're part of both worlds and so is the wolf. That's what I was trying to tell you earlier. To some extent the legend is still just that. At this stage, what you are is...unprecedented."

"Terrific," Josh said as he reached out for Skye's hand. "We have something in common though. And if I try real hard, with any luck, maybe one day I'll be able to read your mind—eventually, maybe we'll be able to mind-link. You know, like the Vulcan mind meld. After all, the three of us are connected now in a huge way."

Skye rolled her eyes. "If you'd focus on something other than sci-fi for five minutes we might be able to figure this out."

"All legends have some factual base to them. And my knowledge of sci-fi is bound to come in handy at some point because—"

Travis held up his hands for peace. "Please kids, if I could be allowed to continue. Don't be surprised if Kiya regains her strength, she may possibly be able to take a corporeal form now and again." When both of them turned to stare at him, Travis added, "Again, Josh's influence. I just can't be one hundred percent certain. In the meantime, why don't the two of you plan to stay here for a couple of days? If for no other reason than to remain off the radar, that way I'll keep pumping the elders for answers, see what information I'm able to pull out of them without sharing too much detail." He looked straight at Josh. "Yes, I know I'll need to be discreet with them. And I will. What I'd like to do while you're here is try a cleansing ritual. If nothing else it might help keep you balanced and in this world. Or, if we're lucky the Great Spirit will show you your true path."

Josh and Skye traded glances. The look on her face told Josh that Skye was leaving the decision up to him. Finally, Josh huffed out a breath. "Okay, we'll stay for a few days but I've already explained to Skye I don't see how an herbal remedy is the answer. But hell, I suppose I'll try anything once."

Travis got up out of his chair. He walked to Josh, slapped him on the back, put his hand out. "That's the spirit. We'll make a Nez Perce out of you yet."

Josh took the man's outstretched hand and said, "I could live with that."

But Skye had been rolling around a thought. "I have a question. Something just clicked. Travis, are you aware the Internet has been full of stories recently where people report seeing a silver wolf around inner city Seattle? My spirit guide's never been corporeal. Now you're telling me with Josh's spirit infused in her, she might be. Are these people seeing Kiya or another wolf running around from somewhere?" A little embarrassed to tell him what Kiya had indicated to her, she hesitated before saying, "Is this wolf connected to me in some way or is it even Kiya at all?"

Travis rolled his eyes. "You want to know too much information. I don't have all the answers either, at least not off the top of my spinning head. But who says the connection is to you. It might be to Josh. And connected could mean anything. Connected might be akin to ESP, a foretelling, a vision maybe, a bridge to the spirit world."

"Ah," Skye said. She looked over at Josh who was reading one of Travis's books he'd taken down out of the bookcase. It was still hard to get used to him sans wire-rims. "What do you intend to tell people, Josh, when they ask about your glasses and why you aren't wearing them?"

"I'll tell them I finally got up the nerve to get Lasik."

"So your eyesight is now perfect?" Travis asked.

"Oh yeah, among other things. Not since third grade have I been able to see distance without my glasses."

Turning to Travis, with a nod of her head toward Josh, Skye deadpanned, "This guy has a slew of fancy rugs at his place. Does he need to be concerned about peeing on every single one of them to mark his territory?"

Josh bumped her shoulder. "I like my rugs."

"Sure you do, that's why I need to know if I should put down newspaper so you don't mess 'em up."

Travis shook his head. "If I were you, I'd really be more concerned about the potential for howling. It's been my experience that never goes over well with the neighbors."

While they waited for Travis to come up with the right ingredients to perform the ritual cleanse, Skye and Josh had plenty to keep them busy.

They used Travis's computer, keeping tabs on the Whitfield case via the media. They put in time at the gun range. Not to mention training like fiends for a battle they weren't sure would ever come. But if visions and dreams were any indication, there were still kids out there locked up—in filth and abused—waiting for someone to come to their aid. How long would their abductors keep them around before shipping them out to foreign destinations?

They were running out of time. With everything else going on, that fact alone caused Skye several restless nights.

That's the excuse she used as she and Josh tossed each other around in Travis's weight room, spacious enough to allow them to practice their martial arts techniques on each other.

Skye went down on her butt again for the third time in a row. "Okay, so you're getting a little bit better as we go."

"How does it feel down there on the mat?" Josh asked in a playful tone. "Be grateful for the mat. Every time you bested me, I landed on a thin scrap of AstroTurf spread out over concrete." He grinned and reached out to help her up.

"How is it you seem to know my next move beforehand?"

"Instincts. Besides, you telegraph them. I'm surprised I didn't catch on sooner."

"Since when?"

"Since I started paying closer attention."

She stood up in a huff, rested her hands on her hip. When he continued to stare at her, she took the opportunity to dive at him in a menacing attack. But he countered by simply picking her up and throwing her over his shoulder. Instead of tossing her over on her back though, Josh let her dangle there, which only frustrated her more.

"Damn it," she shouted. "You can put me down now. I suppose I should be grateful my partner is so adept at hand-to-hand now."

He took the opportunity to pat her on the butt before setting her feet first on the floor. "I won't be surprised or taken off guard again. Not by anyone," Josh determined. "We're both lucky to be here able to argue with one another like this."

"You think I don't know that," she said pushing her hair off her face. "We owe Kiya a debt we may never be able to repay."

"We repay her by continuing your path, your destiny. Together, side-by-side."

"We continue the hunt. Together."

"Yeah."

That night as the sun dropped over the horizon the cleansing ritual began.

Travis led them down a flight of steps and into the in-ground lodge as flutes soared in the background. From the depths of the earth, twelve feet down, Josh and Skye waited as Travis dipped a finger into a clay pot containing burned sage. He used his thumb to smudge their foreheads with the ash to ward off evil. After that, they dropped down cross-legged where they stood, and took their places around a circle where twelve large stones glistened with glowing embers. As the fire simmered with fragrant cedar, sending out smoke trails, it sizzled and popped, while soft shadows danced on the dirt walls almost in time to the music. With elements of lavender for healing, juniper for protection, and sweet grass thrown in to attract the mother spirit, the smells wafted together, thick and strong, purifying the air.

Travis loaded the sacred Chanunpa pipe with ripe tobacco and lit it. He inhaled deeply taking in one puff, then two, before handing it to Skye, who did the same before passing it on to Josh.

Travis began to chant. "We call now to Grandfather Sky and Grandmother Earth, our ancestors, our forefathers. We wish for our questions, our quest, our prayers to be carried to the Great Spirit on the smoke from the tobacco and be heard and answered."

Travis waved his hands through the air to make sure the smoke moved and began to sing. "Ee ah hay, ee ah hay, ee ah, ee ah hay. Oh Great Spirit, we come before you to help young Josh Ander become in the way of our people. Ee ah hay, ee ah hay, ee ah, ee ah hay. Guide Josh Ander along his different path. Lead him strong into the Land of the People. Ee ah hay, ee ah hay, ee ah, ee ah hay. Renew Kiya's spirit and return her so that she may continue to walk her destiny. Lead the wolf to the Land of the Spirits so that she may continue to guide and be strong. Ee ah hay, ee ah hay, ee ah, ee ah hay."

The three of them took up the refrain while alternately smoking the pipe. Even though the ceremony lasted less than forty-five minutes, by the time Josh mounted the steps to the top, he was more than ready to get outside. The air felt good when it rushed past his face even though it had a bite to it. The breeze felt like he'd hit an oasis after spending days in the desert. He longed for something cold to drink.

As if she read his mind, Skye pushed a bottle of water into his hand. "Are you okay?" she asked before chugging down the liquid from her own bottle.

"I'm not sure...how I feel...that wasn't as intense as I thought it would be. Yet I do feel—something."

"That's the point, although to be honest, I have no idea how or why it works." She took another gulp of water as if postponing what was on her mind.

Josh gave her a few long minutes to let her gather her thoughts until finally she spoke.

"Travis and my mom and dad brought me here after it happened, after I got out of the hospital. As a kid, I remember being fairly skeptical of the whole process back then. But then…after spending time in the lodge…I felt renewed. You know…changed…for the better. Back then I needed to come here, the perfect place for me to get well. But that was the last time I was ever in the lodge with my parents."

Josh noted the tears glistening in the corners of those beautiful eyes. The sad look told Josh she needed comforting. So he put his arms around her waist and pulled her to him. Lifting her chin, he covered her mouth. Because his brain seemed empty of thoughts, hollowed out, no words came to mind that wouldn't sound lame. So he said nothing. But he intended to show her how he felt so he led her into the house and into the bedroom.

After slipping a CD he'd found in Travis's den into an old-fashioned boom box that sat on the dresser, Josh reached out for her hand. They began to undress each other as the pipes started out low and haunting in the background.

He grazed along her jaw, chewed along her throat before easing her down on the mattress. As the lilt of flutes soared and mixed with the steady beat of drums, it didn't take long for them to weave their own sweet, slow dance and build it to match rhythm and song.

From his own room Travis heard the woodwinds and couldn't settle. A blind man from ten miles down the road would've been able to see how Skye felt about Ander and it seemed how Ander felt about her.

He didn't begrudge Skye her private life. He just didn't want to see her hurt. As the music continued to climb from the guest room, Travis accepted that there was nothing he could do about it anyway. His little girl had somehow grown up. She was entitled to a relationship, to finally have a normal life. As he took out headphones from his desk to cover his ears to protect his heart from anymore sounds that might drift his way, his eyes landed on a photograph taken years earlier. Daniel and Jodi Cree stared back at him, the couple sitting together outside in their garden, young and vibrant as they had been in life.

From the moment that day in the park when Skye had disappeared and they realized she'd been taken, Travis had worried, and cried, and had feared the worst right along with her parents. For three days through the horror of not knowing her fate, he'd sat side by side with Jodi and Daniel and grieved for the child.

But staring at the picture now made Travis want more. Didn't he deserve more after all the time that had passed? If not now, when? "I've done everything you asked of me. I even allowed her to go live with people who treated her as though she were less. I didn't fight the courts even though I could have. She spent five long years with them. She shouldn't have had to do that. So I'm not sure how much longer I can continue to keep silent. I think she deserves to know what we did. No, I'm not ready to let her go just yet, not when a lie stands between us and I haven't been allowed to stand in front of her with the truth. But I believe you both can rest now as she's finally reached womanhood. Our child is no longer anyone's little girl."

As a tear ran down his cheek, Travis Nakota sat in the dark of his bedroom, too sad about that to bother with the headphones.

Josh wasn't exactly sure what time they finally fell asleep, but that night he dreamed. He ran through a forest lush in its emerald greens and cool jades, over hills peppered in yellow flowers and vines laden with ripe berries. He felt his own heart thud as he ran as fast as the wind and as light as air.

Abruptly, he was no longer running and no longer on earth. Standing between two worlds, one foot in this universe, the other in another sphere entirely, he was able to look down from a great height. He detected hurt...pain...suffering...and ultimately evil.

He'd left his life behind as he knew it for another path, one that he hadn't counted on taking. Instead of unease there was elation at the prospect of following something new with someone new.

Suddenly he took off in a sprint again but this time he wasn't alone. A silver wolf ran at his side. Behind him there were several more of various colors and sizes. By his count, half a dozen trailed after him, but it was he and Kiya together who led the pack.

They were chasing a scent unfamiliar to Josh. The foul odor left an unpleasant taste in his mouth. The further into the thicket of woods they got, the more the timber and surrounding area turned barren with decay and disease. No longer brilliant in colors of spring, the land became a dull brown in various stages of dying off. Even the undergrowth stank of rotting earth.

Whatever they were pursuing led them to the opening of a cave. The smell here was overwhelming.

This is your path now. This is your pack. You must not deviate from it. You have only begun your quest. Open your mind to all that is new. What's inside the cave represents the evil you have yet to find. Now when you cross paths with it, you will be able to recognize how it smells and how it feels when you are near it.

As the dream lifted, Josh blinked awake—and realized he was outside—and naked. He glanced to his right and found a fully dressed Skye standing over him, staring, holding a blanket.

"What are you doing out here?" she asked as she knelt down to wrap the quilt around his shoulders.

He huddled under the wool and said, "I'd ask you the same."

"I woke up and you weren't in bed. I looked over at the sliding glass door in time to see you step outside. I tried to stop you. But it was like you were sleepwalking, naked as the day you were born. No matter what I said or did or how loud I shouted, you were determined to get out into the night. By the time I threw some clothes on and followed you, you had already crossed over into the pastureland. You were heading into the woods toward the coast. I had a helluva time keeping up with you, since you were running as though the devil himself was after you."

Josh got to his feet and looked around. It was pitch dark except for a slice of full moon that tried to peek out past lazy clouds. A sliver of moonlight speared down onto both of them as the sound of the waves crashed up against the cliffs in the distance. Even though the scene should have been serene, there was something not right. Off. Everything felt surreal. He spotted the cave entrance from his dream. "Kiya's spirit was here with me," he mumbled in a low voice. "She was showing me the way to the darkness and how it would feel to find it."

As trees swayed and bent in the shadows, Skye realized Josh was still in a bit of a daze. She tugged on his arm to get him moving. "Josh, we need to go. You have to be freezing cold."

But while a patch of stars glittered as a backdrop, he stubbornly stood rooted to the same spot. "There's evil still out there, Skye."

"I know. Tell me what happened in your vision."

He told her about the dream and then added, "I knew what it was, that it wasn't really happening. But I could hear Kiya's voice as if it were real. I understood all the symbolism the wolf used to show me the whole thing about being in two worlds, the decaying forest representing the evil. I was the hunter, like you. And still the thing that got to me the most was the realization of how powerful the evil is and how it can build if you don't take a stand to stop it."

Skye glanced up at the strip of stars overhead. "I go out every night and walk the streets, hoping to be able to make a difference, to somehow stop that evil from touching so many others. But you know what, Josh? Evil doesn't wait for the midnight hour to strike. It can happen in broad daylight on the walk to school. It can happen at anytime of day. It can happen in the blink of an eye by trusting the wrong someone and getting into a car you know you shouldn't have. But not everything happens in the dark of night. It's like not being able to grasp that the face of a monster can have blond hair and blue eyes instead of fangs and horns."

"That's exactly why we'll keep at it. My vision just reinforces what we said earlier. We walk our paths together, side by side. And we start by finding those missing girls."

CHAPTER TWENTY-THREE

Still chained to the cot bolted into the concrete, Heather woke to muffled voices coming from outside her door. She heard crying, a string of moans, and then the sounds of a hand meeting flesh—firm. The slaps caused more grunts and groans. Someone in the room next to hers was either praying or babbling incoherently, she couldn't tell which.

She'd been held in this place for more than a week, at least she thought it was more than a week. She'd been here so long she doubted she'd ever see the light of day again.

Just then, the male voices grew louder, angrier, took exception to the girl who wouldn't stop chanting. A string of swear words let loose, the likes of which Heather had never heard uttered even by the football players at school.

She rested her head on the wall next to the bed to listen, to get a better handle on what the men were saying. From what she could make out there was some delay in the boat docking that had screwed everything up and kept them here longer than ever before. One was sure it was a bad omen. But what really had them worried was that someone had died, some person of importance, someone in charge of the entire operation that caused the men some anxious moments along with having second thoughts and cold feet.

"They've detained Renaldi for some reason."

"Yeah? Well, they probably caught him smuggling the drugs. It's only a matter of time before this thing might be falling apart before our very eyes. We need a backup plan, a way to get out of here in case this whole thing implodes."

"I can't believe you're running this scared?"

"Damn right, I'm scared. I'm not serving time again."

"Come on, use common sense. We pay off Talbot to look the other way, always have, everything will work out, you'll see. Boss says so."

"When did he say that? Before he got his throat ripped out, killed by some animal? Not a likely story if you ask me. Now Renaldi's been picked up as soon as the ship docked this morning. I'm telling you something's going on. This doesn't feel right to me, not anymore. Maybe Talbot didn't get enough money this time, or maybe he had a change of heart, got cold feet. Without a captain and a boat how the hell do we get these girls to fucking South America?"

"It looks bad I know, but have a little faith. Talbot hasn't let us down yet. And he's one of us. What we do is wait for the signal, the all-clear, like always. Then we load these bitches into the vans, head to the docks as soon as we get the word. Soon as we get our money, you'll feel a lot better. Trust me."

But at the moment he didn't feel much like trusting anyone. Something didn't feel right. And he'd learned a long time ago to listen to his instincts. The only time he hadn't, he'd ended up spending eight years in the penitentiary. He sure as hell didn't want to go back.

Harry couldn't help it, he worried. He fretted. It had been almost a week since he'd last talked to Skye Cree. It wasn't like her to completely disappear like this. In fact, he couldn't remember her ever having done so before. And yet, wherever she was, she'd even turned off her cell phone.

He'd tried talking to her friends—Travis, Velma, Lena—and each one of them, for whatever reason, had shut him down, closed ranks. It didn't get past Harry they were purposely not giving up anything about their friend.

Probably with that damn Josh Ander, Harry supposed. The two had been like Siamese twins ever since she'd met the guy.

Didn't the arrogant jerk know Skye wasn't like other women? She hadn't exactly had a standard to live by for a dozen years now. He knew he was being unreasonable in his worry. Not only was Skye a grown adult woman, Josh Ander was a wealthy business owner, a stand-up guy. Even Harry knew it was time Skye experienced all those things other single women took for granted. If that meant losing her heart to the likes of Josh Ander, so be it.

Harry wasn't her father, not even an uncle. But he was her friend. Or so he'd thought. Although he had been pretty hard on Skye after she'd found the Prescott girl. Damn it, he was a cop. He had to question how she'd found Erin. Anyone would've done the same.

But where was she anyway? It couldn't be a coincidence that Josh Ander couldn't be found either. When he'd questioned Josh's staff at Ander All Games about the man's whereabouts, they had all told him the same story. Josh had simply called in with the excuse he'd be taking time off. No further explanation. Nothing.

Harry had already run Josh Ander through a background check. It didn't matter that the guy had come up whistle clean. If Skye didn't surface within the next twenty-four hours, he'd put out a BOLO on both of them.

Had Skye known Harry was so suspicious and on the verge of putting out an all-points bulletin, she would gladly have picked up the phone and called in. Checking in would have meant she could avoid leaving their little retreat, a quaint cottage hidden from the rest of the world, or so it seemed to her.

It might've been the first time she'd visited Orcas Island, but she wondered why she hadn't made coming here a priority until now. The place was like a picture postcard.

They had their own little wooden pier with a boat that bobbed up and down in the water. They could have taken it out to fish. They could have explored the beach, or hiked a dozen nearby trails.

But they'd done none of that.

Since they'd left The Painted Crow Josh had packed her up and brought her here to his family's cabin in the rural rolling hills of Olga, a tiny hamlet tucked away amid old barns that doubled as artist hangouts and forest land meant for backpacking.

It might not have been tropical. It might not have been the ideal spring break destination for lovers. But the place offered seclusion, isolation, and a chance to recharge and ponder Josh's emerging persona, one that neither of them was comfortable with yet.

Since their arrival on the island, they'd slept late, talked until the wee hours of the night, danced to the Red Hot Chili Peppers, relaxed to *Every Minute in Paris* by David Cohen, and made love while Mozart concertos or Chopin sonatas drifted in the background.

Sitting on the back deck with a perfect view of their own little inlet bay, Skye glanced over at Josh stretched out in a deck chair, his eyes closed, his feet dangling over the end. Solitude had given them what the city couldn't over the past few days. Peace.

Just looking at all that black hair curling around his collar, those gray piercing eyes when awake, his lean body, something moved inside her. More than attraction, more than lust. Love. He'd killed—for her—killed the man she detested more than any other on earth. Josh had ended Whitfield without a thought or a backward glance.

With Whitfield's death something inside her had lifted.

But because they'd both been under so much stress since the man's demise, the setting here at the cabin helped to soothe her.

As Skye looked out at the San Juan Islands, she realized a chapter of her life had come to an end, over—done with—while another was just beginning.

That pain she'd carried around for more than a dozen years, the hurt she'd closed off, she could set that free now. She no longer needed her anger or the pain of it all for motivation, not anymore. The drive would have to come from something else. Or rather someone else, maybe more than one someone else. All the Jenna Donofrios, the Erin Prescotts, all those missing that had yet to be accounted for would have to make up for her own rage as the impetus as she moved forward. But it was enough. The Jennas and Erins and Haileys and Alis were more than enough.

After the shock of it all had passed the realization that Ronny Wayne Whitfield would never again be able to put his hands on another child seemed to be settling in.

Josh and Kiya had seen to that.

She glanced back over at Josh only to find him wide awake and staring at her.

"You went off to that place you sometimes go where I'm not allowed." The frown he saw crossing her face prompted him to add, "It's okay. Everyone's entitled to have someplace special of their very own. We aren't joined at the hip, Skye."

That's what she loved about the guy. He seemed to let her be Skye Cree without trying to change all her bad habits and quirks, which were many. "Hmm, you play your cards right, we could be joined some other way." She wiggled her eyebrows up and down.

Since the merge there were certain urges that had gotten stronger for him. Sex was one of those. He found that no matter how many times they made love, he couldn't get enough of Skye. "Come here you saucy wench."

Her lower belly fluttered as if butterflies were trying to escape a nest of spiders. As much as she wanted to act on her urges there were things they needed to discuss.

"The entire time you were sleeping you were giving off this aura. Are you aware of that?"

He shot her a look. "How do you pick up on that? Sure, I've been aware of it—for days now. I just didn't think you were."

"You have part of Kiya inside you. Don't forget, I've had her spirit inside me my entire life. This whole thing is my fault that it happened in the first place. I'm responsible."

"Skye…"

She held up a hand. "No, hear me out. I should never have let you get involved in any of this. It was never your fight. I got caught up in having a lover, a man interested in me and I dragged you into this mess that's my life. You never would've confronted Whitfield if not for me." Tears came into her eyes. "You were dead, Josh. I thought I'd lost you. I won't lie, the idea of losing you weakened me, almost brought me to my knees while at the same time made me fight like I've never fought before. Yet I was losing. He was so much stronger. If you hadn't gotten Whitfield off me when you did—"

"You'd be dead. You think I don't know that? You think I'll ever get that picture out of my head? I won't. Not ever."

"Same here. Then you know?"

"First of all, you didn't drag me there forcibly. I went because I wanted to go. If I hadn't gotten sloppy, if I hadn't been talking a mile a minute like we were taking a walk in the park, I'd never have let him sneak up on us…he never would have hit me with that damn metal pipe."

Losing patience with him, she shouted, "That's just it, we should never have been there in the first place. You aren't paying attention to what I'm trying to tell you. I've been obsessed with that man and it got you killed."

"Do I look dead to you?"

"You aren't thickheaded. You know exactly what I mean." She rubbed her forehead feeling a headache building. "You've changed and you know it. Plus, you killed a man. Josh Ander, the gamer, the geek, the business owner. You had a fabulous life any man would envy before I came into it that night in the alley. And now...you killed a man because of me. Do you think I can live with that?"

"I see we'll be having this discussion for the fifth time in as many days. You'll have to live with it, Skye. I killed scum. I took out a very bad man. I can live with that. I thought you could, too."

"Are you deliberately misunderstanding what I'm trying to tell you?" She tried again. "I would've taken that man down if I could have without a backward glance. I can live with the fact he's dead. But you did it for *me*. Now this aura surrounding you is sending off wolf vibes. I can feel it." When she saw his eyes narrow, she added, "Don't look at me like that. I've lived with Kiya's vibes my entire life. You think I don't recognize how strong it is in you. Because I do. It's stronger in you than it ever was in me."

"I don't doubt that. And I'm telling you it's all right. That aura you picked up is because I...was...reliving the Donofrio abduction, like seeing it on video, watching it play out. It was disturbing. There's something else...tell me straight, Skye. You're plagued by the same kinds of dreams, by voices from the victims. How long? Since your own abduction?"

"How...? Do you...know that?" When he just stared at her, she said flatly, "I guess...there's no denying it." She smoothed back her hair and prepared to tell him all of it. "About six weeks after my parents died I started having these dreams, all kinds of them from other victims of abuse. The pictures were almost intolerable...unbearable."

"Especially after what you'd gone through yourself."

"That too. But I'd just completed a year of therapy when my parents…were killed. By this time I was stuck in Yakima with my aunt and uncle, no access to my counselor, or anyone else really to talk to. For a while I thought I might be having some kind of mental breakdown. But Kiya began appearing to me each night to sort of talk me through what I saw in the dreams. She told me the victims were communicating with me because I could relate, because I was destined to find them. I was the hunter…the person they looked to for help."

"That's a heavy burden for a thirteen-year-old child." When she just glowered at him, he added, "You were still a child, Skye. You'd been through the trauma of rape, add to that, the death of your parents was a lot to deal with for one so young."

"I know. But there wasn't anything I could do about it anyway unless I left Yakima and ran away from Ginny and Bob's. During this time Kiya made it possible for me to accept the dreams, the voices. There were a lot of victims, Josh. The visions of what they were dealing with seemed to flood me, especially at night. I took to calling in tips to the cops from what I'd seen in the dreams, especially if I could identify the girls and connect them to a story I'd read online."

Impressed, he asked, "How did you manage to do that when your aunt and uncle watched your every move?"

"Well, they did have to send me to school. I got to be really good on the computer so I volunteered to teach senior citizens the basic skills about the Internet and computer software. It didn't happen overnight. The job started out as a summer thing after my teachers recommended me for the slot. Then that fall I was a freshman in high school. By this time I was looking for any extra credit I could get so I could graduate early and get out of there. Teaching the class got me off campus and into a senior complex my aunt and uncle knew nothing about. During the time I spent with the old folks, I'd look up missing persons cases. If I had info from the dreams,

I'd call in an anonymous tip to whatever agency was involved in the investigation. They never knew it was me."

"Clever girl and smart to use what you saw in the dreams. Were there ever any resolutions?"

"Oh yeah. Three found alive. They found the girls where I said they'd be."

"Amazing. So that's how you found Ali Crandon and Hailey and Erin. It's why you don't want credit—"

"For a talent that doesn't really belong to me but now it seems it belongs to you—and more pronounced." It took a few minutes for realization to dawn on what he'd said. "Are you saying you're able to see Brandon Hiller in the *act* of killing…Jenna?"

Anger, revulsion moved into his eyes. "I saw it all, everything, except for where he buried her. God. I wished I hadn't." He rubbed at his forehead as if he too were battling a migraine.

"You get headaches when you see what happens."

"I do. That child was so scared during all of it. I saw the terror in her eyes, the hurt, the pain. Don't make me repeat what he did to her."

"I…I wouldn't. I have a pretty good idea."

He got up then, went to her. He plucked her off her feet, devoured her mouth. They fell back onto the chair while she slid boneless onto his lap, wrapping around him like a glove.

"I want you to know that whatever I felt once," she reached for his hand, placed it over her heart. "Here inside me, that thing that drove me to find…that piece of shit…is gone because of you. It's lifted. I have a new perspective now, Josh. The Jennas out there still need justice. For me, the question now is what do I do about all of it?"

"You mean we, what do we do about it? And what do we do about what I see, what I'm able to see because of Kiya? If you think I can live with this gift and not be a part of bringing the bad guys in, think again. Without question, we go after Hiller. Then we find this human-trafficking ring, see if we can rescue as many as we can. Period. There's no other option."

She grinned. "That's what I hoped you'd say."

"And no guilt from either one of us no matter what drastic measures we use?"

"I'm on board with that. Although I do think we'll have to handle the rescues a little differently."

"Why's that?"

"It's actually your fault." When she noticed the crease lines form on his forehead, she felt a slight case of pity for him and explained, "The Artemis Foundation is high profile now, Josh. I'm the face of the foundation and you among others sit on the board. From this point going forward, will we really be able to use such harsh measures to deal with scum and fly under the radar? I don't think so."

"Ah. I see what you mean. We'll have to take a more covert approach."

"And we'll have to handle Hiller differently as well."

"You're right."

"If we turn these guys trafficking into the cops, we'll need proof, evidence to help put them away for life, otherwise they'll walk. I've been around Harry enough to know cops need evidence to take to the DA. If the DA doesn't think the case is strong enough they won't even bother prosecuting. If the evidence doesn't hold up that opens the door for these guys to plead; when they plead, they get lighter sentences and with it a pass to re-offend down the road at some later date. More victims."

"And if we don't turn them over to the cops we'd be considered vigilantes by some members of society."

"Some might consider that. But I like to think what we're doing is protecting. Plus, I'm not sure if I care at this point what people think about me. Do you?"

He shook his head. "What do you think those upstanding members of society would think about a wolf bringing me back from the dead? I have a wolf's spirit running through my body that's as strong as anything I've ever felt."

"Then I guess we're in agreement."

"We do whatever it is we have to do."

"Agreed."

Somehow in a short span of time, Lena Bowers, the widow and grieving mom, had bonded with the streetwise, troubled Zoe. Having Zoe in the house brought Lena a happiness she hadn't felt since before her son, Jason, had shipped off to Afghanistan only to be brought back to Seattle in a box.

It was an unusual pairing to say the least. But it seemed to be working. When the detective Harry Drummond had stopped by to question Lena about Skye's whereabouts, Zoe had looked on as Lena staunchly stonewalled the cop on Skye's behalf. The loyalty hadn't gone unnoticed by Zoe, who now had a roof over her head, clean clothes, all the food she could eat, and she didn't have to fend off advances from a man three times her age. That might have been the major reason Lena and Zoe had been able to form such an unlikely attachment to each other.

But now that more than a week had gone by, the two were going nuts trying to figure out where Skye and Josh had gotten off to. Neither one had answered their cell phones in almost six days. They weren't at home either. Lena and Zoe had stopped by both places and checked.

"Where could they be?"

"I'm not sure. Sometimes Skye goes for a whole week without contacting me. But she wanted to go with me to the lawyer's office, that Doug Jenkins, to make the introductions and she never showed up. That's unlike her."

"I hope they're okay."

"Me too, sweetie. I know Skye can take care of herself, but I wish she'd call and let us know she's okay."

"Where else is there to look? I could go out tonight, walk some of the streets—"

"No! Skye would not want you doing that. If she hasn't gotten in touch by tomorrow, we'll both go out looking for her."

Even at the cabin there were work-related issues a mile long that Josh had dodged for far too long and cranky business partners that had to be dealt with. While Skye spent the afternoon returning phone calls, Josh sat at his laptop. In between catching up on emails and sorting through marketing strategies, he learned as much information as he could about Brandon Hiller. His habits, such as they were, included living out of his van, a van as it turns out he'd borrowed from his sister's husband.

By that night Josh had a plate number for the van as well as Hiller's debit card number. It was only a matter of time before Hiller used it and when that happened they'd have a location to stake out and a reason to leave Orcas.

When Skye learned what all he'd accomplished over a span of a couple of hours, she couldn't help but be blown away by Josh's talent at tracking info on the predator so quickly. She had to admit, he was better at using his skills than she'd given him credit for. Even though she'd been using Kiya's spirit for years to find the missing, Josh had been able to find Whitfield with a few keystrokes on the Internet. And now, thanks to technology and Josh's skills, they might be able to get Hiller off the streets—for good.

But while Kiya had been a strong enough energy in spirit, Josh on the other hand was both a presence and a force to be reckoned with.

No way would she want to encounter him in one of those dark alleys she routinely walked down every night. He could more than hold his own with anyone or anything. The fact that the visions were keeping him up nights, disturbing his sleep, was a problem, but one she could help him handle just as Kiya had done with her all those years ago.

But if the connection between the two of them was so strong, so fierce, how is it the man could not know, not be able to pick up on the fact that she was in love with him?

CHAPTER TWENTY-FOUR

The narrow lane lined with rows of houses and parked cars was silent as a mausoleum while the residents still dozed in their beds. The suburban neighborhood might have been around for decades, the homes all old, but the lawns and flowerbeds were well trimmed and there was still evidence children lived behind those doors. Tricycles and bikes had been left out on porches while a few toys littered the sidewalks and were left strewn along the grassy curbs. These were starter homes where young couples made children, sent them out to play with brothers and sisters, packed them off to school, and prayed they'd chosen well for an area so the kids would stay safe through all of it.

Not a good place to find Brandon Randle Hiller lurking about.

A hint of sun pinked and reddened the fringe of clouds to the east, which made for a picture- perfect springtime sunrise. If Skye hadn't been so juiced about finally cornering Brandon Hiller, she might've enjoyed what promised to be the first decent day of spring they'd seen in two weeks. She glanced over at Josh, sitting behind the wheel. The look on his face told her he was just as amped as she was.

It was Josh who zeroed in on Hiller's blue van. "There. Parked five cars up, sandwiched between the red Mazda and the gray pickup. He's still asleep."

"How can you tell that from here?"

Josh gave her a withering stare. "I hear him snoring."

It would take some getting used to, she surmised to reconcile the nerd with wolf tendencies.

"I guess I'd be wasting my breath to suggest you wait in the car."

Now it was Skye's turn to return the dismissive glare. "You know the answer to that already."

"Then let me be the one to approach the back of the van. Wait until I get the door open."

"It's probably locked."

"Of course it's locked. But I won't need a key."

"My, but we are feeling awfully cocky this early in the morning, aren't we?"

"You just have the cops on speed dial. I'll get the information we need out of Hiller, then turn him over to Drummond just as we agreed."

They crawled out of the Fusion at the same time from opposite doors, and started up the street. The minute Josh reached the double doors of the van, with his bare hands he wrenched open the handle until the lock popped open. He peeled back the metal like a tin can.

Hiller was stretched out in the back, or had been. The noisy crunching to get inside woke Hiller just in time for him to try to evade through the front driver's seat. But Josh was quicker. He reached in, grabbed the man's leg and pulled him out onto the street, banging Hiller's head on the rusted bumper.

Josh caught Hiller's shirt collar, bunched it into his fists, brought him closer to his face. "You know a guy named Whitfield?"

"No. Why're you hassling me just because I need a place to sleep? I'm just trying to catch a few winks here. I'll move on, I promise."

Not in this lifetime, thought Josh as he closed his grip around the man's throat.

Hiller rasped out, "You guys cops?"

"Nope. You won't hear a Miranda warning out of us. Do we understand each other?"

"Sure. What do you want?"

"Answers. Where does Whitfield keep the girls while they're waiting for transport out of the country?"

Hiller swallowed hard. Josh noticed the man's pupils get bigger, felt his heart race with fear right before he saw the man's crotch area grow damp. A yellow stream of pee began to trickle onto the cement indicating the grown man had wet his pants.

"If I tell you, will you let me go?" Hiller asked.

"Not a chance. Time's up, Hiller. It happens to all of us sooner or later, particularly to very bad men like you. Your time was up when you started killing little kids. But right this minute, I want to know where Whitfield holds the girls." Josh applied even more pressure, cutting off more of the man's air.

"There's a warehouse along the docks."

"There's a ton of warehouses along the docks, be more specific."

Up till then Skye had been silent letting Josh scare the crap out of the guy or in this case the pee, but now she wanted to know, "How close to where you were holding Erin did he keep the girls?"

Hiller attempted to move his head, but struggled for his next breath as Josh tightened his hold yet again. Instead Hiller let his eyes wander over to Skye. "Four...maybe...five miles away."

"I'm thinking Brandon here wants you to loosen your vise-like grip on his throat so he can draw us a map to the area he's talking about and show us...precisely."

"Is that so?" Josh said. "Is that what you want to do Brandon?"

Hiller nodded.

While Skye dashed back to the car to get a pen and piece of paper, Josh looked into Hiller's vacant eyes and cautioned. "That's a good start, Brandon, a real good start. But keep this in mind. If you should make a mistake drawing that map and I'm not able to locate those girls, if I have to come back, I'll snap your neck like a twig. Got it?"

"Yeah," Brandon screeched out. "Who are you guys?"

"Concerned citizens."

The minute Skye ran back she put her hand on Josh's arm. "I have to ask him something else." They'd gone over the order of things and so far it had worked. Keeping to what they'd preplanned, Skye turned to Hiller. "The day you took Erin, by any chance was Whitfield with you...beforehand?"

Hiller nodded again. "Sure."

"Where? Why?"

Hiller shrugged one shoulder. "He had to point out the one he wanted me to take, didn't he? He had an order for a redhead so...that's what we went after."

Sensing the man might be playing her, she countered, "Erin was at school that day. There was no way Whitfield could have been around Erin to point her out."

Hiller snorted. "Look, we'd been scoping out chicks at the marketplace for a couple of hours during lunch. But there were no redheads young enough to fit Whitfield's order. That's when he suggested I hang around the school—and wait. See what I could find there. Lo and behold, she comes hotfooting it across campus. Knowing what he was looking for, I followed her to the train."

"So Whitfield was right there just like you thought that day," Josh pointed out.

"Fifth and Cherry. Looks like." Skye turned back to Hiller. "But you made the mistake of going out that Saturday night and left Erin alone, didn't you? Erin gets away, escapes..."

"I heard on the news you got her out, otherwise that scared little rabbit would have stayed planted right there where I left her."

"Me?" Skye asked in mock surprise. "I don't know what you're talking about. I saw on the news it was that Skye Cree person. But Whitfield couldn't have been very happy with you about that?"

"Are you kidding? Whitfield was fucking furious. He had to settle for a hooker, which he doesn't like to do."

Skye's brow knitted. "Ah, the redheaded hooker named Lucy," Skye said flatly. "Is Lucy still alive?"

"How the fuck would I know? She was alive when I handed her over to Whitfield. That's all I know. He usually doesn't kill 'em unless they give him a problem or…"

"Or what?" Josh asked, cocking a brow.

Hiller's eyes darted away. "Unless the guys get a little too carried away—you know, a little too rough during…"

That disgusting thought brought Skye right back to what they believed Hiller had done to Jenna. Skye needed to get him back on track. "Now for the bonus round, Hiller. And this is the biggie. What did you do with Jenna Donofrio's body?"

"Hey, who said anything about that? I'm not…"

Skye watched as Josh squeezed the man's throat again, letting his fingers wrap tighter until Hiller's eyes started to bug out. "We know you killed Jenna, Brandon. You might as well tell us where she is, otherwise this guy here might get upset and he won't be able to control his innate tendencies."

"How…how…do you…know…about Jenna?" Brandon stammered.

This time Josh ran his thumb up the man's Adam's apple and pressed down—harder. "The woman here has psychic abilities. Seriously though, that's not the answer we want to hear right now. I could howl for you and show you I mean business, but I really don't want to wake up the entire neighborhood this early. Now answer the question. Where did you bury Jenna?"

"Okay. Okay. She's at Whitfield's place. I put her there myself."

Josh's eyes locked with Skye's. "Looks like Brandon will be drawing two maps instead of one."

After Josh left Brandon Hiller tied up inside his van so there was no chance of him getting away, he drove Skye to a pay phone so she could place an anonymous call to the police. In a span of exactly one hundred and twenty-eight seconds, she informed them where they could find the pedophile but also explained that he was the one responsible for the murder of Jenna Donofrio. To prove it, they stopped at an office center chain, scanned the map into a document format, and then found a coffee shop with wifi where they could use a dummy account to send the map via email to Harry directly as an attachment.

When they'd finished with that, they followed Hiller's directions to an old abandoned manufacturing area near the docks. They parked the car two streets over and set out on foot to see if they could locate where Whitfield had been holding the girls.

"What's the plan?"

"You mean after you made Hiller wet his pants?"

Josh grinned. "Not such a tough guy around an adult."

"An adult who snarls," Skye said. "Great touch, by the way. Look, maybe we should call the police to get these girls out. *If* they're still there at all, this could get messy real quick."

He squeezed her hand. "We'll play it by ear, how's that? I don't think we should call the cops until we know for sure they haven't already shipped the girls out, otherwise it would just be another false lead to nowhere. This way, we check the place out, if they're inside, we stick to the plan, then we make the call. How's that sound?"

It turned out that the structure Hiller had told them about had once been used as a distribution center for a retail outlet that had gone out of business a decade earlier and was now owned by one R.W. Whitfield. The abandoned storefront hugged the waterfront. The front door had been boarded up and secured by a stretch of ironwork. Since there was no way of getting past that short of a blowtorch and a lot of noise, they decided the best approach was from the rear. But figuring out how to get into the warehouse without attracting attention would be tricky.

Once they reached the back of the facility, the structure was still a good seventy yards in the distance and across a concrete drainage canal in disrepair. Not only that, but it looked as though at one time it had been a gathering place for vagrants and taggers. The spot was loaded with graffiti and littered with broken bottles, trash of all kinds, and a layer of used condoms.

"The water's no more than a foot deep." Skye pointed out. But the drop off was at least eight feet down. "We can slide but how do we get up the embankment once we reach the other side?" Skye wanted to know.

"I'll get us both up. Just be careful maneuvering over all the cracked concrete strewn on the bottom. That's a great way to break an ankle. And we don't know what's in that murky water." He sniffed the air, stared into the dirty stream. "See there. Snakes."

"Just great," Skye muttered as she followed Josh's lead and slipped down the abutment, careful not to stay in one spot for long. They scrambled through the water using any jutting surface to step, balance, and then leap from one piece of cement to the other until they got to the other side where Josh vaulted up and onto the flat landing above. "Give me your hand and I'll boost you up."

"Showoff," Skye grumbled slapping her hand into Josh's. "Something tells me you could've just jumped this ditch on your own."

He shot her a sly grin. "But you couldn't."

"Aw, thanks. You're all heart. No one said being a spirit guide would be such a thankless task or a walk in the park, huh?" she said, grinning back.

"It has its advantages." He scanned the area, taking his time to check out every possible way to get in closer without being spotted. After several long minutes, he pointed. "There, we approach through that grove of trees, stick to the side of the building until we find an opening where we can look inside."

"Geez, that place must be what, a hundred thousand square feet? Whitfield owns this? The sex trade must be very lucrative."

"Yeah. The sad thing is the guy probably picked up the property at a huge discount because of the downturn in the economy."

"What about all those loading docks? Maybe you could pry one of the bays open."

"We check those out, too. But right now we're looking to make the least amount of noise we can, look for an open fire door, a busted window, anything that can get us in— quietly."

"Split up?"

"No."

Without saying another word, they started through the wooded area, sneaking up to the rear parking lot. After crossing over to a small loading area, they reached the building. Using hand gestures, Skye pointed to the busted glass littering the pavement. Then with her thumb she pointed upward to where the glass had likely come from, a window on the second story, and a way inside. She looked around for something to use for a ladder. In a whisper, she asked, "Can you reach that with your one-leap-in-a-single-bound trick or do you want to boost me up?"

His answer was to jump in the air and land on the roof.

Skye shook her head. How long would it take to get used to those kinds of antics? she wondered, while wishing she had that same ability.

From the roof of the warehouse, Josh leaned over the truss so he could see inside the broken window. He heard male voices in a heated argument discussing whether or not sufficient payment had already been deposited in an offshore account to cover their take. He listened as the discussion got more intense.

"Without Whitfield how do we know the money's even there?" one man shouted.

"Well, I'm not walking away. I have too much time invested in this already to simply drop out and run. I want my goddamn money! We've been waiting for two weeks and now we're fucked."

For the first time the reality of the situation hit Josh. Inside this innocent-looking distribution center in broad daylight in a city the size of Seattle a group of men held out hope that they could still reconnect with the buyers, reestablish Whitfield's link, and salvage the operation by going ahead and selling the teenage girls so they could make a profit.

Josh realized something else. There was no time to make a call to the cops. This would be up to the two of them to do without help. But they still had to find a way to get into the building.

About that time, he heard the faintest of steps coming from the opposite corner some thirty yards away. He watched Skye make her way onto the roof. Somehow she'd found something to use to climb up. He put his finger to his lips to indicate she needed to be quiet and then pointed down into the building. Using hand signals he motioned that there were at least five men inside.

Skye nodded, signaled that he could add three more by her count, standing guard at the front of the building which meant two against eight. She didn't like those odds. When she said as much through more sign language, Josh shook her off.

In a crawl, she made her way over to Josh. "Are you nuts?" she whispered.

"Listen. They've come to a parting of the ways. It's either now or never."

That's when Skye cocked her head and heard the second group of men talking about doing away with the girls.

"I vote we move the merchandise now or else we kill them all," one of the men suggested.

"Same here. They've seen our faces and it's too risky to hang onto them without knowing if the ship's ready or not. I didn't sign on for getting caught. No way am I going back to prison for a fucked-up plan that never had a chance of working without Whitfield."

"This whole thing has gone south. I'm for slitting their throats, right here, right now," another man stated, weighing in with his opinion.

Skye grabbed Josh's arm. "You're right, they sound desperate. Who knows what they'd do in the next five minutes? How many have guns?" Skye wanted to know.

"The two advocating the throat-slitting. But we have surprise in our favor."

She gave him a withering stare. "Remember what Travis said. Don't let your wolf instincts take over and get us both killed. Try to think logically, intelligently, both of which you possess in spades. This is just plain crazy," Skye muttered. "There's eight of them and only two of us."

"Not if we draw a few of them out first."

With that, Josh grabbed her hand, wrapped her to his chest. "Hold on." They both went off the roof, dropped to the ground, feet first.

Skye rolled her eyes. "There was a perfectly good fire escape on the other side. How do you think I got up there?"

"We'll argue about it later. Right now, follow my lead." He kissed her on the mouth before, bold as brass, he knocked on the back door.

Inside, the group of men were still in an intense debate when one of them held up a hand. "What was that? Did you hear that?"

"The only thing I hear is your gums flapping," the other replied.

But the two that were armed with weapons ignored the others and moved to the back door. One flung it open and both men burst outside where Skye and Josh were waiting on either side.

Skye let the first man take two steps before she elbowed him in the ribs and kicked out with her leg, knocking the nine-millimeter Smith and Wesson from his hand. Josh did the same with the man holding the Ruger revolver. Unarmed now, both men came up swinging.

Skye drew a knife from her boot, heaved it end over end until it flew through the air, hitting its mark. The blade landed in the man's heart.

Josh's arms went around the other man he held up against his chest. With one twist, Josh broke the man's neck.

That left three to rush outside to see what was happening. When two advanced on Josh at once, he took out the first one with a kick to the man's jaw and throat. The man dropped like a rock. The other, Josh picked up and simply threw the guy into the side of the building where bone crunched against concrete as his body slid down into a crumpled mass.

A third man tried to come at Josh from behind, but Skye took care of him by drawing a second knife from inside her coat and flinging it into the guy's throat. He staggered back, his hands trying to pull out the knife before collapsing on the ground.

By that time, three other men rounded the corner of the building from the opposite end to check out the commotion. They spotted Skye and Josh standing over the littered bodies and took off back the way they'd come, ostensibly to their cars.

"I've got this," Josh said as he hustled after the trio. Over his shoulder, he shouted, "Go see if you can find the girls."

With speed unknown to him before the transformation, Josh easily caught up with two of the three men who were out of shape and much older. Josh sprang at both, taking them down face first into the concrete. The two fell hard and while they tried to untangle a mass of limbs, Josh snapped the neck of one before turning to the other to repeat the process. He got to his feet and went after the one scurrying to one of the vehicles parked in front.

"You can't leave now, the fun's just getting started," Josh bellowed before he pounced onto the guy's back, took his head in his hands, and once again, broke the guy's neck.

Inside her prison, Heather knew something was up because there was a ton of shouting coming from outside her locked doorway. Were they getting ready to move them? It sounded like chaos to her. All morning the voices had indicated some of the men were panicking. She'd even heard fighting among the men where there had been only unity two days before. But then her captors had been acting weird for more days than she could count.

Skye stepped into the vast building and cast her eyes around, cautious in case they'd overlooked anyone they hadn't accounted for yet. But Skye saw nothing to indicate that. Instead, the large and rather stark distribution center seemed empty. As she moved through the layout, checking out rooms that used to be former offices, a funny odor hit her nostrils. The smell of urine and feces almost knocked her down.

She walked past restrooms, down a narrow hallway that led to individual storage units that once had held items waiting for their inspections from customs. At least that was her first impression. Here, she picked up the odor of death.

Skye counted twelve bright orange, metal roll-up doors each with its own heavy padlock—which explained the orange in her dream. On impulse she called out, "Lucy! Heather! Elena! Anyone! Are you here?"

Skye heard shrieks, gasps, and then voices coming from behind at least six of the locked rooms at almost the same time.

"Here!"

"I'm in here!" said a girl's quivering voice.

"Please, please let me out, please!" another begged in a pitiful moan.

At all the cries for help, Skye had to shout over the din, "I have to find the keys first. It's okay. You're safe now.

Just give me a minute to get these locks open." She started running back down the hallway, but Josh was already standing there holding a crowbar. Skye slid to a stop. Their eyes met. She grabbed his arm, put a finger to her lips, and whispered, "They might be scared to hear a man's voice right about now."

Josh nodded and said in a low whisper, "Can't say I blame them after spending time in this hellhole. The smell in here is awful. Is it just me or do you smell—death?"

"No, it's here," Skye whispered before pitching her voice louder. "Okay, listen to me, girls. I brought a strong guy with me to help you. Don't freak. He's one of the good guys. We're going to get you out. Here's what I want you to do though. You need to move all the way back into your cell, away from the door, as far as you can get."

"They have us chained up," a weak voice explained from behind one of the doors. "It's hard to move around."

"Like animals," sobbed another.

"Then get as far back as you can away from the opening," Skye suggested.

"Those men kept giving us drugs but they ran out a couple of days ago. We've been awake ever since."

"We've all been praying for someone to come help us and take us out of this place."

At the first unit, Josh wedged the iron rod into the space between the lock and the sliding latch. With all the strength he possessed he forced the iron down until the lock and latch broke loose from the frame. With a grinding screech, metal separated from metal.

Skye quickly yanked up the door on its tracks to reveal a filthy single mattress, and ten-year-old Elena Palomar hiding beneath the cot.

Josh did the same thing with the next unit, where they discovered Lucy Border, huddling against the wall. Inside the adjacent unit, they found Heather Moore crouched in the corner. He continued to the fourth, and on and on, until he had broken into each unit. Some were blessedly empty. They freed three other girls they didn't recognize. It took a bolt cutter to cut through the chains that shackled all of them to their beds.

Once Skye led the girls out into the hallway, Josh instructed, "You want to take them out through that side door over there and lead them out into the parking lot. Get them a good thirty yards away. At least," Josh suggested in a low voice. "I'll pull the bodies back into the warehouse before I set the explosive device to blow."

Skye nodded. "I spotted two laptops on a desk in their office area. Grab those. There might be something we can use."

"Got it."

With that, Skye started herding the group outside and into what was blinding sunlight for those who hadn't seen daylight in several weeks.

As they marched away from the building, it soon became clear all of the girls, especially the younger ones, were still in shock. They were all crying and couldn't seem to stop. Despite that though, the older ones seemed unable to keep quiet after such a long time penned up.

"Who are you?" one of the little ones asked.

"We get to go home now, right? You aren't here to hurt us?" Heather Moore wanted to know.

"You're all going home soon," Skye said, touching the girl's cheek. "Your mother is worried sick."

"You talked to her?"

"I did. You'll be home in time for your brother's birthday."

"Did you kill those horrible men?" one of the girls piped up in a trembling voice.

"I hope they're all dead, every last one of them. They raped us. They were going to sell us and ship us out of the country," a brown-haired girl of about fourteen added.

"No, I heard them. They'd already decided to kill us," Lucy corrected.

Since Josh had mentioned the same, Skye reassured them, "I promise they won't do anything to you now."

"What happened to the bad men?" Elena finally spoke, her eyes darting around in fear before squinting them closed at the sun. "Are they still here? Will they grab me again?"

"It's okay," Skye told the youngest one. "I promise you, they won't hurt you ever again."

"It's so great to be outside, to see the sun," Heather said taking a huge breath of fresh air. She picked up Skye's hand. "Are you a cop?"

"No. In fact, I want all of you to put your hands over your ears." Skye glanced at her watch. "In about two minutes there's going to be a huge explosion. I don't want you to be scared."

"You're blowing up the building?" Heather asked. "That is so cool. I never want to see this place again."

When Skye spotted Josh strolling across the lot to join them, she knew the time had come. "I don't believe that'll be a problem. Okay, girls, let's huddle together, hands over your ears, prepare to hear a very large boom. In three, two, one—"

About that time, a blast ripped the air, shaking the ground.

"It's time to go," Josh uttered as soon as he reached the group.

"I know but..."

Josh shook his head, leaned in where only Skye could hear. "No buts, I'm making the nine-one-one call now." He withdrew a disposable cell phone from his jacket pocket. "Come on, we talked about this. I know it's tough to leave them but we need to move. Now! Choppers will be airborne in less than fifteen minutes, be over this area in less than twenty. The girls will be okay for that long."

When Skye started to get up to follow Josh, one of the girls screamed, "Wait! Don't go! Please don't leave us. Take us with you."

Skye picked up her hand, soothing her as best she could. "The cops and fire department are on their way. Stay back from that building. Don't leave this spot. You stay right here until they come for you. As soon as they get here, you'll all go to a hospital so you'll each get checked out. You'll all get to see your families again…very soon. I promise."

"Wait. What…what…about you and him?" Lucy asked pointing to Josh. "I know you. You're Dee Dee's friend. The one she talks to some of the time. Dee Dee trusts you."

Skye shook her head. "You're confused, honey. I don't know a Dee Dee. And you never saw us here. You understand, right?"

Lucy met Skye's eyes. Used to avoiding the cops, the young hooker nodded. "Okay. Sure. Whatever you say, but…you know…thanks for getting us out of there. We were going to die if you hadn't."

"Yeah, thanks to both of you for rescuing us," Heather repeated. "And thanks for blowing up that hellhole. I wanna go home."

Reluctantly, Skye started following Josh through the wooded area, retracing their movements from earlier to get back to the car. They trekked over the same ground, sliding back down into the drainage ditch, sloshing through the water, and up the incline.

"Sorry I wasn't able to help you with the bodies," Skye said.

He reached into his pocket, pulled out the two knives she'd used to take down the two men. "Here. These might come in handy later. Nice moves by the way. I've never seen anyone that accurate in real life with a knife before. You looked absolutely amazing."

Skye allowed herself to take a deep breath before getting into the car. "You realize there's no turning back now," she said as she heard sirens in the distance.

Pulling the car out onto the road, Josh agreed, "We were never turning back from this, Skye. It's too important. Besides, it's done now." Hitting the gas, Josh sped away and had them out of the area in less than two minutes.

CHAPTER TWENTY-FIVE

Back in tiny Olga, among the picturesque coastline, the ridgelines and the valleys, Josh wasn't surprised when he opened the door of the cabin to see Harry Drummond standing on the porch.

"Mr. Ander."

"Detective Drummond. What brings you all the way to Orcas?"

"Seems some very nasty people turned up dead."

"Really?"

"Yeah. The same kind of people Skye would have an interest in. Have you seen her? She hasn't been around her apartment for several days now."

"By all means, come in. You've come to the right place to find Skye. She's been here for almost a week enjoying the solitude of the cabin, the island."

As soon as Harry's eyes landed on Skye sitting on the sofa with her legs tucked up underneath her, he said, "We've had quite a bit of excitement on the mainland. I'm sure you've seen the news."

"Actually," Josh replied, arms spread wide, "I'm afraid there's no television here."

Harry's eyes zipped around the room to verify. "Okay, then I'll hit the highlights for you. Yesterday two unidentified Good Samaritans found their way inside an abandoned distribution center near the harbor where six girls had been held for God knows how long and suffered all manner of deviant acts. Each one of those girls had gone missing over the past two weeks. Our unknown Good Samaritans were somehow able to set the girls free and help them flee their captors. Before the girls escaped, it seems their abductors got into a very heated argument about what to do with the girls."

"How do you know that?"

"The older girls confirmed they heard the men arguing. Anyway, during this heated exchange, someone pulled a knife, followed by a gun and we think one or two might have escaped alive. We're not sure about that…yet."

"You think two captors escaped?" Josh asked, clearly perplexed.

"According to the girls, there were more than a dozen different men at any given time that used them. The doctors determined all of them were in terrible shape. Elena Palomar underwent surgery."

Skye sucked in a breath. This was all a little too familiar—and tragic.

"They also were in a state of dehydration, some even starvation. They hadn't been fed in days. It seems at one point their captors seemed to have forgotten about that little detail. Over the course of their captivity, each of the girls was given various drugs, everything from Rohypnol to ecstasy to heroin. They were raped multiple times during their incarceration. All of them tell the same story. They were being held at that location until arrangements could be made for them to be shipped somewhere out of the country."

"They lived like that in fear, all the while thinking they might die at any moment and they'd never get to see their families," Skye added, her breath hitching with each word. "That's horrible."

"Yes," Harry said soberly. "But for some reason, we're not sure what or why, the plan fell apart. Probably due to Whitfield's death, without their leader in charge, they didn't know how exactly to proceed. We know that because we found evidence on Whitfield's computer linking him to the sex trade. Anyway, inside their prison, a disagreement broke out about what to do with the girls. All of the girls are convinced that some of the jailers wanted to kill them, slit their throats to be exact."

"Because they'd seen their captors' faces," Skye reasoned. "Well, you've certainly been a busy man, Harry. The families must be ecstatic to have their daughters back."

"Oh they are. The girls tell a very strange story about their two rescuers though. Did I mention there were two, one male and one female?"

"Well, don't keep us in the dark," Josh said. "Who were these people?"

Harry slanted him a look. "That's the weird thing. All six disagree on what they looked like. The older three thought the woman wore a blonde wig. The younger ones gave me a description that could have fit Skye here to a tee. Three thought the man had bleached his hair white. I thought that was the best stretch of the truth. The other three described a guy with long black hair, about your height and weight, Mr. Ander."

"Wow, small world," Josh said. "Wish we could take credit for freeing them, but…Skye and I never left the island."

"You're sure of that, are you?" Harry asked with some skepticism. "I could check the log from the ferry."

"You could," Josh stated. "But that wouldn't really be definitive since there are all manner of private boats on the island that we could've used to take us to the mainland. I should know because…"

"The Ander family owns one," Skye offered. "It's a beauty, too. Josh has promised to take me out on the water first chance we get. It's such a heartwarming thing to hear Good Samaritans are out there, that they cared enough about those girls to get them out of that awful place, bring them back home to their worried families. It warms my heart. How about you, Josh?"

"Oh it does. Story like that reaffirms my faith in mankind."

"You guys wouldn't be trying to stonewall me, would you?" When Harry met with flinty silence, undeterred, he went on, "You should know I still have crime scene investigators going over that warehouse with a fine-tooth comb, if there's anything there, even one small piece of DNA, they'll find it. A fire and explosion don't always wipe out all the evidence."

"There was an explosion? You didn't mention that before, Detective," Josh said.

"You do realize Brandon Hiller described the people who left him tied up in his van, don't you? And it fits you two to a tee."

"Oh that. Come on, Harry. You'd believe Brandon Hiller over me? I'm surprised at you. I'm pretty sure that guy would sell out his own mother if he got the chance."

"And his mother is probably the only one who still admits to knowing and liking him," Josh wisecracked. "By the way, I'm curious. Who owned this distribution center where the girls were held?"

"Whitfield."

"So, did you learn anything about the sex-trafficking ring?" Skye asked trying for a casual interest. "Because that's really what your department should be focusing on, not wasting time trying to ID the Good Samaritans, in my opinion."

"I'm getting to that."

"What about the Jenna Donofrio case? Any leads there?" Josh asked, trying to keep the questions coming.

"Now that is one of the reasons I wanted to see Skye. It turns out there's been a break in the case. A couple of days ago, a map arrives in my inbox via email attachment. Says Jenna's buried on Whitfield land, gives me directions as to where—exactly. Didn't take forensics but half a morning before they turned up a mass grave, a serial killer's private garden. As of last count, at least four bodies so far. When I confronted Hiller with the map and the bodies, he confessed to killing little Jenna and helping to bury two other young girls just since he got out. But chances are Whitfield has been at this for at least five years, so there's no telling what the body count will be before we're done."

"Don't tell me Hiller wants to cut a deal with the DA's office?"

"Okay, I won't tell you. But he does. Not only that, he says he has other evidence implicating a cop up in Kirkland on Whitfield's payroll, a detective named Talbot."

At the name, Skye and Josh traded looks and Harry caught the exchange. "It seems this Talbot was responsible for seeing to all the details of getting the girls loaded aboard the cargo ships. The port authority also arrested a ship captain called Renaldi who thankfully doesn't seem to be able to keep his mouth shut confirming Talbot's role in this whole stinking operation."

"Filling out phony manifests," Josh finished.

Harry nodded. "You're a smart man, Mr. Ander. Just how smart remains to be seen." With that, he turned to Skye.

"What exactly is that supposed to mean, Harry?" Skye asked.

Harry ignored the question. Instead he jingled the change in his pocket and went on, "Today I had to tell Stephen Donofrio his daughter wasn't coming home. Did you know the man lost his wife to cancer three years ago? Jenna was nine when she had to bury her mother. Stephen Donofrio's been raising that little girl all by himself. Now he's lost her." Harry paused trying to rein in his emotions before he continued. "Just promise me you'll both stay the hell out of this from here on out. If you don't, I assure you it will get very nasty and messy for both of you."

"You know what, Harry?"

"What?"

"I think you should make a point to come back here to Orcas in June, to see the wildflowers and wild berries in bloom. Bring your wife. Plan to stay at one of the nice B &

B's in the area while you're here. Get away from the rat race, Harry, and don't forget your camera."

He pointed a finger at her and said, "You aren't as cool as you're pretending. This is too serious. I want you to listen to me." He turned to Josh. "And you, too. If I find one link, just one shred of evidence that says you two had anything to do with the deaths of those eight people inside that warehouse…I'll arrest you for…"

"For what, Drummond? For rescuing six victims of sexual abuse, girls that had suffered physical and mental trauma, tortured over a two-week period at the hands of brutal men who used them for their own sick pleasure? You want to put the people who saved those girls on trial? I don't know. I wouldn't mind sitting on that jury. How about you, Skye?"

"I'd vote not guilty in a heartbeat. But I have a question for you, Harry. What would you do if one of those girls belonged to you? What if one of them happened to be your daughter or niece or sister who went missing and ended up raped, sent out of the country to God knows where?"

Harry let out a sigh so loud it filled the room. "That's below the belt and you know it."

"Ask the families how they feel about having their girls back, I know how mine felt."

"Promise me, you will not do this again," Harry said.

Skye said nothing for several minutes. She shook her head. "Sorry, Harry. I can't make that kind of promise, not even for you."

To take Harry's focus off Skye, Josh wanted to know, "How exactly will they ever locate all those girls that have already landed in other countries? What about them? What about what kind of life they'll have for the next few years until some miracle brings them home?"

"We're in the process of scouring Whitfield's computer, wading through his client lists, name-by-name."

"That could take months."

"Maybe even years."

"I hope they use excellent forensic analysis. I could help there, too, if you'll let me," Josh offered, reaching over to link his fingers with Skye's.

"Maybe you could help us with the two laptops that mysteriously appeared on my doorstep recently," Harry said as he moved to the front door. Standing there holding onto the knob for a bit, as if trying to decide what to say next, he turned back. "I understand The Artemis Foundation already has a full board of directors. You'll do good work there, Skye." He narrowed his eyes on Josh and announced, "Do not let her do anything stupid. I'm counting on both of you to use common sense. Don't let your emotions get the better of you." And with that, Harry opened the door and walked out.

"That was intense."

"He didn't arrest us," Skye pointed out.

"For now, I guess that's something to celebrate," Josh said, running a finger down her cheek. "Hiller will probably plead out and get a lighter sentence."

Skye ran a finger down his chest. "Probably. Maybe we should contact the DA's office to make sure Hiller's in for life this time."

"Sounds like a plan," Josh said and wrapped Skye up. He held up his left hand, fingers spread, wiggled them for her to see. "I took off my wedding ring, Skye. I put it away because…I'm crazy in love with you."

Skye opened her mouth to speak but couldn't get the words to escape. So he *had* sensed how she felt. She took his face in her hands, and kissed him, nestled into his body.

"And if you don't like my loft, that's okay. I'll get you a house in the country where you can grow ten acres of…herbs if that's what you want."

"You'd leave your loft? That…isn't necessary. The city is…fine."

"Not even my loft is a place to make a garden. And you need space to grow things."

"People do it all the time. Besides, you wouldn't recognize kale from cabbage."

"No, but you would. Why would anyone purposely grow kale and cabbage? Just saying."

She pushed her hair back, looked up into his silver eyes. "I want to say…I haven't had anyone really close to me since my parents died. I haven't had anyone care about me the way you do. I'd almost forgotten what it was like to be part of a unit. You brought that back for me, Josh."

"I was distraught after Annabelle died. I'm not anymore. And there's this connection we have to a legendary spirit guide that no one else sees but us. I'd say that makes us perfect for each other."

"I'm not used to perfect."

"You'll get there."

She put her arms around his neck. "I love you, Joshua Sebastian Ander with all my heart."

"I love you, Skye Melody Cree, with all my heart. What do you imagine Travis will say when we tell him?"

"Travis? I'm sure he'll be happy for both of us. Why?"

Josh wasn't so sure about that. But he grabbed her hand and led her outside to the deck where they could watch the sun drop down over the mountains. It didn't matter, he decided as he looked out over the peaceful calm of the San Juans. At the moment he didn't much care about anyone or anything, except the woman who stood at his side.

Dear Reader:

If you enjoyed *The Bones of Others*, please take the time to leave a review. A review shows others you've liked my work. By recommending it to your friends and family it helps spread the word. Please Tweet/share that you've finished *The Bones of Others*.

If you do write a review, by all means let me know via Facebook or my website. I'd love to hear from you!!

For a complete list of the author's other books visit her website.
Want to connect with the author to leave a comment?

http://www.vickiemckeehan.com/
www.facebook.com/VickieMcKeehan
www.vickiemckeehan.wordpress.com/ blog

Go to the next page for a preview of
The Bones Will Tell
A Skye Cree Novel

THE BONES WILL TELL

PROLOGUE

Six months earlier
Seattle, Washington

He'd gotten his first taste for killing when he was eight. On a visit to his grandparents' farm, he snared a rabbit in a trap he'd built himself. He'd taken out his trusty Swiss Army knife then and there and slit its throat right before he skinned it.

But that was twenty years ago. Since then he'd graduated to bigger and better rabbits. He chuckled at his own joke as he made another pass on foot, past the house where the blonde lived that he'd been spying on for the better part of a week.

He'd already been inside her townhouse. He knew her name was Carrie Bennington and that she lived alone, except for the occasional men she brought home for pleasure and companionship, always on the weekends. He smiled. Carrie didn't have to worry too much longer about whether she would be alone or not, or how she spent her time, or how dedicated she was at her job as an administrative assistant.

Because the clock ticked and the grim reaper waited for Carrie like a long lost friend, or maybe it was a nice friendly labradoodle. Either way, he'd picked Carrie after she caught his eye at the marketplace and he'd followed her home. That had been a week ago last Saturday. He'd waited until that Monday morning after she'd left for work before he picked the lock on her sliding glass door and slipped inside. That had been the first time. Carrie's neighbors were none the wiser. So much for the neighborhood watch program.

Because he was good at climbing, athletic and lean, he didn't let things like a two-story apartment building dissuade him from getting at his quarry, not if he really wanted to get inside. He'd been a long distance runner in high school and still kept in shape. But even so, he liked to keep it simple. He preferred it when his victims had the good sense to own their own homes. Like Carrie who lived in a stylish two-story condo with an undersized courtyard.

He'd spent hours there going through her closets, her dresser drawers, even her refrigerator. He'd used her bathroom. After all, when the urge to take a dump hit a guy, he had to go.

Every day this week he'd spent some time in Carrie's home. He'd watched. He'd waited. That's how he knew what time she left for work each morning, what time she unlocked her front door every evening, and where she picked up men during happy hour on Friday and Saturday nights.

He knew she kept a vibrator in her nightstand, the one on the left hand side of the bed. He knew which store she'd purchased her last pair of underwear from.

It excited him that he could come and go as he liked. He touched the ring he carried inside the pocket of his hoodie, the ring he'd taken from her jewelry box, some dime store trinket he'd known when he took it that she'd never miss. The ring kept him focused, had for a week. Not that he needed incentive or purpose to think of what he wanted to do to Carrie. But the ring was a reminder that he could come and go in her things, get inside the place where she should've been the safest whenever he needed or wanted.

Standing under the light from a street lamp, he watched as Carrie's bedroom light went out right on schedule. Ten-thirty. He shook his head. One thing about Carrie, she was dependable. He walked to the end of the block, sliding into the shadows of the alley behind her co-op. When he reached the six-foot fence, he took the time to stretch on a pair of gloves. He had help vaulting over the barrier by using crates he'd had the forethought to stack along the alleyway beforehand.

Once in the backyard, he took out his penlight. He went over to the little outdoor shed Carrie used as a greenhouse, found the metal pipe he'd spotted there a week earlier. He hefted the weight onto his shoulder—and stepped to the sliding glass door. He didn't need the tool to break the glass. Only amateurs made too much noise. And he was no novice at B & E or killing. No, he had another use in mind for the heavy rod. From the inside of his pocket, he took out his mask, pulled it down over his head. He pulled out his picklock and went to work on the door he'd already breached once before.

Inside the living room, he scanned the area using his penlight even though he had familiarized himself with the location of the sofa, the coffee table, the bookcase, which wall held the flat-screen television, which side the fireplace was on. But knowing the layout made it easier for him to make his way to the staircase in short order. He managed to avoid the steps that creaked along the way up and kept to the path that worked.

When he stepped into Carrie Bennington's bedroom and stood over her sleeping form, he paused long enough to appreciate her golden hair, her soft skin, her long neck. By the time he placed his hand over her mouth it was too late. He thrilled at the terror he saw reflected in her green eyes. Not only that, but it excited him to know his face would be the last one she'd ever see.

Don't miss these other exciting titles by bestselling author

Vickie McKeehan

The Pelican Pointe Series
PROMISE COVE
HIDDEN MOON BAY
DANCING TIDES
LIGHTHOUSE REEF
STARLIGHT DUNES
LAST CHANCE HARBOR
SEA GLASS COTTAGE
LAVENDER BEACH
SANDCASTLES UNDER THE CHRISTMAS MOON
BENEATH WINTER SAND
KEEPING CAPE SUMMER (2018)

The Evil Secrets Trilogy
JUST EVIL Book One
DEEPER EVIL Book Two
ENDING EVIL Book Three
EVIL SECRETS TRILOGY BOXED SET

The Skye Cree Novels
THE BONES OF OTHERS
THE BONES WILL TELL
THE BOX OF BONES
HIS GARDEN OF BONES
TRUTH IN THE BONES
SEA OF BONES (2018)

The Indigo Brothers Trilogy
INDIGO FIRE
INDIGO HEAT
INDIGO JUSTICE
INDIGO BROTHERS TRILOGY BOXED SET

Coyote Wells Mysteries
MYSTIC FALLS
SHADOW CANYON
SPIRIT LAKE (2018)

ABOUT THE AUTHOR

Vickie McKeehan has twenty-two novels to her credit and counting. Vickie's novels have consistently appeared on Amazon's Top 100 lists in Contemporary Romance, Romantic Suspense and Mystery / Thriller. She writes what she loves to read—heartwarming romance laced with suspense, heart-pounding thrillers, and riveting mysteries. Vickie loves to write about compelling and down-to-earth characters in settings that stay with her readers long after they've finished her books. She makes her home in Southern California.

You can visit the author at:
www.vickiemckeehan.com
www.facebook.com/VickieMcKeehan
http://vickiemckeehan.wordpress.com/
www.twitter.com/VickieMcKeehan

22646500R00202

Made in the USA
San Bernardino, CA
15 January 2019